A
Dinah Harris
MYSTERY

THE Dark Heart

Julie Cave

First printing: May 2017

ISBN: 9781683440130
ISBN: 978-1-61458-600-5 (digital)
Library of Congress Number: 2017940500

Printed in the United States of America

Please visit our website for other great titles:
www.masterbooks.com

For information regarding author interviews,
please contact the publicity department at (870) 438-5288

Master
Books®
A Division of New Leaf Publishing Group
www.masterbooks.com

Acknowledgments

For my own daughters, Jasmine and Sienna, who are more precious to me than words can adequately say. For Terry: And now these three remain: faith, hope and love. But the greatest of these is love.

CONTENTS

A bank of low, dark clouds hid the moon and threatened rain. When Jordan stepped out into the brisk air, he took a deep breath and wondered if he was going to get wet. It had been windy and dry for weeks, and thus, he'd been too busy to even eat lunch most days. The Santa Ana winds were bothering asthmatics, wreaking havoc on emphysema sufferers, and creating recurring attacks of pneumonia. He was one of only a few respiratory therapists on staff at the private hospital, and he went home after each shift exhausted. And his day wasn't done yet: the staff parking lot was a long way from the hospital; a three-block walk.

Jordan walked down the street, one eye on the belligerent clouds, his backpack slung casually over his shoulder. He'd made the walk many times, and he daydreamed about the big supper his mama had waiting for him at home. His stomach rumbled in anticipation.

One block over from the hospital, Jordan came across a car with its hood up, and he wondered what it was doing in this neighborhood. It was a commercial district, deserted at night and apart from hospital staff scurrying to and from work, there was little reason for anyone else to be around. Then he saw the two girls bent over it, the dim glow of a flashlight revealing confused faces. When they heard Jordan approach, they both straightened up and he could see them a little better. One was tall with red hair, and one was small and petite, built like a bird. The taller one called out: "Excuse me?"

Jordan slowed down. "Are you okay?"

"Could you please help us?" she asked. "Our car has broken down and we don't know what to do."

The smaller woman shivered. "I'm scared."

Jordan smiled. "Sure. What are you doing around here anyway?"

"We're lost," said the smaller woman.

"Well, let's see what we can do for you," Jordan said. He put down his backpack and walked around to the front of the car. There were no obvious signs that something was wrong; no steam billowing from the radiator. *Perhaps they've run out of gas*, he thought.

"Hmmm . . ." he mused, mostly to himself. He bent over farther. "Let's have a look at. . . ."

He didn't get to finish his sentence. A blow to the back of his head sent bright, hot flashes of lightning off in front of his eyes. Pain unfurled in his skull like a sail caught by the Santa Ana wind. *What was that?* His panicked brain shouted, although he only seemed to hear his thoughts dimly. *Did the hood fall on my head?*

A panting breath in his ear explained the situation. Someone had attacked him from behind: *a coward's move*, his brain noted, coldly. Some instinct within him urged him to flee, but his legs had turned to limp spaghetti. He could only collapse onto the blacktop below. He became aware that he was being dragged away from the car and into the darkness. With great effort, he realized that the two women were watching, but they weren't calling for help or screaming.

It had been a trap.

He ducked away from a fist aimed at his nose. He caught the flow on his chin and lower lip, which split like an overripe melon. Warm blood flowed onto his shirt. *My work shirt*, he thought. *Mama's going to kill me.*

He tried to fight, although he knew that he didn't stand a chance. There were two attackers, he thought, and both were big and strong. He tried to scramble to his feet, though his head felt heavy and disconnected from anything his legs were trying to do. In desperation, he tried to work out what they wanted from him.

"Money!" he cried. "Money. In my wallet."

It was a mugging, Jordan thought. Perhaps they thought he was a rich young doctor.

The snarling response was pure hatred.

Oh, thought Jordan. A boot crashed into his side, and he felt sure he heard the snap of his rib. *They hate me because my skin is a different shade from theirs.*

He almost wished it was a mugging, because the truth was so incomprehensible. It was such a waste of time and energy, to hate somebody for no reason other than their skin color or facial features. The urgent need for quick cash made more sense.

His attempt to defend himself quickly waned. He simply could not fight off two attackers. While adrenaline flooded his veins, numbing the pain, he remembered the stories he'd heard at his grandmother's knee. He remembered how in times past, his family wasn't allowed in the same bathrooms as other people. He knew that some of his ancestors had been slaves. The echoes of those times were still heard today: sometimes a patient shrank back when he came into the treatment room. Sometimes he was assumed to be the orderly, not the therapist. Yet for some reason, he still dreamed of medical school. His mama had taught him that nothing was beyond his reach.

Yet, this attack reminded him that nothing had really changed. Racism was still here; hatred still lived in the hearts of men and women; and violence could erupt in its ugly fury. Jordan came to understand in that moment that his picture would appear in the evening news tomorrow night, right next to his weeping mother, and his name would be added to the roll call of those who'd died because of how they looked.

Jordan could feel his consciousness slipping; his eyes swam and his ears roared like the sea. As though he was in someone else's dream, he wondered: *Can't they see my blood is red? Can't they see that we are all the same underneath?*

Jordan struggled to keep his eyes open. It was nearly over, he realized. He fought to stay conscious for as long as he could, and he found himself looking at the faces of the two women who'd led him into the trap.

The taller one looked toward him grimly, her face a mask of stone, but she couldn't look directly at him.

The smaller one stared right back at him, and Jordan was astonished to see tears falling down her face, glistening in the dim light thrown by the street light. She stood straight and rigidly still, arms by her side, not trying to hide the evidence of her tears.

Jordan was mystified for a moment, but another bright explosion of pain erupted at the back of his head, and everything went dark.

****

FEBRUARY 2017

Malia Shaw felt rising panic grip her in its intimate and painful embrace.

She raised herself on one elbow and squinted at the blinds: they were partially closed but still allowed a few long sheaths of light through, long and lean as fingers, to spill on the filthy floor. *It is morning then,* she thought. She'd survived another night. Her addiction to heroin was so great that a distant part of her knew that any time she shot up could be her last. To be truthful, each time she awoke from heavy sleep she was surprised that she was still alive. *Despite my best efforts.*

She sat up with a groan, the long tendrils of a cold ache wrapping around the deep of her joints. The room was dim and musty and smelled like sour milk. The floor was almost unrecognizable as such, littered with old takeout fast food boxes, discarded clothing, and empty water and soda bottles. Malia had ceased to notice it anymore. There was only one thing she thought about when she awoke in the morning, one thing that got her through the miserable, lonely day, and one thing that helped her escape vivid nightmares during the cold night. As she reached for her cell phone, she saw that her hands were shaking. A wave of nausea crashed over her with the chill of the Atlantic winter.

She needed more smack, and she needed it now.

Malia texted her dealer and then stood up. Despite the pain, she knew she had to find some cash for him. She began to search through pockets of clothes and handbags, looking for spare cash.

She found some in the pocket of a pair of jeans and waited near the door, hopping from one foot to the other. Her nerves were starting to blaze with agony when the doorbell rang.

Simon stood outside, wearing a huge coat. A biting wind tore past him into the tiny apartment, almost knocking Malia over. He looked at Malia, dressed in a thin shirt and shook his head. "Your apartment is freezing," he said. "Don't you have heat?"

She hugged herself. Being cold was nothing compared to withdrawals from heroin. "I think the heat got cut off," she said. "Have you got some stuff for me?"

Simon handed her a paper bag. She peered in, saw what she was looking for, and gave him the cash.

Her dealer looked around again, askance at what he saw. "Seriously, put more clothes on," he said. "You'll catch your death of cold."

But Malia held in her hand something that would warm her up quicker than any sweater or coat. She spent a few minutes looking for a vein that hadn't collapsed, and then injected the heroin. Simon stood awkwardly, silhouetted by pale morning light, watching her.

Moments later, liquid fire surged through her body. It took away the pain, made her limbs feel pleasantly heavy, and it lifted her mind to a happy, safe place. She waved a farewell to Simon, who closed the door gently behind him.

She relaxed into the couch, enjoying the sensation of being taken away. The dull, thumping ache of regret that beat in synchronicity to her heart stopped. The memory of the wet thunk made by shattering bones beneath heavy boots retreated into a deep corner of her mind. The relentless fear, which disturbed her sleep and bit at her with tiny vicious teeth, finally left her alone.

Her eyes closed, and she drifted into sleep.

Sometime later, she heard the front door close, and she wondered if Simon had come back to take pity on her. When a figure appeared, profiled in the doorframe, she tried to sit up. Confused and disoriented, she realized that she was lying in her bed. She couldn't remember how she had moved from the couch to the bed. As the planes of light changed on his face, she recognized him.

The Dark Heart

She wasn't expecting the person who stood, silently looking at her. There was something not right with him, but her slowed mind couldn't figure out why. Perhaps it was the stiff, tense way he stood, his fists white-knuckled at his side. Perhaps it was that his usual smile was absent. Perhaps it was the expression on his face. Lots of people looked at her like that — their gazes full of scorn and pity, disgust and fear. They crossed the street to get away from her. She was a worthless addict, a junkie in every sense of the word. *Human junk.* But *he* had never looked at her like that. He'd always been warm and compassionate.

Suddenly, he was inside the bedroom, closing the door behind him. For the first time, through her haze, Malia felt a sharp stab of fear. "What's wrong?" she asked, scooting backwards from him until her bare shoulder blades rested against the headboard of the bed.

He took off his jacket and slung it casually across the end of the bed. "How long did you think you could keep running?" he asked. "Did you think I'd never catch up with you?"

She gaped at him. "But I thought — I *trusted* you —"

He smiled broadly. "Of course you did." From his pocket, he pulled out a curled photograph. Smoothing it, he showed it to her.

Malia gasped.

"Recognize it, do you?" he said. "I guess the smack hasn't erased *all* of your memory. This is your past and you can't outrun it."

"Listen," said Malia, her voice brittle with desperation. She knew all about desperation, didn't she? Her life had been one frantic act of survival, one after the other, for as long as she could remember. How well she knew she would never flee her past; it was locked in her memory and it assaulted her viciously daily.

"You don't get to opt out," he continued. "You don't get to decide to walk away. What you did, though, was worse than walking away. What you did was unforgivable."

"I didn't. . . . I wasn't, I . . . *please*," stammered Malia. The realization of why the man was here suddenly assailed her. The heroin haze lifted as adrenaline dumped into her system. She looked around hopelessly for a weapon, but what good would a cushion do? There was a lamp just out of arms' reach, but it was cheap and light, and against the bulk of the man was likely to do little. She searched for an escape route, but the door to the bathroom was a dead end, and a man she'd thought was her friend blocked the only other exit.

"Listen," she said, again. "I'm sorry. Please, you must know how sorry I am. I know I hurt you terribly."

His laugh was harsh, guttural. "You think you know how much I hurt?"

"I know I turned a blind eye to your suffering," continued Malia, her throat tight. "But you have to know that I was scared and hurt. I didn't know what to do except what they told me to do."

Something seemed to snap inside him and he snarled: "Shut up! Just shut up!"

"I'm sorry I was so weak. Please. I hate myself more than you could possibly ever hate me." Malia begged, tears dripping down her face.

He was upon her in only a few seconds. He had brought no weapons with him but his hands, and with astonishing strength, he seized Malia around the neck.

Instinct kicked in, and Malia's hands flew to her throat, trying to peel away the man's grip. Desperate, choking whimpers were all the noise she could make as she tried to kick out, but it was no use. She thrashed around, in the hands of a much stronger person, much like a fish caught on a hook, fighting until the inevitable end.

Despite her best efforts, the past had caught up with her, and it was intent on extracting revenge.

Starbursts of purple light flashed in front of her eyes as her oxygen-starved brain began to shut down. As the light began to die, she tried to cry out.

The brilliant flares of light in front of her eyes contained within them images from her life: herself as a small girl on a dirt floor, abandoned, frightened, hungry, and dirty, morphing to an angry and hurting teenager, an easy victim for a predator.

Then she was falling backward into darkness that engulfed her, while the light slowly faded into tiny points. She fell and fell, forever, it seemed, and she was not scared.

Then, it was over.

****

Darkness had always been her friend.

She had never been afraid of it, nor scared of being alone in it. The air, which seemed somehow lighter once the sun had gone down, was refreshing to breathe and made her feel clean. Night air felt so much more easygoing than the heavy air of daytime, with all of its loaded expectations and responsibilities. Night air was clarity, freedom, renewal.

It was why Dinah Harris was out jogging through the small town of Ten Mile Hollow, Virginia, at midnight. It was late fall and bitterly cold, but Dinah didn't mind. Ten Mile Hollow was a picturesque town, especially now that it was dressed in all its fall finery of deep red, copper, and gold. At midnight it was silent, and all Dinah could hear was the slapping of her sneakers on the road. The sound reminded her of the years of grief following the deaths of her husband and son, when the only time she could face leaving the house was late at night. Although the streets were arguably more dangerous in Washington D.C. than the rural hamlet of Ten Mile Hollow, she had walked its streets night after night — the only time she felt free of the heavy cloak of shame and judgment.

Thankfully, that cloak had loosened its hold on her in recent times, though it wasn't above a sneaky attack out of the blue, when the feeling of rising anxiety was literally a noose around her neck.

Jogging helped. Jogging at night particularly helped. It gave her time to think, reflect, process, and pray — to rid herself of the day's difficulties. She always returned from a night jog feeling less burdened and more content.

There was also the fact that she no longer slept very well; an insomniac of some years. Instead of frustrated fighting with the bedsheets because her brain refused to wind down, a jog helped to calm her.

The beautiful, cold silence of the night was shattered by the sound of her cell phone ringing. Dinah stopped running and glanced at the time before she answered the phone. It was 20 minutes past midnight.

"Hello?"

"Dinah? Where are you?" It was her friend and host, Elise Jones. Dinah and Elise had been friends years ago, when they went through FBI training at Quantico. They'd lost touch in the intervening years, but Elise had found Dinah through social media. They'd rebuilt their friendship as they exchanged their history — Dinah as a former star of the FBI, her spectacular fall from grace, and her new life as a private investigator, consulting mostly to other law enforcement. Elise had also left the FBI, although in less scandalous circumstances, and was now the detective in the Ten Mile Hollow Sherriff's Department. As the only detective, she handled everything from breaking and entering to murder.

Elise had invited Dinah to stay with her for a few days. In between cases, Dinah had agreed, remembering how much she enjoyed Elise's company. This was her first night, having spent the evening getting to know Elise's husband, Lewis, and 15-year-old daughter, Chloe.

"I'm . . . um, I'm running," said Dinah, realizing it probably sounded weird.

"Oh. Are you in town somewhere?"

Dinah looked around, trying to get a sense of where she was in a town she didn't know. "Let's see . . . I'm outside a little strip of shops, there's a little place called Wheeler Diner?"

"Oh yeah, I know where you are. I'm going to come pick you up."

Dinah frowned. "I'm okay. You don't need to worry about me. I do this all the time in D.C."

Elise gave a brief, dry chuckle. "I have no doubt of that, Dinah. I only ask because the dispatcher just called me to let me know a 911 call was received regarding a dead body. I thought you might be interested in coming along."

"Sure," said Dinah, feeling a familiar thrill. "A murder?"

"I don't know. The caller didn't say much."

"Okay. I'll wait here for you." Dinah hung up and looked around the cold, clear night. Above, a tapestry of stars shone gently in the velvet sky, the faintest whisper of a breeze caressing her cheek. It was at moments like this that she was simply glad to be alive. In spite of past sadness and struggle, she was still here, picking up the pieces of a shattered life and thriving.

By the grace of God.

She shoved her hands into the pockets of her windbreaker and waited, watching her breath bloom in front of her face like a flower made of mist.

A few minutes later, a white Ford appeared. It careened toward Dinah and stopped suddenly, tires squealing. Elise waved at her from the driver's seat.

Yikes.

As she drove, and Dinah hung onto the sides of her bucket seat for dear life, Elise explained that the body would probably turn out to be a suicide or an accident. In the small town of Ten Mile Hollow, Virginia, murders were rare, save for the odd drunken fight. Periodically, she pushed a hand into her hair, trying to keep the tight, springy ringlets the color of honey out of her eyes. It meant she only had one hand on the steering wheel, and with the careless regard she had for speed limits, life, and limb, Dinah felt sure they would not actually arrive at their destination in one piece.

I am destined to be scraped up off the road by the fire department.

When Elise had finished speaking, to distract herself from her impending doom, Dinah asked, "Do they call you by the nickname you had at Quantico?"

Elise had pulled on a puffer jacket to protect against the chill settling into the fall air, and although it did make her look slightly bulkier, it didn't hide the fact that she was short and thin as spaghetti. At Quantico, she'd been known as Bonesy Jonesy, often shortened to just Bonesy.

Elise snorted. "It follows me wherever I go. Could be worse I suppose."

They passed through Main Street, where tranquility ruled in the sparkling fountain outside the courthouse, in the small, green park next to the medical center, and in the striped awning of Esther's Eat Inn (*get it? — so small town clever*). They crossed to the western side of town, now literally the wrong side of the tracks according to Elise. Apartment buildings that had once been starter homes for young couples had fallen into disrepair and become havens for drug addicts and petty criminals. Elise knew that gang activity was beginning to crop up in the town, a consequence of failing families and poor employment prospects.

The apartment they'd been called to was a crumbling, red brick, two-story walk up. The street was quiet and deserted, except for the wail of a baby somewhere inside the apartment building. In the darkness, a light was switched on in a window. Elise parked, Dinah said a prayer of thanksgiving for her survival, and they walked up the stairs. Elise knocked on the door, and a shower of peeling paint flakes fell at their feet.

There was no answer. They waited as Elise knocked again. When there was only silence from within, she tried the doorknob. It was locked, but the deadbolts weren't.

Elise raised her eyebrows at Dinah and bent down to peer through the keyhole. A moment later, she motioned for Dinah to do the same. Dinah pressed her eye to the keyhole and saw what could easily have passed for a waste facility. It was trashed.

"We need to get through the door," Elise said. "Lend me your shoulder?"

"Sure."

Dinah and Elise hit the door three times with their combined bulk. It was a cheap door and a flimsy lock, and it was eventually defeated. Dinah stood on the threshold of the apartment, her eyes scanning the scene. Though the apartment was dark and cold, it didn't take long to see the body of a woman and the pale, waxy hue of her skin, lying on the couch. She was definitely dead.

Elise turned to Dinah. She spoke in the careful, calm voice of a person used to dealing with crisis. "I'm going to take a look at her and then call for backup."

Dinah nodded. "I'm right behind you."

As she navigated the room behind Elise, Dinah took careful note of the surroundings. The apartment was in disarray, filthy and messy. She saw at least one used needle on the coffee table.

Perhaps Elise is right. This is probably just an overdose.

Dinah knelt down by the body and looked at the dead woman while Elise checked for a pulse. The victim was not a young woman, but heroin often aged someone considerably. Recent and faded track marks scored both arms. She was very thin. She had long, dark hair that was fanned around her face.

Dinah couldn't see an immediate cause of death — there was no pool of blood.

Elise suddenly motioned with one hand. "Look," she hissed.

Dinah leaned closer, and then she saw the long, purplish bruises around the woman's throat. *Definitely not a suicide or overdose. This is murder.*

Carefully, she raised the eyelid on one of the woman's half-closed eyes and saw red, broken blood vessels — the telltale signs of death by asphyxiation.

Elise looked at her, and understanding passed between them without a word having to be spoken. Elise rocked back on her heels and pulled out her cell phone.

Dinah stood up and took a careful step back from the body. She listened as Elise called in backup, forensic technicians, and the medical examiner.

Dinah began to look carefully around the room, taking out her cell phone to record her observations. Her immediate impression was one of neglect and filth. It would appear that the dead woman lived alone in squalor, which wasn't unusual for hard-line heroin addicts.

The kitchenette contained a hotplate and refrigerator that both looked unused. Judging by the number of empty takeout bags and containers around the room, the dead woman had lived almost entirely on Chinese food.

The living room contained only a couch, coffee table, and a small TV. Dinah picked her way gingerly across the room, mindful both of needles that were likely strewn around and not disturbing the crime scene. There was nothing that stood out immediately to her as being out of place, but it was so hard to know given the state of the room. On a crate serving as a coffee table, Dinah found a small purse. Inside, she found a social security card and an ATM card in the name of Malia Shaw.

She gave the purse to Elise, who dropped it into a plastic evidence bag, and headed for the bedroom.

The queen-sized box-spring mattress took up most of the bedroom, with sheets spread haphazardly across it. The small, attached bathroom was grimy and virtually empty, save for a bar of soap. The dead woman apparently hadn't bothered with the niceties of makeup or perfume.

Dinah returned to where Elise was standing, just inside the door. She couldn't shake a feeling of disquiet. The dead woman had lived a solitary, sad life, she thought.

"Well, what do you think?" Elise asked. Two deputy cars had parked below them; Elise waved at them to come up.

"She was a hard-core heroin addict," said Dinah, "so it could be a drug deal gone bad. Or simply being in the wrong place at the wrong time."

"There's nothing to take, except a stash of drugs, perhaps," observed Elise.

"Do you know who she was?"

Elise sucked in a lip for a moment and said, "Not offhand. I'm willing to bet that if we plug her name into the computer, there'll be a record. She had to be supporting her habit somehow."

Dinah nodded, distracted by the feeling that she had missed something. *What is it?*

She went back inside the apartment and knelt beside the dead woman again. Without touching her, she looked over the body more closely, wondering if there was anything there she had overlooked.

"Found anything I should know about?" a cheerful voice sounded above her. It belonged to a tall man in his late forties, with a thick thatch of silvery hair with a matching beard and a beaming smile.

"This is the medical examiner, Dr. Theo Walker," explained Elise. "Doc, this is my FBI buddy, Dinah Harris. She's a private consultant now."

Dr. Walker smiled as he snapped on his gloves. "Nice to meet you. What did you do for the Bureau?"

"Gangs mostly, but I also did some profiling for serial homicide." *Ah, glory days. All gone. Nothing lasts forever.*

"Excellent. Well, what do you think of our body here?"

"So far, only that she's a murder victim," said Dinah. She pointed out the bruising on the woman's neck.

Walker knelt down next to her and nodded.

"I saw it when I tried to find a pulse," explained Elise.

Silence fell in the tiny, suffocating room as the county medical examiner carefully looked over the dead woman's body. From time to time, he shook his head, as if noting the sadness of the woman's wasted life.

"My immediate impression is that she was strangled manually," said Dr. Walker finally, as he examined the neck carefully. "These bruises look like finger marks, as opposed to rope or cord."

He began a second careful examination of the body, this time speaking into his iPhone as he made notes. Dinah watched as the man gathered evidence slowly and methodically.

"Any thoughts?" she asked, at length.

Walker rocked back on his heels. "Off the record, I think she was probably killed at least a couple of days ago, though the cold temperatures in here would have sped up the cooling process. Rigor mortis has passed. No sign of insect activity, but that is due more to the temperature than anything else. There are no other obvious signs of trauma. I'd be surprised if the killer inflicted any violence on her other than that by which she died."

Dinah nodded. "He probably wouldn't have needed to — she's so small." She stood up and walked to the door of the apartment to breathe in some fresh air, which suddenly felt cold and sweet compared to the odor of death.

"The crime scene tech is on her way," Elise noted, after looking at her phone. "She's coming from another job over in Norfolk."

Dinah knew that Ten Mile Hollow was too small to employ a full-time crime scene technician, so they used the county resources. The tech worked from the same office as Dr. Walker in Norfolk.

From her perch by the door, Dinah looked around the street: still dark and quiet with not a soul in sight. If this murder had occurred in the middle-class districts, neighbors would have crowded around the scene, curiosity getting the better of them. Here, most of the neighbors had something to hide and stayed behind firmly shut doors.

Across the street, an apartment above a pawnshop had tried to cheer up the bleak façade of the building with flower boxes. For some reason, this attempt at homeyness made Dinah feel unspeakably sad. Somehow, the loneliness of this street struck a chord with her own isolation, and it echoed in her heart like a beautiful song left unsung.

****

The eastern horizon was blushing with the pink promise of a new day. In the hour before dawn the temperature plummeted even further, and dressed only in her jogging gear, Dinah began to shiver.

Wearily, Dinah and Elise stood in the threshold of the dead woman's apartment as the crime scene technician finished up. Black fingerprint powder was dusted over every surface, but it was virtually unnoticeable amid the original grime. The crime scene technician nodded somberly at them as she left, the medical examiner had already removed the body, and the remaining apartment and its contents were Elise's to process. Although she had notified him, the sheriff had no interest in combing through the dead woman's belongings, and had made an excuse not to be there.

"He'd be here in a flash if it were an important member of society," grumbled Elise. "Apparently lonely heroin addicts don't make the cut."

Dinah knew this only too well. It seemed that humanity was collectively keen to assign value to human beings based on a list of subjective criteria.

The apartment had been sealed all night with a sheriff's deputy guarding the door. *No doubt his presence severely dampened the usual trade of the drug dealers during the night*, Dinah thought with a smile.

Though the dawn had teased them with feminine shades, the day failed to deliver. Clouds rolled in, turning the sky low and gray. Dinah felt as though she was now completely frozen. Her extremities were numb. Her nose could drop right off her face and she wouldn't even notice.

"All right," said Elise. "Let's do this."

She gave Dinah gloves. They decided to start in opposite ends of the apartment, go through each room carefully and compare notes at the end. Dinah was to start in the kitchen.

After only a few minutes, she decided the autopsy would have to show signs of significant malnutrition. There was literally no food in the apartment, the spoiled remains of a milk carton notwithstanding. The small refrigerator was bare, and there was no evidence of a pantry at all. Underneath the sink languished a solitary bottle of disinfectant. Another cupboard yielded a few mismatched cups and plates. The countertops and sink were covered with the detritus of fast food. Dinah sifted through all of it, looking for anything odd. She opened a large trash bag and dropped each piece of rubbish in after a thorough inspection.

She found nothing there.

She moved into the threadbare living room. First, she looked through the rubbish that littered the couch and coffee table, and put it carefully into the trash bag, mindful of needle stick injury. Once the floor and the couch were clear, she stood back to look. The furniture was cheap, the couch cushions ripped in places and sagging in others. The floor was covered with thin, worn carpet, the original color of which was anyone's guess. Now it was a sickly gray-brown. *At the age of 39, this woman should have had a significant other, some kids, a warm and cheerful home.* Dinah sighed. In this, she and the dead woman were alike.

There were few places to hide anything of note. There was no murder weapon to look for, no ballistics. She hoped that the crime scene tech had found some hair or fingerprints.

Dinah decided the only thing to do was to pull the couch apart. Gingerly, afraid of used needles flying out at her, she pulled up the cushions, leaving the frame bare.

It paid off. A thin black cell phone had been hidden or had fallen underneath one of the cushions. Dinah opened it and began to look through the contacts. There weren't many, and she felt encouraged by this. She dropped the phone into a plastic evidence bag.

She walked into the bedroom with its tiny attached bathroom. The sheets on the bed were dirty and covered in tiny flecks of blood — perhaps from needle wounds. Dinah carefully bagged it up as evidence. Perhaps, as a stroke of luck, the killer had left his own speck of blood. Clothes littered the floor of the bedroom, but in totality, Malia Shaw had owned little in the way of clothing. Dinah found a pair of jeans, several T-shirts, a couple of sweatshirts and an old coat, a pair of boots, and a pair of sneakers. She bagged each item, carefully wrote the record book, and was left with the mattress.

With a sigh, she rocked back on her heels, wondering why she suddenly felt so warm and claustrophobic. Dinah had always thought that a person's home shared a soul with its owner, and therefore had a personality of its own. In her own house, visitors would instantly see that she loved cooking. She owned every cookbook ever published, and displayed them in her kitchen. Much of the color was provided by a potted chili plant in one corner, and a collection of potted herbs in the courtyard. A throw blanket was always carelessly draped across the couch for use on cold nights. A beautiful and rare painting by an indigeneous Australian artist adorned one wall, the earthy ochre, burnt gold, deep brown, and dark red reminding her of an exotic and faraway land. It was a home that was lived in.

That was what was bothering her. There was absolutely no indication in this apartment that Malia Shaw had cared one little bit about herself. The apartment was bereft of love, cold and shuttered. There was nothing sentimental, nothing personal. There were no photos or mementos or souvenirs. There were no books or music — not even a computer. No indication that a human being, with a soul, with a personality, with preferences and desires and fears, had lived here. *Is this what a life reduced to a heroin addiction looks like?*

A spreading sadness trickled through every vein. *How could you call this a life? Was there anyone who loved you?*

Dinah took apart the box spring, searching for any cuts or frays in the fabric in which something could be hidden. She didn't find anything.

The final room to search was the bathroom, which consisted of a shower stall, a toilet, and a sink, all of which were moldy and dirty. Dinah found nothing in the stall or toilet tank, and turned her attention to the small cupboard underneath the sink.

It was bare — a bottle of shampoo, a body moisturizer, and several new bars of soap. For lack of anything else to look at, Dinah picked up the bars of soap and threw them back into the cupboard in frustration. The soap hit the back wall of the cupboard with a hollow *thunk* and Dinah frowned.

The back wall of the cupboard sounded loose and spongy. She reached in to test it and the particleboard shuddered at her touch.

Dinah retrieved her flashlight from her bag in the living room and looked around the cupboard before realizing that the particleboard was bent *toward* her, in a concave fashion.

Shuffling on her knees, she pressed herself up against the bathroom wall and shone the flashlight in the small crack between the wall and the back of the bathroom cupboard. She could see something there, a dark mass that had bent the particleboard inward.

In the process of pulling the dark mass out, Dinah scraped her glove-clad knuckles and bent her elbow at impossible angles. With great concentration, she managed to inch the mass out from behind the particleboard slowly.

It was a large, sealed plastic bag, and at first Dinah thought it would be a stash of drugs, kept safe from anyone who might steal it. But the feel was wrong; it was too stiff and thick to be drugs. When she pulled the contents from the bag out, she stared for several moments in total confusion. Two U.S. passports and three social security cards emerged from the bag, all bearing Malia Shaw's photo. However, the documents contained three aliases: one passport and social security card read Theresa Scott, the other passport and another social security card named her as Lexi Hollingsworth, and the final lone social security card pegged her as Amanda Wallace.

The documents all had varying addresses, all within Virginia; but all had the same birth date. Dinah examined the documents carefully. They were professionally made; indiscernible fakes. She slumped back against the bathroom wall, her heart galloping like a thoroughbred, thundering in her ears.

Who was Malia Shaw?

Angus Whitehall arrived home as the last golden filament of dusk disappeared, absorbed by the cold blackness of night. He felt a usual rush of warmth as he made the juxtaposition from dark to the cheerful light of his home. As he walked from the driveway to the porch, he could feel the burden of responsibility of his work as the pastor of Ten Mile Hollow First Baptist Church begin to lift. The responsibility of being the leader, the motivator, and the example to an entire town was, at times, exhausting — particularly since he was pretending to be a fine, upstanding citizen when he knew very well that he was not anything of the sort.

His wife, Louise, was both fixing dinner and supervising the homework of their children, 15-year-old Grace and 10-year-old Marcus. He shrugged off his coat, kissed Louise, and poured himself a glass of water.

"How was your day?" he asked.

"Oh, you know. It was fine," said Louise. She was distracted, stirring broth into a simmering pan and answering Marcus's questions about fifth-grade math. "How was your day?"

Angus shrugged. "It was okay. I finished my sermon for Sunday, so that's a big relief."

"Uh-huh, that sounds great," said Louise. She flitted from one saucepan to the next. "I'm sorry, honey. Can we talk later?"

"Of course. Can I help with dinner?"

"Oh, it's all under control. Do you know anything at all about math? I really don't." She smiled at him.

"I may remember something." He stood up and took another swallow of water. "Hey, Marcus. Need a hand?"

For 15 minutes, he helped Marcus wrestle fractions into submission and checked on Grace, who was in her room. While he waited for dinner, he decided to relax for a few minutes.

In the living room, he sat down on a couch and turned on the television. He mindlessly watched without really digesting the latest political news from Washington, tales of economic woe from Europe, and a scandal surrounding a famous football player.

"In local news," the newscaster said, "the body of a woman was discovered this morning in the small town of Ten Mile Hollow, just outside Norfolk, and police report that her death is a suspected homicide. Ten Mile Hollow Sheriff Wilder says that the woman was strangled about two days ago in an apartment on the west side of town. She has been identified as Malia Shaw, and she was 39 years old."

The glass slipped from Angus's hand and shattered on the hardwood floor.

The latest photo of Malia Shaw appeared on the screen, and he saw gaunt cheekbones, dull skin, and weary eyes. The photo was lifted directly from her driver's license, and her hair was disheveled. *She looks almost dead,* Angus thought and then shuddered with horror at the thought. *Now she really is dead.*

Suddenly the television screen was too large, too sharp, too clear. Did they really have to blow up her face to such dimensions? Did they want the general public to see death already residing in her eyes?

"Angus?"

He snapped back to reality and saw Louise standing next to him, looking at the broken glass in confusion.

"What's wrong?" she asked. "You look like you've seen a ghost."

Angus wanted to laugh, hysteria bubbling up in him. *A ghost, indeed. A ghost from the past, who represented memories he'd almost succeeded in repressing.*

"Uh," he said. "I'm fine. Just an accident."

Louise looked at the television screen. "You were watching footage of the woman who was murdered?"

"Yes." He looked down at the broken glass and thought he should start cleaning it up. Yet, he couldn't will his limbs to move.

"It was a shock, wasn't it?" Louise said. "A murder, in our little town."

Angus felt relief wash over him. "Yes," he agreed. "Terrible. You wouldn't think it could happen here."

Finally, he managed to drop to a knee and begin cleaning up the glass. Louise came in with a small broom and took over, directing him to the dinner table. Over dinner, he tried to behave normally, but he caught Louise throwing him a few odd glances, as if there were something slightly off-kilter about him. Was he talking too fast, laughing too loudly? Did the smile on his face reach his eyes?

He kissed the kids goodnight and sat brooding on the couch. *What is going to happen? Will the police link Malia to me? What if people find out? What if my family finds out?* The thought made him go cold all over, his stomach flipping like a fish on a hook. He wasn't sure if he wanted to laugh, cry, or vomit. All options felt entirely possible.

Louise had curled up on the couch next to him with a cup of tea, watching him carefully. "Is everything okay?" she asked him, when he smiled briefly at her.

"Of course," he lied.

"Did you know the murdered woman?"

"No!" he replied, a bit too quickly. He waited a moment. "No. Why do you ask?"

"No reason," she said. "I just thought you might have come across her during your ministry work on the west side. She looked like she lived a hard life."

A hard life doesn't even begin to explain what she — what we — did. But his wife had unknowingly thrown him a lifeline. *Ministry on the west side.*

"I didn't know her," he said. "I guess she might have been a recipient of our ministry services, but if so, I didn't recognize her."

He had lied to many people, including Louise, throughout the course of his life. It was only because the truth was too hard to bear for anyone except him, and he'd resigned himself to carry the burden alone. But this lie sat heavily on his shoulders like an ill-fitting coat, because of the possible consequences of discovery.

The last time I saw her she was alive, talking. She had the same eyes though: death lived there.

He and Louise slid into comfortable movie watching, although Angus's mind was elsewhere. He stared blindly at the television screen, seeing people move and speak and do things. He had no idea what was going on.

Instead, he was wondering if he'd covered his tracks well enough. He wondered if he'd left behind anything of himself, though he thought he had been as careful as he could be. He wondered if anyone had seen him, if they could identify him. He wondered if any clues existed on the woman's dead body.

Fear thrummed through him like a high-tension electrical wire. He couldn't afford for any of this to be revealed. It would be devastating if his secret were exposed. He had spent so many years building a careful veneer of respectability, and he couldn't imagine what would happen if it all came crashing down.

He was the pastor of Ten Mile Hollow First Baptist Church, a husband, and a father. Since those terrible times with Malia, he had tried to make amends in every way he knew how. He had spent all his energy giving to others, trying desperately for love to outweigh the hatred. Now he had to acknowledge that, as in many things, his efforts fell short.

Oh God I'm so scared. Please help me. Please show me what to do.

What he couldn't say, couldn't find the courage to articulate or the temerity to ask for was a plea for protection for himself.

****

Chloe Jones glanced at the front steps of the E. Crenshaw Ten Mile Hollow High School. When she saw who was sitting there, her heart tripped a little and then went icy cold. *If only there was another entrance,* she thought.

Each morning, before the bell, Jessica Hunter and her minions would station themselves on the steps. What followed was great sport to them — making nasty comments, laughing, teasing, mocking — and dread to those who would fall victim.

Chloe was one of their favorite targets.

She narrowed her eyes and stared at the girl who ruled the tenth grade. She was beautiful and popular and confident. Long, blue-black hair cascaded in effortless waves around a face with flawless olive skin. Her blue eyes were startlingly lovely, and her white teeth were perfect. She was a cheerleader and dated a senior football star. Her clothes displayed long, lean legs and a tiny torso. She was vicious and mean, feared by almost everyone in the tenth grade.

Chloe knew she made an obvious victim. Her hair was blunt and short and spunky. Her figure could best be described as curvy, though Chloe thought of herself as simply fat. She was as pale as the full moon. She wore glasses and favored a chunky frame. She liked to wear clothes that were retro, and therefore not at all cool. She was smarter than Jessica, and beat her in every class.

In return for these slights, Jessica tormented her at every possible moment.

Chloe glanced around, trying to see if a more likely victim was about to make his or her way up the stairs. She waited five minutes, but finally, she knew she had to take a deep breath and enter the building.

As she approached the stairs, the tenth-grade chess club president began to climb the wide, stone staircase and she silently yelled out a thank you. He was sure to attract more taunts than her.

It was going perfectly until she reached the step third from the top. She was so tense, waiting to hear her name called out, that she forgot to concentrate on what her feet were doing and she tripped. She dropped her book bag and fell on her hands — not a large fall, by any means.

But it brought the vultures circling.

A loud burst of laughter erupted from Jessica's group, sounding like a rookery of raucous crows.

"You don't just look like a cow," called Jessica. "You're as clumsy as one, too!"

Blood rushed to Chloe's face as she picked up her book bag. A brief thought flitted through her mind — *that doesn't even make sense* — but she didn't dare retort. *Are cows clumsy? Really?*

On cue, Jessica's minions began to moo loudly. As Chloe fled into the school building, she heard the *mooing* intensify amid squeals of laughter. Once inside, she realized she was shaking, while humility burned her cheeks. Other students streamed past, most of them probably thankful that they'd avoided the wrath of Jessica on this particular day.

"Hey, you don't look great," a familiar voice said at her side. Chloe turned to see her best friend in the whole world, Grace Whitehall, fall in beside her. Grace could have been one of Jessica's minions; she was pretty enough and had the interest of plenty of boys. Jessica had never thrown any taunts her way.

Instead, Grace had chosen to be Chloe's friend. They'd known each other for only a few years, but had clicked almost instantly. They'd been inseparable ever since.

Chloe looked at the petite, blonde girl and said, "Jessica."

Grace frowned. "Yeah, I heard the last part of it. Are you okay?"

"I guess." At the lockers, Chloe suddenly felt drained. She had invested so much energy into trying to escape Jessica that she actually felt sick.

"She'd be nothing without her minions, you know," Grace said. "A bully is a coward."

"And her stupid football star boyfriend," added Chloe, with a frown.

Grace sighed. "Yeah, it totally bites. I'm sorry."

Chloe patted her friend on the shoulder. "Not your fault! What doesn't kill us makes us stronger, right?"

Just as she was about to feel better, she saw Jessica stalking down the corridor toward her. Her blue eyes were narrow and mean as she searched for her prey. Chloe tried to melt into her locker, sending up a prayer to whoever might be listening. *Please, please, please, please leave me alone.*

Instead, she heard the sweet voice of her friend Grace say, "Hey, Jessica!"

Chloe went mute with horror.

"Hi, Grace. When are you going to cheerleader tryouts?" Jessica asked, her voice suddenly warm as pudding.

"Never," snapped Grace. "And leave Chloe alone!"

Chloe turned around slowly, if only to witness the situation unfolding grotesquely like a train wreck. Except that a train wreck could never be as horrifying as this situation unfolding before her.

Jessica smirked and flicked a contemptuous look Chloe's way. "I don't know why you're friends with her. She's dragging you down. Aren't you embarrassed to be seen with her?"

Embarrassed? thought Chloe. She felt hot, as though she was standing directly underneath the sun on a hot summer's day.

"Don't be ridiculous," said Grace, sharply.

Jessica stared at the blonde girl for a second, then tossed her hair. "Whatever." Her minions followed her sashaying walk down the corridor.

"You didn't have to do that," Chloe said, almost collapsing against her locker. Every limb felt like a wet noodle. "Seriously. She's going to have it in for you now."

Grace shook her head fiercely. "I don't care. Now, let's forget about her. What's new?"

Chloe smiled in spite of herself. *Thank goodness for Grace.* "Mom's got a lady staying with us at the moment. An old friend from when she was an FBI agent."

"Really? That's so cool. Is the friend still an FBI agent?"

"Don't think so." Chloe frowned, realizing she didn't really know for sure.

"What's her name?"

"Dinah Harris." Together they began to walk to their first class. "She seems nice."

****

The office was quiet when Dinah and Elise arrived at the police department later that day. Both had returned to Elise's home for a quick nap and now had arrived to continue their investigation. Dinah had only been able to sleep for half an hour. She was preoccupied with the new case, her thoughts all over the place.

Elise looked around the office and snorted. "The sheriff has obviously decided two hours of work today is sufficient."

Dinah smiled. "What would you like me to do?"

Elise laid the bags containing the cell phone and the identification documents on her desk. "My first job is to try and locate some next of kin," she said. "While I do that, could you start with arrest records for Malia Shaw?"

"Sure." Dinah sat at a spare desk and using Elise's log on details, opened up the arrest records database.

The Dark Heart

The first and most obvious question was whether the woman's name had actually been Malia Shaw, or whether that was another alias.

She'd been arrested twice, both on minor drugs charges. She'd been identified as Malia Shaw in both those arrests. Dinah typed in the other names she'd found on the bogus identification but found no matches. Therefore, while the dead woman had lived in Ten Mile Hollow, she'd only used one name — with the police, anyway.

Dinah searched through the records and saw that at both arrests she had not been bailed out nor visited. The charges had been minor, and she hadn't served a great deal of time in jail, due to non-custodial sentences. Dinah got the initial impression of a woman who had lived a very solitary life.

There was nothing in the arrest records that revealed Malia Shaw's next of kin. Wherever she had come from, Ten Mile Hollow clearly was not home to parents, siblings, or even a romantic interest. Dinah recorded the information for Elise, closed the files and turned her attention to the cell phone.

The first thing she checked was the phone contacts. It was a pitifully small list: only three names — Simon, Al, and Lola. There was no entry for Mom or Dad, nor anyone else who seemed like a family member. No aunt or uncle. No Grandma or Grandpa.

Dinah called Simon first. The phone rang out, with no voice mail message. *Interesting.*

Next, she called Al. The phone rang, then a male answered: "Hello?"

"Hello, this is the Ten Mile Hollow Sheriff's Department and—" *Click.*

"Hello? Hello?" Dinah listened and heard nothing. Al had hung up on her. *Very interesting.*

Dinah called Lola, the final name in the contacts list. The phone rang out, and like Simon, it did not go to voicemail. She pursed her lips thoughtfully as she wrote out the numbers to follow up with the phone company.

She looked at the text messages next, and saw that almost every single text message was to or from Simon.

Need stuff, wrote Malia Shaw.
30 minutes, Simon replied.

You be around today? Malia had asked on another occasion.
Yes need something? Simon said.
Yes.

Her drug dealer, Dinah thought. It was no wonder he hadn't answered his phone.

Occasionally, a text message popped up from Al or Lola. The purpose of those messages appeared to be checking in on Malia, asking her whether she was okay.

When Dinah checked the phone log, she found calls to and from Al and Lola on a semi-regular basis. Al seemed to be in contact with Malia several times a week, while Lola appeared once or twice a week. She wondered the significance of their relationship. Although they had been in regular contact, neither Al nor Lola had visited Malia in jail or tried to bail her out.

Dinah had a burning desire to follow up the phone numbers and pay a visit to Simon, Al, and Lola; but first, she had to wait for Elise, who had been on the phone the whole time.

Finally, she hung up and shook her head in frustration. "I got nowhere," Elise said. "This woman did a good job of cutting off her whole family or she was dropped off here by the stork."

Elise drummed her fingers on her desk for a moment. "All right. Let's go talk to the owner of the building in which Malia lived. I figure she had to fill out a rental application and they usually ask for next of kin details."

While Dinah waited, Elise accessed the county records database, which showed that the owner lived on the opposite side of town to his grubby, crumbling apartment block.

It was late afternoon when they stepped outside, and the sun was relinquishing its job in a seemingly hurried fashion. It was very cold, and a series of scudding gray clouds promised rain before nightfall. The approaching dusk had almost completely leeched what little light was left as Elise and Dinah pulled up in front of an immaculately kept bungalow.

Owen Karakarides was a short, bald man with a head shaped like an egg and a huge cigar protruding from his mouth, around which was clamped a set of yellow teeth.

He glowered at them. "You the detective?"

He looked both women up and down like he didn't like what he saw. Dinah raised her eyebrows, silently daring the man to make a rude comment. *Give me a reason, old man.*

When the silence stretched out, Elise said, "Evening. I'm Detective Elise Jones of the Sheriff's Department. This is Dinah Harris, former FBI agent and consultant on this case. I need to talk to you about the tenant of one of your buildings."

"Uh-huh," he said, looking at Elise and then Dinah, through narrowed, suspicious eyes.

Dinah felt her patience sap and her ire rise. "Shall we go inside, or do you want your neighbors knowing your business?"

Grudgingly, he stepped aside, showing a well-furnished living room. "This about that dead lady?"

Dinah glanced around the room and sat down with some reluctance on an overstuffed armchair. "Yes. Her name was Malia Shaw."

He snorted. "I never really knew her name. She, and all the rest of them in that building, they're all the same."

"Same in what way?"

"Junkies," Karakarides sniffed. He puffed on his cigar.

Dinah let out a slow breath, amazed at the man's ability to completely irritate her to the point of violence in only five minutes.

Elise jumped in. "Okay. So do you remember Malia Shaw?"

He waved his hand in a vague gesture. "Sure. Single lady. Obviously a junkie. No job."

"Why on earth would you rent to her if she was so clearly a drug addict and had no job?" Elise asked.

Karakarides thought about that. "As I recall, she paid her rent six months in advance, in cash."

Elise and Dinah exchanged a glance. "Six month's rent in cash? How much would that have been?"

"Well, the monthly was $300, so you do the math," Karakarides said, with a smirk.

Dinah bit her lip viciously to prevent herself from saying what she thought. She very much wanted to knock the man in his yellow teeth at that moment. To hide her irritation, she wrote the figure in her notebook, thinking about the information the owner had just given her.

Eighteen hundred dollars: not a lot of money by some standards, but to a drug addict, a fortune. Dinah thought about the tiny, sparse apartment, furnished cheaply. How had she come up with $1800 in cash? How had she resisted the temptation to trade it for heroin?

"When was the lease due for renewal?" she asked.

"I think March."

"So did you ask her if she was going to stay in the apartment?"

"Not me, personally," said Karakarides. "But the super — well, he's only a part time super, on account of the place being a dump — he told me that she told him she wanted to stay. And that she had cash."

Curious. Both Dinah and Elise had tossed the apartment and there had been no hidden stash of money. From where would she have gotten the money?

"Do you have the rental application?" she asked.

Karakarides sighed. "Well, I guess it's in my office somewhere." He didn't move.

Dinah almost growled aloud. Even Elise, who seemed more patient, snapped, "Well, I'm gonna need it."

Karakarides made it a big production to get up and shuffle off down the dark hallway to another room.

Dinah thought about the dead woman's finances while Karakarides was away, wondering if Malia Shaw had been dealing drugs on the side or engaged in some other crime to feed her habit. It would open up a world of possibilities when it came to suspects if that were the case. Finally, the owner returned, waving a thin file at them.

Elise took it from him. "Thank you," she said. "I'll return it when I'm done."

"Really? Can't you take a copy?" Karakarides whined.

Elise smiled. "Sorry," she said. She sounded suspiciously like she didn't mean it. Dinah rose and together they saw themselves out of the bungalow, leaving Karakarides standing behind them with his hands on his hips, puffing on his cigar, and filling his home with the acrid smoke.

In the car, with Elise dangerously behind the wheel, Dinah opened the file and read the application quickly. Some of the information would require further clarification, but it was bare where it counted for now.

No next-of-kin was listed — in fact, the page was totally void of writing. Dinah supposed the property owner hadn't cared, since he'd received his rent in advance.

"Nothing here," she told Elise, as the car lurched forward, tires squealing. "I suppose since the owner received the rent in advance, he didn't care too much about the missing spaces on the rental application."

Elise managed to avoid a tree and pedestrian with only inches to spare. "So our dead victim is still a ghost."

Dinah had to agree. Malia Shaw was turning out to be a shadow, a wraith, a ghost, a woman with no past, no family and no future.

How did she end up here in Ten Mile Hollow, and why?

****

Darkness had stolen across the sky on the silent feet of a thief by the time Elise turned the car into her driveway. Dinah muttered a brief prayer of thanks that somehow they hadn't both been killed. Elise had a careless disregard for yellow traffic lights.

Elise lived in a pretty, two-story A-frame house. Flower boxes adorned every window and the front door and shutters were all painted a cheery yellow. Light spilled from the windows into the cold dark, promising warmth, hearth, and home.

Elise's husband, Lewis, was a firefighter and paramedic with the Ten Mile Hollow Fire Department, and worked shift hours. His car was not in the driveway tonight, and Dinah surmised that he was on shift down at the fire station.

Once inside the house, Dinah sat at the kitchen table to await further instructions regarding dinner, while Elise flipped through her mail.

"Hello?" Elise called up the stairs. "Chloe? Are you up there?"

"Hi, Mom!" Chloe shouted back. "I'm doing my homework."

"Okay. Dinner in about half an hour, okay?"

"Sure!"

Elise returned to the kitchen and began to rummage through the refrigerator for something for dinner. She pulled out some lettuce, tomatoes, peppers, and a carrot and popped them in front of Dinah. "Would you mind slicing these up for a salad?" she asked.

"Sure," said Dinah, selecting a knife from the block.

She began to chop while Elise prepared to grill some chicken to add to the salad. Using garlic, lemon juice, and continental parsley as a dressing, she also took out of the refrigerator a bottle of white wine.

Dinah watched with some trepidation as Elise put a wine glass in front of her.

"Would you like a drink?" Elise opened the bottle and waited.

"Uh . . . no thanks." Dinah took a deep breath. "I don't drink."

"Oh, okay. Do you mind if I have a glass?"

"Not at all." Dinah concentrated on chopping. There was a momentary silence.

"So you've given up drinking altogether?" Elise asked, putting the chicken on the grill.

Dinah nodded. "Yes. I can't drink at all." She debated whether to tell her friend the truth — it was always hard to talk about. But honesty seemed to lead to conversations about the deeper issues of life. "I had some problems with alcohol after Luke and Sammy died."

Elise turned to look at her, her expression one of sympathy. "I'm sorry. I can't say I blame you, but it must have been a terribly difficult time."

The tiny, deadly claws of shame were always looking for an opportunity to sink themselves into Dinah's brain. Now they pounced, sending twin rivers of electrical pain through her head and right down into her stomach. "I didn't handle it very well," she admitted to Elise. "I made some terrible mistakes." *And death followed me and took my family and very nearly took me, too.*

"You seem to be doing much better now," said Elise, turning the chicken on the grill.

"Well, thank you. I think so." Dinah stared hard at the wine bottle. It would always be a struggle to resist the temptation of alcohol, and she had to admit that she thought of it often — especially when shame and guilt took hold of her.

"How did you overcome it?"

"Two things. I became a Christian and I went to rehab," explained Dinah. "But in reality, I owe my life to becoming a Christian."

Elise nodded. "I've heard faith in a higher power can help with addiction."

"Well, it's more than that to me. It's not just simple belief in something out there, or blind faith in something I can't explain. It's personal. It's a relationship with God, who made Himself real to me."

Elise looked at her quizzically, but there was no more time to talk. Dinner was ready and Chloe was clattering down the stairs with the earnest enthusiasm of youth. Dinah tossed the salad into a bowl and then buttered bread rolls while Elise chopped up the sizzling chicken. When it was ready, they sat down at the kitchen table.

Elise asked her daughter: "How was your day?"

Chloe glanced up. "Okay. How was your day?"

"Long."

Dinah suddenly realized she, too, was exhausted. A night of no sleep followed by only a short nap was not enough.

"Is Dad at work tonight?" Chloe asked.

"Yes. How's your homework?"

"It's fine." Chloe waved her hand in a dismissive gesture. "Can I be excused?"

Elise frowned. Chloe had already finished dinner and was looking impatiently at her cell phone. "No. Where are your manners? How about you talk to our guest?"

Dinah hid a smile while Chloe tried to hide a long-suffering eye roll. "How are you enjoying Ten Mile Hollow, Ms. Harris?"

"Please call me Dinah. I like it very much. It's a beautiful town."

Chloe snorted. It was an identical snort to the one Elise often gave and it made Dinah smile. "It's pretty boring. I can't wait to get out of here."

"Where would you like to go?"

"Well, college. I want to go to college someplace fun."

"What would you like to do at college?" Dinah asked.

"I dunno." Chloe cocked her head to one side. "I like science. I like computers. I'm pretty good at both. Maybe something to do with that."

"Sounds great. I'm sure you'll do well no matter what you choose."

Chloe gave a faint smile. "Thanks. Can I be excused now?" she asked of her mother, now that the chore of talking to the dinner guest was over.

"Sure." This time it was Elise giving an exaggerated eye roll to Dinah.

Chloe disappeared in a flash, and Dinah stared after her for a few moments. She would forever miss out on Sammy's teenage years — she would never see the attempts to find his independence and identity, nor the awkward, gangly teenage limbs, nor the awkwardness of a first date.

After cleaning up the kitchen and watching a sitcom with unseeing eyes, both she and Elise decided to turn into bed early. Dinah was relieved, in all honesty. The comfort and familiarity of home for Elise, Lewis, and Chloe brought pangs of sadness for Dinah.

In the guest bedroom, she turned off the lights and slipped between the sheets. Despite her tiredness, her mind was racing.

Thoughts of her own solitude inevitably led her to think of Malia Shaw, who had been far more isolated than she: the cold, blank apartment; communication with no one other than the supplier of her drugs; nothing of sentimental value around her at all.

Where are her parents, who once must have loved her? Had she ever loved somebody more than she'd loved drugs? Had everyone who'd known her forsaken her?

Dinah wrestled her mind back to the case. For one thing, the death of a drug addict seemed that it would be more complex than it first appeared. Why did Malia Shaw have fake passports and social security cards with aliases? How could she have afforded to pay six months' rent in advance, with cash? By all indications, she was getting ready to do the same when her lease expired in only two months' time. Where would she have gotten her hands on a further $1800? It was wildly implausible that a hard-core drug addict like Malia Shaw could possibly avoid the temptation to turn the cash into heroin.

Finally, she had suffered a lonely, violent death at the hands of another. It was such an enormous waste of precious human life. In the harsh light of day, Dinah could be tough, unemotional, jaded. But in the soft darkness of this foreign guest room, she allowed herself to feel the pain of humanity whose mistakes gave her employment.

Perhaps, she also realized, that she and Malia Shaw were not so different.

She rolled over. *God,* she cried out silently. *Tonight it hurts. Please send me some of Your great comfort and strength. Thank You that even in the midst of pain, You are name above all names, the great Creator of the universe, the One worthy of all our praise.*

As she slipped away into sleep finally, she was conscious of one last thought that she knew to be irretrievably true: *Always remember that you are forgiven, daughter.*

Chloe stopped typing her homework on the computer and listened intently. She heard her mother's soft footsteps slowly walk past her room and she waited for her door to swing open. Any Internet surfing was strictly forbidden during homework time, and her mom often checked in on her before going to bed. But tonight, the door remained firmly closed. She heard her mom's door close and a faucet turn on in the bathroom.

Chloe quit her homework, logged onto the Internet, and opened up the Facebook home page. She'd hoped Grace would be online for a chat, but there was no sign of her.

She rolled her eyes at the usual inanity that her classmates shared. There were a few memes that were actually funny. She was about to go back to her homework when she caught sight of a post that made her breath catch at the back of her throat.

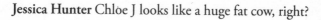

> **Jessica Hunter** Chloe J looks like a huge fat cow, right?

Chloe felt her hands go clammy. Should she post something or just leave it alone? If she posted something, she'd probably cop it even worse at school tomorrow. Then she realized there were comments piling up underneath Jessica's post.

> **Jessica Hunter** Chloe J looks like a huge fat cow, right?
> **Sarah Mallister** I was going to say a pig, but you right on
> **Shaun Kruger** U.G.L.Y. U know it
> **Jessica Hunter** What's with her stupid hair? I just want to slap her
> **Alice Greendale** LOL! I'd love to see that
> **Shaun Kruger** She'd totally do it
> **Jessica Hunter** I would, but stupid school would dog on me and like, suspend me
> **Sarah Mallister** Whatever. Do it anyways
> **Shaun Kruger** Yeah, what she said
> **Jessica Hunter** Maybe I'll get lucky and she'll just die
> **Alice Greendale** We should all wish for that now *wishes Chloe J would die*
> **Sarah Mallister** *wishes Chloe J would die*
> **Shaun Kruger** *wishes Chloe J would die*
> **Jessica Hunter** *wishes Chloe J would DIE*

Blood roared in Chloe's ears and she gripped the edge of the desk to keep herself from falling from her chair. Dimly, she heard her mother calling her. She couldn't seem to get her head together. A cold, sick dread coiled itself in her stomach like a nest of snakes.

Her door swung open, and her mother stuck her head in. "I was calling to see if you wanted a drink? I'm making hot chocolate. I can't sleep or read. I have a headache."

Chloe's throat had almost closed, due to the huge lump that had arisen. So, she just nodded her head.

Mom looked at her closely. "You look pale. Are you okay?"

Chloe wasn't sure how to answer that. *I'm great, unless you take into account that half the school thinks I should just die.* Eventually, she mumbled, "Yeah."

She followed her mom downstairs for the hot chocolate. During winter, they'd often chat together over steaming hot mugs. It had become a fun tradition, although it seemed like they hadn't done it for a while. Tonight, Chloe couldn't manage more than a monosyllabic reply. In the end, Mom gave up and they drank in silence.

Chloe's thoughts swam in her head like vicious piranha fish snapping after each other. Mostly, all her thoughts boiled down to: *What am I going to do?*

She calculated that at least 80 percent of her class would see the comments. Tomorrow, those people would look at her with a mixture of pity and contempt and *I'm glad it's not me.*

"Do I have to go to school tomorrow?" she asked.

Her mother looked at her strangely. "Of course. Why?"

I'd rather not set foot in that place ever again in my life. "No reason, I guess."

"Have you finished your homework?"

There was no way Chloe could bring herself to log back onto the computer, so she said, "Yeah."

She looked up at her mother and realized that Mom herself looked tired and pale. "What's wrong?" she asked.

Mom rubbed her eyes. "Oh, honey, I'm just tired. I can't wait for your dad to get home."

Chloe felt bad. She wondered if she should tell her dad about Facebook, Jessica, and the minions. At one time, she'd told her dad everything, secure in the knowledge that he was the font of all wisdom.

Now she realized she didn't want her dad to know she was such a loser.

"Are you sure *you're* okay?" Mom asked. Chloe realized her mother had been studying her.

Chloe debated telling her about Jessica Hunter and her minions. But Mom tended to overreact to things. She was likely to march down to the school and demand that the principal take immediate action. She probably would also call Jessica's parents. Chloe shuddered. *It would make everything ten times worse. This is my problem, and I'll handle it.*

It was something she'd have to work out on her own.

She helped Mom wash the mugs, and climbed the stairs to her bedroom. She heard the television click on and she felt guilty for being relieved that her mom wouldn't keep trying to talk to her. She closed the door to her room and walked to her dresser. There, she stared at herself in the mirror. Black hair, chopped into a blunt bob. Two streaks of blue through the front — the color changed every now and then. Before they were blue they'd been hot pink. The color in her hair was one of Jessica Hunter's favorite targets, but for some reason she fiercely guarded her right to do it.

She stared at her face. It was round and . . . full. Round and chubby. Round and *fat*, don't shy away from the truth, she told herself. Round, soft, pale, and fat. The square-frame glasses that looked funky at the mall didn't make *her* look funky. She just looked like a fat nerd.

Then there was her body. She had never been particularly tall. She'd always been a chubby girl. Her mother liked to say she was strong or robust. Chloe knew these were just nice ways of saying that she was fat. What made it worse was that her mother was tiny, and had never struggled with her weight. Her nickname was *Bonesy* for goodness sake. Chloe had inherited her broad build from her father. So, it was hard to talk about it with Mom, who could never understand the quiet despair of weight that just wouldn't shift.

She scrutinized herself. Flabby, old-lady arms. No waist. Chunky thighs. Wobbly calves. How many pounds would she have to lose to look like Jessica Hunter? *Probably 30 pounds. Maybe 40.* The thought depressed her. She'd have to stop eating altogether for weeks to lose the weight. *Guess that's why they call me a cow. That's what I look like.*

A sharp knock at her door startled her and she turned away from her reflection.

"It's Mom. I'm going to bed. Good night."

"Sure. Good night." Chloe found herself wanting to run to the door and tell her mom everything. How she was starting to hate everything about herself. How she wished she could walk away from this school and this town and never look back. How she felt so alone that her heart cried. She wished she could run to her mom like she had when she was little. She thought about the first time she could remember feeling that she was not quite the same as the other girls. In the fourth grade she wore a cute balloon skirt to school in place of the usual jeans. She remembered feeling the warm sun on her legs.

I hadn't been in the school gate more than five minutes when a sixth grader I didn't even know pointed at me and laughed. Her gaggle of friends all looked at me and laughed, too.

I hadn't heard what she said, but my friend Grace did. Grace turned red with indignation, but fourth graders didn't usually challenge sixth graders, so we walked harmlessly by. Once past, I asked her, "What did she say?"

"Don't worry about it," Grace said. I already needed protection by a prettier friend, even at the tender age of nine.

But I nagged at her until finally she gave in. "Chloe," Grace said. "They said that you look fat. That's all."

I tried to pretend that it didn't matter, but I was wounded. I gave a brittle laugh, as if there were no words in the world that could hurt me. But it was like I had just eaten from the tree of the knowledge of good and evil, as Eve had done. My eyes were suddenly open to everything shallow, conceited, and self-conscious. I was aware that I just wasn't good enough. I didn't look right.

It was that day that I understood more clearly how the world worked. How it favored the thin and pretty; how it rejected anyone who refused to conform to its ideals. It was because of that day that I could never quite look at myself in the mirror again, that every ice cream I ate carried with it an atomic bomb's weight of guilt, that I was acutely aware that cute dresses would never look good on me.

It was that day that I began to hate myself.

Instead, she listened to her mother's exhausted steps down the hallway and she kept her silence.

****

By the following morning, the dark clouds had disappeared and given way to a clear, cold day. The sun, a pale, yellow disk, seemed too far away and coldly indifferent to the affairs of men.

Dinah still felt tired even after two cups of black coffee. She and Elise arrived at the Sheriff's Department, where Elise was immediately whisked away into some meeting. Dinah didn't mind — it gave her a chance to concentrate on the next task. Her thoughts were solely focused on the murder case, and the first order of business was to obtain the addresses of the three numbers in Malia Shaw's cell phone.

Dinah called the phone company, and went through several layers of the management hierarchy before finally talking to the head of the Public Relations Department.

She had to start her story again. "I'm Dinah Harris and I'm calling from the Ten Mile Hollow Sheriff's Office," she said. "I am investigating a murder, and I need some information about the victim's cell phone."

"I see," the woman said, coolly. "I'm not sure I can do that."

Don't even go there with me this morning. Just don't.

"Well, I can of course get subpoenas and come down to your office," said Dinah. "I'll bring every deputy we've got, and we can go through your files one by one. Shouldn't take more than a few weeks. It'd be disruptive, but there's not much that I can do about that."

"Or I can just tell you what you want to know, right?" guessed the head of Public Relations.

"Right. Here is what I need: there are three numbers in the victim's cell phone. I need to know if those numbers are registered with your company or not, and if so, their full names and addresses. Now, I'll hang up and give you an hour to find that information. Then you call the Sheriff's Office here at Ten Mile Hollow and ask for me. That way, you'll know I'm genuine."

It was strangely satisfying to order the head of Public Relations around, Dinah thought as she hung up. She missed being able to boss people around.

The woman did call back within the hour, but with less good news than Dinah hoped. Of the three numbers, only the one belonging to Lola was registered with the same phone company. Still, it was a start. Lola's address was on the western side of the railway tracks, just as Malia's had been. Dinah waited impatiently for Elise's meeting to be finished, and when the other woman finally emerged from the office, Dinah grabbed her. On the way, she explained to Elise that they were headed toward Lola's place.

Lola lived in a duplex that was nicer than Malia Shaw's apartment, but still a little shabby. The apricot-colored paint was peeling, the lawn was struggling, and one of the shutters on the front window hung askew.

Elise knocked on the front door and they waited for a few minutes. There was no answer, and she knocked again.

"Looking for somebody?" a voice behind them barked.

Dinah jumped, startled, and turned around. Behind her stood a wizened old woman from whose face a pair of dark eyes glared at her ferociously.

"I'm looking for Lola," said Elise.

"And you are?"

"Detective Elise Jones, Sheriff's Office, and Dinah Harris, consultant." Elise showed her badge to the old lady, who looked at it suspiciously and sniffed.

"I'm Ada Whittaker," she said. "And I'm looking for Lola, too."

"Why is that?"

"I live next door," Ada Whittaker said, inclining her head toward the adjoining duplex. "I own this place, and I think Lola has split."

"Why is that?" repeated Elise.

"She's fallen behind in her rent. Owes me a month," said Ada, sourly. "Her mail's been piling up, and I haven't seen hide nor hair of her for well over a week. Maybe it's been two weeks now, when I think about it."

"Have you been inside?"

"Nope, but now that you're here, you can do it," said Ada. "I've got no desire to be seeing things that'll give me nightmares. Not at my age."

While Ada found the right key and fiddled with the lock, Elise asked, "What is Lola's last name?"

"Lola Albright," said the old lady.

"Do you remember from the rental application whether she worked or not?"

"I may be old, but I still have my memory," said Ada. She turned the key and eased the door open. "Lola was an office worker for one of those temporary placement places. You know, they work a month at one office, and then go to another office. The placement agency handles it all."

Elise nodded. "Thank you, ma'am. We'll take it from here."

"I'll be waiting," said Ada, her voice crisp.

Dinah and Elise walked inside the duplex, which was quiet and dark. It was furnished cheaply, but pleasantly. The kitchen, dining room and living room were all tidy and clean, except for a week's worth of dust. The bedroom, bathroom, and study nook were similarly attractively furnished, tidy and clean.

Dinah did a cursory search and found no purse or cell phone. More importantly, she didn't find a body. She looked through the closet in the only bedroom. There were still clothes hanging there, with no obvious gaps; but it was impossible to know whether Lola packed a bag in a hurry and left of her own accord or simply vanished.

Elise was also flummoxed. Back outside, in the pale, struggling sunlight, Elise asked Ada, "Did Lola drive a car?"

"Yes, an old Toyota, I think. I haven't seen it since Lola vanished into thin air."

While Dinah continued looking around the duplex, Elise asked Ada to find the lease agreement. Dinah inspected bookshelves, countertops, drawers, and couch cushions. Nothing seemed disturbed or out of place. It was just as a house would normally look if its occupant had left for work. And didn't mind a bit of dust.

A thought struck Dinah, and she frowned. There was one odd thing: like Malia Shaw's apartment, there were no photos, no knick-knacks, and no mementoes of any kind. That's what was odd — the place had a sterile feel to it.

Ada returned with a copy of the lease and rental application.

Elise inspected the documents and then gave them to Dinah. Dinah was unsurprised when she saw that Lola hadn't filled in the next-of-kin details either. Her birth date put her at around the same age as Malia Shaw. *Another ghost?*

"Did you ever see Lola doing any drugs?" Dinah asked.

The old woman shook her head. "I don't tolerate that kind of thing around here," she said. "I kept as close an eye on her as I could. I didn't see anything that looked like drugs. She went to work and she came home. She didn't have any visitors. To me, she seemed kind of lonely."

That seems to be a recurring theme, thought Dinah.

"Did you see anyone suspicious hanging around?" she asked. "Or did you see Lola acting like she was afraid?"

"Not that I can recall," said Ada. "I'd know if there were any unsavory types hanging around here."

Dinah took one more glance around the duplex and thanked Ada Whittaker for her help. Elise promised to return the lease and rental application when she was finished with it, and both women went back to her car. As she turned the ignition, Elise said, "I know there have been no missing persons reports filed for anyone matching Lola's age and gender. I'd know, because any report would have come across my desk."

"So, she disappeared a week — or perhaps two weeks — ago," mused Dinah. "Before Malia Shaw died?"

"Are you thinking of her as a suspect or a victim?" Elise asked. She drove over a residential speed bump like it was a scrap of paper and something in the car made a loud bang.

Dinah clenched her teeth together. "I suppose both are possibilities, but I'm leaning toward Lola leaving in a hurry because she knew of some danger. It seems she left before Malia Shaw was murdered, so unless she came back to kill Malia, the timeline doesn't really fit."

Elise nodded and they fell into thoughtful silence.

Dinah stared through the windshield at the pale blue sky, seemingly blanched of its color by the vicious cold.

Two women in their late thirties. Both lived alone, in sterile and shabby surroundings. Neither seemed to have any family or friends. Both seemed isolated, except for a tenuous link with each other. Now one was dead; the other vanished.

What was the connection between them?

****

Angus Whitehall had managed to spend the first few hours of the day dealing with pleasantries and pretending to be normal. His cheeks hurt from smiling widely and falsely, and he was heartily sick of shallow platitudes. *How are you? Just great! How are you?* It was essential to convincing everyone at work that he was fine, that a dead woman found on the wrong side of town had absolutely nothing to do with him.

When he had finally gotten some time alone, he locked himself in his office at the Ten Mile Hollow First Baptist Church and sat down at his desk. It was a relaxing space: the walls lined with books on theology, philosophy, morality, and ethics; two table lamps throwing warm pools of light onto the carpet; an old, battered, deeply comfortable Chesterfield couch.

But Angus did not feel relaxed today.

The panicky feeling in his chest, which felt like a desperate bird thrumming in his rib cage trying to escape, hadn't reduced in intensity. It left him short of breath, a little like he was slowly drowning on perfectly dry land.

The detective had called yesterday. His panic had flared intensely in that moment, like a flashpoint, and he had hung up on her. If there were anything that would flag a detective's interest, it would be an alarmed hang-up. Now he was wondering what he was going to do.

Last night he'd fully expected several police cars, lights flashing and sirens blaring, to crash into his front yard. He'd been waiting, on edge, for that moment in time in which he'd be arrested in front of his children and wife. It hadn't happened, but he was a fool if he thought the detective wouldn't come sniffing around.

As he had many times before, he felt tired, bone-weary. He was so sick of running and fighting, hoping to stay ahead, wondering if he'd be safe. It felt like he was in the midst of a hurricane, the roaring wind ripping and pulling at his thin veneer of respectability, threatening to tear it off and expose the rotten core hidden beneath. Had he really been so stupid to think that marriage and a family and a reputable job would shield him? Now that stupidity would put Louise, Grace, and Marcus in harm's way. *I am not the person they think I am. They think I'm good, but I'm bad. They think I'm wise, but I'm a fool.*

Louise cannot understand the frequency of nightmares I have — too many for an adult, surely? Not when you've done the things I've done.

Louise is frightened of me when I become angry. She can see the monster in me. She doesn't know what I'm capable of, but she can sense something is not quite right. I know that my anger is lethal and treacherous, as menacing as a shark in dark waters. It has exploded with deadly force before. But nobody must know about that. Nobody must find out the things I've done!

I'm walking a tightrope nobody knows about, where to fall is destruction, despair, death. To stay steady I must grit my teeth and fix my eyes upon the end. Often, the battle not to fall, not to give in to my old nature, leaves me exhausted.

I am under no illusion that I will keep this façade up forever. One day, the truth will surface and you will have to decide to forgive or to walk away. Perhaps, one day, I'll lose the battle on the tightrope, and I'll fall. I pray you'll understand how long I've fought myself, and know that I did it for you.

He tried to gather his thoughts, to keep focus and think sensibly. He needed to work out what he would tell the detective when she inevitably contacted him again. *God,* he implored, *I know I need to tell the truth. But I'm so scared.*

How willing was he to expose everything about himself? Inwardly, he cringed, knowing that he was a coward, and always had been.

He had been in Malia's apartment, and he was pretty sure the police would discover that. Despite his efforts to be careful, he had to think that they would find a stray fingerprint or some other DNA. There might even be a witness who'd seen him come and go from that apartment. His first priority was to come up with a plausible story about why he'd been at her apartment. He cast around for ideas, each sounding wilder than the last.

Finally, he settled on the only one that seemed likely — that he'd counseled her, he a concerned minister and she a drug addict, trying to help her change her life.

He rubbed his burning eyes, realizing he'd been staring at the same spot. *What a ridiculous story!* Why would a minister go to a dingy apartment to counsel a drug addict when the church had so many outreach programs running from within this very building? It was laughable. He had to come up with a better story.

Angus shook his head. His thoughts were buckshot, spraying through his head with no target and no aim. He needed to think about what the police definitely knew.

First, they knew that he had known Malia. They had gotten his phone number from somewhere, and it was likely from her apartment or cell phone. There had probably been witnesses over time who had seen him with her and going into her apartment.

Second, they would find out that he'd been in her apartment. He'd always been careful not to leave much of himself there, but there would almost certainly be a fingerprint or some DNA that would connect him with her.

What they *didn't* know was how he knew her.

This was the exact story that couldn't get out. It would ruin his career and reputation. It would destroy his family, none of whom knew about his past.

But there was one thing he knew for sure. *I didn't kill her. I wasn't there when she died. They have no way of proving that I had anything to do with her death.*

Angus realized with a start that he'd spent every minute since he'd learned of her death thinking about how it would affect him. He hadn't once thought about the fact that she had died violently at the hands of another. He hadn't grieved for her. He wasn't sure he could. In truth, her death was a relief. He no longer had to worry about being seen with her, about her saying the wrong thing to the wrong person in a heroin haze.

He thought of her, finally, as the broken bird she'd always been. What they'd been through together, he'd survived. But she had been more fragile, more easily bruised, and had not outlasted her pain. That was why he'd continued to help her, despite the fact he knew she wouldn't live much longer. He'd always thought he'd find her dead from an overdose, the needle still in her arm. He'd never thought that their past would find her first.

The question now was, if he hadn't killed her, who had? Had the past he'd been trying to hide for so long finally caught up with him in this small town? Was he himself in danger?

This led him to think of Lola — the third person in their triumvirate of violence and secrecy. He wondered if she knew, and whether she was scared. He debated whether to call her, to warn her. But perhaps that would put her in worse danger, for surely he was the main target for the killer.

Angus thought of Malia again, of the girl he'd once known. She'd been bright, vivacious, and cute. In those days, he'd been younger, handsome, and arrogant, with a forceful personality. In those days, he'd been rougher, with less finesse. She had loved him, worshiped the ground he'd walked on. He'd taken advantage of her naivety; he'd always loved himself more. He'd dragged her down into a dark place, from which she'd never recovered.

He'd fooled himself into thinking that somehow they'd escaped from their past, that it would remain successfully hidden.

Instead, it rose from the murky depths, like a sea serpent from the old myths, ready to destroy.

****

Late in the afternoon, when those who did their work in the shadows shook themselves from sleep and emerged into the dying light, Elise and Dinah ventured into the seedy neighborhood Simon called home. Dinah had called the phone company, been put on hold and eventually received Simon's address after two hours of polite requests, negotiation, and finally threats of bringing the full force of the law crashing down upon them. Elise had listened the whole time while she caught up on her paperwork, grinning.

Dinah had assumed from the nature of the text messages between Malia and Simon, that he had been her dealer. That made him a prime suspect, in her eyes. For protection and intimidation, Elise decided to take along one of the sheriff's deputies, a building-sized officer named Peyton Hauser. He was big, and he was quick with his gun. He wasn't the sharpest knife in the drawer, but he possessed a frighteningly impassive glare that promised violence and a horrible death to anyone who dared cross him.

When Simon opened his door and saw the police on his doorstep, he seemed weary and resigned, as though he'd been waiting for them. "Come in," he said, though his tone indicated that he very much wished they would do the opposite.

His place was bigger than Malia's, and kept in better condition. The furniture wasn't much to speak of, but Simon clearly had a thing for gadgetry: electronics of every description crowded the living room.

Hauser whistled. "Nice stuff you've got here, Simon. What is it you do for a living?"

Simon was tall and twig-thin, with watery, pale blue eyes, scruffy, patchy facial hair, and a thin mouth. He waved vaguely at a fake-leather couch, an invitation to sit down.

He smiled. "I'm in the import/export business, sir."

Elise snorted. "Of course you are. Lucky for you we're not here to inspect your goods. We're here about a woman named Malia Shaw."

Simon swallowed. "What about her?"

"How did you know her?" Dinah asked. "Before you start lying through your teeth, you should know we have dozens of text messages between the two of you."

Simon considered this for a long moment and nodded. "Yeah, I knew her."

"How long have you known her?"

Again he took a moment to think. "Musta been three, four years ago."

"How did you come to meet her?"

Simon smiled and stayed silent.

Deputy Hauser shifted his bulk close to the other man. "Answer the lady, Simon. You don't want to make me get upset."

Simon eyed the officer's muscle-bound arms and said, "I, uh, helped her get the stuff she wanted."

"By stuff, you mean heroin," prompted Dinah.

Simon's eyes slid nervously around the room. "Yeah. She was into it in a big way when I met her. Already a big-time junkie."

"How did she pay you for the drugs?"

"Cash. I don't accept nothin' else."

"Right. She ever have a problem paying you?"

"No, she always had cash."

"Where did she get cash from? Did she work?"

Simon considered this. "I don't know. I'm pretty sure she never had a proper job. She was too, you know, too much of a junkie."

"What about other sources of income? Did she sell drugs? Steal? Beg?"

"No," he said immediately. "I know who's dealin' drugs around here. She didn't have the control to sell smack, anyways. She saw smack, it went straight in her arm. Don't know about stealing stuff, but I don't think that sounds right."

Dinah thought for a moment. It matched Malia's condition as a hard-core drug user. What didn't match was the foresight or control to pay rent in advance.

"What about herself?"

Simon shook his head. "I don't think so. I know she wasn't on the street. I'd a known about that."

Dinah nodded. How on earth had Malia paid for a steady stream of heroin? She had to be getting the cash from somewhere.

"So you never had a problem with payment with Malia?"

"Nope, never," said Simon.

"Ever have any disagreements with her?"

"No. We didn't really know each other well, know what I'm sayin'? She texted me when she needed stuff. I'd go over, get my cash. That was it."

"You ever try to stiff her? Cut her drugs with talc, sugar, or anything?"

Simon had the arrogance to look offended. "No way! I got a good name in this business. My stuff is always good; I'm reliable. I charge a premium for it, so I only get clients who can pay."

This mystified Dinah. Malia didn't fit the stereotype of someone who could afford premium heroin.

"You ever want more from her, Simon?" Elise asked, leaning forward and watching his eyes intently. "More than a business relationship and she turned you down?"

Simon looked pained. "I don't mix business with pleasure. Anyway have you —?"

"Have I what, Simon?"

Simon's face stained faintly red. "Ah . . . I was just gonna say . . . she wasn't my type."

"So you're saying you didn't touch her?"

"Yeah, yeah, that's what I'm sayin'."

"If that's true, the DNA will prove it. DNA doesn't lie, you know."

That didn't scare Simon. "It'll tell you true, then. I didn't touch her." His eyes widened. "I didn't kill her either, if that's what you be thinkin'."

"You didn't get upset with her, smack her around a bit?"

"No way! In fact, I never used to even go into her place hardly. Used to stand on the porch, do the deal quick. In fact, it was me who —"

Simon suddenly clamped his mouth shut.

"Who what, Simon?" Elise asked.

Deputy Hauser moved closer to the other man and flexed his bicep. Simon swallowed noisily. He was silent for a few moments, and said: "It was me who called 911."

"Really?" Dinah knew that the emergency call had been anonymous. "Tell me what happened."

"She texted me for stuff a couple a days before I called," Simon said. "I took it over, she gave me cash. It was usually every two, three days. I'd give her enough to last her a few days. I didn't hear from her after that, I went over to check."

"Why did you do that?"

Simon looked embarrassed. "She was a good client. Made lotta money from her."

"So what happened?"

"Knocked on her door. Looked through the little window next to the door."

Dinah thought about Malia's apartment and recalled the small pane of frosted glass next to the front door. How had he seen through the frosted glass? She frowned and started to ask him, but he must have read her thoughts.

"There's a strip of glass right around the edge that ain't frosted," Simon explained. "Like about half an inch wide. I couldn't see her at all. I knocked and knocked, and she didn't come to the door. I thought it was pretty weird. I didn't know what happened. For all I knew she overdosed or hit her head or somethin'. So I called it in, but I swear I never knew she'd a been murdered."

Dinah thought his story rang true. He would be stupid to kill off such a regular customer, unless there had been a problem between them. She needed to dig a little deeper into the real Simon.

"Where were you last Monday?" she asked.

"I was with . . . clients most of the day," he said. "She'd a been one of the first ones."

"I need names, addresses, and phone numbers," Elise said.

Simon suddenly looked shaken. "I . . . I can't!"

"Unless you want a murder rap on your sheet, you can," said Elise.

"You don't understand," said Simon, his voice high-pitched and desperate. "These aren't down-and-out junkies like Malia. Most of my clients are . . . regular people, with jobs and families and stuff. They don't wanta be found out!"

Wrong, Simon, they're all addicts. I would know, wouldn't I?

"Simon, let's do a deal," suggested Elise. "I'll be discreet with them, if you'll be upfront. Their secret lives will remain safe with me. But if you mess around with me, I'll make all kinds of noise and organize lots of drug raids and not only will you be finished, but you'll be in jail for supply anyway. Then I start thinking all kinds of unhealthy thoughts about how you murdered this woman. You understand me?"

Simon sighed. He got up, took out a red notebook from a desk drawer and gave it to Elise.

He'd seen nine contacts during Monday, he told her, including Malia. Dinah looked through the book once Elise had finished copying the details of those contacts. Once, she might have been stunned. Since her own fall from grace, nothing about the human condition surprised her anymore.

Most of Simon's clients were middle-class — teachers, mothers, lawyers, bankers. Not the sort of people you normally assumed used drugs.

But things had changed, Dinah thought. Life was cheap and the strong victimized the weak. She had seen men smack the teeth out of their wives, kids film each other kicking a hapless victim in the head, women put out their cigarettes on their kids' legs. It was a mad world.

"Now, Simon," Elise said, by way of farewell. "You make sure you stick around, okay? We'll be watching you. Any funny behavior, we'll take you straight in on any number of drugs charges. You keep playing straight with me, we're okay."

He nodded as Elise, Dinah, and Hauser made their own way out of his apartment.

A cold night filled with soft mist had fallen as Elise and Dinah drove toward Norfolk. The slick blacktop hissed underneath the wheels, a noise that had always seemed comforting to Dinah. It reminded her of long road trips she'd taken as a child with her parents, a peaceful quiet reigning in the car, save for the sweet sound of her mother singing softly. At this moment, though, she was buzzed and wide-awake. The autopsy of Malia Shaw had been done, and she and Elise wanted to be there in person for the results.

On the way, Elise called home to check in with Lewis and Chloe. This filled Dinah with a considerable amount of anxiety, as Elise's distracted driving became even worse. She hung on, clenched her teeth, and somehow they arrived in one piece.

A freezing rain was falling when they pulled into the parking lot at the Medical Examiner's Office in Norfolk. Elise stopped the car and they ran across the wet parking lot into the building, where cheerful light spilled from the windows in sharp contrast to the miserable weather.

Dr. Theo Walker was alone there; everyone else had gone home for the night. Elise had explained that he was the doctor who usually did the autopsies for the occasional mysterious deaths that occurred in Ten Mile Hollow. Usually, the autopsy was a formality, a confirmation that the bar fight had gone terribly wrong, or that a husband had finally hit his wife too hard. This one would be different.

"Evening, detective," he greeted, cheerily. He looked at Dinah. "Hello. Nice to see you again!"

Dr. Walker's cheerfulness only seemed to increase with every dead body he saw, Dinah thought.

"Evening, doctor," Elise replied, shaking the rain from her hair. "Thanks for fitting us in."

"No problem," said the doctor. "Follow me. We'll go have a look at her."

Elise and Dinah followed the tall doctor back to an examining room, fitted out in blinding white and stainless steel. It was immaculate, which made the jarring juxtaposition between the spotless room and the ruined body of a human being on the table even more pronounced.

"Let's begin with the basics," said Dr. Walker. "Your victim was female, aged in her late thirties. She had never given birth to a child."

Lonely, lonely, lonely, the room seemed to echo.

"The cause of death was asphyxiation due to strangulation," continued Dr. Walker. He motioned at the throat of Malia Shaw. "You can see the bruises on her neck, which indicate force was applied, probably with another person's hands, rather than an instrument like rope or cord. Further evidence of asphyxiation can be found in the eyes — you can see petechial hemorrhages."

Dinah saw that the small, red capillary blood vessels in Malia Shaw's eyes had burst. It was a telltale sign of strangulation.

"Further, there was some cyanosis to her lips and extremities, indicating a depleted level of oxygen in her body. Again, that's indicative of asphyxiation. I believe the victim died sometime last Monday. I couldn't narrow it down much further than that 24-hour period. I mentioned at the crime scene that rigor mortis had passed by the time we got there, indicative that it was at least 48 hours since her death. The cold of the apartment had slowed decomposition, however, so it may be impossible to pin down the exact time. In any case, I have to think that this particular victim wouldn't have lived much longer."

"Drug addiction?" Elise said.

"Right. This lady was a heavy, long-time drug abuser," said Dr. Walker. "I'm thinking at least 10 years, but could be as many as 20 years." He pointed at the inside of her arms. "You can see scar tissue here, to the point that most of the veins in these areas had collapsed. I also found scar tissue in her feet, legs, and stomach, all showing evidence of being used as injection sites. She has other hallmarks of a chronic heroin user: she's very thin, there are contusions all over her body from scratching and picking."

These were evident upon the body — deep, weeping sores because heroin addicts often felt like their skin was crawling and couldn't help but scratch.

Dr. Walker consulted his notes. "Internally, she was a mess, to put it mildly. She had contracted hepatitis C, and had not received treatment for it. Her liver was in a diseased state. Her heart was also damaged and I saw some mild inflammation of the lining, which would worsen with time. She had an obvious decrease in muscle mass. I wouldn't have been at all surprised if one day soon, she'd shot up, her heart stopped, and she'd not woken up."

Dinah let out a long breath. She felt immense pity for the woman, who seemed to be bent on self-destruction. For anyone who had struggled with addiction, she knew how hard it was to beat. For someone like Malia Shaw, who had been isolated, it must have seemed an insurmountable hurdle.

"Physically, there is only one other item of note to report," Dr. Walker said. He rolled her arm back over, so that the outside was more visible. "I found strange scarring that is very old, maybe 15 or 20 years."

Dinah looked at the dead woman's arms closely.

"You won't see traditional scar tissue," said the doctor. "What's occurred is a bleaching of the skin."

Dinah saw what Dr. Walker was referring to — on each upper arm, a large patch of skin that was a shade whiter than the rest of her body appeared. It was more pronounced than a tan line; somehow it seemed much more permanent.

"What caused this?" she asked.

"Most commonly, laser removal of tattoos," said Dr. Walker. "Today, it can be done with minimal scarring and a reasonable result. Twenty years ago, the procedure was much more invasive and left this distinctive scar."

"Oh!" Elise sounded surprised. "Wouldn't that be expensive?"

"It would be," agreed Dr. Walker. "Certainly 20 years ago, it would have been more expensive than it is today."

Dinah made a note of this, wondering what it meant, if anything. It did seem coincidental that 20 years ago, Malia had gotten tattoos removed and commenced taking heroin. What had happened 20 years ago?

"Now, you'll want to know if I found any DNA or evidence you can use," Dr. Walker continued. "I took scrapings from underneath the fingernails and found some DNA there. I'll run it through the system tomorrow and see if we get any hits. I didn't find any other prints, hairs, or fibers on the body itself."

Elise nodded. "Thanks, Doctor. You've been very helpful."

"Sure," said Dr. Walker. "I'll call you tomorrow."

Driving home in icy rain, the conditions seemed fitting. Dinah's mind whirled around like a hurricane, attempting to reach the elusive eye of the storm. Who was Malia Shaw? How did she have access to cash? Why did she have tattoos removed? Why had she become a heroin addict?

And how did this all relate to her death?

****

Chloe was dressed in sweat pants, a long-sleeved T-shirt, and a hooded sweatshirt. The garments did nothing to keep her warm, but she reasoned that she should warm up soon. She glanced around her. The track was empty — the serious school athletes trained inside warm gyms during the winter months. Plus, it was still very early in the morning. The sun had only just appeared reluctantly above the eastern horizon.

She was here because there was no way she wanted to work out in front of people. Here, with just her, the grass, and the sky, she felt comfortable enough to run. The last time she'd been here, the track had looked completely different. In the bleachers, parents and students yelled and cheered. The athletes, their taut and lean bodies in action, had sprinted and jumped and thrown. Chloe spent the day making sarcastic comments to hide her jealousy.

She'd calculated that if she learned to run two miles every day, she should be able to lose two pounds a week. The website she'd found — onemileonepound.com — practically guaranteed it.

She did some basic stretches and started to run. In truth, she was a total klutz and looked like a total nerd when she jogged. *Nobody wants to see a fat girl run*, she thought. Here, in the quiet early morning, she enjoyed the solitude.

It didn't take long for her breath to become ragged. She'd barely completed one-fourth of her goal. There was a painful stitch in her side. Her legs felt like they had been dipped in cement.

I need to complete half, then I'll take a rest. So she pushed herself until her lungs seemed to have been burned away to a third of their original size and she felt sure her heart would just beat right out of her chest and plop to the ground. Then she allowed herself to stop, hunch over, and suck in sweet mouthfuls of cold air.

The upside was that she was warm. *Probably red as a beet*, she thought.

She managed to run one and a half miles before she honestly thought she might die. *This is only the first day of many*, she told herself. *No need to kill yourself.*

As she walked home, her lungs still felt newly scalded but despite that, she felt flushed with excitement. She'd jogged, done something healthy, and now it felt great! *This must be the endorphin high I keep hearing about.*

It was almost time to leave for school by the time she arrived home, and she noticed the house was empty. Her mother and Dinah had already gone to work; her father had either gone or would be home soon depending on his shift.

Chloe turned on the computer and decided to check Facebook for a quick scan while she ate a piece of toast.

For the second time in as many days, she wished she hadn't.

Jessica Hunter had posted a video, shot on her cell phone. As if she were watching a grotesque car wreck that simultaneously repulsed and thrilled her, Chloe clicked "play."

The Dark Heart

The video was of her, running around the track field. The shaky camera zoomed in on her thighs, then her stomach, and then her face. With sick fascination, she observed that her thighs were thunderous, her stomach wobbly, and her face red and tortured.

The comment Jessica had attached to the video read: *Run, cow, run!*

Underneath, her minions had weighed in. Shaun Kruger wrote, *mmoooo! Mmmm — ooooooo! I think I just threw up a little in my mouth.*

Alice Greendale wrote, *Maybe the cow will keel over and die! Lol!*

Sarah Mallister wrote, *That's disgusting. I think my eyeballs r bleeding.*

A cold, numb dread settled over Chloe. A bitter, metallic taste rose in her mouth — the taste of humiliation and disgrace. In her head, she tried to calculate how many people that she went to school with would see the video.

It'll go viral. It won't just be my school; it'll be everyone in the whole town and probably the whole country.

Her stomach rolled and heaved; she wanted to throw up. For one crazy moment, she wondered if she withdrew all the money in her bank account whether she could start a new life in a different country. Maybe New Zealand. Surely they wouldn't see the video there. But of course the paltry $350 in her account wouldn't get her to New Zealand, or even Canada.

Miserably, she logged out of Facebook and stared at the blank computer screen. Her thoughts were jittery and danced crazily like bugs trapped near a light bulb.

She decided to call Grace on her cell phone. Grace was probably at school already.

Grace answered. "Hey, Chloe?"

"Hey, how you doing?"

"Good! Where are you? Are you here yet?"

"Uh . . . no, not yet."

There was a pause. "Are you okay? You don't sound so good."

"Uh, have you been on Facebook yet?" Chloe asked.

"No. Why?"

"There's a video of me on there."

"What video?"

Chloe explained the video that Jessica had posted on Facebook.

"What? That's totally uncool. I'm going to tell her so."

"It's okay," said Chloe, sadly. "It's not your fight."

"Of course it is!" Grace was indignant. "You're my friend. What happens to you, happens to me."

Chloe felt some of her anxiety ease as she spoke to her friend.

"Have you told your mom yet?" Grace asked.

"About Jessica Hunter? No. I've tried a few times, but she's been so tired lately. I don't want to disturb her."

"You have to tell someone," urged Grace. "Or Jessica will get away with it."

"I know. I'll try to talk to her tonight."

"Oh — hey," said Grace. "The bell just rang. Are you coming to school?"

Chloe thought about going, but the horror of seeing Jessica's mocking smile and hearing the jeering laughter was too much.

"No, I might stay home. I'm not . . . feeling good," she said.

"Listen," said Grace. "I'm going to talk to Jessica today. I don't know if it'll do any good, but I'll try. Okay?"

Chloe hung up, feeling slightly better.

She went upstairs to shower. At the mirror, she sucked in her stomach and scrutinized her thighs. Had she lost weight today?

To make totally sure, I'll skip lunch, she decided. She'd read somewhere that reducing food intake drastically was a good way to lose weight fast.

If I had the money, I'd just get liposuction. Then I'd be instantly skinny and not be videoed running around the track like a loser.

She decided to work on an assignment and managed to concentrate. When hunger pangs lashed out in her stomach, she realized it was lunchtime. She thought about eating, but she liked the feeling of an empty stomach. It made her realize that she was in control, that she had power over her body. And eventually, the hunger pangs went away and Chloe knew she'd won the first battle.

If she could just do that every day, she'd be skinny in no time at all.

****

Angus had spent the morning in a meeting about town planning permits, and he had no idea what he'd said. Similarly, he'd gone through the family motions last night, watching TV with Louise, acting as normally as possible.

The Dark Heart

Inside was a different story. Anxiety gnawed at him like termites on a wooden post. Waiting for the police to come knocking was driving him crazy. Were they doing this to him on purpose? The anticipation of their visit made him jumpy, hyper-aware, unable to sleep properly.

He'd napped for a few hours close to dawn. He woke as the sky changed from gray to pink. Groggy, shaky, and with a headache, he'd quietly left the house. Now that he was in his office, he had a mission. He needed to get in contact with Lola, to make sure she didn't say anything stupid, to remind her to keep up her end of the bargain. *But mostly to protect me, if you want to know the truth,* he thought. A sick shiver of shame rolled over him.

He called her cell phone, which rang out. There was no option to leave a message. He debated for far too long about whether to send her a text message, and eventually he fired off a very short one: *call me*.

He looked up the name of the agency that handled her temporary work positions and called them. "I'm trying to reach Lola Albright," he said. "Can you tell me where she's working at the moment?"

The receptionist ceased loudly chewing her gum briefly to tell him the name of a stationery supply business on the east side of town.

Angus called there. "I'm looking for Lola Albright," she said.

The man who answered snorted loudly. "You and me both, buddy," he said. "She hasn't turned up to work here all week. *She's* supposed to be answering this phone."

"Have you contacted her agency? I don't think they're aware she hasn't been to work," said Angus.

"I'm gonna call them next week," said the man. "It's not unusual for temp staff to go AWOL." His tone changed, hardened. "Why do you want to know? What did you say your name was?"

Angus hung up. The only other contact he had for Lola was her landlord, an old woman who lived next door. He called her. "This is Ada Whittaker," the cracked voice of the old lady answered.

"I'm looking for Lola Albright," Angus said. "Is she home?"

"No, she isn't," snapped Ada Whittaker. "Do *you* know where she is? She owes me a month of rent."

"I'm concerned for her safety," said Angus, using his most pastoral tone. "When did you see her last?"

"Over a week ago. Probably two weeks ago," said Ada. "I saw her leave in her car. Thought she was going to work like she did every other morning. But I didn't see her come home, and her car hasn't been home either."

"Have you checked her apartment?" Angus asked.

"No need, son," Ada said. "The police already came to check the place. She wasn't there."

Angus's heart plummeted to his shoes like an out-of-control elevator. "Sorry, what did you say?"

"The police already came to check her place," Ada said. "She wasn't there. I gave them the key, we went in and looked around."

Angus wanted to throw up. "Thanks anyway," he said, hanging up the phone.

The *police* had been there? How had they made the connection between Malia and Lola so quickly? How long would it be before they connected him?

One woman dead, one woman missing. This doesn't bode well. What have I done? Why am I still being punished for this? Why can I never escape the past?

Angus's thoughts turned to his own safety. Would they come after him next? If they'd found Malia and Lola so easily, he'd be even easier to locate. Or would they come after his family?

That thought caused him to go cold with fear. Going after his family was precisely the kind of thing *they* would do.

But how could he warn Louise and protect his kids without telling them the whole story? Louise didn't know about his past. She wouldn't have married him if she had known. It wasn't the sort of thing he could just come clean about now — not to mention that his career would come to a screeching halt. It was too big and there had been too much deception. No church congregant in their right mind would want somebody like Angus as their minister if they knew the truth.

Perhaps he could surprise them with a vacation? But that was a risky move for someone who was under police suspicion. Angus drummed his fingers on the desk, his anxiety building. This was an impossible situation.

Angus suddenly couldn't stand the confines of his office, and he decided to go for a drive. Perhaps he could look for Lola's car, a beat-up Toyota. The police wouldn't yet have a clear picture of her usual haunts.

Angus drove into town, circling Main Street several times, despite knowing it was unlikely Lola was simply having coffee in one of the local cafes. One did not usually go out for coffee for weeks on end. It was futile, but he felt that doing something — anything — was better than sitting on his butt. He visited several office buildings where he knew she'd done work in the past, but he didn't dare go in; he was scared of being recognized. So he cruised through the parking lots of each building, searching for her car and seeing nothing.

He drove past the gym where she liked to put in hours on the treadmill, as if she could somehow outrun her past. Her car wasn't there. He drove to the bus terminal, and checked the parking lot where people who caught buses into Richmond left their cars. Her Toyota wasn't there.

Finally, he couldn't think of another place where she might be. It seemed she had gone, melted away like snow. Had the person who'd killed Malia spooked her? Had she been killed already, and just not found yet? Full of dread, Angus turned around and drove home. It was mid-afternoon; the kids would be home from school. He could play basketball and help with homework and try to forget about this hideous, impossible problem.

He drove down his street and his stomach gave a lurch when he saw the unmarked police car parked outside his house.

Finally, the police had come for him.

****

Dinah saw the headlights of Angus's car turn into the driveway. She had found a seat in the living room, where his wife Louise had been hovering, both offering hospitality and worry in equal amounts. Elise sat opposite her, perched on the edge of a fabric couch. Dinah, amidst the detritus of family life, was running out of ways to decline Louise's suggestion of a cup of coffee. She couldn't help but feel sorry for the woman, fluttering around like a frightened bird.

Thankfully, when she saw his car, Louise flew outside onto the porch, wringing her hands. "Angus, the police are here," Dinah heard her call. "Where have you been? I've been trying to call you."

Dinah didn't hear his reply, but heard his footsteps approaching the front door.

Louise reappeared first, her head turned toward her husband.

Angus Whitehall was tall and patrician, with a full head of dark hair, intelligent dark eyes, and a charismatic smile. He spoke with a voice as smooth and sweet as honey. He was only in his late thirties, and Elise had told Dinah on the way that he was an immensely popular pastor. Elise knew the pastor vaguely; their daughters were the same age and were good friends.

"Is everything okay?" Louise asked her husband, her brow creased with worry lines.

"I'm sure it is," said Angus Whitehall. He smiled casually, although to Dinah's trained eye it seemed more a grimace than a smile.

She stood to shake his hand.

"Hello, Mr. Whitehall," Elise said. "I'm Detective Elise Jones with the sherriff's office, and this is Dinah Harris, a former FBI agent who is consulting with me. I'm sorry to disturb you this late in the evening, but I wonder if I might have a few words with you?"

"Sure, Detective. I know who you are. Aren't our girls friends?" he said, sitting down on the couch opposite her. Louise sat down next to him.

Elise cleared her throat. "Yes, that's correct. Your Grace and my Chloe have been friends for a while now." She paused for a moment. "I'm sorry, Mrs. Whitehall. I need to speak with your husband privately."

Louise jumped to her feet, her face blooming red. "Oh . . . of course. Will you be okay, dear?"

"Yes," said Whitehall. "Though it's been a long day and I'd sure appreciate a cup of coffee. Would you mind bringing a pot for us?"

At least we know there is plenty of coffee waiting, thought Dinah.

"Certainly," she said. She threw a look at Dinah that seemed to say *I told you so! I knew you wanted coffee all along!*

While Louise busied herself in the kitchen, Elise asked the pastor, "How is Grace?"

"Very well, thanks. How is Chloe?"

Elise smiled. "Great. Busy day at the office?"

Mr. Whitehall almost replied immediately, and then seemed to catch himself. "Well, the office was busy, yes. I wasn't there, specifically; I was attending to other matters today."

An odd answer, thought Dinah. She made a note to find out more about the pastor's activities that day.

Once the coffee had arrived and Louise had anxiously retreated, Elise got down to business. "Mr. Whitehall, I'm here because I'm investigating the murder of a woman named Malia Shaw," she said. "I believe you knew her." *Good, Elise — start as you mean to continue,* Dinah thought, impressed.

"I did," agreed the pastor, after a tiny hesitation. His features jumped around, as if trying to decide in which position to settle.

"Did you know that she had been murdered?"

"I found out on the Wednesday night newscast," said Mr. Whitehall.

"The police tried to call your phone recently," said Elise.

A flush tinged his face for a moment. "Did you? My cell phone?"

"Yes." Dinah watched him closely.

"I'm sorry, my cell phone has been dropping in and out recently. I've barely been using it; it's become so annoying." The words came out smoothly, but Mr. Whitehall's face slowly stained a light red.

Not a smooth liar, thought Dinah.

"Had you seen her recently?"

A pause. Whitehall said at length: "I saw her about twice a week."

"Did you go to her apartment to see her, or did she come to you?"

"I usually went to her apartment. She found travel . . . difficult."

"Prior to her death, when was your last visit?"

He considered. "It would have been Sunday afternoon."

Dinah made some notes, thinking any fresh DNA they might find could well be explained, if Mr. Whitehall was telling the truth.

"Your name was found in her cell phone," said Elise. "The call log shows that you were in communication with the victim on a regular basis. What was the nature of your relationship with her?"

"I was concerned with her well-being," said Mr. Whitehall. "I check on her every few days to make sure she's okay. You must know by now that she was a heavy heroin user. I wouldn't have been surprised to hear of her death at any time."

"Her death from what?"

"Well, an overdose," said the pastor, his light red flush turning rosy. "Or simply her body giving up. She's been using drugs for many years."

"So you've known her for a long time?" Elise pounced.

Mr. Whitehall seemed to realize he'd given away more information than he'd wanted to. "I think it's obvious to anyone that she's been using drugs for a long time," he said, evenly. "But sure, I've known her for a while."

"And how exactly did you know her?"

He stiffened and ducked his head. The silence stretched into awkwardness.

"Mr. Whitehall?"

"We went to college together, a long time ago."

"Really? Where was that?"

"At UC San Diego."

"Do you know a person named Lola Albright?"

There was a tiny pause. "Uh . . . no, I don't believe so." His eyes were wide and looked straight into Elise's, unblinking. However, his hands danced on his knees, picking and smoothing, tapping and flicking.

"She was also in frequent contact with Malia," explained Elise.

The pastor shrugged. "Sorry. I don't think I know her."

Dinah stared at him. He was lying, and not doing a good job hiding it. His hands continued to skip and dart on his lap.

Elise glanced at Dinah and sighed. "Mr. Whitehall, where were you on Monday?"

"All day?" he asked. "I was at work, with various different people. I can give you my schedule. Or you can ask my secretary for it. She has the details."

Elise nodded and stood up. "Thanks for your time, Mr. Whitehall. I have no doubt I'll be back with more questions."

"Yes, Detective, I understand."

He walked her to the front door. As she ducked through the doorjamb, Whitehall said, "There is something else I'd like to say."

"Yes?"

Mr. Whitehall drew himself up and Dinah saw in that moment the tall, handsome man whom his congregation liked so much. "I didn't kill her, Detective."

Dinah looked into his eyes searchingly, looking for deceit. She didn't find any, but that meant nothing if Whitehall had managed to convince himself that this was the truth.

As she walked to the car with Elise, she had to admit that it was incongruous to think that the pastor of Ten Mile Hollow First Baptist Church could be involved in murder. Most small-town murderers here were hardly criminal masterminds. But equally, it was not inconceivable. How many community leaders like pastors and politicians had covered up bad behavior to protect their careers? There was a plethora of examples of those who had done terrible things to cover up their shame.

Did that extend to the pastor of Ten Mile Hollow First Baptist Church?

At some point during the night the rain turned to sleet, and it made Dinah's midnight run rather uncomfortable. Still, she kept running, her mind processing the things they knew so far about the case. Her instinct told her that Angus Whitehall was telling the truth about not killing Malia Shaw, but lying about virtually everything else. It made her wonder why. She slowed down to a walk, pulled out her earphones, and called Aaron.

Aaron Sinclair was an FBI agent who specialized in explosives. She'd met him several months ago, and the chemistry between them had flared immediately. But Dinah had been a recently recovered alcoholic and a new Christian, and a romantic relationship was something she just couldn't contemplate. They'd settled into friendship instead, taking it very slowly.

He was currently in Oregon, investigating a series of bombings thought to be perpetrated by eco-terrorists. So far they'd damaged two slaughterhouses and a pig farm.

"Hey, I've been wondering how you were doing," Aaron's warm voice answered.

Dinah felt a simultaneous thrill of hearing his voice and a warmth at the comfort she felt talking to him. "Sorry it's so late," she said.

Aaron laughed. "I expect nothing less from you. Have you been running?"

"Yeah, just on my way back to the house now. How is Oregon?"

"Cold," he said. "But we're getting closer to our targets, I think. How is Virginia?"

"Also cold." Dinah filled him in on the generalities of the case. Aaron listened without interrupting. Dinah loved that he didn't interrupt.

He was silent for a few moments after she'd finished. "Sounds interesting," he said. "There's some kind of history that needs to be explored. Something that happened 20 years ago."

"You're right," agreed Dinah. She paused. "I miss you."

"I miss you, too," said Aaron. "Thanks for calling me."

"I better get some sleep now," said Dinah. "Good night."

"Good night."

Back at Elise's house, thoroughly soaked and cold, she had a hot shower and went to bed, falling into a deep, dreamless sleep.

She woke at six-thirty and had eggs and coffee for breakfast with Elise and Chloe. The teenager was particularly quiet this morning, Dinah noted. Who understood the creature that is an adolescent girl?

At the sheriff's office, Elise's phone rang. She listened for a moment and then put it on speaker and motioned for Dinah to listen.

"Hi, it's Dr. Walker," the voice of the medical examiner said, cheerily. "Sorry it took some time to get back to you."

"That's fine, Doctor," said Elise.

"I took the liberty of waiting for the analysis of the crime scene to come through, as well as of the body. I had the results expedited for you," continued Dr. Walker.

"Great," said Elise, raising her eyebrows at Dinah. Here was the opportunity to accelerate the case. Dinah leaned forward in anticipation.

"So, crime scene first. You can imagine how difficult it was to wade through the detritus in the apartment, most of it irrelevant to the case," said Dr. Walker. "But anyway, we persisted. We found some good fingerprints in and around the front door, and the system told us that they belong to Simon Wakowski, a guy with a drug record as long as I am tall, from what I can gather."

"No surprises there," said Elise. "He was her drug dealer; we haven't ruled him out as a possible suspect."

"Right. Well, the only other items of interest we found that didn't belong to Malia Shaw were some short black strands of hair," said Dr. Walker. "Probably male. There weren't any hits on the system."

Elise didn't say anything, but Dinah knew they would both be thinking the same thing: Angus Whitehall's hair was short and black.

"Did you find anything on her body?" she asked.

The doctor sighed. "I have no good news, I'm afraid. I would say the woman was murdered quickly and efficiently. Strangulation leaves no mess, no marks. There is no weapon to trace."

"Oh," said Elise, disappointed.

"But I don't come to you completely empty-handed," said Dr. Walker. "The fake IDs you found in Malia's apartment yielded some results. I sent them over to the local FBI field office. Apparently, fake documents often contain some certain methods of manufacture that help us to identify where they came from. The FBI people were pretty certain the documents were made by a local outfit who is also known to launder money and sell weapons illegally, among other things. The agent told me that if you wish to speak to this outfit in Richmond, that they'll accompany you and assist you."

"Okay, thanks," said Elise. "We're both FBI alumni. I'm sure one of us will be able to smooth the path there." She smiled at Dinah.

Unless they know about how I was kicked out of the FBI in disgrace, thought Dinah. *They may not be so happy to talk to me then.*

"That's all I've got for you, Detective. I hope it was in some way helpful."

"Of course," said Elise. "You never know what will pan out." She hung up. "I sent you an email," she said to Dinah. "Malia Shaw's bank statements. Do you want to go over them and tell me what you think?"

"Sure," said Dinah. "I may need a second cup of coffee though."

"Feel free to drink the acid we've got here," smiled Elise.

Dinah poured herself a cup of said acid and sat down at the desk she was using. The bank statements were not complex or hard to read.

It was immediately obvious that most of Malia's life had revolved around cash. There were very few entries in her bank statements, but what was there was telling.

There was no money from either a workplace or the government being deposited into the account, which didn't surprise Dinah. There was no evidence that Malia Shaw had had a job or collected welfare payments. Yet there were regular deposits of cash arriving in her account, every two weeks or so; five hundred dollars a fortnight. Not much to most people, Dinah noted, but a fortune to someone who was interested in shooting the money directly into her veins.

An uncomfortable thought arose: what had Malia Shaw done in return for the money? Did she have an arrangement with somebody that got her killed? She knew from bitter experience that there were no limits to what people would do for gratification.

Though paying the money into her bank account was supremely stupid, a client who could afford that kind of money surely knew cash deposited into a bank account could be traced.

A light bulb flicked on in her mind. Perhaps this was the client's first foray into the forbidden. Perhaps although he led an exemplary life on the surface, he was hiding a dark secret. Like Angus Whitehall? He was a pastor who had lied to the police. Could he have fallen victim to his own desires, only to resent the toll his secret life was taking? What if Malia Shaw had tried to get more money from him, tried to blackmail him? It would destroy his entire life — his marriage, his job, and his reputation. Perhaps under the fear of losing it all, he had taken Malia's life to ensure his own wouldn't be disrupted in any way.

He wouldn't be the first person in his position to succumb to temptation.

Dinah recorded her observations in her notebook. They would run a trace on where the bank account deposits had come from, and this would answer a great number of questions.

Is it you, Angus Whitehall? What have you done?

****

The next morning, Elise woke Dinah and Chloe to suggest that they go out for breakfast. Lewis had only just gotten home from a double shift and was exhausted.

"I'll take you to my favorite café," whispered Elise.

They left the house quietly and Elise drove the car like it was a rocket ship to Main Street. It was her favorite cafe because the coffee was strong and hot and the eggs perfectly cooked. "I don't have any other requirements," she joked.

Elise was right though — Dinah enjoyed the breakfast of eggs, toast, and coffee.

Chloe ordered scrambled eggs and spent an hour pushing them around her plate. "What's going on at school today?" Elise asked her.

Chloe looked up, jolted from what seemed like deep thought. "Oh . . . the usual," she said. She glanced at her watch. "I suppose I'd better go. See you."

"Have a great day. Love you!" said Elise.

"Love you too." Chloe said in a flat voice, and trudged to the door.

Elise watched her go with a frown on her face but said nothing. Dinah waited while she ordered another pot of coffee.

"So," Elise said. "The client list that Simon the drug dealer gave us. I'd like to double check his movements on the day Malia Shaw died, see if his alibi checks out."

"Okay," agreed Dinah.

Elise read out the names. "Do you remember when drug addiction was a problem for a distinct few?"

Dinah sighed. She'd been a cop too long — and she knew well from personal experience — to think that heroin and cocaine weren't just the drug of choice for social outcasts. The list Elise was holding in her hand contained the names of a teacher, a lawyer, a banker, and a mother. The long tentacles of addiction had an insidious reach into many homes and families across the nation.

Fortified with three cups of hot coffee and a hearty breakfast, Dinah and Elise got to work. Elise drove to one of the middle-class neighborhoods where the cars were new, the lawns lovingly cared for, and the houses large and comfortable. Melissa Lopez lived here with her husband and three children, and apparently bought a steady supply of cocaine from Simon. A woman with frosted tips in her hair and artfully done makeup answered the door. She was in her late thirties.

Behind her, a swell of noise broke over them with an ear-shattering crescendo.

Dinah looked into her eyes and saw a bone-deep tiredness.

"Hello, I'm Detective Elise Jones with the Sheriff's Office and this is Dinah Harris, a consultant working with me. I need a few minutes of your time." Elise held up her badge to identify herself.

The woman's eyes flashed but she smiled and said, "Of course. Come in."

The noise got louder as Dinah walked in. The three children were shouting, screaming, and playing at full volume; two in a room that looked like a playroom and was completely trashed, and the youngest one running up and down the hallway shrieking, wearing only a diaper.

"Sorry about the noise," said Melissa Lopez. "I wish they came with a volume button." She barked a laugh that was utterly without mirth.

Dinah smiled. "They look young."

"Yeah. Three kids under three. Bad idea, trust me."

Melissa started clearing breakfast dishes from the kitchen table. "Can I get you a drink?"

"No, thanks," said Elise. "I just want to ask you if you know a Simon Wakowski."

Melissa tried to remain casual, but Dinah saw her throat move as the other woman swallowed. She continued stacking bowls with exaggerated concentration. "No, why?"

"Are you sure?" Elise asked. She produced Simon's mug shot and gave it to Melissa. "Perhaps this will jog your memory?"

Melissa Lopez studied the photo carefully. Dinah watched her, and saw the other woman was thinking very hard.

"No," Melissa said, eventually. "I don't know him."

"Simon Wakowski has said that he knows you," said Elise. "In fact, he alleges that you buy cocaine from him."

Melissa couldn't stop the red flush that spread up her throat as she struggled to keep a neutral look on her face. "That's absurd! I don't know why he would tell you that."

Elise leaned forward. "Let me be very blunt with you, Mrs. Lopez. I'm not here to bust you over the cocaine. I'm investigating a murder, and all I want to know is whether you saw Simon Wakowski last Monday. If you are helpful, I'll overlook the drugs. If you choose to be difficult, I can look around here, see if I can find some drugs, haul you down to the station, give your husband a call, and let him know what's happening."

"No!" gasped Melissa, almost dropping the bowls to the floor. She put them back down on the table. There was a silence as she tried to work out what to tell the detective. Finally, she said: "I'm not admitting to anything. But I saw Simon last Monday."

"What time?"

"About eight thirty in the morning."

"Where?"

"Here. We have a . . . system. He dresses in a courier's uniform and delivers packages, so the neighbors don't get nosy."

"So he's here for a couple of minutes?"

"Yeah."

"And it's always Simon? He doesn't send someone else?"

"No, it's always Simon. I don't trust anyone else."

"How long was he here for?"

"No longer than five minutes. It's a simple exchange."

Elise nodded and stood up. "Thanks for your time, Mrs. Lopez. Listen, you should know that if something happens to your kids while you're high, the state will take your kids away from you. If you cause an accident while you're high, you'll go to jail for a very long time. You might want to think about kicking this habit before you destroy someone else's life."

Melissa's eyes filled with tears. "I know, Detective. I *know*. But my kids . . . they're so hard. I can't cope with them. They're so . . . noisy and demanding! I just need . . . I need some help to get through the day."

Dinah felt compassion for the woman, but she had seen too many similar scenarios turn deadly. A mother who left kids in the bath to take another hit of coke and returned to drowned children. A mother who left the gas on in a heroin haze and suffocated everyone in her house, herself included. A father who left his children in the car while he tried to score more meth, oblivious to the rapidly rising and searing heat inside that eventually killed his kids. And what of herself? She had screamed at her son to shut up and half an hour later he was dead. Dinah shivered.

Elise remained impassive. "Just think about what I've said. Thanks for your help."

A sudden shriek ripped through the dull roar coming from the other room and Melissa jumped to her feet.

"We'll see ourselves out," said Elise. "You go to your children."

They picked their way back across the toy-strewn lawn and climbed back into the car. Neither woman spoke.

The next address belonged to one of the town's bankers, Tim Aubusson. He was in his office, and welcomed Elise and Dinah inside warmly. The morning was still early enough that the bank was virtually deserted. Three bank tellers were counting their money, bored.

"How can I help you, Detective?" Tim Aubusson asked.

Elise slid the mug shot of Simon Wakowski across the desk. "I'm wondering if you know this man, Simon Wakowski?"

Aubusson adopted a curious expression. "No, sorry, I don't."

Here we go again, Dinah thought.

"This man claims to sell heroin to you," she said, flatly.

Aubusson's eyes bulged and he dug at the tie around his neck, as though it was suddenly too tight. *"What?"*

Elise repeated her words, while Aubusson cringed and looked around for any possibility of eavesdropping. Elise reprised her speech on not caring about the drugs, and caring only for accounting for the whereabouts of Simon on the day a murder occurred. "I don't want to make your life difficult," she finished. "But I can, if you decide not to help me."

As addicts usually did, Aubusson wilted under the threat of being exposed. "Yes, I know him."

"Did you see him last Monday?"

"Yes. At about ten."

"What was the purpose of that meeting?"

"He delivered me some . . . you know. He dresses like a courier and brings it in a package. So the staff doesn't get curious."

"He was here for only a few minutes?"

"Yes."

"Is it always Simon, or does he send someone else?"

"Always Simon. I wouldn't buy from anyone else."

Elise nodded and she and Dinah stood. "Thanks for your time, Mr. Aubusson."

Tim Aubusson stood and looked uncomfortable. Finally, he stammered: "You're not . . . will you . . . can I ask . . . please don't tell anyone?"

Elise gave him a steady stare. "I won't tell anyone, Mr. Aubusson. But if you think this secret will stay hidden forever, you are sadly mistaken. This drug will expose you sooner or later, and my suggestion is that you deal with it sooner before it destroys your life."

Aubusson looked vastly relieved. "Thank you, Detective."

Dinah knew that the addict in Aubusson had heard what he wanted to hear and discarded the rest. How long would it take before he found himself sitting amid the scraps of what used to be his life? *Don't wait until you hit rock bottom, like me.* But she knew he would.

Elise had three others on her list to visit — a lawyer, a teacher with whom she'd once been in a book club, and a college student — and all three reiterated the same story. Simon had visited them last Monday, dressed as a courier, delivering a package of either heroin or cocaine. It had definitely been Simon. While Elise conducted the interviews, Dinah calculated the driving time and delivery time and decided Simon had indeed spent the best part of the day making his deliveries.

However, it didn't completely clear him, either. Malia Shaw had been his first delivery; he would have had plenty of time and opportunity to kill her before continuing on his way.

The neighbors wouldn't have noticed anything was amiss — Simon blended into that neighborhood like a fish belongs in the sea. His presence would have either gone ignored or unnoticed.

Dinah made a note to check with the neighbors, to see whether he'd gone back to Malia Shaw's apartment that day.

They headed back to Main Street to grab a late lunch.

****

Chloe had spent the morning basically wishing for a natural disaster. An earthquake would be awesome. A tornado would do nicely. Anything that would take the attention of this miserable place away from her.

Overnight, the video of her jog around the track had gone viral and the entire school had seen it, and probably the entire town, and possibly the entire world. Though she pretended she didn't care, the giggles, whispers, and taunts that had been directed at her wounded her deeply. Humiliation coiled in her belly like a snake.

Grace had spent the morning running defense, snapping at those who had laughed at her friend, challenging those who had taunted her, glaring at those who whispered behind their hands. Chloe was desperately grateful for her best friend, but she also knew that Grace could never truly understand the depths of her fear and hurt.

Grace was thin and willowy and good at gym class. The boys looked at Grace admiringly. Grace had feathery blonde hair that shone in the sunlight. Grace had perfect teeth and golden, tanned skin.

Not me, thought Chloe, as they sat down to lunch in the cafeteria. *I'm fat and clumsy and terrible at gym class. The boys look at me with contempt. My hair is short and boring, my skin as white as milk, a face like a chipmunk.*

It often puzzled Chloe: Grace could ditch her and be friends with Jessica Hunter. She could enjoy the trappings of popularity — the envy of the girls, the attention of the boys. She could attain the power that popularity could command in high school.

Yet she chooses to hang out with a loser like me, lamented Chloe. It wouldn't be forever, though. Eventually Grace would see that Chloe was dragging her down and would switch her allegiance to Jessica. Chloe wasn't sure she could actually turn up to school every day if it weren't for Grace. She had become such a target for Jessica and her minions that even the glee club kids and chess club kids avoided her.

Grace was one of those girls who everyone instinctively liked; she smiled easily, she was warm and caring, she always knew the right thing to say, and she was pretty. Everyone wanted to be friends with her. For some inexplicable reason, she chose to be friends with Chloe: *loser of the century*, she lamented.

It is enough for me to live in the heat of Grace's radiance, to bask in her glory. I've learned to deal with the laughter and spiteful comments because I know that those girls are only jealous of her, and they know enough to vent their frustration at the planet in her orbit, rather than at the sun herself.

I can live with it because I get to be friends with her, and that's all that matters to me. I've always measured my worth, found my identity in her. Caught in the morass of her beauty and power, I've never considered what would happen should I ever stand alone.

Suddenly, I'm struck by the desperation with which I need her. This perverse pride I've built up in being someone different is just a sham. It's a devastating thought. One of the only reasons I've been able to deal with all the mockery is to tell myself that I have strength in knowing who I am. But I don't — I don't know who I am at all.

I'm only somebody because of her. And should I lose that distinction, what do I have? Nothing besides some bad color in my hair, chunky legs, and a pasty face, someone that everybody else hates.

The truth is, when I think about the fact that everybody hates me, it becomes pretty hard to like myself. If others can't see anything in me to love, why would I?

"Oh no," muttered Grace, snapping out of her reverie, Chloe looked up at her.

"What's wrong?" she asked. Grace was looking over Chloe's shoulder.

Chloe turned around and saw Jessica Hunter weaving through the cafeteria directly toward them.

Chloe felt dread rise in her, releasing a metallic taste into her mouth and making her head swim briefly.

She could *feel* Jessica's presence, a dark shadow, a prescient malevolence.

"Do you really think you should be eating so much lunch, Chloe?" Jessica inquired, sickly sweet. "You know there are starving children in Africa who could use that food."

There was predictable laughter from the minions.

"Why don't you stop eating for a week and send the food you'd normally eat over to the starving children?" Jessica continued. "You could feed the whole of Ethiopia. And maybe you'd lose some of that disgusting weight."

That doesn't even make sense, thought Chloe. *How would I send food? Bundle up sandwiches and mail them to Ethiopia?*

She looked at her lunch tray and felt shame heat up her face like fire. She *had* served herself too much food. It *was* disgusting. *She* was disgusting.

"Are you going back to the track field to burn off some of that food this afternoon?" inquired Jessica.

More predictable laughter.

"Give it a rest, Jessica," snapped Grace. "This is getting so *boring*."

Jessica's eyes flicked over to Grace, but paid no attention to her. Her quarrel wasn't with Grace.

"Why aren't you eating, *cow*?" Jessica demanded. "Or is this your second helping?"

Chloe felt a strange compulsion to actually pick up her fork and eat, if only to make Jessica quit. Instead, she balled her hands into fists at her side and remained silently still. Her lack of reaction seemed to stir Jessica into a greater fury.

"I *hate* fat useless cows like you," she snarled. She suddenly picked up Chloe's lunch tray and dumped it into Chloe's lap.

Chloe gasped — the macaroni and cheese was still piping hot. She jumped to her feet, sending the tray to the floor. Macaroni and cheese slid down her legs wetly, leaving behind yellow trails. The pasta shells lay curved like snail shells on her skirt. Chloe felt a heave of revulsion.

The whole cafeteria erupted into laughter, their mocking glee hanging heavily in the air. Chloe burst into tears and ran from the cafeteria, with Grace following her.

She heard the hoots and catcalls follow her as she fled. She couldn't think of anything at all, except to escape this hateful place. She heard Grace calling after her, urgently, asking her to stop.

Chloe didn't stop. She ran and ran, out into the freezing wind, toward the school gates. She ran through them, down the street, realizing that Grace had stopped chasing her.

Still, the bitter taste of humiliation followed her, and she kept running, toward home. She was suddenly thankful that her mother worked during the day because it meant she could hide here for the rest of the afternoon.

Once the front door was closed and locked behind her, Chloe sagged against it and tried to catch her breath.

The freezing air had burnt her lungs with its cold fire, and it took some time before her breathing returned to normal. When it did, she walked on jelly legs to the kitchen. Grimly, she opened the freezer, looking for the tub of cookie dough ice cream. She took it out and ate the whole thing, straight from the tub, without stopping, barely breathing. When she had finished, sick guilt swept through her like a summer squall.

Upstairs, she leaned over the toilet, stuck her fingers down her throat and tried to make herself vomit. It took three or four attempts, but finally, she purged the ice cream from her stomach.

Chloe walked shakily to her bedroom and lay on her bed. Throwing up made her feel more calm and in control, despite the fact that her throat was burning. Staring out at the sky through her window, she dreamed of all the ways she would exact revenge on Jessica, if only she was brave enough.

When her mom came home that night and asked how her day had been, Chloe smiled and lied.

****

Neighborhoods like the one Malia Shaw had lived in took on a bunker-like effect when the sun had gone down. Doors and windows latched tightly, trying to ward off the danger that lurked in the streets under cover of darkness.

Unfortunately, it also meant that neighbors turned a blind eye to the various illegal activities that took place there, much to Elise's frustration. Shadows retreated on street corners as she parked the car into the safety of the alleys. It was freezing tonight; a cold sleeting rain fell periodically, but it didn't seem to dampen business.

Elise and Dinah had brought with them the human mountain, Deputy Peyton Hauser, to canvass the neighbors. First, they tried the one directly above Malia Shaw's apartment.

The door opened a crack, and a fearful brown eye peered through. The light inside the apartment seemed almost as gloomy as the night in which Elise and Dinah stood.

Elise pushed her gold shield up to the crack. "I'm Detective Jones," she said. "I'd like to ask a few questions about the woman who lived below you."

The door opened slightly farther to reveal a tall woman with a worn face. "Is that the one who died?" she asked, her eyes darting around with fear.

"Yes. What is your name?"

"Yelena Damascus," she said. "I didn't know her."

"You didn't speak to her much?"

Yelena shook her head. She had beautifully fine facial features with tired eyes.

"Did you notice anything about her that you thought unusual?"

Yelena Damascus gave a grin. "You spend much time here, Detective? Everythin' around here is unusual. Listen, I know what she was. She was a junkie, right?"

"Yes. I'm more interested in the day she died — last Monday. Do you recall anything unusual on that particular day?"

Yelena shook her head again. "No, but I was workin'. You want to know the only thin' I noticed with her?"

"Sure."

"She had visitors — only two of 'em. Two guys used to come round all the time."

Dinah showed her the mug shot of Simon. "Was this one of the men?"

"Yup. That was one of 'em."

"What did the other one look like?"

"More upper class than what we're used to." Damascus grinned. "I used to see him and think, he's slummin' again. He was a white boy, tall, dark hair, pretty broad."

Dinah wished she had a picture of Angus Whitehall — it was a pretty good description of him.

"You didn't recognize him at all?" she asked.

Yelena shook her head. "Nope."

Dinah had a sudden idea. While Elise kept talking, Dinah took out her phone and began to Google.

"How often were these two guys at the apartment downstairs?" Elise asked.

"That skinny one . . . maybe once or twice a week?" Yelena guessed. "The rich lookin' guy, maybe . . . once a week. But look, I'm workin' every day, so I mighta missed him if he came during the day."

"Did you ever hear any shouting or fighting from downstairs?"

"No," said Yelena. "That poor girl . . . she was quiet. Some days, so quiet I wondered if she . . . you know, was dead." The woman suddenly looked sorrowful.

"Did the woman downstairs ever talk to you, tell you anything about herself?"

"Nope. We said hello maybe once or twice on the stairs. That's it. We all got problems round here, you know. We keep to ourselves."

Bingo. Dinah found it. On the website of the Ten Mile Hollow local newspaper, she had found a picture of Angus Whitehall. It was a clipping of Angus taken over last Christmas, standing in front of the Nativity scene outside his church.

"Was that the second man you saw come to visit Malia Shaw?" she asked, holding up her phone.

Yelena squinted and looked hard for a few moments. "Yeah . . . I think it is."

Elise looked at Dinah, her eyebrows raised. "Nice work."

She thanked Yelena for her time, and she and Dinah trudged down the stairs to the basement apartment. The door there was opened by a young white man, a baby fussing on his hip. The smell of chili wafted through the door. "Help you?" he asked.

Elise showed him her badge and introduced herself, noting the gang tattoo on his forearm. He seemed wary, but not alarmed by her presence.

"What's your name?"

"Hank," he said, shortly. "This is Maria." He waved in the direction of the kitchen.

"I want to ask you a few questions about the woman who lived above you," Elise said, as a young woman appeared from the tiny kitchen, a dishtowel in her hands. "Did you ever speak with her?"

"No, but we just moved here," said Hank. "Like, a month ago."

"She didn't come out much," offered Maria.

"Did you notice anything unusual about her?"

Hank shrugged. "We knew she was usin'," he said. "Ain't hard to figger that out."

"Her dealer, he tried to hustle us," added Maria. "Tried to sell us some stuff."

Elise showed them the picture of Simon. "This guy?"

"Yeah." Hank snorted in contempt. "I know what that stuff does to you. Told him we weren't interested."

"Did any other visitors ever show up?"

Hank shrugged. "I didn't see anyone."

"I did," said Maria. "I'm stuck here with the baby all day. I saw another guy come by all the time."

Dinah showed the woman the picture of Angus Whitehall on her phone.

"Yup, he the one," said Maria.

"How often did he come by?" Elise asked.

"Probably twice a week," said Maria. "Sometimes during the day, sometimes at night."

"Did you hear any shouting or fighting coming from the apartment?"

"No," said Maria. "It was always quiet there."

Hank nodded his agreement.

"What about last Monday? Do you remember if either of these guys came by last Monday?"

Hank shrugged, but Maria looked thoughtful. "I was home," she said, thinking aloud. "Oh, yeah. I remember last Monday because little Rafael here was teething. I was up and down all night and day with him." She swatted the baby affectionately. "I seen both of them here that day."

Dinah felt a surge of hope. "Really? Do you remember what time?"

"That skinny guy, her dealer, right? He came during the morning," said Maria. "About seven or seven thirty, I think? The other guy came later, about an hour after that. I remember because I had just fed Raf his snack and I was watching TV. I saw this guy come up the stairs. He was wearing a nice black coat. I remember thinking it was a fine coat."

"How long was he there?" Dinah pressed.

"A while. Half an hour?"

Dinah exchanged a glance with Elise. *This is getting mysterious-er and mysterious-er.* Elise thanked the young couple for their time and they walked back to the car, both deep in thought.

Why are you lying to us, Angus? What are you hiding?

The phone call from the medical examiner's office in Norfolk came just as Elise and Dinah had arrived in the office the following morning. "I thought you'd be interested to know," said Dr. Walker on speakerphone, cheery as ever. Dinah wondered if the man ever had a bad mood.

"What's that?" Elise asked.

"The DNA scraped from underneath the victim's fingernails and the dark hairs found in the victim's apartment? They match; it's the same DNA. Whoever left hair in her apartment also left skin underneath her nails."

"That *is* interesting," mused Elise. "No hits in the system?"

"No. Whoever he or she is, he's been clean up till now."

Dinah thought for a moment. When they had enough evidence for a search warrant, it would include a warrant for a DNA swab.

"Thanks, Doctor," Elise said. "You've been very helpful."

"It's no trouble," said Dr. Walker.

Dinah wrote everything the doctor had said in her notebook, and then glanced at her watch. Elise caught the gesture and nodded. "Time to go."

It was time to go to the Ten Mile Hollow First Baptist Church, where she had organized meetings with Angus's colleagues to check his alibi.

Angus had said he'd been at work all day the Monday Malia Shaw had been murdered. But Shaw's neighbors reported seeing someone matching Angus's description at the apartment. It would be interesting to see what the pastor's colleagues said.

Angus met them at the door. "Hello, detectives." He looked like he hadn't slept well for several days. "I've given you an office in which to conduct your interviews." His tone was flat and tired.

"Thank you, Mr. Whitehall," said Elise. "How is Grace?"

Dinah remembered that the pastor's daughter and Elise's daughter were friends. Whitehall seemed to flinch. "Oh, she's doing well. How is Chloe?"

"She's fine. Thanks again. I'll be in touch if we need anything else."

Whitehall nodded and left. The office he'd given them was small and well-heated, equipped with several chairs arranged in a circle.

Elise had arranged consecutive appointments with Whitehall's secretary, associate pastor, and a church elder. She started with the secretary, a young, terrified woman by the name of Shana Woolcroft. Barely in her twenties, she crept into the office and stared fearfully at the detective.

"Hello, Miss Woolcroft," said Elise, gently. "Today, I want to ask you a few questions about Mr. Whitehall's movements on last Monday. Please just be truthful, and nobody will get into any trouble. It'll be very easy, just you and me having a chat, okay?"

Shana Woolcroft murmured something.

"Pardon me?"

"Sure," whispered Shana, still looking at the floor.

Elise glanced at Dinah, suppressing a smile. "Now, were you at the office last Monday when he arrived at work?"

"Yes," whispered Shana.

"Excellent. What time was that?"

"About nine," said Shana. "I arrive at eight-thirty to make coffee."

"You're doing great, Shana," said Elise. "What did he do once he arrived at work? Did he go to his office, or hang around talking?"

"He said good morning to me, took some coffee, and went to his office," said Shana. "There was nobody else here."

"Your desk is directly outside his office?"

"Yes."

"So you know when he goes in or out of his office?"

"Yes."

"Did he come out of his office at all during the morning?"

"Yes," said Shana. "He came out for a meeting with John."

"John Rowland?"

"Yes."

John Rowland was the associate pastor with whom Elise had set up a meeting right after Shana.

"Where did they go for the meeting?"

"Here," said Shana. "Well, the boardroom. Across the hall."

"How long did the meeting last?"

"About half an hour?" guessed Shana.

"And they both came out together?"

"Yes. Mr. Rowland left; Mr. Whitehall went back to his office."

"Did Mr. Whitehall come out of his office after the meeting?"

"Yes, he went to early lunch." Shana bit a nail.

Dinah felt a stirring in her gut, a tingling sensation that meant something was off.

"Did he go alone?"

"Yes."

"Do you know if he was meeting anyone?"

"I don't know."

"How long was he away for?"

"About an hour," said Shana. "He came back. Went into his office."

"How long did he stay in his office?"

"All afternoon," said Shana. "On Mondays he spends the after-noon returning phone calls and emails from the weekend. I didn't see him again until about five, when I told him I was going home, and he agreed and walked with me to the parking lot."

"How long have you known Mr. Whitehall?"

Shana raised her eyebrows. "Uh . . . I've only been working here for like, six months."

"You only met him when you started working here?"

"Yeah. I just moved here."

"Thank you, Shana. You've been very helpful."

Shana looked up, a frown on her face. "That's it? We're done?"

"Yes. I told you it would be easy!" Elise smiled at the young woman. Shana didn't smile back, but clutched her sweater around her and slunk out of the room.

As if on cue, John Rowland marched into the room. According to the church website, he'd been in ministry his whole life and had helped to shape Ten Mile Hollow First Baptist Church for better and worse. In semi-retirement, he had taken the associate role to support Angus and to reduce the demands on his time. He was a tall man in his seventies with a sharply angled face and an austere gaze. As if to belie his severe countenance, he possessed a soft, gentle voice.

"How can I help, Detective?" he asked.

"I want to ask you about last Monday, Mr. Rowland," said Elise. "Specifically, whether you saw Mr. Whitehall."

"I did," said Rowland. "We had a nine o'clock meeting, which went for about half an hour or so."

"Here at the church?"

"Yes, in the boardroom."

"What was the meeting about?"

He leveled a gaze at her. "Church business, ministry and pastoral issues I can't really talk about. Suffice to say that it was a meeting focused on the church."

"What happened at the end of the meeting? Did you have lunch together?"

Rowland shook his head. "No, I went to another meeting. I'm not sure what Angus did."

"How long have you known Mr. Whitehall?"

A flicker of uncertainty lanced across the man's face. "Well," he said. "He's been here, in this church, about 12 years. First in an associate role to me, and then as the senior pastor. Prior to that, he was studying for his theology degree. I don't know what he did before that."

Elise watched him intently. "So, 12 years?"

"Yes," said Rowland.

"What sort of character would you describe him as having?"

"He has always been a man of integrity. He has been very popular among the congregation and town, I'm sure you know. I've certainly never had a problem with him," said Rowland, without hesitation. "Is there anything else?"

"Thanks, Mr. Rowland," Elise said. "You've been very helpful."

The board member, a middle-aged man named Brad Bowen, entered the room next. He was perplexed; he had barely seen Angus Whitehall at all during last Monday. He'd been there briefly to check the financial reports in his role as treasurer.

Dinah knew this and her questions were designed to catch out any lies told by Shana Woolcroft or John Rowland. But Bowen's version of the day's events meshed exactly with what she'd already been told.

She hung on as Elise drove back to the office, her mind a tumult over Angus Whitehall — seemingly perfect life, lived without reproach since arriving in Ten Mile Hollow.

She had a hunch that the key to the mystery of Malia's death lay in events that had happened years ago.

But she had no idea what.

****

It was almost seven o'clock when Chloe heard her mom and Dinah arrive home. In her room, Chloe heard the front door close, then a big sigh and a double thud as Mom's shoes were tossed into the corner.

"Chloe!" Mom called. "Are you there?"

Chloe stared at her assignment, decided she'd done enough for now, and trotted downstairs. "Hi, Mom. Hi, Ms. Harris."

"Please, call me Dinah," said Mom's friend with a smile.

Chloe looked carefully at her mom, who looked haggard. Her eyes were bloodshot, there were big puffy circles underneath her eyes, and her face seemed older.

"What is for dinner?" she asked, after a moment

"I think Dad is bringing some takeout food for dinner. How's your homework going?"

Chloe shrugged. "Okay, I guess."

Moments later, the front door banged open again, accompanied by a gust a cold wind. "I'm home!" yelled Dad. He had several bags of food that smelled amazing. She shook herself. It might smell amazing, she told herself, but it'll make you *fat*.

Chloe followed her dad into the kitchen, trying to hide the disappointment she felt. Of course, neither of them had the energy to cook tonight, but takeout food was not going to help her get skinnier.

The chicken and fries were doled out into four portions, and they ate together at the kitchen table.

"So how was your week at school?" Mom asked.

The worst week of my life, thought Chloe. "It's been okay," she said, instead.

Mom looked at her sharply, seeming to sense the tone in her daughter's voice. But thankfully, she misread it. "Are you still finding school boring?"

Thankful for the diversion, she nodded. "Haven't I always?"

Mom smiled and shook her head. "Honey, it won't always be this way. Once you get to college, it can be as hard as you want it to be. And you'll find you won't be the only smart kid."

"Yeah, I know." Chloe was looking forward to college in an almost mythical fashion, the same way that kids were sure mermaids and unicorns were real. For now, it seemed so far away, so unattainable, so unlikely. She had two more years of high school to get through — two more years of Jessica Hunter and her minions — before she could escape.

Chloe stared at the plate of fries and chicken, noticing the big pools of grease underneath the food. Though she was starving, the thought of *not* eating the takeout filled her with a pleasurable sense of control.

She ate a few chunks of chicken, without the skin, and some fries. That took care of the stabbing hunger pangs, and she decided that would be enough. Sharp-eyed, her mother frowned. "What's wrong? Aren't you hungry?"

"No . . . not really. I had a sandwich before you came home," said Chloe.

"A sandwich isn't enough for dinner," said Mom. "You need to eat some more."

Chloe picked at her food again, moving the food around on the plate and hiding some of the fries beneath the chicken breast. Thankfully, it seemed her mom didn't have the energy to keep nagging at her, and Chloe was able to tip the rest of her dinner in the trash.

"Do you remember when we were at Quantico," began her mom, facing Dinah and leaning back in her chair.

Oh no. Nostalgia. Save me, thought Chloe, rolling her eyes. "May I be excused?" she interrupted. Her mom stopped, shocked by Chloe's uncharacteristic rudeness. "I still have some homework to do," she added.

Mom pressed her lips together, and for a moment Chloe was sure she was going to get told off. But she must have decided not to do it in front of Dinah. "All right. You may be excused."

"Thanks, Mom," said Chloe.

She went upstairs and closed the door in the bathroom. She stood on the scales, hoping to find that she'd lost some weight. After all, she'd done the jogging thing during the week; she'd been a bit more careful about how she ate. She stared at the numbers and felt all her hopes plummet like a balloon rapidly losing air. She hadn't lost any weight. None at all. *How is this possible?* She wondered. She sat on the edge of the bathtub and mentally went through everything she'd eaten during the last week.

It was clear she was still eating too much. Breakfast: normally a bowl of cereal. *I can just skip breakfast,* she thought. It would be the easiest meal to do without — her mother wouldn't know and couldn't nag her about it.

Lunch: normally taken in the school cafeteria, and everyone knew the food wasn't exactly healthy. Her favorite was macaroni and cheese. She decided she'd swap it for the watery looking chicken noodle soup. If she just ate the noodles and the broth, and left the chicken in the bowl, she could eliminate more calories.

Dinner would be more problematic. Her mom would notice she wasn't eating at much as usual. The good thing was that Mom insisted on serving vegetables the nights they didn't have takeout. So she could eat all the vegetables, which were low in calories, and she could pretend somehow to eat the meat and carbs.

Disheartened, she trudged to her room and logged onto her computer. She wondered if she Googled it, whether there would be some ways of hiding food from parents. The search engine came up with 2 million hits, much to Chloe's surprise. She clicked on the first one and was shocked when the website loaded. It was dedicated to the pursuit of thin, to the point of anorexia.

Chloe looked at the pictures posted by the members of the websites of themselves: impossibly thin, with angular hips and jutting collarbones. She scrolled through them with a mixture of jealousy and revulsion. *I don't want to take it that far,* she thought. *I don't need to be that skinny. But I bet there are some good ideas on here for people to lose weight quickly.*

She wasn't disappointed. The website was full of weight loss tips, some of them drastic.

Chloe found some ideas for hiding food — cutting it into tiny pieces made it easier to dispose of in a napkin, so that parents would think the meal had been eaten. Chloe kept reading, thoroughly absorbed. Some girls ate their meals but made themselves vomit or used laxatives so that the food couldn't be absorbed. Chloe wrinkled her nose in disgust. It would surely be easier not to eat at all, rather than having to vomit it back up.

She spent a few hours on the site, reading and realizing that she wasn't alone in her desire to be skinny. Fortified by this knowledge, she went to bed, vowing to herself that tomorrow, she would begin in earnest.

I will be skinny, even if it kills me.

****

A rarely glorious Saturday made Dinah feel sad for a moment that she would be working a homicide investigation instead of enjoying the day off. The sky was clear, a deep azure that promised a cold, sunny day. *Who am I kidding?* She chuckled. *I love working homicide investigations.*

In the kitchen, Lewis had made pancakes. "Good morning!" he greeted her, brightly. He was a broad man, no taller than Dinah herself, with a closely cropped beard and shaggy eyebrows. "How did you sleep?"

"Very well, thanks." Dinah accepted a plate of pancakes. "These look delicious."

"These are my patented, cure-all, fix-em-up pancakes, right, Chlo-Bow?" he grinned.

Chloe rolled her eyes but couldn't help smiling. "Right, Dad."

"While you ladies are off chasing down murderers, terrorists, and other assorted criminals, Chloe and I will be quite happily hiking and gardening together today."

"Hiking *and* gardening?" Chloe grumbled, but without venom. "I've got homework, you know."

"Well, we'll be hiking, gardening, and homeworking!" Lewis laughed. Chloe smiled.

Elise sighed and turned to face Dinah. "Well, in the face of that hilarity and good cheer, we'd better do some work."

On the hair-raising ride to work, Elise's phone rang. "Hello?" she answered through the hands-free, so that Dinah could hear.

"Hi, is this the detective who's investigating the murder of that woman?" a thin, nervous male voice asked.

"Yes, this is Detective Elise Jones," she said. "How can I help you?"

"Look, I don't know . . . I wasn't sure if I should call," the man said. "I mean, I don't know if it'll help. But . . . I thought . . ."

"I'm happy to hear any information," she said. "What is your name?"

"Um, Blake Watson."

"Okay, Mr. Watson. Now, what did you want to tell me?"

"Just that . . . there's often a car — I mean, there *was* often a car outside the woman's place," said Watson.

"How did you see this car, Mr. Watson?"

"Oh, I run a shop across the street," he said.

"Are you there now?"

"Yeah, why?"

"I'm coming to visit you. Stay right where you are."

Elise broke several road rules in her hurry to meet Blake Watson. Dinah's heart galloped throughout the journey. *If I don't die in a car wreck, I'll die of a heart attack.* She closed her eyes as Elise floored the accelerator through orange lights or pulled out abruptly to pass slow cars. She crossed over Main Street and headed back over to the crumbling neighborhood in which Malia Shaw's life had ended, and pulled to a halt outside the apartment with a final, tortured screech of protest from the tires.

Dinah let out a breath she had apparently been holding for the entire trip.

Directly opposite Malia Shaw's apartment were two businesses — a liquor store and a pawnbroker. A tall man with skin the shade of chocolate stood outside the pawnbroker shop, scanning the street. Elise and Dinah approached him. "Are you Blake Watson?"

In a deep, rich baritone, Watson replied, "Yeah. You must be the detective. Come in." He looked with curiosity at Dinah.

"I'm Dinah Harris," she told him. "I was an FBI agent and now I'm consulting on this case."

Watson's small shop was crammed with items that had once had value to their owners — everything from jewelry to coin collections to antique firearms. The goods were catalogued neatly, and everything was clean and gleaming.

"Please tell me what you saw," Elise suggested. "From the beginning."

"Well, I just take notice of things," Watson began. "In this neighborhood, it pays to keep your eyes open. So I took notice of a car that was always around outside the apartment where the dead woman lived."

"Why did it get your attention?" asked Elise.

"It was a new car, and the man inside looked rich, at least to us," said Watson. "A little unusual around here. He was here two times a week, on average. I didn't think much of it until that lady turned up dead."

"Did the man inside visit Malia Shaw, specifically?"

Watson thought about that. "He definitely went up the stairs. A few times, I saw them together outside her building."

"What sort of car was it?"

"Ford Taurus, gray," said Watson. "It was a nice-looking car."

"Was the car there last Monday?"

Watson thought about this. "Yes, I believe so. Is that the day the lady died?"

"Right. Has the car been here since the woman died?" Elise asked. "Since last Monday?"

Watson shook his head. "No. That's why I thought it was a little weird."

"Could it have been this man?" Dinah asked, showing Watson a photo of Simon Wakowski.

Watson looked at the photo intently. "I don't think so," he said. "I've seen this guy around the neighborhood and I know what he does for a living. No, the guy in the Taurus is taller, broader. I never got to see his face properly, but he was richer looking than anyone else who gets around here, you know what I mean?"

"How did he look richer?"

"Well, his car for one thing. But the way he dressed, too. He had a nice black coat; it looked expensive. He wore good shoes. I saw what looked like a decent watch."

"Did you ever speak to him?"

Watson snorted. "I don't think a guy like that would be seen dead in a place like this."

Dinah thought about this information. The man who matched Angus Whitehall's description, seen by the neighbors visiting Malia Shaw often, had worn a nice, black coat. Dinah guessed that Angus Whitehall also drove a late model gray Ford Taurus.

However, did it actually mean anything? Angus Whitehall had claimed that the dead woman was an old friend and that he'd felt responsible for her. In fact, she seemed to talk to nobody else in her life except her drug dealer, Angus, and the missing woman, Lola. Unless it was a completely random crime, it was likely that one of those three had killed Malia Shaw.

Simon Wakowski, though he'd claimed his drug clients as his alibi, had still a window of opportunity in which he could have killed Malia. It wasn't uncommon to see him visiting Shaw. But what was his motive? She had been a good client, always paying him on time. Why would he get rid of such a reliable customer? The only motive could be a relationship that soured or was stunted — though he had denied that.

Angus Whitehall too, although providing an alibi, had unaccounted time during which he could have killed Shaw. He too, was a regular visitor to the apartment. His motives seemed more likely — a clandestine relationship that had perhaps gotten out of control, to a point where he worried about losing his family and his job. That would be enough motive to kill the woman.

And what of Lola, the woman who'd vanished under cover of a frosty night? Had she disappeared because she was scared, or because she was fleeing from the scene of the crime, or because she herself was dead?

Dinah brought up the photo of Angus Whitehall and his nativity scene on her phone. "Do you recognize this man?"

Watson stared at the picture for several seconds. "He looks familiar . . . yes, I think that's the man who drove the Taurus."

"How positive are you?" Dinah asked.

He nodded. "I'm almost certain."

Dinah glanced at Elise, who raised her eyebrows thoughtfully.

"Thanks very much for your information. You never know how useful even small bits of information can be in an investigation," said Elise.

"No problem," Watson rumbled.

Elise and Dinah left the store and stood outside on the sidewalk, trying to get a better feel of what he would have seen. The street, like in the entire town, was wide and lined on both sides with cars. As a result, it wasn't particularly easy to see exactly what was happening on the other side of the road, but Dinah could see the stairs of the old building. Blake Watson would have had a pretty good view of whomever came and went from the apartments.

Dinah sighed and stared up at the sky. The air was bone cold and she soon found herself shivering.

Elise drove them both back to the office, and for once Dinah didn't notice the bad driving. Her thoughts consumed by a gray Ford Taurus, a potential shadowy relationship, and a woman who lived and died for heroin.

****

Deputy Peyton Hauser was waiting for them when Elise and Dinah arrived back at the office. He didn't look very happy.

"What's wrong?" Elise asked him.

He sighed. "I'm missing my son's Little League game," he said, mournfully hitching his shoulders. "But aside from that, I can't locate next-of-kin."

"For Malia Shaw?" guessed Elise.

"Yup. I've scoured every record in this county — medical, government, you name it. There is nothing."

Dinah thought about Malia Shaw's rental application, where she'd left next-of-kin blank. "We may have to go public nationally instead of locally," she suggested. "Although even that might not help. Malia Shaw might not even be her real name."

Deputy Hauser nodded. "You want me to contact the television station and the newspaper?"

"Yes, please. Send them the most recent photo we have, as well as a list of the aliases she may have used," said Elise. "She has to be someone's daughter or sister or wife."

Hauser looked at her gravely. "Maybe not anymore."

Dinah had to agree. Fractious family breakdowns, abuse, neglect, indifference. She'd seen it all; it would be sadly unsurprising to find that Malia Shaw had no family who would claim her.

On the computer she was using, she ran a trace of Ford Taurus's registered in the county. From there, she narrowed it down to Ten Mile Hollow, where she found five Ford Taurus's registered to citizens of the town. One black, two white, one gray, one red. The gray one was registered to Angus Whitehall, pastor of Ten Mile Hollow First Baptist Church.

It gave her an initial thrill, but it didn't really prove much, other than the fact that he'd been at the apartment, which he'd admitted. She told Elise about her finding. Elise gave a big smile. "Let's go visit him again and see if we can get anything else from him."

Dinah was convinced that Whitehall was lying about something, but what did it have to do with the murder? She brooded on this all the way to Whitehall's home. They stopped outside his house and Dinah looked at it thoughtfully. The gray Ford Taurus was parked on the driveway, in full view. It seemed incredibly stupid to be so blatant in his dealings with a murdered woman, but then, most murderers were stupid. And perhaps Whitehall's naïveté contributed.

His wife Louise answered the door and immediately looked fearful.

"I just want to speak with Angus again," Elise said.

Solicitously, Louise offered them both coffee before ushering them into the living room, where Angus was waiting. He had been reading a book, now turned face-down on a side table.

"Hi, Detective," he said, wearily. "I didn't expect to see you back here so soon."

"Well," said Elise. "I've got a few more questions for you."

Louise came in with mugs of hot coffee and then seemed to hover anxiously.

"Everything's fine, honey," he said to her. "Why don't you take Marcus to get some ice cream?"

Louise seemed relieved to have something to do, and she left the room. Deep in some other room, Dinah could hear her talking to her son.

"Do I need my lawyer present?" Angus asked, his face guarded.

Elise smiled. "No, I'm just here for a friendly chat."

Angus gave a half-hearted smile.

"So, we know that you visited Malia Shaw on the day she died," said Elise.

"Do you?" Angus asked. He seemed watchful, afraid of using too many words.

"Yes. Why did you visit her?"

"I went to check on her," said Angus. "As I do — did — every week."

"You didn't think you should tell me that in our original interview?"

"I wasn't sure what our original interview was about, Detective," said Angus.

"What did you find when you got there?"

Angus sighed heavily. "She was passed out. She had probably shot up not long before I got there. It wasn't unusual to find her heavily sedated. She was using a large amount of heroin toward the end, Detective. It's no wonder it knocked her out."

"What did you do when you got there?" *And is it your DNA underneath her fingernails?* Dinah added silently.

"Nothing," said Angus. "She'd slumped, half off the couch. I checked her pulse to make sure she was still alive. There was a needle nearby. I tried to make her more comfortable, so I picked her up and took her into the bedroom. I figured she'd be safe there."

Yeah, not so much.

"And then you left?"

"Right. There was nothing more I could do for her."

"What time was that?"

"Mid morning? No, probably later in the morning," Angus said, thoughtfully. "I think I remember I had an early lunch, and used the time to check on her."

Dinah wrote this down carefully in her notebook, as a reminder to cross check with the statements they'd gotten from Whitehall's colleagues.

Generally, his story matched the observations of Malia Shaw's neighbors.

"Do you know if she has any family members?" she asked. "We're having trouble locating next of kin."

Angus's face remained impassive, but his hands began to tap dance on his knees. "No. I don't know. I never met any."

"Haven't you been friends with her for a long time?"

"Yes. But I've never met any family members." Angus looked away. "I know a little about her past, Detective. I don't believe her relationship with either parent was stable, or loving."

"Do you know where either her mother or father might be now?"

"No, sorry."

Elise paused a beat. "Do you know why Malia might have had false identification in her possession?"

Angus's hands were Irish dancing now. Dinah found herself watching his hands with fascination. "No. What do you mean?"

"Like fake passports or drivers licenses. Do you know why she would have had these?"

"Gosh," he said. "I have no idea."

"Do you know how Malia Shaw knew Lola Albright?"

"No. I don't know Lola Albright."

Angus stood up and walked over to the picture window that looked out onto the back lawn. "Detective," he said. "I've been remarkably patient with you. Now, I must ask: are you here under some misguided notion that I'm a suspect?"

Elise smiled. "Not at all, sir. I'm just trying to learn more about the victim."

Are you feeling nervous? Dinah wondered.

"The more we know about a victim's life, the more likely it is we find the killer," she added.

"It would seem apparent that there were other people in her life more likely to be murderers than I," said Angus. *Ah, self-righteousness: the hiding place of the guilty,* thought Dinah.

"Do you have any suggestions?" Elise inquired.

"Well, her drug dealer for one," snapped Angus. "I don't know. It's not my job, is it? I'm sure she must have known all kinds of shady characters."

"Well, we're looking into the drug dealer," admitted Dinah. "As for other shady characters, the only one we know of for sure is you."

Angus flushed. "I think we're done here," he said, through clenched teeth.

Elise met his gaze for several long moments before she bid the pastor farewell, thanking him for his time. She and Dinah sat in the car for several minutes, both lost in thought. At length, Elise started the car's engine. "You know, I just cannot shake my gut feeling that Angus Whitehall knows who killed Malia Shaw — and that indeed, he might very well be the killer."

"I have to agree with you there," said Dinah. "What is he hiding?"

It was thus far the great unanswerable question.

The next morning, as Dinah ate breakfast in the companionable chaos of family life next to Lewis and Chloe, Elise's cell phone began to ring. She looked at it and frowned.

"Hello?" Elise listened for a few moments. "Oh, thanks for calling." She looked at Dinah and waved her over. "Do you mind if I put you on speaker?"

Dinah followed her into the living room where it was quieter. Elise pulled the phone away from her ear. "Would you mind starting from the beginning so that my colleague can hear you?"

"Hello, this is FBI Special Agent Max Shorten," came a brisk, male voice.

"I'm Detective Elise Jones, from Ten Mile Hollow Sherriff's Department. With me is former FBI agent Dinah Harris. She's consulting on the case."

There was a brief pause as the FBI agent processed that. "Hello, Detective. Hello, Ms. Harris," he said. "I'm based in Richmond. Which office did you work out of?"

"I was at headquarters in D.C.," said Dinah, wondering if he'd heard about her fall from grace. She felt the familiar burning anxiety start up in her stomach. *It doesn't matter if he has. There's nothing you can do about it now.*

"Well, glad to meet you," said Shorten. "The reason for my call is that the medical examiner's office sent us some counterfeit documentation to analyze for you."

"That's right. Did you find anything useful?" Elise asked.

"Well," said Shorten, "as I told the medical examiner, we were pretty sure we knew who did these. Every counterfeiter has his own distinct style. Nevertheless, we checked it out to confirm our suspicions. I called you to find out whether you want to come up here and take a visit with me."

"Yes, we absolutely would," said Elise, grinning at Dinah. "When?"

"Can you come up right now?" he asked. "If you leave now, it'll only take a couple of hours. It's Sunday, so there shouldn't be too much traffic."

Elise got directions to the field office from the FBI agent, and she and Dinah quickly finished the rest of breakfast.

The drive up to Richmond on I-95 was uneventful. Dinah and Elise spent the drive singing at the top of their lungs to music that helped them through training at Quantico — Guns N' Roses, Springsteen, Mellencamp. It was a surprising reminder to Dinah that she missed having friends. In her grief and alcohol addiction, she'd pushed away everyone who cared about her. The simple joy of belting out classic tunes with her old friend was astonishing. It also took her mind off the fact that Elise was doing 20 miles over the speed limit, and often changed lanes without warning or the use of turn signals.

Special Agent Max Shorten met them at the Richmond FBI field office, and gave them a quick tour. Dinah didn't recognize any of his colleagues, and then he whisked them out to one of the Bureau's unmarked cars. On the way, he gave them a quick lesson in document counterfeiting. Usually, counterfeiters were multi-tasking criminals who were involved in lots of other crimes. This particular outfit, he told her, also dealt in illegal weapons, money laundering, and drug dealing.

"They're a sophisticated outfit," said Shorten. "They run everything through a talent agency, if you can believe that. It *is* a legitimate business, but their most profitable branches of business are the illegal ones."

"What are you watching them do?" Dinah asked.

"At the moment, we're watching them bring in arms from Iraq," he said. "We're in the data-gathering stage. I'm sure you remember the mind-numbing, boring surveillance. It's the most unglamorous part of the job, but it builds the spine of our case against them."

"Going there today won't spook them?"

Max laughed. "It will, but they'll think that's all we know about. They'll be so keen to hide the arms deal that they'll confess to this meager crime." He paused. "At least, that's what I'm hoping."

The talent agency did indeed look very legitimate, and apparently, there were auditions being undertaken in one of the rooms, according to a sign that encouraged quiet. Someone behind the door was doing a good job of torturing a Mariah Carey song to death.

Special Agent Max Shorten flashed his badge at the receptionist, who looked thoroughly bored, and gained admittance to a small boardroom. A few moments later, a small, bald man with a harmless looking, dark-featured face entered the room.

"Haven't seen you for a while, Special Agent," he said, with a smile. "Who have you brought with you today?"

"Well, Guido, you did tell me that you'd cleaned up your operations," said Shorten. "Thought I'd take a look. This is Detective Elise Jones, from down in Ten Mile Hollow, and former FBI agent Dinah Harris, who is consulting on the case."

"I don't think we do business there," said Guido.

"Some of your *customers* do, though," said Shorten. "We found some fake passports and social security cards."

Guido didn't look the least bit worried. "Uh-huh. What's that got to do with me?"

"You guys did them," said Shorten, sharply. "I know your work, Guido. Don't treat me like I'm stupid, or it'll go badly for you, understand?"

Dinah got the impression that Guido saw this conversation as simply another business deal. She imagined his mind was already calculating what he could get in return for his co-operation.

"So what do you want from me?" he asked.

"I want to know about the people who bought them," said Shorten. "And maybe this time I'll let it slide."

Shorten slid one of Malia Shaw's fake passports across the desk. Guido picked it up and examined it thoroughly.

"This is pretty good work," he said, at length. "You can't seriously expect me to remember who bought them. It's a cash business, Special Agent. I'm sure you understand we don't keep records."

"Do you recognize the woman in the documents?"

Guido shook his head. "No."

"These have been done pretty recently," said Shorten. "They look pretty new."

Guido looked over them again. "Yeah. But I don't recognize the lady in the photos."

"You don't think she bought them from you?"

"Nope. For some reason, I'm thinking they were bought by a man."

"Do you think it was this man?" Elise asked, showing Guido Simon Wakowski's latest mug shot.

"Nope, wasn't him."

"What about this man?" Dinah showed him a picture of Angus Whitehall on her phone.

Guido looked at the picture for a long time. "You know, this guy *does* look familiar. It could have been him."

"You got cameras in here at all, Guido?" Shorten asked.

"What do you mean, cameras?"

"Like CCTV. Keeping an eye on your *illegal* employees?"

Guido smiled, showing a gold tooth. "Nice try. All my employees have the correct documentation, but you're welcome to look. Yes, we have CCTV in some areas of our business."

"Would your cameras have seen someone looking for new fake documents?"

"If he walked in the front door, yeah."

"Great. How old would you say these documents are?"

Guido tossed the documents on the table. "Two years?"

"Great. I need the tapes from two years ago."

"The whole year?" Guido whined.

"Until I see this guy," interjected Elise, pointing at Whitehall's picture. Guido pouted like a five-year-old girl, but in the end, he agreed.

Outside, Elise suddenly seemed unsure. "It's going to take me a long time to go through those tapes."

Shorten smiled. "I'll help you out. I'm sure there's some stuff on there I'd like to see and I like helping out two former colleagues." He smiled.

Dinah couldn't shake the sensation of running through quicksand, sinking deeper with every step beneath the weight of deception and misery and lifetimes wasted on the sharp end of a needle.

****

The need to find Lola rendered Angus incapable of anything else. Somehow he managed to preach on Sunday morning, though he couldn't remember what he'd said. He spent Sunday night restlessly tossing in bed, unable to sleep. On Monday morning, he got up early and, with a headache thumping behind his eyes, he drove to the duplex in which Lola had lived.

The proprietor, the elderly woman who lived next door, was watering her flowers and her eyes narrowed with suspicion as he approached her.

"Good morning," he said. "Mrs. Whittaker?"

"Ada Whittaker," she confirmed. "You looking for the lady who used to live here?"

"Yes. I spoke to you on the phone a few days ago," said Angus. "Right after the police came. I'm very worried for her, but the police won't file a report yet. Do you mind if I ask you a few questions?"

Ada Whittaker frowned at him. "How do I know you're not the one who is wanting to do her harm?"

Angus paused. "You don't," he agreed. "But if you look at who paid the deposit for this place, you'll see my name, Angus Whitehall. I am her friend."

Ada barely blinked. "Yeah, I remember the name. Well, son, I don't know if anything I tell you will help anyway. I haven't seen her for two weeks, and she owes a month's worth of rent."

"Have you ever had any conversation with her, just in passing?" Angus asked.

"Well, sure," said Ada. "She seemed a nice lady, though lonely. So I took it upon myself to befriend her a little. She didn't seem to have any family, either."

She doesn't, thought Angus.

"Last Christmas I asked if she would be seeing her folks," said Ada. "She just shook her head, told me she'd be having dinner at some place called Joaquin's."

Angus filed this away — how long had Lola been hanging out at Joaquin's? How was it that he knew nothing about her life anymore?

"Other than that," continued Ada, "all we talked about was the weather or something we'd seen in the news." She suddenly looked stricken. "I hope she's okay."

"So do I," said Angus. "Thanks for your help. I'll try to find you the money that you're owed."

Ada shrugged. "Good luck, sonny."

As Angus walked away, she yelled: "Hey!"

He turned around. "Yeah?"

"You look familiar. Do I know you?" The old lady stood peering at him with her hands on her hips.

He bent his face away from her. "I don't think so."

Angus drove to the temporary placement agency where Lola had received her assignments. On the fringes of downtown, it was a basic office set up to find staff for businesses that needed a temporary worker.

The receptionist had ruler-straight black hair and purple lipstick. She raised one eyebrow when Angus asked about Lola, and suggested laconically, "You need to see the Personnel Manager."

"Is that possible?"

The receptionist waved him through to an empty meeting room, and a stressed-out woman with frantic eyes joined him moments later. "Hello, sir," she said. "My name is Megan Marshall. I'm the Personnel Manager here. I'm very sorry about Lola Albright; she was always one of our most reliable workers. If your office has lost money due to her absences, I'm sure we can find some way of —"

"Ms. Marshall," interrupted Angus, gently. "I'm not from a company. I'm a friend of Lola's, and I'm concerned for her wellbeing."

Megan Marshall took a moment to shift gears. "What? You think something happened to her?"

"I hope not," said Angus. "But as you said, she was usually reliable. Nobody has seen her for two weeks, and it's not normal for her to simply vanish like that."

"I see," said Megan Marshall. "So what can I do for you, then?"

"I'm wondering when you saw her most recently, and if you noticed anything unusual," said Angus.

"Well, the thing is, I don't see our temporary workers very often at all. I organize placements for them, and call them to tell them where to go next. That's pretty much the extent of our relationship." Megan suddenly looked uncertain, as if she were afraid of getting into trouble.

"Sure," said Angus. "I understand. Did the office here get any strange phone calls for Lola? Was there any place she didn't particularly want to go?"

"If there were, she didn't tell me," said Megan. "I don't know about anything like that."

Angus felt increasingly desperate, but it was becoming clear that Lola Albright held people at arm's length, not allowing them into her life. He thanked Megan Marshall and drove to the only other place he knew Lola went — Joaquin's.

Joaquin's was a Mexican cantina near the edge of town, frequented by blue-collar workers. The groups of eaters were large and noisy, and they barely noticed Angus's arrival. Lola could have slipped in and out of the place without anybody realizing she'd been there at all, Angus realized. That was probably the attraction of it.

Angus approached the bar and asked the harried barmaid if she knew Lola Albright. The look of confusion and irritation was enough for Angus. This was not a place for building slow friendships, and Lola had probably chosen it precisely because she could be anonymous.

As Angus drove back to the office, he felt adrift, at sea without a rudder or anchor, simply bobbing about uselessly in a vast and unfriendly ocean. He was desperate to know that Lola was okay, but deep down, the tendrils of fear had snaked around his heart. The three of them had fled their past together, creating new lives in this small Virginian town. Now one was dead, the other missing. What did that mean for the remaining person?

Is my life in danger? Angus wondered. *Is my family in danger? Are they going to come after me? What does Lola know, if she is still alive? Has she talked to anyone? Does anyone know the truth about me? Why did I think I could ever get away with it?*

The experts say that a marriage built on deceit cannot last. Sometimes, it seems there is no better choice. I could never find the courage to tell Louise about Malia or Lola, because they represent the very worst parts of me. They are women who trusted me, needed me, at times, even loved me. I gave them nothing in return but violence and misery. Lola was the stronger of the two; but Malia was lost from the start. I took terrible advantage of her and destroyed her. I have spent so much time thinking of violent red blooms of blood; the bitter taste of hatred; hasty deals done in the darkness of my heart. I've been thinking of lives destroyed, money exchanged for the last breath of life, cheap hotels and needles that rob a person of everything that made her human.

Sometimes I feel like I've bathed in other people's blood, like it's dripping from me, like it's staining my skin and darkening my heart. I can't get rid of it, I can't outrun it, and I can't wash myself of it. It haunts my sleep and ghosts my days. Yet, somehow I've fooled everyone, haven't I? Nobody would guess my origins; nobody would believe the things I've done.

The truth is that the false life we set up here in Ten Mile Hollow all those years ago became real for me, but it didn't become real for them.

Malia couldn't deal with everything we had done — she found a dealer and slipped into her addiction, despite the many times I tried to help her. It was as if she knew that life had nothing else to offer her. We tried the charade of getting her a job, finding her a nice place to live, only to hear a few weeks later that she'd been fired or evicted or both. But I kept going back, trying to help, because it was all my fault, don't you see?

Lola didn't fall into the hole of addiction, but she didn't really settle here either. She only accepted temporary jobs, she moved houses all the time. She didn't have any relationships or close friends. Perhaps she could sense she was living on borrowed time.

I've thought about it for years and years, you know; why I could settle down and live a normal life, and why Malia and Lola couldn't. I believe there really is no difference between us except for one thing.

The capacity for evil in my heart is much greater than theirs. While their lives were consumed with guilt and horror at what we'd done, my aptitude for denial and self-justification and pride is stellar. The instinct for self-preservation is strongest in me, and I'm so ashamed I can barely stand myself.

Angus shook away his shadowy thoughts, parked his car in the lot at church, and stared sightlessly through the windshield. He knew the truth of it, deep down, whether he was truly in danger or not. He had allowed the two women to be thrown to the wolves, while he cowered behind his family and office.

As I have always been — a coward and an egotist. A bad combination; a dangerous, violent combination.

****

On Monday morning, Chloe was horrified when her mother suggested that they go shopping together during her free periods. Ever since she'd learned to hate mirrors, Chloe also hated shopping. *Pale, fat, round girls did not enjoy shopping,* Chloe thought darkly.

But for her mom, shopping was an all too rare bonding experience, and Chloe didn't want to disappoint her. And it was rare that Mom had time off during the week.

Thankfully it usually only happened two or three times a year, as the weather changed. Winter was on the downhill slide toward spring, which meant that Mom instantly decided Chloe needed new clothes.

Down at the mall, Chloe resolved to be as agreeable as possible so that the shopping thing could be finished as quickly as possible. But for some reason today, Mom decided to stroll along casually, looking in almost every store.

"Oh, my!" Mom exclaimed, stopping outside a Kohl's store. "Look at those adorable dresses. Come on!"

Chloe really wanted to say, *I look terrible in dresses,* but instead she said weakly, "Sure."

Like a woman on a mission, Mom gathered up spring dresses left and right, amassing armfuls for Chloe to try on. Chloe looked at the dresses askance, seeing pretty floral prints, and floaty skirts that would look absolutely awful on her.

Still, to humor her mother, she disappeared into the changing room to try on the dresses.

"Make sure you come out and show me!" called Mom through the door.

Chloe rolled her eyes and pulled on a pink and yellow floral dress that only seemed to accentuate her flabby arms and thick ankles. With a deep sigh, she opened the dressing room door.

Her mom looked up with a bright smile and Chloe took a sudden step backward, filled with dread. Standing with her mom were Jessica Hunter and two of her minions, Sarah Mallister and Alice Greendale. All of them wore fake, syrupy smiles to go with their lean, willowy legs and long glossy hair.

"Chloe, your friends happened to be here, too!" said Mom, cheerfully. "Isn't that great? That's a lovely dress. What do you think, girls?"

Chloe would have been quite happy to die on the spot. Was it possible to will yourself to death? If it were, she would've done it immediately. Jessica grinned, full of spite and glee.

"Hi Chloe!" she said, as if she were an old friend. "Your mom said you were trying on some dresses. We couldn't resist the opportunity to see you!"

Before Chloe realized what she was doing, she pulled out her cell phone and took a quick photo. "Lovely!" she said, her tone suggesting otherwise. Clueless, her mom beamed.

"Well, I hate this dress," Chloe announced, and stepped back behind the curtain. She ripped off the dress and pulled back on her regular clothes.

As she reappeared, her mom looked confused. "What about all those other dresses?" she asked. "Aren't you going to try them on?"

"Yeah," chimed in Jessica. "You looked so great in the last one. There were some really pretty ones there, too!"

Chloe felt hot, and she was sure her face was bright red. "I don't want to try on any more dresses," she snapped. "Let's go."

"Chloe," Mom said, bewildered. "Please don't be rude to your friends."

Jessica managed to slide a hurt look onto her face. "Sorry Chloe, I didn't mean to upset you."

Chloe felt herself quite capable of physical violence at that very moment. Briefly, she imagined Jessica being consumed by a fire or caught in a tornado or buried in a landslide. Instead, she turned and stormed out of the store.

The tinkling of their laughter followed her as Mom caught up with her and grabbed her arm. "Chloe! What on earth is the matter with you?" she demanded. "You were very rude to all of us."

Chloe thought of all the things she could say about Jessica and her minions, but instead said: "I hate dresses, okay? I hate wearing those stupid flowery dresses that make me look terrible. I wish you'd stop trying to make me into something I'm not!"

"Chloe, I don't think —" Mom began.

"Just drop it okay? I don't want to talk about it," snapped Chloe. Close to bursting into tears, she turned away.

"I wasn't trying to make you into something you're not," continued Mom, her voice calm. "There's no need to be rude to me."

Chloe's anger and humiliation boiled over. "Why don't you just admit you don't know anything about me?" she yelled, oblivious to the people around her. "You want me to wear ridiculous dresses; you don't even realize I hate them! Those girls aren't my friends, but you don't even know that! You have no idea about me at all! Why don't you just go back to work and leave me alone!"

Her mom looked stunned at the outburst. It was unusual for Chloe, even adolescent Chloe, to explode like that. But she didn't care. It felt good to tell the truth for once, instead of humoring her and pretending everything was fine.

Chloe stomped back to the car. Mom followed her, a look of tight displeasure on her face. The car trip to school was filled with awkward silence, Mom shooting glances at Chloe every so often. Thankfully, she seemed to sense that Chloe didn't want to talk and she stayed silent.

At school, Chloe went straight to the library, shaking her head at her mother's total ignorance. She sat at a computer cubicle right at the back of the library and logged onto Facebook even though it was against the rules, grimly certain she'd find something posted about her by Jessica. Grotesque fascination made her do it, as if she couldn't look away. If nothing else, she needed to know what the kids at school would be laughing at all day.

Jessica Hunter didn't disappoint.

She'd photo-shopped the image of Chloe in the dress, adding crudely drawn fairy wings and a wand. At the bottom of the photo, she'd written: **YOUR FAIRY HOG-MOTHER** and posted it on Facebook.

Chloe inspected the photo with a harsh and critical eye. She'd been right — her legs were too round and short, her arms soft and saggy. The dress seemed to accentuate every site where flesh squeezed against the seams. She could even see rolls of fat around her stomach, every crease noticeable through the thin fabric.

The jeering comments underneath the photo were coming thick and fast. It seemed that she was fast becoming an object of ridicule not just among Jessica's minions, but almost everybody at the school.

Chloe closed her computer and sat back in her chair, staring up at the ceiling. She heard the bell calling her to class, but she resolutely ignored it and the consequences, dreaming of a parallel universe in which she was tall, thin, beautiful, and popular.

****

The bank manager called on Monday afternoon, for which Dinah was thankful. Elise had been in a quiet and snappy mood since her shopping trip with her daughter. Dinah didn't know what had happened, but they'd both arrived home looking unhappy. Since then, the silence in the house had been full of tension.

"I didn't think you'd be calling until tomorrow at least," Elise said into the speaker phone.

The bank manager, who had identified himself as Raoul Gomez, laughed. "The vice-president told me to call you as soon as the traces were complete," he said. "I've got the paperwork here. Would you like to take a look at it?"

"Yes, please," Elise said. "Shall we meet somewhere?"

"Flannery's is open for a late lunch or early dinner," suggested Raoul. "It'll be quiet, seeing it's a Monday."

Elise and Dinah left ten minutes later, and met Raoul at a round table away from the bar. The Irish bar was often busy over the weekend, but on Monday nights, quiet tables were available. Most of the patrons were clustered around the television, watching Monday night football.

Raoul Gomez was tall, dark-complexioned, and floridly handsome. In his mid-thirties, he'd managed the Ten Mile Hollow Savings Trust Bank for five years. He sat behind a stack of paper. "Hi, Detective," he greeted Elise. He glanced at Dinah with curiosity. "Hope the information I've found is useful."

"I'm sure it is," she said. "Thanks for calling me. This is Dinah Harris, a former FBI agent who is consulting on this case for me."

"Nice to meet you," Gomez said, standing up to shake Dinah's hand.

They all sat and ordered root beer from the waitress.

"Well, let's start at the beginning," Gomez said, showing Elise and Dinah a copy of Malia Shaw's bank statements. "You can see regular deposits into her account, of about five hundred dollars a fortnight."

Dinah saw the regular injections of cash and nodded.

"You'll notice the numbers after the word 'deposit' on the statement," continued Raoul. "This is a descriptor, which tells me that the money was transferred from another account, as opposed to being deposited in-person in a bank."

Dinah and Elise nodded again.

"Secondly, the descriptor tells me the money came from another bank, not the Ten Mile Hollow Savings Trust. When we perform the trace, we basically decode the numbers."

Dinah, a little impatient, kept a pleasant smile on her face. *Let's hurry this up, Raoul!*

"So the bank the money came from is Bank of America, from an account held in a branch in Richmond," continued Raoul.

"Who is the holder of that account?" Elise asked.

"A company, Sons & Daughters Ltd," said Raoul. "Does that ring any bells for you?"

Elise frowned and shook her head.

"I didn't think so," said Raoul. "So I did some further checking with a friend who works at Bank of America. The signatories on the account are a man and woman, by the names of Robert Langer and Theresa Scott."

Dinah frowned, her brain in overdrive. Those names didn't sound familiar either, yet something flagged deep in the back of her mind.

"This Sons & Daughters, Ltd account is the only one in that name, and neither Robert Langer nor Theresa Scott have accounts there in their own names."

"How much money did the account have in it, and where did it come from?" Elise asked.

"I'm glad you thought of that, because I did, too," grinned Raoul, who seemed to be enjoying himself immensely. "The account has been open for close to 20 years, and there is a deposit of roughly $15,000 every year. So we ran a trace on the deposit of $15,000."

Dinah nodded. *Spit it out, man!*

"*That* deposit comes from a Wells Fargo branch held in D.C. The Wells Fargo account is held in the name of The Wellness Group

Trust, and the signatories on that account are Lola Albright and Robert Langer."

Lola! Dinah sat up straighter. "I know a Lola Albright," she said. Elise agreed with a nod.

"Well, here is something interesting," said Raoul. "The money in that account is also about $15,000 a year and the trace led to another account, an investment account with Goldman Sachs. It was opened about 20 years ago — I'm starting to see a pattern here — in the name of Robert Langer, with an opening balance of $225,000, at a branch in California."

That got Elise's attention. "*Really?*" she said, eyebrows raised. "What do you think that means?"

"The attempt to hide the source of the money is not particularly sophisticated," said Raoul. "Though this information is not widely available, any bank staffer could trace the money pretty easily. But where did the $225,000 come from? It was a series of cash deposits — all under the amount of $10,000, of course. Anything over that we have to report. So we see a wide range of cash deposits from banks and branches all over the country, all for between $8,000 and $9,000 each. Collectively, it adds up to $225,000. And *that's* the interesting thing."

"Is there any pattern to those deposits being made?" Dinah asked. "Indicative of a journey from somewhere else, for example?"

"No," said Raoul. "I checked. It's all here, but as an example, you can see that in March, a deposit was made in New Orleans. Two days later, another deposit in Seattle. It bounces around all over the country in the same way over a period of about six months."

There was silence as both Elise and Dinah thought about this. "So the trace stops eventually with a huge amount of cash in Robert Langer's name," said Dinah.

"Right. One thing I can't tell you is where that cash came from, but perhaps this Robert Langer will explain," said Raoul.

A long-time heroin addict receives five hundred dollars a fortnight from a man and Lola, thought Dinah. *But it comes from a nest egg of almost a quarter of a million dollars, deposited 20 years ago in cash.*

A thought suddenly struck her. She stood and shook Raoul's hand. "Thanks for all your help," she said. "Can I take this paperwork with me? I'd like to go to the office and look through it."

Elise looked up at her, a puzzled expression on her face. But she stood too.

"Of course," said Raoul. "It was kind of fun, you know, doing some proper investigating."

Outside, Elise asked: "What? You thought of something?"

"Let's get back to the office and I'll explain," said Dinah.

Elise drove urgently to her office, which meant her driving was even worse than normal. Still, she arrived in record time. The office was empty save for the deputies on duty and the night dispatcher, who chewed gum frantically as though her life depended upon it. Dinah flicked on the lights over her desk and rifled through the evidence they'd already collected while Elise watched.

She finally found what she was looking for — the fake identification documents she'd found in Malia Shaw's apartment. Her suspicion was confirmed — the signatory known as Theresa Scott was one of the aliases Malia Shaw had used. She showed the document to Elise.

Elise immediately called Raoul on his cell phone.

"Raoul?" she said. "Listen, I need one more thing from you. Can you locate the identification documentation Robert Langer used when he opened the account at Bank of America? I think I know who he is, but I need a picture to confirm it."

Though the evening was getting late, Raoul managed to get the information from the West Coast by close of business. As the sun died a fiery death in the west, the fax machine chattered into life. The document that came through clarified Dinah's hunch. When Robert Langer had opened the account, he'd been required to provide identification. He'd given a passport and a driver's license, which had been photocopied by the bank employee. And even the grainy, poor-quality photocopy of the passport photo could not hide his identity. Robert Langer was Angus Whitehall. His fake identification seemed to be as professional as those found in Malia Shaw's apartment; certainly, the bank employee had seen no reason to be suspicious.

Dinah sat down hard at her desk, her mind spinning like a child's toy. Who were Angus, Malia, and Lola? What were they hiding?

And why had it led to Malia's death and Lola's disappearance?

D on't tell me," groaned Angus. His knuckles turned white where he gripped his desk. "Please not today."

"I'm sorry, sir," said Shana, in her wobbly, uncertain voice. She often made the sentences she said sound like questions. "He's already on his way in?"

"Thanks," whispered Angus. He took a deep breath and waited, counting grimly. He wasn't sure his overwhelmed mind could take much more. In one corner, the shocking murder of Malia Shaw tried to elbow its way into the foreground. It competed with the needs of the church, and all of the responsibilities that entailed. In yet another corner, the concerned and probing looks his wife gave him caused him concern. In a third, his concern for Lola Albright throbbed like a heart. Above all of these, a red neon light flashed over and over: *what if they find out about me?*

Two minutes later, the door of his office opened. A tall man with crew cut gray hair, large eyebrows that looked like gray squirrel tails, and a hawkish nose stood in the doorway.

"Morning, Pastor," he said. "Mind if I come in?"

He was in before Angus could formally address the question. Angus stood up to shake the man's hand and then sank back down into his chair. "Hello, Mr. O'Toole. How are you today?"

Samuel R. O'Toole III was one of the richest men in Ten Mile Hollow, owning the John Deere dealership out on Industrial Way and acres of land throughout the town and beyond. He was a regular attendee at Ten Mile Hollow First Baptist Church and a generous benefactor. He happily donated time, money, land, and whatever else he could to the church and to the ministry. If Angus needed something, Samuel O'Toole was the man he turned to for help. There was only one small problem — O'Toole desperately wanted Angus to confirm his opinion that white people were the God-ordained master race and that all others were inferior.

The irony, thought Angus, when he heard O'Toole was on his way in. *The irony burns.*

Angus wouldn't comply with the man's wishes, and therefore every so often, O'Toole would appear in his office to ask why not.

"Well, sir," said O'Toole, seating himself down opposite Angus. Only the desk between them offered Angus any respite. "I have to say, I can't quite agree with some of the things you said there on Sunday morning."

Angus stifled a sigh. "Which parts, Mr. O'Toole?"

"Call me Samuel, now," the big man said. "Well, I have to take issue with you telling us that all the races are equal. I have no shame in telling you that my ancestors had slaves, and I know that's how the good Lord wanted it to be."

"Mr. O'Toole, let's not start by saying that we are of different races," Angus suggested. "That is a term that only serves to divide us. We're all one race, the human race descended from Adam and Eve. I think you must agree with me on that."

"Well, but you're suggesting that I'm the same race as the slaves my great-great-grandfather owned!" O'Toole shook his head. His squirrel-tail eyebrows danced up and then down. "I have to remind you that they couldn't even read!"

Angus looked the other man in the eye. "Sir, you know full well that's because they were afforded neither an education nor opportunity. Frankly, you *are* the same race." Angus tried to recall the exact figures. "If you were to examine your DNA and the DNA of another person regardless of their ethnicity, you'd find very little difference indeed. From memory, about 0.1 percent."

O'Toole gave a little chuckle. "I don't know much about the science behind it, but I do know about the curse of Ham. Oh yes. Noah cursed Ham, and that's why there are black people. Now I'm not part of any curse, so I can't be the same."

Angus cleared his throat and took his Bible from the drawer. "I'm glad you brought this up," he said. He flipped through the Bible to the passage O'Toole referred to — Genesis chapter nine. He handed the book over to O'Toole.

"Would you read it to me, please?" he asked.

O'Toole obliged. "'When Noah awoke from his wine and found out what his youngest son had done to him, he said, 'Cursed be Canaan! The lowest of slaves will he be to his brothers.' " He looked up triumphantly.

"Please read me the part where this curse has anything to do with skin color or race," said Angus, his voice mild.

O'Toole re-read the passage to himself but remained silent, as Angus knew he would. Although Genesis chapter nine was often used to justify slavery and racism of dark-skinned people, in truth it did nothing of the sort. It pronounced a curse upon Canaan and its people the Canaanites, but the curse had nothing to do with their skin color. Descendants of Canaan had been found in many parts of the world — Asia, the Middle East, and Africa — and shared a diverse range of physical characteristics.

Angus continued: "Of course, the Bible *does* tell us quite a lot about human beings. It refers to us as being of 'one blood' in Acts 17:26. Paul makes the point in Romans that 'there is no difference between the Jew and the Greek.' But most importantly, he reminds us that we've *all* sinned and fallen short of the glory of God and that Jesus died for sinners."

O'Toole still looked skeptical.

"Tell me, sir," Angus finished. "Do you think only light-skinned people get to go to heaven?"

Samuel O'Toole sighed. "Well, now, don't put words in my mouth. Listen, don't you take me for a racist. I don't hate them. I just . . . they're just . . . we're just not the same, no matter what you say."

The phone on Angus's desk rang. "You've got your next meeting?" Shana said.

"Thanks." He hung up and stood. "Mr. O'Toole, I'm sorry to cut this short. But I have another meeting to go to. Thanks for stopping by."

Mr. O'Toole shook Angus's hand. "I appreciate your time, sir." He paused for a moment. "I guess it's lucky we got soft-hearted people like you around." He left with a chuckle.

Angus wanted to collapse on the ground but he wasn't sure whether it was with hysterical laughter or angry weeping.

I tell you about this because I must undo all the terrible things I've done. Because you must never know who I truly am.

****

Dinah dreamed about fake bank accounts, suitcases full of money, and shadowy figures that never quite allowed their faces to be seen. She tossed and turned all night and woke early, the urge to uncover the mystery of the money strong. While it was still dark outside, she changed into her running clothes, sent Elise a text message telling her that she'd meet her at the office, and went out into the bracing morning air.

A smidge of grayish-pink on the eastern horizon was all that hinted at the coming sunrise. There was no wind, but the cold bit at Dinah's bones within seconds. She began to run, taking slow, measured breaths of the cold air, enjoying the quiet solitude of early morning in a small town. Back home in D.C., it was never really quiet or still. Traffic still moved, a siren would wail, 24-hour convenience stores never turned off their blinking neon lights. But in Ten Mile Hollow, nothing moved or made a sound. It truly was dark and quiet.

She called Aaron again and they spoke briefly. Aaron was tense, gearing up for a raid that morning on the office of an environmental lawyer. He was getting into the zone, that space of hyper-awareness that preceded the possibility of violence. It didn't bother Dinah that they couldn't talk much — just hearing his voice made her feel calmer.

She ran five miles around town before having a quick shower at the sheriff's office, changing her clothes, and picking up a breakfast burrito from Main Street.

By the time she got back to the office, Elise was waiting for her. "Look," she said, without preamble. "The owner of Malia Shaw's building, that cranky old guy — what was his name? Kracker Ides or something?"

"Yes," said Dinah. "Karakarides."

"Right. So he told us that Malia Shaw had paid her rent six months in advance."

"Yes," repeated Dinah. "A fortune for someone who was otherwise occupied with getting as much heroin as she could."

"So when you rent an apartment, you have to provide proof of a job or pay a deposit or have a guarantee, right?" Elise continued. "I mean, you have to make *some* representation that you'll pay your rent."

"I had the same thought myself," agreed Dinah.

Elise thrust the rental agreement toward Dinah. "Yeah, so *look*."

Someone had indeed guaranteed Malia Shaw's rental application. On the back page of the rental application was a section for guarantors to fill in their details. On this application, Angus Whitehall had completed it.

Dinah thoughtfully committed this piece of information to her memory. Angus Whitehall had guaranteed Malia Shaw's lease from the moment she needed a place to live in Ten Mile Hollow. That would indicate that he'd known her well before she'd moved here. Well enough to guarantee an addict's lease.

"Let's give him a call," she suggested.

Elise called Angus Whitehall's number and turned on the speaker. "Hello?" He sounded tired.

"It's Detective Elise Jones," she said. Without further pleasantries, she continued: "I note that you signed a guarantee for Malia Shaw's lease."

There was a long silence. "Yes," admitted Whitehall, his words tense and clipped. "I did."

"She needed a place to live and you felt sorry for her?" Elise asked. "Yes."

"How long did you know her before she moved to Ten Mile Hollow?"

"I didn't, not really," he hedged. "She came to me for help. We had known each other in college many years before. I felt sorry for her."

"Did you both move here at the same time, to live in Ten Mile Hollow?"

"I'm not sure," said Whitehall, his voice trembling. "I don't know."

"Why would she move here? She has no family here, no friends. No job. How did she end up here?"

"I don't know. I really don't."

Why are you lying? thought Dinah. *If you didn't kill her, why are you lying?*

"How did she meet or get to know Lola?"

"I don't —"

"Let me ask you something else," said Elise, abruptly. "Do you think I'm going to find withdrawals of about $1,800 every six months or so from your account?"

The silence on the other end of the phone made Elise shoot a triumphant smile at Dinah.

"So you'll guarantee her lease because you're paying the rent," she said. "Fair enough. Don't you think it's odd for someone to go to so much trouble for the sake of an addict, for someone you barely knew?"

"She wasn't just an addict!" said Angus, fiercely. "To me, she was still a human being who needed help! It was worth making sure she had a place to live. I couldn't control what she spent the rest of her money on, but at least —"

"Why did you care so much?"

"It's my job to care!" cried the pastor. "It's what I do!"

But you don't guarantee a lease or pay the rent of anyone else. Only Malia Shaw. Why?

"How did you know she even had any more money?" Elise asked. "Where did she get her money from?"

Angus fell silent, and the air between them was heavy with suspicion. "I'm not comfortable talking to you any further without my lawyer present," he said after a pause.

"Sure, Mr. Whitehall," Elise said. "Let me say one thing before you hang up. The money trail never lies, and I'm following it. Do you understand?"

She hung up the phone noisily.

"Well, that was fun," she grinned.

"I want to know where that quarter of a million dollars came from," said Dinah. She felt that there were only a few missing pieces of the puzzle to the money mystery, and it was frustrating that she didn't have them. "Who deposited the money? Why?"

She thought about what the bank manager had told them — that the funds had been deposited in different banks all over the country, in amounts of $9,000 at a time so that the transaction wouldn't be reported to the authorities.

"You know what's really weird?" mused Elise. She was idly doodling on a blank piece of paper in her notebook. "That quarter of a million dollars has been untouched for 20 years. I mean, apart from paying Malia Shaw's rent. Could *you* resist the temptation to withdraw some money here and there for a pair of new shoes or to renovate your house?"

"No, I couldn't," said Dinah. "Nobody could."

She sat back in her chair, drumming her fingers impatiently on the desk. She knew that, equally, finding both Lola and the money would solve this murder mystery.

But it was easy to lose oneself in this great country, particularly if she had access to high-quality fake identification as Angus and Malia did. She could have jumped on a bus, train, plane, or taxi and be in New York City or Los Angeles or Canada by now. Did she have access to cash? If so, she could live completely off the grid, in utter anonymity.

Struck with a sudden idea, Dinah phoned Raoul Gomez at the bank again, and asked if Lola Albright had an account there.

"Yes," he said, cheerfully. "The agency she works for requires all their staff to have an account here."

"Any unusual activity in her account? Large transactions?" Dinah asked.

"Well, just her salary up until a couple of weeks ago," said Raoul. "But then she withdrew all of it in one hit."

Perhaps Lola knew she was in danger and was preparing to flee. The question is, did she make it?

"Where did she do that?"

"An ATM in . . . let's see, an ATM just outside Norfolk."

There is an international airport in Norfolk, thought Dinah.

"Did she have any credit cards?"

"Yes, she did. But she stopped using it a couple of weeks ago."

Dinah felt her heart rate speed up a little. Clutching the phone a little harder, she asked, "Can you see the transaction history of the card?"

"Sure. What am I looking for?"

"Ticket purchases, like plane or bus tickets. Hotel bookings. Car hire deposits. Stuff like that."

There was a pause as Raoul scanned through the transaction history. Finally, he said, "No, nothing like that. Just groceries, a haircut, some clothes."

Disappointed, Dinah thanked Raoul and hung up. She relayed the conversation to Elise and both women lapsed into silence, thinking about the money trail, the fake documentation, and what it could possibly mean.

The money had a story it wanted to tell, Dinah was sure of it.

****

Angus arrived home long after night had fallen, as a light snow fell silently over the landscape. The flakes dissolved the moment they touched the ground, as if too delicate for the reality of life on earth. The moon jutted itself around a cloud, fat and full. As the snow fell, it muffled noise and turned the streets into the gray, bleak terrain of a distant planet. Inside, dinner had been eaten, the dishes washed and put away, and the children were upstairs watching TV or doing homework.

Louise was scrubbing out the pantry. This was not a good sign, Angus knew. Compulsive cleaning meant Louise was angry about something. There had been times when, during an argument, she'd started cleaning windows or the oven in an attempt to handle the conflict. She hated fighting, and it was partly his fault, he knew. He was often too aggressive, despite his best attempts at self-control.

"Hi," he said, entering the kitchen. "Sorry I'm late. It's been a crazy day at the office."

That didn't seem to help the situation appreciably. Louise scrubbed harder. Eventually, she said, "I've kept your dinner warm in the oven."

Angus was too sick with dread to be hungry, but he found the plate and began eating. Louise didn't pause in her scrubbing or look at him.

"What's up?" he asked, at length. "Are you upset about something?"

"No," she said. "I'm fine."

Angus ate another mouthful. Clearly, she didn't mean she was fine. She meant that everything was not at all fine. He was male, and women generally mystified him, but this much he knew. "Louise. Please. Stop it and tell me what's wrong." He took a drink of water from his glass.

She pushed back a strand of hair and straightened up. She snapped off her rubber gloves and asked, "Where were you today?"

"It was a busy day at the office," said Angus. "I was in meetings and —"

"Don't lie to me!" snapped Louise, with more venom in her voice than Angus could remember ever hearing. "Your secretary called *here*, wanting to know where you were!"

Oh, thought Angus.

"So, where were you?" Louise demanded.

"I'm sorry, Louise," he said. His old friend *shame* wrapped thick, suffocating layers of disquiet around his chest. It became more difficult to breathe. "I've been trying to protect you from this ugly business with the murdered woman and a friend of hers, Lola, who has gone missing. I've spent the last few days in the car, looking for her."

"Last time I checked, you were the pastor of a church," said Louise. Her voice was so cold, so unlike Louise. She stood rigidly, her tension obvious. "Not a detective. What business is it of yours?"

"Well . . . uh, I knew them. I feel somewhat responsible," said Angus. "So I suppose I feel as if I need to help find whoever did this to her."

Louise's eyes were like laser points, boring into him, seeking to lay bare his secrets. "Really? How did you know them?"

Angus opened his mouth and realized he was about to lie. It was so natural now, to lie about Malia and Lola and what they'd shared. But to lie to his wife so blatantly was crossing a line. "Louise," he said, his voice shaky. "I knew both of them from many years ago. We are old friends."

"Why have you never introduced them to me, if they're such good friends?"

"No, they're friends from a long time ago," corrected Angus. "They aren't *good* friends. In fact, they're only friends in a bad kind of way."

Louise, usually the very image of gentleness, had somehow transformed into a terrier, refusing to let go. "What does that mean?"

"I felt responsible for them," he said. "I felt I should make sure that they were okay. The murdered woman, Malia Shaw, was a heroin addict. I checked on her, to make sure she was okay, and by okay, I mean whether she was still alive or not. Lola used to do the same. Occasionally, we'd talk about how we could help Malia. But that was it."

Louise was silent for a time, studying him as if she'd never really seen him before. Of course, Angus knew that she'd only ever known the thin veneer of respectable Angus. The murky undercurrents of his real self had remained opaque, hidden. Only he knew the depths of disgrace he had sunk to in years past.

"Was there anything else to your relationship with either of them?" she asked, her face so drawn and tight that her skin seemed translucent under the harsh kitchen lighting.

"No!" exclaimed Angus. "No, Louise . . . I promise to you on my life, absolutely not."

The news didn't appear to mollify Louise in any way, but she nodded. It seemed she could accept this as truth. "Do the police think that you killed Malia?"

Angus sagged under the weight of the words. "I don't know."

"Did you?" Louise's eyes were darkly smoldering.

"No! Absolutely not!"

Louise considered him, and Angus realized that for the first time in their marriage she was weighing up whether to believe him or not. That her trust in him had received a mortal wound shook Angus to his core. To hide his fear, he stood up and advanced a few steps toward her.

"Please, look at me," he implored. "I'm not a murderer." *Well, not anymore.*

"But the police continue to call you, to visit here. What is it they think you know?" Louise took a tiny step back. Angus felt another blow deep in his chest, seeing the fear and distrust in her causing her to move away from him.

"I don't know," he said. "I think they've latched onto me just because I knew the woman and cared for her wellbeing."

Louise looked at him oddly for a moment. "What about Lola? Didn't she care about this woman too?"

He sighed. "Yes, but she has gone missing."

"*Missing?*" Louise shook her head as if she couldn't quite believe that this was happening. "What does that mean? Has she been killed too?"

"I don't know." Angus closed his eyes briefly, at once weighed down by the burden of the past. It was too heavy to carry.

She turned her eyes away from him, her mouth sagging at the corners. "I think you're telling me the truth," she said, and his relief was instant. "I think I know you well enough."

"Thank you," he said. She moved toward him, and they hugged. She was a slight woman and he had always marveled at how delicate she felt in his arms. *I don't ever want to hurt you. It would kill me to hurt you. But I fear that if you ever knew the truth of who I once was, you would hate me. And I love you so much that I couldn't bear it.*

"I love you, Louise," he said. *I'm sorry, so sorry.*

"I love you, too," she said.

****

That afternoon Chloe walked the long way home from school. There was no chance she could take the normal route when Grace wasn't with her — it was tantamount to asking for a verbal beating, or worse. Grace hadn't been at school today, and despite Chloe's text messages to her, hadn't replied. Chloe hoped she was okay.

She'd spent the last few hours after school in the library — the only sanctuary where she knew Jessica would not set foot. Finally, when the librarian had cleared her throat a few times and rattled her keys, Chloe realized that it was time to leave.

As she walked, her shoulders slumped. School was almost unbearable when Grace was away; Jessica Hunter and her minions had no reason to censor their behavior. As a result, the jibes had been heavy and constant today, leaving Chloe feeling drained and exhausted. Worse than the mocking were the looks in the eyes of other students, who heard the taunts and stayed silent. Chloe could see the pity and embarrassment written on their faces, and it burned worse than Jessica's words. *Would none of them speak up?* The burden resting across her shoulders was becoming too heavy for her to bear alone.

She arrived home from school and was used to letting herself into the house and rattling around in there on her own until her mom or dad got home. Today, she was surprised to see her mother's car in the driveway.

Chloe opened the front door and called, "Mom? I'm home!"

There was no reply, but the sound of scuffling from the kitchen.

Frowning, Chloe dropped her book bag near the front door and peered into the kitchen.

"Mom?"

Her mother was standing at the counter, her back to her daughter. Her arms were spread on the counter, as if they were holding her up.

"Hi, honey," she said, falsely bright.

"Where's Dinah?"

There was a pause, then her mom turned around. "She is still at the office," she said. "I came home early because I need to talk to you."

Uh-oh, thought Chloe. She immediately began to catalogue in her brain all the things her mother might have discovered: the binging? Skipping meals? What had she done that would make her mom angry?

"Okay," she said, sinking down onto one of the kitchen table chairs.

Her mom must have read the exhaustion in her face and she quickly said, "How are *you*?"

"Okay." Chloe took a few deep breaths. "Okay."

"I . . . have a situation at work, that may affect you," her mom said.

Chloe bit her lip. *At least she doesn't know I've only been pretending to eat dinner.*

"What?"

"It's Grace's dad. I know that you are good friends with Grace, so I thought you should know. I'm investigating him for murder. We're only in the beginning stages of the investigation, but since Grace might bring it up, I thought I should tell you."

Chloe was shocked. "*Murder*? That's insane!" She thought of Mr. Whitehall's friendly eyes, ready laugh, and obvious adoration for his kids. It was impossible!

Mom sighed. "Nevertheless, it's true. And I have to do my job."

"But Mom, he's the *pastor* of a church!"

"I know. But everyone is capable of doing the wrong thing. Even pastors."

Chloe thought about that. "So you'll be trying to put Mr. White-hall in jail?"

"Not necessarily. I'm working to find out if he is innocent."

"Will you have to testify against him in court?"

"I'm not sure. Not yet."

"Well, can you ask to be taken off the case?"

Her mom smiled slightly. "I can't, honey. I'm the only detective in town."

"Oh."

"I'm sorry, Chloe. This may affect your friendship with Grace."

"Oh." Chloe felt the fear start hammering at her again. *Please don't let Grace be angry with me. She wouldn't, would she? Surely she must know that my Mom is just doing her job.*

Her first instinct was to dig out her cell phone, but instead she stayed to ask, "Are you okay, Mom?"

"Yes, honey. I know this puts you in a difficult situation. But there isn't anything else I can do about it. I'm sorry."

Chloe rarely saw her mother in any other state than perfect control, and this new vulnerability unnerved her. She crossed the length of the kitchen and hugged her mom tightly. She could feel the tension in her mother's back and it worried her.

"Okay, let's get ice cream!" her mom said brightly.

In the car, Chloe took out her cell phone and sent a quick text to Grace. *How R U? Missed U at school.*

Fifteen minutes later, Grace had not texted her. That was unusual. Grace always had her phone with her, and always responded. A low frequency of anxiety began to hum in her like an improperly tuned radio. She ate her ice cream and laughed with her mom. Both mother and daughter forced their laughter and faked their good cheer; while the sham was self-evident, both chose to ignore it.

By the time they got home, Chloe's phone remained annoyingly silent. While her mom started dinner, Chloe logged onto Facebook to track Grace down. She vaguely heard her father come home, the front door thudding shut behind him, and the deep rumble of his voice drifted upstairs. Then Dinah arrived, and she could hear her Mom and Dinah talking in the kitchen.

She scrolled down the news feed, thankfully noting that she wasn't mentioned anywhere by Jessica or her minions. However, equally, she couldn't find Grace.

Don't panic! She can't be available to you whenever you want.

Chloe's anxiety was turning into a low-throated scream. To take her mind off it, she eased herself into the bathroom to weigh herself. She found she'd gained half a pound and was disgusted with herself. It was the ice cream, she thought. Why on earth did she agree to eat ice cream?

Staring at herself in the mirror, she pinched the skin underneath her chin. It was really fat, she thought. It was basically a double chin. She wondered how much it would cost to get liposuction.

She checked her phone. No answer from Grace.

Chloe knew that some girls from school made themselves throw up in the bathroom after lunch. They often spoke about it as if it made them cool. Chloe had always regarded them as sad and pathetic, but she wondered if she had the guts to make it a habit of sticking her fingers down her throat and forcing herself to vomit. Probably not — just another thing in which she would never be cool.

She checked her phone. Still nothing from Grace.

New diet starts tomorrow, she told herself sternly. *Mom invites you for ice cream, you suggest salad.*

"Chloe!" her mom called. "Dinner's ready!"

This is your opportunity, Chloe thought. *Start by not stuffing your face full.*

Before she went downstairs, she checked her phone. Still nothing.

Then something made her check Facebook one more time. And she saw that Grace had written on her wall. What she saw felt like a physical blow to her stomach, making it difficult to breathe.

Grace Whitehall -> Chloe Jones Don't talk to me ever again. I hate you and I hate your mom.

****

Dinah lay in bed in her dark room, an opened but unread book lying on her chest. She stared up at the ceiling, her thoughts zooming around in her head like race cars on the Indianapolis track. There seemed to be so much circumstantial evidence tying Angus Whitehall to the murder, but none of it was quite good enough to stick. There was something slightly off-kilter about the man; a very good facade seemed to hide a rotted core, she thought. But there was also a quiet and determined gut instinct somewhere deep within her that told her that whatever Angus was hiding, it wasn't the murder of Malia Shaw. If he wasn't the killer, then who? They had no other leads, no other suspects, no other possible motives.

She rolled over, picked up her phone, and called Aaron.

"Hello!" he answered. His familiar voice made her smile.

"Hi! How did the raid go?"

"Well, there were no casualties," said Aaron. "So that is a good thing. But we didn't get the evidence we thought we'd find."

"I'm sorry," said Dinah.

"Yeah, me too, mostly because it means I'm stuck here for longer." Aaron sighed. "It's beautiful, but remote. We're at the base of the Blue Mountains, and if I wasn't working, I'd like to hike them. One day I'd like to show them to you."

Dinah smiled. "I'd really like that."

"How is your case going?"

"More and more curious."

"Oh yeah? Tell me."

Dinah smiled again. Aaron never failed to be interested in the details of her life and cases, even the most mundane. Having someone to talk to was priceless.

She told him about the money trail.

"They're running from something," mused Aaron. "But what?"

"I was hoping you could tell me," said Dinah. "Then the mystery would be solved. I think —"

She was interrupted by a knock at her door. It startled Dinah and she stared at it momentarily before it registered that Elise was softly calling her name.

"Hang on a sec," she said into the phone. She jumped off the bed and opened the door. She expected to see Elise in her pajamas, but she was fully dressed.

"The night dispatcher just called me," Elise said. "Someone found another dead body."

Dinah went into full FBI agent mode. "I've got to go," she said into the phone.

"I heard," said Aaron. "Talk to you soon."

Dinah hung up and got dressed quickly while Elise waited. When Dinah arrived downstairs, Elise was filling two thermoses with hot tea. "It's snowing out," she said.

"Thank you," said Dinah. "What are the details?"

"The dead body of a woman was found out on Rushcutters Road about half an hour ago by a guy looking for firewood," said Elise.

Lola? Dinah thought.

Elise seemed to read her mind and nodded. "I had the same thought. Unfortunately, we will have to pick up the sheriff on the way."

Dinah laughed.

In the hallway, Chloe suddenly appeared, her face gray and drained. "What's going on?" she asked.

"Oh, honey, you should be asleep," said Elise, putting her arm around her daughter. "I have to go to an emergency. Hopefully I'll see you in the morning."

Chloe nodded, her face anxious. "Is this about Grace's dad?"

"I don't think so. Make sure you get some sleep tonight, okay?"

Chloe nodded and trudged back upstairs.

Elise drove them quickly to the sheriff's house, where Wilder was clearly unhappy about being roused out of bed. Dinah felt no sympathy for him. If she had to go out in the freezing cold, in the snow and ice and sleet, so did he. He shambled out to her car with an expression on his face not unlike a two-year-old about to throw a tantrum.

"This better be important," Sheriff Wilder said by way of greeting as he settled into the car. "Do you know how cold it is tonight?"

Obviously. I'm out in it too. Dinah rolled her eyes.

"The body of a dead woman has been found out on Rushcutters Road," said Elise. She must have been making a great effort to remain calm. "My suspicions are that it's a murder victim."

"Really? Who?"

"My gut tells me it's Lola Albright," said Elise, turning the car toward the outskirts of town.

As Elise drove them through the cold night, where snowfall made bare tree branches look like skeletons and nebulous brush appear to be hiding faces, Dinah's heart pumped with just one rhythm: *Lola, are you dead? Lola, are you dead?*

The body of the woman lay spread out over soft, melting snow, serene in her stillness, and for one moment she looked like a child trying to make a snow angel. Only her silhouette was visible in the darkness, her figure shrouded by night and shadows. A nearby homeowner had found her as he searched for firewood on his property. On the outskirts of Ten Mile Hollow, small cabins perched on large lots of land, some sharing their space with trailers or rusted-out car bodies. The owner, Hank Castro, was a small, scraggly looking man with a lit cigarette hanging out of the corner of his mouth. He'd been searching for firewood in a small copse of trees on the southern end of the lot, and he claimed he hadn't been down there for several weeks.

"Had plenty of wood until tonight," he told Elise and Dinah. "I forgot I hadn't got enough to get me through the night. Thought this place would be my best bet, so I moseyed on down here about an hour or so ago."

It was absolutely freezing. Dinah shoved her hands into her coat pockets and glanced around askance. "In this weather?" she asked. She could hear Wilder wheezing behind her.

He shrugged. "Better than shivering through the night."

Dinah saw that he was holding a flashlight. "Mind if you shine this on the body?"

He took a long suck on his cigarette, as if for fortitude, and did as she asked. The light was harsh and made a difficult scene worse. As Dinah moved toward the woman, she heard Castro make a few strangling noises, as though he was choking on his cigarette. The sheriff stayed with the man, for which Dinah was both thankful and disdainful.

The woman was gray in death, but would have been very pale in life, with fair skin and deep, auburn hair, which lay fanned out on the snow like flame. Her eyes looked dark — possibly dark blue or dark gray, thought Dinah. It was hard to tell in the flickering light. She wore blue jeans and a navy blue turtleneck sweater. Her feet were bare. She looked as though she hadn't been dead for very long, although the cold weather would have slowed down any decomposition.

Dinah knelt down beside the body and asked Castro to direct the light toward the woman's head. Leaning over, Dinah could see that there were broken red capillaries in her eyes, telltale marks of petechial hemorrhaging. She gently rolled down the turtleneck and saw long, thin bruises. These initial marks were almost identical to those of Malia Shaw, suggesting death by manual strangulation. She glanced at Elise, who was kneeling on the other side of the body. Elise nodded in silent agreement.

"Do you know who this woman is?" Elise asked Castro.

He shook his head. "No idea. Sorry."

Elise looked at Wilder, who shrugged. *Helpful as always*, said the scornful look on her face.

"You said you hadn't been down to this particular part of your property for a few weeks?" Elise asked of Castro, rising to her feet. Her knees cracked loudly.

"Yeah. I rarely come down here to the trees."

"Have you seen any people on your property in the last few days?"

Castro shrugged. "Nope. But somebody could easily slip in here from the road and I wouldn't likely know about it."

That seemed right to Dinah. She tried to get her bearings. Rush-cutters Road ran along the property's southern border, and the copse of trees skirted the fence line. Castro was correct. A vehicle could park by the trees, be unseen from the house, and allow a person to sneak in and out, all under the cover of snowy evergreens.

"Do you have dogs?" Elise asked.

"No, my old boy died last spring," said Castro. "I haven't got another one."

Elise glanced over at Wilder, who was leaning against a tree yawning. A flash of anger lit up her face for a moment.

"Sheriff," she said. "While we're waiting for the medical examiner, would you mind marking out the scene with tape? I'd like to talk with Mr. Castro further."

Sheriff Wilder looked enormously displeased with this suggestion. With a great sigh, he heaved himself up and strolled interminably slowly toward the body. Dinah felt frustration boil up from her stomach. Had he no respect for the dead? Did he not understand the immense privilege of bringing justice for the victim?

With great effort, she turned her attention back to Elise and Castro.

"You have noticed nothing strange in your life in the last few days?" Elise asked. "Strange vehicles? Anyone you wouldn't normally see?"

Hank Castro stroked a struggling mustache while he thought about that. "Not as I can recall."

"What do you do for work, Mr. Castro?"

From the corner of her eye, Dinah could see the sheriff lazily slinging crime scene tape from one tree to another, taking no care to avoid adding footprints to the scene. She suppressed a growl and focused on Castro.

"— mechanic in town," he was saying. "I work there Monday through Saturday morning. The rest of the time, I hang around here. You know."

Dinah noticed the medical examiner, Dr. Theo Walker, approaching through the snow, his face split into a grin. *Is that man ever sour?* Dinah lifted a hand to wave at him.

Dr. Walker went to work immediately while Dinah continued to watch Sheriff Wilder and feed the fires of annoyance that lived in her belly. Hank Castro fidgeted nearby, chain-smoking. Dinah didn't want to create a scene by shouting at the sherriff, so she looked through the evergreen copse for footprints. Unfortunately, continuing snowfall had likely obliterated any evidence left behind. Still, she inspected as much as she could until Elise called her back to the body.

Dr. Walker had completed his initial examination. He stood up, rolled his shoulders and said, "I'm done. I'm happy to take her to the morgue for autopsy."

"It seemed to me that this death is very similar to that of Malia Shaw," said Dinah. Her lips and nose might well have fallen off by now; they were completely numb. Her speech came out a little thick and slow as a result. "What do you think?"

"I tend to agree," said Dr. Walker. "My thoughts at this point are that this lady died by manual strangulation, by someone's hands rather than by rope, cord, or wire. Do you know who she is?"

"No idea," said Elise.

Lola, did you face death here in the lonely snow?

"Do you think she died here or was brought here?" Dinah asked.

Dr. Walker inclined his head while he considered. "I don't know," he said, at length. "She hasn't been dead for very long — perhaps 24 hours. The snow we've had since then might have obscured drag marks. Hopefully the forensic techs will be able to tell you more."

He lifted his arm to indicate to the morgue workers to begin the removal of the body, and then caught himself suddenly. "I almost forgot," he said, with a sunny smile. "I found this in her back pocket."

He gave Elise a small, red, leather-bound book.

"Don't know if it's helpful, but you never know."

He grinned again.

Into the cold, shadowy night, the morgue workers disappeared with the body.

****

The two women made their way to the office from the field where the woman's body was found. The air was as still and sharp as ice, and it took a hot shower and two cups of coffee for Dinah to warm up after she sat down at her desk. In front of her lay the little book found in the dead woman's jeans.

Both Dinah and Elise had glanced through it while they waited for the medical examiner to finish, and it hadn't immediately given up any secrets. It appeared to be a name and address book, with a list of names, phone numbers, addresses, and most intriguingly, short descriptions. She hadn't had a chance the previous night to read them. She now had a much closer look at the entries and realized that the names were all male.

One name had been handwritten on each page, with a phone number directly underneath, and an address. The addresses were all in or around Ten Mile Hollow, which told Dinah it was likely that the dead woman was a local.

The descriptions were the most interesting. The paragraphs seemed to center on the man's personal circumstances and possible past.

> Shaun Holdsworth
> 275-3146
> 98 Wellington Ave
> Ten Mile Hollow VA
> *Forty-two years old. Married. One child in college in San Francisco. Contacts in California? Lived in TMH for twelve years. Works in local accountant's firm. Wife grew up here and wanted to return here. He is from Oregon? Washington? Couldn't find hostility, latent or overt. Requires more info about past.*

The next page entry read:

> Miles Reading
> 275-2118
> 11/2578 Forest Glade Rd
> Ten Mile Hollow VA
> *Thirty-eight years old. Single. Carpenter working at Aristocrat's Kitchens. Grew up here and has never left, as far as I can tell. Standard learnt hostility. Seems to be a loner. Bears watching.*

Dinah read ten more entries that were similar. *Curious.* What were these men hostile to? Why were their backgrounds being checked? Why was the dead woman playing amateur sleuth? Was that why she died?

And the most important question: "Are you Lola?" Dinah muttered.

"Are you talking to me?" Elise asked.

Dinah jumped, startled. "Good morning!"

"I bring you doughnuts," said Elise. "In the name of peace and goodwill for all mankind."

Dinah realized she was hungry. "Thanks. I'm starving!"

While she ate a cinnamon glazed doughnut, she gave the book to Elise to read through.

Every entry read similarly: a brief description of the men, their families, their work, and their age. The strange research seemed to concentrate on where the men had come from and whether they seemed "hostile," whatever that meant.

Two hours later, when both Elise and Dinah had read the book from cover to cover twice, had come up with very few answers, and couldn't stand the suspense anymore, they climbed into the unmarked police car, and drove to the workplace of the man who appeared first in the book — Shaun Holdsworth. He was an accountant at a local firm in Main Street, a pretty, red brick building with striped awnings and flowerboxes in the windows.

Elise announced herself to the receptionist. With a doubtful look, she phoned Shaun Holdsworth. She had barely hung up the phone when an anxious-looking man appeared from an internal door.

"I'm Shaun Holdsworth," he said. "Is everything okay?"

He was a tall, balding man with large, dark eyes, glasses, a small mouth, and a sweating forehead. He was dressed in the standard professional attire: dark pants, white shirt, and soberly patterned necktie.

"Perhaps there's somewhere quieter where we might talk?" suggested Elise, after identifying herself and showing him her badge.

He waved them through to a small office, furnished with a round table and four chairs. Elise introduced him to Dinah, but the man didn't seem to listen.

"I'm wondering if you know this woman," began Elise, sliding a photo of the red-haired woman across the table.

Shaun Holdsworth drew a sharp breath. "Is that woman . . . dead?"

"Yes. She was murdered and we found her body last night."

Holdsworth's complexion turned gray-green. He swore. "Sorry. I wasn't expecting that. That's awful!"

"Did you know her?"

Holdsworth licked his lips. "Well. I know who she is, but I can't say that I *knew* her."

Dinah and Elise exchanged a glance. "Who is she?"

He gave her a strange look. "You don't know? Her name is Lola Albright."

Yes! Dinah stopped a grin from spreading across her face. *Don't be weird,* she scolded herself.

"How did you know her?"

Holdsworth scratched his nose and licked his lips. "Well. Uh. Is that relevant?"

Elise stared at him hard. "You're wondering why it's relevant that you knew a murdered woman?"

Sweat began to drip down the man's brow. "Well."

I swear if he says "well" one more time, I'm going to slap him. Dinah took a deep breath. She had to stop thinking these violent thoughts.

"Mr. Holdsworth," Elise said, in a stern tone, "I'm interested in who murdered this woman. That's all. I strongly suggest that you be honest with me at this point, unless you'd like to stare down the possibility of being under suspicion for murder."

Holdsworth turned an even more interesting shade of gray-green. "I did *not* kill her. I swear."

"Okay. So how did you know her?"

He licked his lips. "She was a friend of Malia Shaw."

Dinah stared at him, her heart beating even faster. It throbbed in her temples. "Did you know Malia Shaw?" she asked.

"Yes," said Holdsworth, ducking his head.

"Are you aware that she too, was murdered?"

"Yes."

"How did you know Malia Shaw?" Dinah was racking her brain, trying to remember if there had been any mention or sign of Shaun Holdsworth in Shaw's life. She couldn't think of one.

"You won't tell anyone? I mean, is this confidential?" Holdsworth asked.

"I'm not a lawyer, if that's what you're thinking. I can't promise confidentiality, but if it turns out that what you tell me really is irrelevant, then I'll keep it to myself." Elise watched the other man carefully.

He nodded and blew out a breath of air. "I should have known I wouldn't get away with it forever." He closed his eyes briefly. "Detective, I thought that Malia Shaw was propositioning me. That's how I knew her." He stared down at the table.

"Propositioning you?" Elise frowned. "What do you mean?"

"I thought . . . I thought she wanted . . . well, she bought me a drink."

Elise looked a Dinah for a moment. "Did anything happen between you?"

He swallowed. "No. It turns out, I was wrong."

"She didn't want to proposition you?"

"Nope. She — well, her friend, Lola — wanted to interrogate me. It was weird."

"Interrogate you? About what?"

He shook his head. "I still don't really know. It was the weirdest conversation I've ever had in my life. It made me decide never to go back to Joaquins, that's for sure."

Elise and Dinah exchanged another glance.

"You'd better tell us everything."

****

The final bell had rung ten minutes before, but this was Chloe's new time of arrival. For someone who was organized and punctual, arriving deliberately late was excruciating for her. She hated seeing the look of disappointment on her teacher's faces, many of whom had much higher expectations of her. But it was infinitely better than the punishment Jessica Hunter was waiting to inflict on her before class. Since Grace now refused to hang out with her, talk to her, or even *look* at her, Jessica was free to entertain every vicious thought that entered her head.

Chloe slipped into her first period English class and earned a withering look from Mrs. Bellson.

Chloe slunk into her seat and ignored the giggles around her. Mrs. Bellson turned back to the book and immediately Chloe felt something hit her softly on the shoulder.

She saw a bunched-up piece of paper bounce to the floor. She glanced over to her left and saw Alice Greendale, one of Jessica's minions, smiling at her. Chloe frowned and looked away, then saw Alice motioning to her. Chloe glanced at her again and realized she was supposed to open the piece of paper.

With a heavy feeling of dread, Chloe opened the note and read:

FAGLY: Fat And Ugly = YOU

Muffled laughter erupted around Alice Greendale as Chloe's face burned red. She crumpled the note in her hand and let it fall to her desk. Deep inside her, a little voice whispered: *Yes, you are. You know it's true.*

Mrs. Bellson turned around. "Is there a problem, Alice?" she demanded.

"I'm sorry, Mrs. Bellson," Alice said, sweetly.

Chloe kept her eyes on the text, humiliation burning in her stomach like acid. Each time her eyes slid sideways, one of the kids who sat near Alice would whisper: "Fagly!"

Chloe watched the clock, as its hands passed at an agonizing pace. Finally, the bell rang and she waited as the classroom emptied slowly. She heaved herself up from the desk and walked to her locker, wondering why she felt so weary. There was no way she could rule out a chance encounter with Jessica in the hallway, but she didn't seem to have the energy to move any faster.

Each time she got up to walk, her legs felt impossibly heavy. She immediately thought to herself: *Well, of course they do. They each weigh a ton. Lose some weight, fatty!*

Lunch in the cafeteria was the worst of all. Chloe dreaded it every single day.

Today she took her tray to the table at which she and Grace always used to eat their lunch. Now, she ate alone. Even the usual school losers avoided her; Jessica's wrath was too fearsome to risk. Grace had since elected to sit with new friend Jessica, who often looked over at Chloe with a gloating expression on her face. She'd follow that up with a few quietly spoken words, which elicited an eruption of laughter from her minions, all of whom looked scathingly at Chloe. Chloe didn't care what Jessica had said about her, or what the minions thought about her. She only cared about what Grace thought. When her former friend looked her way amidst the laughter, Chloe thought she saw a lot of anger, tinged with pity and discomfort. And she never seemed to laugh as hard as the others. In fact, Grace often didn't laugh at all. Chloe would look her friend right in the eyes, and found that often Grace could not meet her gaze.

She was still utterly perplexed as to why Grace had so unceremoniously dumped her as her friend. Grace utterly refused to speak to her.

Chloe began to eat, quickly and methodically, wanting to escape to the library as soon as she could. She saw Jessica and her friends already seated. Alice Greendale was talking animatedly, probably telling them all about the incident in English class.

Soon enough, like tiny poisonous spiders shooting across the room on silken thread, taunts of "fat" and "ugly" and the two words combined began to float over her way. Chloe could do nothing except pretend she couldn't hear them, despite the flush on her skin, and the clammy cold of her hand, squeezed into a fist in her lap.

She'd almost finished her lunch when a ringing shout caused her to look up in alarm: "Heads up!"

A millisecond later, a blossom of pain unfurled just above her ear with a loud crash. Liquid sloshed down the side of her face, sticky and cold. Involuntarily, she let out a loud cry and clapped her hand to her ear. Her head buzzed, like a chainsaw had been started inside her skull.

At her feet, the offending missile, a half-full can of soda, rolled. Shouts of laugher erupted at Jessica's table like an atomic mushroom cloud; all of them were bent over double from the effort of laughing so hard. Shaun Kruger, a footballer who was as cruel as he was handsome, was collecting high fives.

Chloe hurriedly wiped at her face with napkins, soaking up the soda that was dripping through her hair and onto her shirt. Pressure began to build up in her throat and nose, a sure sign she was about to burst into tears.

Chloe gave up with the napkins, as the laughter resounded in her ears, jumped to her feet and ran out of the cafeteria. But not in time to hide the tears that rolled down her face. Her head throbbing, she had only a few seconds to register the faces of everyone else in the cafeteria as they stared at her making her exit. Many looked disgusted; some were faintly amused. Written plain on all their faces was the same sentiment: *I'm sorry, but I'm glad it's you and not me.*

****

Shaun Holdsworth wiped his brow with a forearm that was surely sodden by now. Dinah was still trying to reconcile the bland accountant in front of her thinking that Malia Shaw was propositioning him. "How did you meet Malia?" she asked.

"It was really an accident," said Holdsworth. He sounded a little like he was trying to convince himself of this truth. "I often stop by Joaquin's for a drink after work — you know where that is?"

"It's a cantina, right?" Dinah didn't know the place at all.

"It's barely more than a shack, a favorite for the hard drinkers," explained Elise. They both looked at Holdsworth. Dinah couldn't imagine him there.

"I met them both there — they were together," said Holdsworth. "I sat next to Malia at the bar, and she offered to buy me a drink." He swallowed.

"You accepted her offer?"

Holdsworth had the grace to turn red. "I did."

"So she bought you a drink. Then what?"

"She asked me if I'd like to sit in a booth with her. It's a bit quieter there. I agreed, and we went there, but Lola was already sitting at the booth. I kind of thought that was weird, but Malia sat down next to me and I guess I just thought it wasn't a big deal."

"So then what happened?"

"The mood changed right away." Holdsworth reddened again. "Lola took over. They started asking me questions about all kinds of things."

"What kinds of things?"

"How old I was, where I was from, if I'd ever lived in California. How I felt about women. Had I ever been violent toward women, that sort of thing."

Odd questions.

"It was Lola asking these questions, or was Malia involved as well?"

"It was all Lola. Malia sort of went off into a daze, I think."

"How did you feel about those questions? Did you try to leave?"

"It was weird, for sure." Holdsworth glanced down at his hands. "But by the time it occurred to me to leave, the questions were over. It was later that I realized how strange it was. I think they must have thought I was somebody else."

"So you've never lived in California?"

"Never. And I've never hurt a woman, or been violent in any way." Holdsworth shook his head.

Dinah paused, trying to gather her thoughts. His answers only made the situation more confusing, rather than clarifying her questions. "Have you seen either of them since that initial meeting?"

"No. I've never been back to Joaquin's, either."

"Both of them are dead now," Elise said. "Both murdered. What are your thoughts on this?"

Holdsworth rubbed his face. "I have no . . . thoughts. I mean, I have no idea. It's terrible. The only thing I can think of is that they found whoever it was they were looking for, and that he must not have been a very nice guy."

"What were your impressions of the women? Did they seem scared, worried, nervous, anything like that?"

"Well, Malia certainly wasn't anxious; she was just drugged out of her mind. To me, it seemed like she just didn't *care*. I mean, I don't even think she cared about whether she lived or died."

"What about Lola?"

"She was . . . *intense*. I didn't get much else from her. I felt like she was a woman you didn't want to cross, that she'd make life pretty difficult for you. She seemed to be a person you wouldn't want to mess with."

Only someone did mess with her, and won.

Dinah rubbed her temples wearily.

"So where were you last Monday night?" Elise continued.

"Me? Uh . . . I was at home."

"With your wife?"

"Please don't tell her!" Holdsworth begged, suddenly desperate. "I didn't tell her that I went to Joaquin's."

"With your wife?" she repeated, implacable.

"Yes! We ate dinner. Watched some TV."

"What did you watch?"

"Uh . . . well. Oh, I think we watched some football. My wife was reading a book beside me."

"What about last night?"

"Well. I was at the gym last night."

"What time was that?"

"I left work a little late — maybe six. I would have been at the gym from then until about seven-thirty. Then I went home and ate dinner with my wife. Then we video-called our daughter."

Remembering the notes in the book, Dinah asked, "Where is your daughter?"

"She's at college in San Francisco. Her first year away. We miss her terribly."

Malia was someone's daughter, once.

"Did Malia or Lola mention anyone else? Any other friends?"

"Not that I can recall." Holdsworth looked up at the ceiling. "No, I don't believe so."

"Do you know how Malia and Lola knew each other? How long they'd been friends?"

"No, I don't know." Holdsworth shook his head. "But my impression was that they'd known each other for a long time."

Elise sighed. "I see. Well, I think that's all the questions I have for the moment. I hope you've told the truth, Mr. Holdsworth, or I might have to visit your home next time and ask questions in front of your wife."

"I've told you the truth, I swear," said Holdsworth, eyes large and beguiling.

Outside, Elise said, "I believe him."

"Yeah, me too," agreed Dinah. "Joaquin's was his walk on the wild side, until it scared him."

"Why were the woman asking him those questions? What were they up to?"

"I don't know. I feel more perplexed now than I did before talking to Holdsworth," admitted Dinah. *And I feel flat, too.*

In the car, she wondered why the conversation with Holdsworth had deflated her.

Maybe it was because Malia seemed so alone, so isolated, so vulnerable. Maybe it was because everyone who had known her in life seemed so quick to absolve themselves in her death. Maybe it was because she had met her death alone, frightened, trapped.

Maybe it was because there were similarities in her own life and in Malia's, and that Malia's lonely death was something that could have easily happened to her.

****

"Science," said Samuel O'Toole. "It proves it."

Angus put down his cell phone with reluctance. "What does it prove?" He wasn't really listening. His mind was stuck on a loop: *Where is Lola? Why hasn't she returned my call? Where is Lola? Is she dead?*

"Natural selection," said O'Toole, triumphantly. "It proves that some races are inferior to the white race."

Angus sighed. "First. There are no races. We are all members of the *same* race — the human one. Second, what are you talking about?"

The Dark Heart

"You can't deny that people who come from Africa *look* different to people who come from Sweden," said O'Toole.

"Of course they do. Do you mean to tell me that you subscribe to that old argument that the Caucasian person is somehow superior to any other?" Angus cringed inwardly as he spoke, because at one time this was precisely what he himself had believed.

"I think it's obvious," declared O'Toole. "The Western civilization has been responsible for the technological and societal advances of the past several hundred years. And you know who makes up the largest section of the Western civilization? White people."

Angus sat back in his chair. "Let me ask you a question. What do you think people like Adam and Eve looked like? And, furthermore, what do you think Jesus looked like?" He didn't wait for a reply before moving on. "Lots of Bibles portray Adam and Eve as blond-haired and blue-eyed. But the truth is that Adam and Eve probably had a middle-brown skin tone from a mixture of "light color" genes and "dark color" genes. Their descendants could then exhibit a wide range of skin tones from very light to very dark with most somewhere in between (as seen in the world today). Adam and Eve likely possessed genetic variation for eye shape and other common distinguishing characteristics as well."

He paused and looked at O'Toole intently for a moment. "As people scattered across the earth after their languages were confused at the Tower of Babel, groups of people became isolated from others and likely married only within their language group. Each group carried a set of physical characteristics determined by their genes. Certain characteristics dominated as they intermarried because of the group's small pool of genes. Over time, different people groups displayed distinct physical characteristics. For example, Asians have almond-shaped eyes, dark hair, and middle-brown skin, whereas those of European descent have round eyes and fair-colored hair and skin.

"It doesn't make any people group better than another."

O'Toole opened his mouth to say something.

"Hang on," said Angus. "I'm nearly finished. You know, most of the world is somewhere in between a dark skin shade and a light skin shade. And underneath all of us — whether we call ourselves white, brown, black or some other shade — we have genes that determine skin tone. My genes are not superior to your genes or anyone else's." *Though once I thought that was true.* "The truth is we are all like cake batter."

"Pardon?" O'Toole raised a sceptical eyebrow.

"Cake batter. We all have the same ingredients, but some have more of something than the other. In fact, just by changing the proportion of ingredients in the cake, we can end up with a large array of different-looking cakes. But they're all still cakes."

He was on a roll now and O'Toole couldn't have stopped him if he'd tried.

"What is more important than what shade of skin we have, is to understand that God created us all as human beings and we are all equal before Him. God does not see one of us as superior to the other — in fact, in His eyes, we can only ever be inferior because of our sin. But Jesus died for sinners equally, and offers salvation and redemption to sinners equally. Do you believe that salvation is available to an African person or an Asian person as freely as a European person?"

"Well . . . I suppose so," admitted O'Toole.

"I think we need to stop looking at the outward appearance of people and see them as God does," continued Angus. "That's true of skin color, hair color, dress sense, and nose piercings. We're *all* sinners, in desperate need of God's grace. Christians especially should reflect the love and grace we've received so freely from Jesus toward other people. If you're a Christian, there's no room in your life for hatred."

Angus saw the conflict in O'Toole's face, the different emotions fighting for control. He could understand how the other man felt. It is difficult to overcome the brainwashing received in childhood that you grew up believing as truth. It is difficult to look around you at a country deeply divided by race and know that all of it was caused by sinful pride lurking deep within the heart.

"How would you feel if your daughter married someone who wasn't white?" Angus asked.

O'Toole blanched. "To be honest, I wouldn't be happy about it."

"Why not?"

"I just . . . don't believe that it's the right thing to do," said O'Toole. "But I don't really know why."

"Let me suggest to you that what would be far worse is if your daughter married someone who wasn't a Christian," said Angus. "In truth, this is the only type of marriage that God tells us should be avoided. It's been the position of many churches over time, unfortunately, that what we know as interracial marriage is wrong. To back up their position, they erroneously use the passage from 2 Corinthians chapter six which says, 'what communion has light with darkness?' The Bible isn't talking about skin shade or people groups here. It's talking about Christians being married to non-Christians."

O'Toole seemed troubled, but he remained silent. "Well, you've given me a lot of think about," he said. "Thank you for your time."

"Ask God to show you the truth in your heart," said Angus. *If God can soften my dark heart from hate to love, then He can do the same for you.*

After O'Toole left, Angus felt exhausted. He put his head on his desk and closed his eyes. God had changed his heart, had softened it and taken away his hatred. But the consequences remained, and no matter how hard Angus had tried to atone for his sin, he felt like the punishment for it would never end.

He feared it would take his life.

The great English writer named C.S. Lewis once said that having integrity means that you do the right thing even when no one is watching.

Angus sat in his office, the door locked, the blinds on the window drawn. O'Toole had gone, and Angus had never felt more like a hypocrite in his whole life.

Nobody can see me. I've never felt more alone.

There was thick fog outside: thick, fat fingers surrounded the building, softly embracing it. Angus felt like he was hiding in the midst of the fog, but the moment the high sun started to burn it away, it would expose him. He was lost in his thoughts, his fears, the dark shame of his past.

We all do it, I think. We present a façade to the world, presenting ourselves as good and acceptable people. We construct walls around our lives that other people might peek over, but will never breach. Each wall represents a compartment in our life that we disguise or twist so that other people see a distortion of the truth.

The truth as other people see it:

I'm a good father. See how he loves his kids!

I'm a loving husband. He really takes care of his wife.

I'm a trustworthy pastor. He speaks the truth to us.

I'm a compassionate citizen. He helps other people all the time.

I'm generous and kind. He never seems to think of himself.

Perhaps our families see part of the truth. Our children sense the truth when we lash out in anger in words or deeds, and fear skates over the shiny surface of their eyes. Our wives see part of the truth when without even raising our voices, we cut them down with our words, and worse, we feel a thrill of satisfaction because we have won. Our friends and colleagues and acquaintances might glimpse the truth occasionally when we tell pithy and self-deprecating stories about ourselves but we never ask about them. As for the towns and cities in which we live, where we are known only by reputation, the citizens there will never see the truth.

We put on a show, a shiny, happy show that masks the truth of who we really are. We lie even to ourselves. We are unkind and ungracious, and blame the other person for being awkward. We lose our tempers because someone else provoked us. We are selfish because nobody else cares for us. It can't possibly be my fault.

This is the lie we tell ourselves. I am a good person.

I've laid awake in the dark dead of the night, and I've stripped away the defenses that cover my heart. I've put aside the lies we tell ourselves about our own goodness, and I've looked at what lies deep in my heart.

I've seen the truth of who I really am. My heart is dark. It is black with sin and violence and pride.

Angus looked around his office, an extension of what he felt was all that was false about him. Books lined the walls: serious books about law and history and philosophy. They told people that he was intelligent and thoughtful and even perhaps wise.

I haven't read the books. I don't know who wrote them. It's all a lie.

The office I hold — the leader of this church. I say the things I know I should say and I smile when I know I should smile. But it's an empty shell.

Nobody knows me or the things I've done or the things I know I'm capable of doing. You never really know this until you are thrust into the furnace of suffering, when the flames are burning away everything but your basest instincts; it is then you come to know yourself intimately. And you see how dark and shameful you really are.

Angus thought that the detective seemed to understand this. Perhaps it was her keen instinct for sniffing out human frailty, but he sensed that she could see in him the latent violence that he had once unleashed. *It's a taint, a smell that you can never truly exterminate, despite the erection of thin walls.*

This dark, sinful heart of mine seeks to do harm. It's self-preservation.

Angus knew that the detective would find out about his past, in spite of all his efforts to conceal it, and he would be forced to confront the truth. Worse, his wife and children and the church would be forced to confront it, too. *And when they find out who I really am, my life will be over.*

This war rages in my soul. My desire to keep lying, to keep running, to keep the walls in place, to keep the show going wrestles with the painful relief of giving up all those burdens. But this one thing I know for certain: if I run, I will forever be tainted with the deaths of Malia and Lola. And I did not kill either. I need to stand and face the truth, no matter what might happen.

Angus lay his head on his desk and closed his eyes, wishing he could escape himself. He wished he could turn off his thoughts and lie down and sleep for a year.

A knock at his door startled him and he sat up. John Rowland poked his head in. "Have you heard?" he asked.

"Heard what?"

"There's been another woman murdered," said Rowland. "On Rushcutters Road. I hope this doesn't cause any panic."

Angus's heart seemed to stop beating altogether. Around a bright pain in his chest, he asked: "Who was it?"

"The murdered woman?" Rowland shrugged. "I don't know who she is. They haven't released a name."

Angus was not sure how he managed to say upright in his chair. He felt like a quivering cup of Jello. *I know who it is. I know.*

"That's awful." His voice sounded like it was coming from someone else, a vast distance away. "What should we do?"

"Let's just wait and see," suggested Rowland. "If there starts to be some panic-mongering in the media, we'll issue something. More police on the streets, that kind of thing."

Angus nodded. "Good, sounds good. Thanks."

Rowland disappeared and Angus sank down into his chair. Every one of his limbs shook and he couldn't seem to catch his breath. *They're coming for me.*

He was seized with a powerful urge to leave this town. His fear and panic was suffocating. But he needed to be done with running. He needed to stand up and tell the truth, be strong for the first time in his life. *It is time to do the right thing.*

****

The setting sun threw long, dark fingers reaching across from the horizon as the temperature fell even further. Darkness had already enveloped the building when Elise glanced out of the window and said to Dinah, "You ready to go?"

As Dinah wound her scarf around her neck, Elise's phone began to buzz on her desk, startling her. It was Dr. Walker. Elise put the speaker on.

"Hello, Detective," he bubbled. "Sorry to interrupt your evening, but there are a few things I thought you should know right away."

"Sure, Dr. Walker," Elise said. Dinah smiled. It was impossible to talk to Dr. Walker without smiling.

"About 25 feet from the woman's body, farther into the woods, we found a purse and a cell phone," said Dr. Walker. "We have a preliminary identification of her: Lola Albright."

It was confirmation of what they already knew, but that didn't stop a satisfying feeling in Dinah's stomach. "That's great," Elise said. "I mean, it's mystifying, but I'm always happy to put a name to the face."

"I thought I'd drop the cell phone over to you, since I'm passing by on the way back to Norfolk," said Dr. Walker. "I'll have the autopsy for you in a few days, I hope."

Fifteen minutes later, Dinah held Lola Albright's cell phone in her hand, hoping that it would divulge more than Malia's phone had.

She started with the list of contacts. Interestingly, Lola had not ascribed a name to any phone number in her contacts list. She had simply given each number an initial.

Next, she moved to the text messages. There were several messages to and from someone with the initial M, which appeared to be Malia. Dinah recognized some of the messages from Malia's phone. Those messages seemed to revolve around Lola checking on her friend.

There was also a number of messages from someone with the initial A. The most recent had come through only a few days ago, and it was short: *call me!* Immediately, Dinah thought of Angus, who had hotly denied knowing Lola Albright.

Elise shared her theory. "I've got an idea," she said. "Let's call that number and see if Angus answers." Dinah sat back in her chair while Elise used the office phone to call the number tagged with the initial A. Listening to a dial tone, she was tense with anticipation.

"Hello?" a male voice answered. It sounded familiar, and anxious. "Hello?"

"Hello, with whom am I speaking?" Elise asked.

There was a pause.

"Angus Whitehall. With whom am *I* speaking?"

"Detective Elise Jones."

There was a long silence while that bombshell was digested.

"How —? I mean —" The pastor actually sounded flabbergasted.

"I would ask the same question of you," snapped Elise. "You told me that you didn't know Lola Albright. Imagine my surprise when I see your name and number in Lola's phone."

There was another long silence.

"And what do you have to say about this phone number I've just called? You have two cell phones. You forgot to tell me about that."

"What happened to Lola?" Angus asked, at length.

"I was hoping you could tell me," said Elise.

"I haven't seen her for weeks!"

"Well, she's dead."

"How?" Angus didn't sound shocked.

"She was murdered. Just like Malia Shaw. Know anything about that, sir?" Elise asked.

"Of course not! When did this happen? *How* did this happen?"

"Where were you last night, Mr. Whitehall?"

"You think I did it?"

"Here's the thing, Mr. Whitehall. You tell me that you have no idea who Lola Albright is, let alone where she is. Suddenly, we discover she's been murdered and the truth is that you *did* know her, well enough to be texting each other several times a week. On a second, secret cell phone. So you'll forgive me if you seem like a bit of a suspect right now."

Another silence. Dinah would have paid the entire contents of her checking account to see the man's face right now. She was willing to bet Angus Whitehall's hands were Irish dancing across his knees.

"So, now that we're being honest with each other," said Elise. "How did you know Lola?"

The silence went on for a long time. Finally, Angus spoke with great reluctance. "The truth is that we are all old friends. Malia, Lola, and I have known each other a long time. We went to college together."

"Where?"

"San Diego, California."

"How did you all end up in Ten Mile Hollow, Virginia?"

"I moved here first. They followed."

"They *both* followed you here to this town?" Dinah scribbled this information down furiously.

"Well, Lola was looking out for Malia, so really Lola followed Malia."

"So you moved here . . . what, about 15 years ago?"

"Yes. I think that's about right. Just before my daughter was born."

"Why did you lie about knowing Lola?"

"I . . . I don't know." Dinah could hear the bald fear in the pastor's voice. "To tell you the truth, I'm a little worried."

"What about?"

"Two friends from college are murdered — don't you think I might be next?"

Dinah and Elise glanced at each other. "Who would want to kill you all?"

"I don't know!"

Dinah shook her head. Now he was veering into untruth.

Elise remained silent, also seemingly skeptical of his story.

"I believe we may need to have another talk," she said, at length. "It sounds like we need to go through your old contacts from college."

"Ah," said Angus. He didn't sound thrilled with this idea, but since he'd brought it up, he now had to go with it. "Well, whenever you are free, Detective. I'm happy to work with you on this." Elise hung up after bidding him goodbye.

Dinah's investigative instincts told her that it was improbable that he'd lied about Lola simply because he was scared. A normal person would have brought her up immediately, worried about her safety as well as his own. He was hiding something — if not murder, what? What motive would he have for killing two college friends? These questions whirling around in her head, she and Elise finally left for the evening.

****

The following morning, Elise had the unenviable job of working her way through the mountain of paperwork on her desk. It fell to Dinah to make the necessary phone calls. Sheriff Wilder sat at his desk nearby, snuffling his way through a packet of chips. The noise was supremely irritating. Dinah listened for a moment — Wilder would crunch through the chip and swallow with a weird snorting sound, like he was a pig eating a treasured truffle. Though Wilder was frowning fiercely at his computer screen, it wasn't because he was concentrating on work. Dinah knew that the Sherriff was playing solitaire. She sighed and tried to concentrate on her own work.

Her first phone call was to the university in San Diego. Apparently, this was where Angus Whitehall, Malia Shaw, and Lola Albright had met and become friends. They had formed such a fast friendship that they had all decided to settle in the same small town in Virginia, half a world away from southern California. Dinah was still skeptical of this story — she had left her own hometown to go to college, and had built her own life. Her college friends hadn't followed her. They'd built their own lives, their own families, and their own paths. *It was all just too weird.*

It was earlier in the morning on the West Coast, but a receptionist transferred the call to Student Services, who in turn, transferred Dinah to the vice dean. With each transfer, Dinah's temper deteriorated. When the vice dean answered the phone, Dinah was hot all over with frustration.

"My name is Dinah Harris and I'm a consultant with the Ten Mile Hollow Sheriff's Department," she said, as pleasantly as she could. "I'd like to ask some questions about some previous students."

The vice dean launched into a predictable speech. "I can't divulge grades or other personal information. That would be a violation —"

"I understand," interrupted Dinah. "Let me explain what I need, Ms. —. I'm sorry I didn't catch your name."

"My name is Victoria McHale." Had there been a superior sniff following this statement, Dinah wouldn't have been at all surprised.

"I'm investigating the backgrounds of three people," said Dinah, "two of whom have recently been murdered." *Using the word "murder" usually gets attention.*

The vice dean wasn't cool enough to hide her gasp of dismay. "Oh dear," she said, her voice a little warmer.

"During our investigation, I've uncovered some information that suggests that these three people attended your university. All I want to know is whether this is true and when it was they attended."

"I see," said Victoria McHale. She seemed a little relieved. "Well, our records only became computerized in about 1990, so I'll do my best."

"I'd like you to check ten years ago to as far back as your records show, please," said Dinah.

"Certainly. What are the names?"

"Angus Whitehall, male."

There were several moments of silence save for the clicking of a keyboard. Dinah watched the sheriff licking out his chip packet while she waited. A porcine snout sniffing through a trough of rubbish would have been more elegant than Wilder. Elise looked over in Dinah's direction and stuck out her tongue in disgust. Dinah smiled.

"Okay," said Ms. McHale. She drew the word out as if she was uncertain, and in that moment, Dinah felt a tiny tickle race up her spine. "I've checked from the year 2000 right back to 1991, which is as far back as I can go on our computerized records. I can't find that we've ever had a student by that name."

Dinah thought about that. "Is there any male at all with the last name Whitehall?"

There was another pause. Thankfully, Wilder had thrown his empty chip bag in the trash and had lumbered out of the office.

"The only Whitehall to attend this campus is a female, and in fact she's still here," said Ms. McHale. "There are a couple of Whites, a Whiteley, and a Whitman."

Dinah wrote this down. "What about Malia Shaw, female?"

After several minutes, Ms. McHale reported the same finding. "Nobody by that name, I'm afraid. There are a few with the same last name."

"And female, Lola Albright?"

Again, the answer was negative. Angus Whitehall, Malia Shaw, and Lola Shaw had not attended UC San Diego — at least not under the names they'd been known by in Ten Mile Hollow. Dinah dug up the false identification documents they'd found in Malia's apartment.

"What about these names?" she asked. "Theresa Scott, Lexi Hollingsworth, Amanda Wallace?"

There was a very long pause. As she waited, Dinah's mind raced. Angus Whitehall had been caught in a blatant lie — but what precisely had he lied about? His attendance at the university? Meeting the women in San Diego?

"Ah," said Victoria McHale, a different tone in her voice. Dinah stilled.

"What?"

"Well, we do have a Theresa Scott. She came to this campus for an undergraduate degree in the mid '90s."

Dinah sat back in her chair, her mind temporarily cleared by the white-hot flare of revelation.

"Detective? Are you still there?" Ms. McHale asked, when the silence had stretched on awkwardly.

"I'm sorry. That is very interesting information. I appreciate your help," said Dinah, not bothering to correct the woman labeling her a detective. "Thank you."

She hung up.

She thought about one dead woman, meeting death alone in a dirty apartment, surrounded by needles, by the despair of her life. She thought of the most recent dead woman, lying like a frozen angel in the woods, stumbled across inadvertently. While across town, the pastor lived in a warmly lit home, his family around him, a worthy and productive life.

He knew why these women died, Dinah was sure of it. He might have had a hand in their deaths — whether directly or by orchestration, she wasn't sure.

I'm going to get the truth, one way or the other.

****

Later that afternoon, Dinah felt her eyelids begin to droop despite the coffee. The late night was catching up with her.

Elise noticed. "I feel much the same way. Want to have an early finish today?"

"Sounds like a plan," agreed Dinah.

She had closed down her computer and turned off her lamp when Elise's phone rang again. "Hello?"

"Hi, is that Detective Jones?" The voice was so full of cheer and good humor that it would only be Dr. Walker, the medical examiner and forensic technician.

"Yes."

"It's Dr. Walker. Again. I seem to be calling you quite a lot, aren't I? Anyway, I thought you would be interested in discovering that we found some strands of hair on the body of Lola Albright. Obviously they haven't been analyzed officially, but I'd bet my left leg that they match those found on the body of Malia Shaw."

Elise sat back down at her desk and stared at Dinah. This was very important. "What do the hairs look like?"

"They are short and dark. I'd say, completely off the record, that they belong to a Caucasian male."

Dinah thought about the drug dealer, Simon Wakowski. He had long, stringy hair. The hairs found on the two bodies were unlikely to belong to him. But Angus Whitehall had short, dark hair, and lyin' eyes, thought Dinah. Just like the song. Lyin' eyes and a smile that was a thin disguise.

"Thanks for calling," Elise said.

"No problem," he said. "Have a good evening!"

Dinah stuck a pencil in her mouth and chewed on it, deep in thought. The confirmation of every piece of evidence seemed to point to Angus Whitehall as the killer of both women, but why would the pastor take such an enormous risk? A man with a church congregation and a wife and family would have to be certifiably insane if he thought he could get away with murder twice. Yet, in police business, truth was very often much stranger than fiction.

She fell into an exhausted sleep at about ten, and woke at about four-thirty, groggy and disoriented. She tried to go back to sleep, but couldn't. When gray light eventually appeared feebly on the horizon, she gave up and wandered downstairs for coffee. In the quiet stillness of early morning, Dinah took the opportunity to read her Bible. She was working through the Book of Galatians.

Chloe appeared downstairs about ten minutes later, showered and ready for school. She made herself a piece of toast. "What are you reading?" she asked.

Dinah looked up. "I'm reading the Bible. A book called Galatians."

"Oh yeah? What does Galatians mean?" Chloe's toast popped.

"It's a letter Paul wrote to the people who live in Galatia," explained Dinah. "They're called Galatians."

"What's it about?" Chloe sat down opposite Dinah and took several tiny bites from her piece of toast.

"Well, I'm up to this verse," said Dinah. "Chapter 2, verse 16: 'We . . . know that a person is not justified by the works of the law but by faith in Jesus Christ. So we, too, have put our faith in Christ Jesus so that we may be justified by faith in Christ and not by the works of the law, because by the works of the law, no one will be justified.' "

Chloe raised her eyebrows. "I have no idea what that means."

Dinah grinned. "What it means is that nobody is good enough or can keep the rules well enough to be considered righteous in God's eyes. It's not the rules that will save you. Only faith in Jesus will save you."

"Well, that's a relief," joked Chloe. "I've broken three commandments before breakfast usually!" She stood up. "I gotta go. See you later."

"Bye," said Dinah. She managed to finish reading chapter two of Galatians before Elise appeared, jingling her keys impatiently.

Mercifully, the sheriff was not in the office when they arrived. Had he examined the interior of a chip packet or opened his fat mouth, there was no telling how Dinah might have reacted, despite her best efforts to keep her temper under control.

Dinah was desperate to talk to Angus Whitehall about the lie he'd been caught in. But first she wanted to rule out other avenues of the investigation. She preferred to be thorough, unlike the good sheriff, who was quite happy to be sloppy and neglectful.

The next entry in the little book found near Lola Albright's body had raised Dinah's suspicions. She had written of the unmarried carpenter,

Miles Reading, that he "bore watching." What did that mean? Had he threatened them? Had she suspected he could be dangerous?

She decided to call the man at his place of work, Aristocrat Kitchens. A man answered the phone with a deep, rich baritone.

"Aristocrat Kitchens."

"Hello. I'd like to speak with Miles Reading, please?"

"He's in the workshop. Can you hold on?"

"Sure."

The hold music was tuned into the local radio station, and a hyperactive DJ was currently screaming about something so passionately he was unintelligible. When Miles Reading picked up the phone, she was utterly nonplussed.

"Miles here." In the background, a saw whined.

"Hello. This is Dinah Harris, a consultant from the Sheriff's office," she said. "I'd like to talk to you about Malia Shaw and Lola Albright."

There was a loud clunking sound, then some rustling. "Sorry," said Miles Reading. "I uh . . . dropped the phone. What did you say you wanted to talk to me about?"

"Specifically, the murders of Malia Shaw and Lola Albright."

"Ah . . . right. I . . . don't know anyone by those names."

Dinah sighed loudly. "Miles, don't start this badly. I *know* you knew them. I don't care how, but I want to know all about it. Do you understand?"

"Uh . . . I don't . . ."

She was not feeling patient. Or gracious. Or sympathetic. With a strident tone, she said, "Miles, did you meet Malia Shaw and Lola Albright at Joaquin's?"

There was a long silence. "Um . . . yes. I —"

"How did you meet Malia Shaw?"

"Um . . . I remember I went there on a Friday night and I was sitting at the bar when Malia approached me."

"For what?"

"She wanted to buy me a drink."

Unbidden, an image of Angus Whitehall floated through Dinah's mind. Had *he* visited Joaquin's?

"What did she say to you?"

"She uh, asked me if I wanted to go sit in a booth."

"I guess you did?"

"Well, yes."

"What happened when you got to the booth?"

"There was another lady there," said Reading.

"Did she introduce herself as Lola Albright?"

"Yeah, she was with her."

"What happened then?"

"Well, that's when it got weird. Malia seemed like she wasn't really all there — I think she was, like, a junkie — and Lola started asking me lots of questions."

"What did she ask?"

"Where I came from, whether I'd lived here my whole life, whether I'd ever lived in California. Really weird stuff like that. Whether I'd ever beat anyone up or been in jail or assault."

"You answered all her questions?"

"Well, once I realized how weird it was, I got up to leave."

"What happened?"

"Lola tried to make me sit down. She seemed like she was used to getting her own way. So I just laughed at her."

"And then?"

"She tried to block me, physically." Miles coughed. "I sort of, uh, pushed her aside."

"You shoved her?"

"Well, just out of the way. She kind of stumbled over. I just wanted to get out of there. It was really weird."

"What was Malia doing during this time?"

"Well, she was just watching. She didn't make much noise. I think she was half-asleep."

"Did you see either of them again after that encounter?"

"I saw them hanging out at Joaquin's again, but I never talked to them again. I stayed well away from them."

"Did you see any other men hanging around Malia and Lola at all?"

"No, I didn't see anyone else. They seemed to keep to themselves the few times I saw them."

"Are you aware that both Malia Shaw and Lola Albright have been murdered?"

"I saw it on the news." There was not even a trace of sadness in the man's voice. *Bears watching,* Lola had written.

"I'd like to know where you were last Monday morning?"

"Me?" Miles Reading seemed to suddenly understand why he was being questioned. "You think I —?"

"Just answer the question, please!" Dinah's low patience threshold had all but petered out.

"Uh . . . well, being a Monday, I was at work."

"What time did you start?"

"I work from seven till three."

"You were at work the entire day? You didn't leave for any reason?"

"I was here, in the workshop. Just ask my boss."

"I will," Dinah promised. "What about the Monday night just gone?"

"Uh, you mean a couple of days ago? I stopped by Joaquin's for a few drinks after work. Then I went home, I guess."

"Did you go home alone?"

"Yup. Ate dinner, went to bed."

No real alibi, but equally no evidence that ties him to the murders, other than an interrogation by Lola.

"Thanks for your time today, Mr. Reading. I may be in touch with you again. I'd like to make it really clear to you that you shouldn't leave town. Do you understand?"

"Yes, yes," agreed Reading, sounding vastly relieved to be done.

Dinah hung up and stuck the pencil back into her mouth.

All the signs still point to Angus Whitehall. Esteemed pastor and family man — murderer?

The next morning found Dinah staring blearily at the coffee pot again, having had a night of restless, broken sleep and bad dreams. She considered for a moment forgoing a cup and simply pouring the contents of the pot directly down her throat. Elise stood beside her, making oatmeal.

Elise's cell phone buzzed on the kitchen counter, startling them both.

"Hello?" Elise put the phone on speaker.

"Detective Jones? It's Special Agent Max Shorten, FBI."

"Hi, Special Agent. How are you?"

"Great. I think you'll be feeling pretty good when I show you this tape."

"Really? From the surveillance of the organized crime's business?" Dinah was at once excited, the adrenaline doing more for her state of awareness than caffeine ever could.

"Yes. Can you come up to Richmond? I'd like to show you."

Twenty minutes later, Elise and Dinah were on I-95, driving north toward the city. Despite Elise's erratic driving, Dinah felt herself drifting off into a doze. The series of nights with little sleep left her feeling exhausted. The doze didn't really help; by the time they reached the FBI office in Richmond, she felt groggy and her eyes felt raw.

When Max Shorten met them outside his office, Elise smiled. "So you sounded pretty happy on the phone," she said. "What have you got?"

He led them into an interview room with a television and other assorted electronic gear set up. "I think you'll be pretty happy, too," he said. "It didn't take too long because we saw your guy come in only about two and a half years ago. We know most of Guido's business associates, so we could fast-forward through lots of them. The ones we didn't know we had a careful look at — and I think this is someone you'll be interested in."

Shorten turned on the television and brought up a still image in grainy black-and-white. It was shot from an awkward angle above Guido's talent agency, but it gave a clear view of the street and entrance. Shorten started to play the tape.

At first, all Dinah saw were several teenage girls coming and going from the agency.

"They probably think they'll be the next supermodel," said Shorten, his voice sour. "In reality, the gang will fleece their parents out of thousands of dollars."

Then a different figure appeared onscreen, walking up the sidewalk toward the agency. It was a male, dressed in chinos, boots with pointy toes, and an open-necked polo shirt. He stopped at the door, glancing around the street before going inside. In that moment, Dinah got a good look at him.

It was Angus Whitehall.

According to the time stamp, Whitehall appeared an hour and a half later, carrying a small white shopping bag just the right size to contain false identification documents.

"Obviously, the tape doesn't prove what he did in there," said Shorten. "But he'll have a devil of a time trying to explain it, I would think."

Dinah thought about that. "Is there a chance he went there on behalf of his daughter? He does have a teenage daughter."

"Of course, there is a chance," admitted Shorten. "But there are far more well-known and highly regarded agencies in this city for an ordinary person to go to. This talent agency doesn't advertise and I don't see how he would know about it, unless it was for less innocent purposes. In any case, I'd imagine if it were for his daughter, he'd actually bring the girl along."

Dinah nodded. "Okay. That makes sense. I don't suppose you've made a copy of the tape for me?"

He handed it to her. "Indeed, I have. Do you think this man is the one who murdered the woman?"

"It's *women* now," corrected Elise. "A friend of the dead woman was found murdered two nights ago. Yes, I think this guy might have done both. There are too many holes in his story. I've caught him out in too many lies."

Shorten stood up. "Well, good luck with the case. I hope you nail whoever did it."

"Thanks, I appreciate your help." Elise and Dinah told him goodbye and headed back out to the car for the trip back down to Ten Mile Hollow.

As Elise drove, Dinah pieced together the case against Angus Whitehall. The pastor was in big trouble.

****

O'Toole was on the phone. Angus wanted to screech down the line at him that he had *far bigger* problems right now than trying to convince the other man that there was no master race. His edginess told him he was close to having a major breakdown.

"I've found evidence of inferior races," O'Toole said. "Even you can't deny it, because it's historical."

Angus closed his eyes. "Which ones are you referring to?"

"Pygmies."

"I don't know how many people you've insulted by saying that word," said Angus, "but African tribes of any sort are not inferior. Nor any people groups indigenous to certain continents."

"But, listen," said O'Toole. "When white civilization came across the pygmy African tribe, they didn't know how to farm, they didn't know any animal husbandry skills, and they certainly had no infrastructure. And this was only at the beginning of the 20th century! We'd been building cities for hundreds of years by then and *they* were still living like savages in the jungle."

"In their own environment," retorted Angus. "The tribes you speak of were exceptional hunters, experts at tracking and trapping, physically agile, and had highly developed social structures. I would dare say that any city-dwelling white man dropped into the African jungle might have a hard time surviving. But we don't judge his ability to survive, do we? Only the other way around — and that is pure racism at its worst.

"Furthermore, what you're implying is that certain people groups are no more than savages. Do you know what that word implies? It implies subhumanity: *not quite human. Savage* is the very word Darwin himself used to describe groups he considered not to be fully-evolved, groups like American Indians, African tribes, and Indigenous Australians. He contended that white people were more fully evolved, more *human* than people with darker shades of skin. The belief that these people groups were subhuman allowed the justification of horrific treatment: slavery, oppression, and genocide. Do you in your heart believe in Darwinism, that we are all descended from an ape-like creature?"

O'Toole was silent for a moment. "I'm a Christian man, sir. I believe that God created us."

Angus nodded. "God does not say that He created one human and one sub-human. He created a man and a woman, and they were fully human."

"But," said O'Toole. "The Bible talks about slavery — there was lots of it in the Old Testament. And the New Testament doesn't forbid slavery, either."

Angus was expecting this argument. "Slavery in the Old Testament was based on vastly different circumstances. The Israelites were slaves in Egypt because there were so many of them and Pharaoh was afraid of their numbers. So he subjugated them. What we think of as slavery — capturing people against their will and selling them to an owner — is not what slavery was in biblical times. In fact, somebody who attempted to do this was to be put to death, according to Old Testament law. In those times, the absence of a social welfare safety net meant that people who were unable to provide for themselves would become slaves in exchange for food and housing. There were a vast number of laws pertaining to the protection of one's slaves: they were not to be injured or killed, they were required to have the Sabbath day off, and they weren't even to speak badly about their slaves.

"The New Testament is set during the period of Roman rule. The Roman empire practiced involuntary slavery — the capture and sale of otherwise unwilling slaves. Early Christians were slaves to Roman masters but were encouraged to serve faithfully in order to show the love of Jesus. Anyone who became a Christian who owned slaves was instructed to treat them with justice and fairness. In fact, it is widely believed that in Paul's letter to Philemon, Paul encourages Philemon to treat an escaped slave with mercy and forgiveness, even to the point of releasing him from slavery. In the first chapter of the Book of Philemon, Paul writes: 'For perhaps he was for this reason separated from you for a while, that you would have him back forever, no longer as a slave, but more than a slave, a beloved brother, especially to me, but how much more to you, both in the flesh and in the Lord.' Does it sound like the Bible endorses slavery, Mr. O'Toole?"

"I suppose not," said O'Toole.

Angus suddenly felt very tired. "May I make the following point: racism isn't harmless. Believing that one group of people is superior to another isn't harmless. The German philosopher Arthur Schopenhauer attributed civilizational primacy to the white people: 'The highest civilization and culture, apart from the ancient Hindus and Egyptians, are found exclusively among the white races; and even with many dark peoples, the ruling caste or race is fairer in color than the rest.' Do you remember what happened in Germany?"

O'Toole cleared his throat. "Are you talking about the Holocaust?"

"Yes, the belief that a certain *race* of people was the master race, that all others were invaluable. It led to the extermination of six million Jews, the extermination of the Roma Gypsies, and anyone of African descent. Eleven million died because of racism, sir. Do you think that's harmless?"

He realized that he was almost yelling now, and he hadn't meant to. O'Toole hastily hung up and Angus thought that he'd probably just lost his most generous benefactor.

He was beyond exhausted. He knew it wasn't harmless. He knew from bloody experience that it wasn't harmless. It seemed he could achieve no atonement for his sins. It seemed that no matter how hard he tried to change the minds of people who would happily describe others as subhuman, he would never succeed.

****

Elise drove straight to Whitehall's office and arrived unannounced. His secretary, Shana Woolcroft, glared at her with hot eyes. "Detective, he is in meetings all day today. You can't just —"

Elise ignored her and walked straight past her, Dinah following, into the office from which Whitehall worked. He was sitting at his desk, his head in his hands. When he saw Elise and Dinah enter, he looked up. His face was tired and haunted, dark shadows like bruises underneath his eyes.

Behind Dinah, Shana squeaked: "I'm sorry, sir, she just barged her way through!"

"Thanks, Shana. It's not a problem. Would you mind making us coffee, please?" His pleasant words belied the fear and anger on his face. A mottled purple flush crept across Whitehall's face.

"What can I do for you, Detective?" he asked. "I'm very busy, and I certainly don't appreciate being interrupted like this."

"I'm sorry," said Elise, and it sounded like she meant precisely the opposite. "Unfortunately, in the course of my investigation into the murders of two women, your name continues to crop up. It's become imperative that I speak with you."

"I see." He waited as Shana brought in a tray of coffee and poured them each a cup.

Dinah poured creamer and sugar into her coffee. Elise continued, "On the phone I asked for your whereabouts on the night Lola was murdered. Where were you two nights ago?"

Whitehall looked down at the desk calendar. "I had a . . . board meeting," he said. "From seven until ten. Then I went home."

They hadn't yet gotten the results of the autopsy, so Dinah didn't know exactly when Lola had died. But the hours between ten and two were sufficient enough to strangle a woman and dump her body. Further, it would be unlikely Louise would testify against her husband if they asked her to disprove the alibi.

"Now, if I recall correctly, you met Malia Shaw and Lola Albright at college?" began Elise. "Whereabouts was that again?"

"At UC San Diego," said the pastor. "As I've already mentioned."

"Indeed. Do you remember what year you attended that campus?"

"It was about 20 years ago — probably in the mid-nineties, I suppose."

"And all three of you attended the same campus?"

"Yes!" He put his cup down with a bang. "What has this got to do with —?"

"Well," interrupted Elise. "I spoke to the vice dean and there is no record of you, Malia Shaw, or Lola Albright ever having attended the college."

Whitehall pressed his lips together. "I'm sure that is simply a mistake."

"Perhaps it could be," agreed Elise. "Though it would be a remarkable coincidence if the same mistake was made three times while searching for three different people, wouldn't it?"

Whitehall's hands dropped to his lap. *Probably to dance,* thought Dinah. *A square dance this time? What about some break dancing? A pop-and-lock?*

"Anyway," said Elise, "as you might remember, I found some false identification documents in Malia's apartment when I searched it, so I thought I'd check to see if any of those names popped up on the college's database."

Whitehall suddenly blanched. "False identification?"

"Now when the vice dean ran those names through her computer, one of them *did* pop up." Dinah watched the pastor very closely. "The name Theresa Scott is listed as attending that college in the mid-nineties. Isn't that interesting?"

Whitehall couldn't seem to find anything to say.

"So it kind of lets you off the hook, though," continued Elise, "because Malia *did* go to UC San Diego, as you said. But it was under a different name. When you met her, what name was she using?"

"I've only ever known her as Malia Shaw," said Whitehall. "If she went to college using a different name, I didn't know about it."

"Really? Well, what name did *you* use to attend?"

Whitehall's face now turned an interesting pale shade of green. "I . . . I told you, it must be a mistake."

No mistakes here, Angus. Just all the lies you're telling are adding up to one catastrophic mistake.

"Well, let me continue. It might become clearer. We traced the false identification documents to a place in Richmond. Did you know that the FBI, who have been extremely helpful, could tell where a counterfeit document was made because each counterfeiter has their own unique way of doing it?"

"I didn't know that," whispered Whitehall.

"Fascinating, right? So the FBI traced the documents to an organized crime outfit up in Richmond. I couldn't quite believe it. Why would Malia Shaw have links to an organized crime outfit?"

Whitehall bravely tried to regroup. "Well, she was involved in drugs, so perhaps that's where she got to know them."

"You think they made these documents for her?"

He shrugged. "I guess if that's where you traced the documents to, then that would make sense. Honestly, a woman involved in drugs — it's hardly surprising that she might have encountered organized crime along the way."

Dinah almost felt like laughing in delight.

"You are quite right," agreed Elise. She was relentless. "Now, the organized crime outfit wasn't particularly helpful. They hide behind a legitimate business, a talent agency. They wouldn't confirm that the documents had been made by them, but I suppose we wouldn't expect anything different."

"No," agreed Angus. Some color was returning to his face. Perhaps he thought he would be okay.

"What wonderful luck that the FBI has had the talent agency under surveillance for the best part of five years, obtaining evidence about their activities," continued Elise.

Whitehall went so pale he looked like the underbelly of a snake. "They — *what?*"

"So it was just a matter of going through the tapes to see if Malia Shaw did in fact visit the talent agency. Of course, she didn't."

Whitehall opened and closed his mouth. *A marvelous rendition of a goldfish.*

"But *you* did." Elise delivered the sucker punch and sat back, waiting.

"I did what?" Sweat was glistening on the pastor's forehead and his eyes had gone glassy. Somewhere inside his head, Dinah thought, he was desperately trying to make up a convincing story to explain all of these little inconsistencies.

"Why would you visit an organized crime outfit to obtain false identification documents for Malia Shaw?" pressed Elise. "Why did Malia Shaw *need* false identification documents? Why would you help her get them?"

"I . . . I . . . Listen," said Angus. "I don't know *why* she needed them. She just asked me for help, and I couldn't turn her down. She seemed scared, for good reason, as it turns out. She told me where to get them from and asked me to do it for her. It was probably a dumb thing to do, but I really just thought I was helping out a friend in need."

Elise sighed in mock sorrow. "That all sounds wonderfully plausible, Mr. Whitehall. But there is still a small problem."

"What?"

"Why is there no record of you attending UC San Diego? What name did you use to attend? Did you even go there, as you claim? Are you using a false name? Why did you lie about knowing Lola Albright in the first place?"

Whitehall worked his mouth, his throat moving up and down, but no sound came out.

"Well, Mr. Whitehall? Do you have anything to say?"

He cleared his throat. "I want a lawyer."

****

Angus Whitehall waited until he was sure the detectives had left. Then he buzzed Shana. "I don't want any more calls or visits," he told her. She nodded and left his office. He locked it behind her.

At his desk, he stared sightlessly at his desk calendar. All his overwhelmed mind could think was, *What am I going to do? What am I going to do?*

First, Malia had been murdered, then, Lola. Was he next? He was the last of them to survive. Yet he had been the worst of the three of them — the leader, the captain. If any of them deserved to die, it was him.

Outside, a chill winter wind howled, lashing tiny chips of sleet at the windows. The intermittent beat on the pane of glass reminded him of fingertips tapping him on the shoulder and whispering, *We know who you are, we know what you've done.*

He shivered. He'd spent the past 20 years hiding, looking over his shoulder, pretending to be something he was not. He'd hidden behind the institution of marriage and family and church, though truth be told, he'd probably made their lives miserable. Yet his enemies had been waiting for him all along.

Angus thought about what the detective had said: Malia had died in her desolate little apartment; Lola had been found in the snow in the middle of the night. Two lives, taken and carelessly thrown away. He knew he was supposed to care, to grieve even, but all he could do was curse them. It was *their* fault he was in the predicament. How could they have been so stupid to let themselves be caught like that, like rats in a trap?

His old friend *anger* bloomed in his chest. Malia had always been weak. *Her life was doomed the moment she met me, and thought I could save her from the place she'd come from.* The things they had done had damaged her in a deep place, from which she had never been able to recover. Her love affair with heroin had commenced soon afterward. Once she had been found, it was just a matter of time for Lola and Angus.

Time had caught up with Lola. She had been more cautious, less likely to get into trouble. But even she had followed him here. He should have made them all split up, knowing that Malia would have died long ago and Lola would probably have drifted into some kind of trouble. Her problem was that she'd always had poor judgment of a person's character and she was sucked in by controlling, manipulative personalities. Angus was smart enough to know who he was: dominant, aggressive, and often cruel. He knew that's why broken and vulnerable women became so attached to him. *I use their devotion to my advantage. They give me their pathetic lives and puppy dog eyes, hoping for love. But I take what they give and I use it for myself. Still they followed me here, like a beaten dog that crawls back to its master.*

He often relived those glory days of his youth, when he was free to do as he pleased. He still remembered the rush of violence, the torrent of pleasure that swept through him. The high would be with him for days afterward. The anticipation of further violence filled him with wild joy. He remembered when he first met Malia, who'd been beautiful and haunted in those days, like a butterfly with a crushed wing. He recalled meeting Lola, who hid her vulnerability behind a facade of false bravado and confidence. He'd taken enormous pleasure in crushing Malia's remaining, beautiful wing and destroying Lola's wall. When laid bare in front of him, their pain and desperation raw and choking, he knew they were his to do with as he wished.

Now, reality had intruded. Those days were long past, and the two women with whom he should have cut ties with years ago had put all their lives in danger. Dread settled like cement in his stomach, heavy and cold. *Will my sin never be done with me? Why does it follow me everywhere I go?*

Of course, he knew the answer: the human heart is desperately wicked. Those who pretended otherwise had not experienced the depths of depravity to which seemingly normal people could sink.

The urge to flee was strong, but he knew that he couldn't. It wasn't the right thing to do. And because his heart was changed, because he desperately wanted to be free, he knew he had to do the right thing.

****

Dinah spent her lunch break looking over the meager finances of Lola Albright. Following her bank account and credit card transaction history, the money trail placed Lola in Norfolk, the last place she had been alive, according to the ATM records. She'd withdrawn all of the cash in her bank account at nine o'clock at night, near a movie theatre in the center of town. What happened to her after that was anyone's guess. Had she been snatched from the street in Norfolk? Or had she returned home, only to fall into the clutches of her killer?

Once she had finished looking through the bank statements, Elise decided to drive back to Lola's duplex. "If she was anything like Malia, she would have fake identification documents hidden somewhere inside," Elise said as they walked to the car.

The sky was low and gray as Dinah climbed into the car, lending an oppressive feel to the cold air. The snow had since mostly vanished, leaving behind the occasional dirty scrap of ice that was too obstinate to melt.

At the duplex, the side of the building in which the property owner, Ada Whittaker, lived in was locked up and quiet. Elise and Dinah slipped in through the front door using the murdered occupant's keys. A stack of mail lay stacked up in the mailbox, and Dinah brought it in with her.

Not much had changed in the sterile home, apart from a layer of dust. It told Dinah that Lola had fled a couple of weeks ago, perhaps sensing that her life was in danger, and hadn't been back since. She hadn't been back to collect her mail, to tell her landlord, or to resign from her job. She'd simply vanished — and then been found by the murderer.

If she had fake documents, why didn't she use them to escape?

They had not found any fake identification in the murdered woman's personal effects.

Dinah looked carefully through the small duplex for any hiding places — behind the refrigerator, behind cupboards, in cracks or crevices, underneath floorboards, in the ceiling cavity. But she found nothing except a sneezing attack brought on by the dust she stirred up during her exploration.

With a sigh, she sat down on the sagging couch next to Elise, who was looking through the mail. There were bills that were now overdue but unopened, and the usual assortment of junk mail.

A hand-written envelope suddenly got Elise's attention. She showed it to Dinah. A hand-written envelope! She wasn't expecting that! Furthermore, it was made out to Rachel Sutton, their first possible clue to another of Lola's identities.

Carefully, Elise turned the envelope over so that they could see the return address.

Flora Keenby
10275 Hastings Rd
Suffolk VA

Dinah could feel excitement blooming within her as Elise withdrew the letter. This could be the bread in the case they needed. It was hand-written, in an old-fashioned cursive script.

Dear Rachel,

How are you, my dear? It feels like a long time since I spoke with you on the phone, and I'm having trouble connecting to your number. Have you changed it? It could be me — I'm an old lady still trying to understand how these new-fangled cell phones work!

I hope you are well, dear? I'm doing well, considering I'm almost eighty. I have a touch of arthritis in my hands and I don't see as well as I used to. I'm so thankful someone thought to put out audio books! I find it hard to read now, so I just pop on my earphones and listen to the book instead. Marvelous.

I'd love to see you sometime. I'm afraid I get a little lonely these days. It's a sad realization that I've outlived most of my family. But I still have you, and I hope you are healthy and happy.

Please drop by or give me a call? I'd love to hear from you.

Your loving Gran

Dinah re-read the note, glanced at her watch and met Elise's eyes.

"We have to go," Elise said.

"Yes," agreed Dinah.

Buzzing with anticipation, Dinah locked the duplex and they both raced to the car. Minutes later, they were on the way to Suffolk. This could be that vital moment when the final missing pieces of the puzzle dropped into place, and Elise's impatience made her drive faster than usual. It would be late afternoon when they arrived, but Dinah hoped Lola's grandmother had nothing else to do but be at home. Holding on in the passenger seat, her thoughts jittered around the strange relationship between Lola, Malia, and Angus. She wanted to call Aaron, to find out his thoughts on the case. She missed his razor-sharp mind, the way he could see past the inconsequential to the facts that really mattered. And she missed lazy conversations over coffee, and the hikes they took on weekends, and the kindness in his eyes when he looked at her. She missed the exploration of the Bible they undertook together. She missed his easy laugh and quick wit. *I basically just miss Aaron,* she realized.

"Wake up, space cadet," Elise said, with a laugh.

With a start, Dinah saw they had arrived at Flora Keenby's home. On a quiet, tidy street, Flora lived in a bungalow with flower baskets hanging in the front porch. Come spring, the baskets would be ablaze with color, Dinah thought. She took some deep breaths and climbed out.

When Elise rang the doorbell, it took some time for the old woman to answer. Dinah could hear her shuffling from a room in the back. She swung open the door and peered at the two women through thick glasses. She was a small lady, hunched over and using a walking stick. It appeared the arthritis was worse than she'd admitted to in her letter.

"I'm Detective Elise Jones, from the Ten Mile Hollow Sheriff's Office, and this is Dinah Harris, a consultant and former FBI agent," she began. "Are you Flora Keenby?"

Flora blinked. "Indeed I am," she said, her voice still strong and clear.

"I'm wondering if you have a few moments to talk?"

"What about, dear?"

"Your granddaughter."

Flora almost managed to straighten up as she reared back in alarm. "Rachel? Is she all right?" she whispered.

"Truthfully, I don't know," said Elise. "That's why I'd like to talk to you. Can we come in?"

Flora Keenby led the way down a small hallway to a musty kitchen. The house was hot, and Dinah immediately began to sweat. Flora indicated the Formica-topped kitchen table. "Sit down," she invited. "Something to drink?"

"No, thanks," said Elise. "Can I get *you* something?"

Flora gestured toward a freshly made pot of tea. "I've got what I need," she said. "Now, is Rachel in some kind of trouble?"

"Before I explain, could I show you a picture of the woman I believe is Rachel?" asked Elise. Seeing the old woman's expression of confusion, she added, "In our town she was known by another name. I want to make sure I have the right person."

She slid across a photo of Lola.

Flora picked it up, examined it carefully and nodded. "That's my Rachel. She went by another name? Why would she do that?"

"Ms. Keenby," said Elise. "I'm very sorry to tell you this, but Lo — uh, Rachel, was found murdered a few nights ago."

Flora gasped, her hands flying to her mouth. "Oh — are you —?" Her walking stick crashed to the floor.

"I'm sorry," said Elise, gently. "Can I get you something?"

Flora took off her glasses and cried quietly for a few minutes. Then, she seemed to square her shoulders. "All right. Now what happened to my girl?"

Elise explained how they had come to find Lola/Rachel.

Flora sighed. "Oh, I had a bad feeling about her, Detective. I used to talk to her on the phone two or three times a week. Unfortunately, I haven't heard from her in a while — probably more than two weeks. What was unusual was that I couldn't get through on her phone."

"You sent a letter to her recently?"

"I didn't know how else to contact her," said Flora. "Her phone stopped working, and I don't go in for that email business."

"Do you remember the last time you spoke to her?"

"It's my hips failing me, not my brain," said Flora dryly. "Of course I remember."

Elise smiled. "How did she sound? Did she sound anxious, depressed, worried?"

Flora thought about that. "Not that I recall. She sounded her usual self, even got a bit touchy when I brought up the transient nature of her life. She's never settled down, you know, never really had a decent job."

"Do you know why?" Dinah asked. They knew next to nothing about this woman who'd vanished and then reappeared, dead.

"Well, she was a troublemaker in her younger days," recalled Flora, shaking her head. "Too wild for any sensible man. But she changed her life in many ways, and I truly believe she'd make an excellent wife and mother now."

"How was she a troublemaker?" Elise asked.

Flora gave a chuckle. "Well, I don't rightly know. I raised her, you know. Her parents died — my son and his wife — in a car wreck when she was only 12. Poor little thing had nowhere else to go and I was sprightly back then. So I raised her until she turned into the aforementioned troublemaker." The old woman looked forlorn. "Something happens to a child when her parents die that can never be healed, you know? I don't think she really was the same after that."

"Did she rebel against you?"

"Well, she waited until she went to college, at least," Flora said. "I knew she was up to no good there, but she wouldn't tell me what. It was a gut instinct I had, based on account of her being a smart girl and getting terrible grades. She was getting money from somewhere, even though she didn't have a job and I wasn't giving it to her. She would go for months without returning my calls or writing to me. I'm not sure to this day what was happening out there."

"Where did she go to college?"

"UC San Diego," said Flora. "She was a long way from me. Anyway, eventually she seemed to change back to the sweet girl I knew, moved around a few times before moving to Ten Mile Hollow. She would never speak about college, though. Not even recently. She just would clam up. So I know it was bad, whatever it was. And ever since she came back from college, she seemed much quieter, even sadder than I'd ever seen before."

Flora sighed. "You never stop worrying about your kids, that's for sure."

Dinah felt the chord of loss sound deep within her. *How I wish I still had my son with me to worry about.*

"Did you ever meet any of her college friends?" Elise asked.

Flora shook her head. "It was a part of her life she kept firmly to herself. I wasn't invited in."

"Is that why you were worried she'd gotten into trouble again?" Elise asked. "You not hearing from her for six months, did it remind you of the bad old days?"

Flora chuckled without mirth. "You're not too dense yourself, Detective. Of course I've been worrying about that."

"Did it ever occur to you to file a missing person's report?" Elise asked. "It does seem odd not to hear from your granddaughter for a few months, if you don't mind me being blunt."

"Oh, I know," said Flora. "But I remember a conversation we had only a few weeks before she disappeared. She sounded pretty sad, which was not uncommon for her. She said to me, 'Gran, there comes a time when I might feel the need to just vanish for a little while. You won't need to worry.' I asked her why, but she wouldn't say any more. I keep thinking about that now, wondering what she meant."

"You think she vanished voluntarily?" Elise asked.

"Yes, Detective. Knowing her, I think that's exactly what she did. Not that it did her any good in the end. But you and I will always be wondering from what she was hiding."

Elise nodded. "Did you know she was living under a different name in Ten Mile Hollow?"

"No, I didn't know that. What was she calling herself?"

"Lola Albright."

Flora shook her head. "I haven't heard that name before. Why would she do that?"

"I don't know. I have a feeling it's connected to her murder in some way." Elise closed her notebook.

"Well, listen," said Flora, standing up slowly. "Wait right here. Rachel gave me something a little while ago and asked me to keep it for her. I don't know what's in it, or whether it might help you."

She shuffled slowly away into another part of the house and emerged some time later with a shoebox-sized parcel. "This was one of the last times I saw her," she said. She took off her glasses and wiped her eyes again.

"Thank you," said Dinah, and gave the other woman a sympathetic touch on her shoulder. She couldn't ease the woman's pain, and even finding the killer often didn't ameliorate the grief. Death was part of life and it happened to everybody, but it didn't make it easy to deal with. Death was the ultimate enemy.

Elise opened up the package, which was tightly bound. When she at last undid the final wrapping, she showed Dinah: a selection of passports, driver's licenses, and social security cards lay within.

"What on earth?" wondered Flora Keenby.

Dinah looked through them. A passport in the name of Rachel Sutton — her real name. Another passport and a driver's license in the name of Deirdre Pucci. A driver's license and social security card in the name of Willa Douglas.

Dinah thought about Angus walking out of the talent agency with fake identification in a package under his arm, and knew without a doubt that he had obtained these for Lola.

But why? What or whom were they hiding from? Why had it ended up with the murder of these women?

Angus knew, Dinah thought. Angus knew everything.

Flora Keenby looked tired and sick with grief, but Dinah reluctantly had to continue to push the old lady, for at this point in time there was nobody alive who was willing to talk about her.

"I'd like to ask you more about her time at USC, please," said Dinah, after making a fresh pot of tea. "Is it fair to say that her time there is when she began to change?"

"Most certainly," agreed Flora. "As I said before, losing her parents was terribly hard for her, so she hadn't always been the easiest child to bring up. But she was a good child, in spite of it all, and we had a good relationship. Of course I was pleased that she got into college, even if it was on the other side of the country."

"What did she study there?"

"Social sciences, I think. Yes, that's right. She majored in Environmental Studies. Initially, she did very well. Her grades were good, we spoke on the phone often, and she'd come home during her vacations."

"How did things change?"

Flora Keenby frowned. "Then . . . she stopped calling me, or returning my calls. I wasn't too worried to begin with. You know kids, they like their independence, they like to think they're in total charge of their own lives." She gave a sad chuckle. "But then she stopped coming home altogether, and I began to feel worried. It's not normal to not speak with your child for months on end, in my book. Eventually I rang the vice chancellor's office. I remember the call clearly because they sounded more worried about her than I did."

"Why is that?" Dinah asked, when Flora Keenby paused.

"Her grades had tumbled," said Flora, her eyes fixed on the ceiling as she remembered. "They were about to put her on academic probation, and had tried to organize meetings with her to discuss it. But she hadn't showed up to any meeting. It was like she . . . was checking out. I had no idea who her friends were, if she had any, or where she was. I was frantic with worry. All I could do was keep calling her."

"You didn't fly over to visit her?"

Flora grimaced and gestured at her walking stick. "I had arthritis then, too. Flying there, or driving there, would have been pure torture." She dabbed at her eyes. "Part of me wonders if Rachel knew that all along."

Dinah wondered that, too.

"Anyway, one day she finally answered the phone. I don't know if I caught her at a weak moment, but she answered. I almost burst into tears at the sound of her voice. I remember I asked her over and over if she was all right." Flora's voice cracked and she cried quietly, as many of her stoic generation often did.

Dinah waited patiently, getting up to retrieve a box of tissues.

"She assured me that she was fine, just busy. She had gotten a job to make ends meet, which sounded reasonable. I certainly didn't have a lot of money to give her. I asked her about her grades and she said she was trying to fit everything in but she'd do better next semester." Flora shook her head. "And there was just something terribly . . . wrong with the way she spoke, her tone. I knew I wasn't talking with the normal, real Rachel."

"What did you think was wrong?" Dinah asked.

"Of course, I thought she was taking drugs," said Flora. "That was my first thought. I asked her and she laughed. She said she wasn't. And then I heard. . . ." She trailed off, thinking. "I heard . . . a male voice in the background. And suddenly she sounded fearful, to me. She got off the phone real quick. I kept calling, and eventually we settled into a semi-regular routine. We spoke about twice a month, which I was okay with, and she seemed okay with it, too. But I did notice that whenever I heard a male voice in the background during the phone calls, she would clam up and find an excuse to get off the phone."

Dinah exchanged a glance with Elise. "So what did you think was happening?"

Flora sighed. "Best as I could tell, she'd gotten herself into a bad relationship. I did some reading, I found out that in some abusive relationships, women aren't allowed to speak to their families or do anything on their own. I thought that's what had happened. I mean, she didn't grow up with a father, so it's not surprising she would fall for any snake oil salesman who came along, you know?"

Dinah thought about that. *What if Rachel had found herself in a relationship with a charismatic and handsome man, like Angus, and what if the bond was so deep that she followed him to Ten Mile Hollow because she couldn't free herself of him?*

"She wouldn't come home during school vacations," continued Flora. "I didn't know if it was because he wouldn't let her or because she didn't want me to ask questions. She always had some excuse or another." She sighed. "But what can you do? She was a grown woman by then, and I couldn't make her do anything she didn't want to do."

Dinah nodded sympathetically. She had seen the aftermath of hundreds of cruel, manipulative people who could make other adults do almost anything. But it wouldn't do to tell Flora that her granddaughter might have suffered like this at the hands of one who was supposed to love her.

"Her grades improved a little — enough so that she wasn't kicked out of school. I never saw her, and I barely heard from her. I was desperately worried about her, so all I could think to do was to continue contacting the school, to make sure she was still there and doing okay. Then, in her junior year something terrible happened."

"What?" Dinah asked, leaning forward with anticipation.

Flora sighed. "Well, if you ever find out you'll know more about it than me."

Dinah tried to hide her disappointment. "What *do* you know?"

"Well, the school kicked her out, for one thing," said Flora. "She turned up here one morning — I remember it was bitterly cold, like it is now, and she rings the bell wrapped in this hooded jumper. She looked for all the world like she was 12 years old again. I've never seen such a frightened face."

"You hadn't seen her for — how long at this point?"

"It had been about two years since she'd been home. I'd spoken to her sporadically on the phone during those years, but that contact had lessened. Suddenly, she's on my doorstep with a duffle bag. I made her some tea and sat her down, so she knew I wasn't going to brook any nonsense. I asked her what was going on. And — oh, dear." Flora started to cry again. After a few moments, she went on: "She laid her head on this very kitchen table and sobbed like a little girl. She couldn't stop. I didn't know what to do except rub her back and wait it out."

Dinah nodded to encourage the old woman along.

"Eventually, she just said, 'Gran, I've done some terrible things. Things you wouldn't believe. I don't want to be that person anymore, so I came home. I'm so sorry.' " Flora sighed again.

"And that's all she ever said about it. Three years of her life, vanished like they didn't happen."

Dinah wrote down some thoughts furiously in her notebook before she forgot them. *A university didn't kick out a student simply because she was trapped in a bad relationship, or even because she was barely passing. There had to have been a severe breach of the rules — perhaps something she deeply regretted.*

But what did she do?

****

Chloe listened to her mom clanging around wearily in the kitchen, making breakfast. Mom and Dinah had gotten in late last night and Chloe had pretended to be asleep when she heard her walking up the stairs. Now she realized she would have to go downstairs and talk to her, if only for a moment. She ventured downstairs to find her mother hunched over the counter, waiting for the coffee to brew. Her eyes were red and raw-looking, with puffy bags underneath so dark they looked like bruises.

"Can I make you anything?" she asked, smiling at her daughter.

"I'll get it," said Chloe. Her mother looked so tired she seemed unable to support her own weight, let alone make breakfast. She moved past Mom and slotted some bread into the toaster. It seemed to take an age to toast. *What a fine pair we make,* thought Chloe. *Mom hunched over the coffeemaker, me slumped over the toaster.*

"Where is Dinah?" she asked Mom.

"I think she went out for a run," said Mom. "I wish I had her energy."

Chloe thought about Dinah's tall, lean physique. *I wish I had her body.*

Chloe scraped some peanut butter onto her toast and sat down at the kitchen table.

Mom's coffee finished brewing and she added creamer and sugar before sitting down opposite Chloe.

"How is the case going?" Chloe asked, around a bite of toast.

Her mom shook her head. "Okay, I think. It's a little too early to tell."

Chloe smiled for a brief moment. "You look tired."

Mom rubbed her eyes and smiled back. "Just a very long day yesterday, and probably another one today. How was your day?"

Chloe shrugged. "Okay."

"Well, what classes did you have yesterday?" Mom sipped her coffee, apparently ravenous for details about her incredibly uninteresting day.

"Uh . . . algebra and history," said Chloe. She couldn't really remember. School seemed to pass by in one of two phases: either blinding panic when she needed to avoid Jessica Hunter and her minions, or an exhausting haze during which she had no idea what was happening.

"What did you learn about in history?"

History had been Chloe's favorite subject once, a lifetime ago. She thought about the class in which she'd sat in a state of fugue, not listening, not caring.

"I think . . . Pearl Harbor?"

Her mom looked up with a frown. "You think?"

"Yeah. Yeah, it was." Why events unfolded as they did at Pearl Harbor, Chloe wasn't sure. She remembered the teacher looking at her quizzically, wondering why her previously enthusiastic student sat limply in the corner, like a puppet with no master.

Her mother sensed there was something wrong, and she seemed to think about saying something before concentrating on her coffee.

Chloe was too tired to get into an argument about whether she was interested in school at the moment. It wasn't the end of the world if she didn't listen in class from time to time. High school was such a pain, anyway: all that pressure over getting good grades and getting into college. Who could be bothered to care so much?

When the conversation eventually petered out, Chloe went upstairs to brush her teeth. She stared at her reflection in the mirror without seeing herself. She avoided looking into her own eyes, because what she found there was depressing. Instead she focused on all the little things she hated: round cheeks — who could tell if there were any cheekbones in there at all — double chin, glasses. She fantasized about being one of those fat girls who went away for the summer and came back thin and beautiful. *Wake up, loser, that'll never happen.* She spat and rinsed, and returned to her room, sitting down on her bed.

From her book bag, she pulled out a notebook and drew a line right down the middle. On the left, she wrote BAD and on the right she wrote GOOD. On the bad side, she wrote:

> Grace doesn't like me anymore
> I don't have any friends
> Jessica Hunter hates me
> Therefore everybody hates me
> I'm fat
> *I'm ugly*

On the good side, she wrote:

> My mom
> My dad
> *I'm smart*

She stared at her handwriting so long the letters began to swim in front of her eyes. The bad side seemed so much longer, so much more serious.

Chloe shoved the book away and logged onto Facebook. She scrolled down the screen, looking at boring and useless updates, including what friends were eating, wearing, and doing. Briefly she wondered what the point of Facebook was. Did anything interesting ever happen? Did she really care about what people she barely knew were thinking? What they were eating? Where they went with their friends?

She clicked on the red notifications flag that told her about activity on Facebook that involved her.

Her heart was seized with a cold, vicious fist as she saw that there had been plenty of activity already this morning.

It had begun with Jessica Hunter:

I had a dream last night that you were dead. I wish you would do everyone a favor and kill yourself!

Utterly shocked, her seat seemingly falling away from underneath her, Chloe continued to read.

Sarah Mallister > Chloe Jones *I wish you would die. Nobody likes you.*

Alice Greendale > Chloe Jones *Everyone thinks you're a loser. And a freak. I think you are a freaking loser.*

Jessica Hunter > Chloe Jones *Want some suggestions on how to do it? You could take some pills. Or walk in front of a train.*

Shaun Kruger > Chloe Jones *Maybe your old man has a gun?*

Jessica Hunter > Chloe Jones *Maybe cut your wrists.*

Sarah Mallister > Chloe Jones *Then I wouldn't have to look at you in school. I'm so sick of looking at your stupid fat face.*

Jessica Hunter > Chloe Jones *Maybe you could starve yourself to death. Then at least you'd look hot for once in your life.*

Shaun Kruger *Nah it'd take too long. Anyways, nothing would make her look hot. She's too ugly.*

Alice Greendale > Chloe Jones *Gas yourself in your mom's car.*

Jessica Hunter > Chloe Jones *Stop wasting air, oxygen thief! You don't deserve to live.*

Chloe kept reading. She could not tear her eyes away as her tormentors began to outdo each other with calling her names until it finally ended with a chorus:

The Dark Heart

Loser, I wish you would die!

Chloe stood suddenly, feeling as if she wasn't even in her own body. She went to the bathroom, and washed her face with shaking hands. She stared at herself in the mirror. *Is that what I am? A loser? Fat? Ugly? Worthless?*

She searched her features for a hint of beauty and couldn't find any. *Nothing, there is nothing there. I am nothing. I am nobody. I am what they say I am. Why do I deserve to live?*

Numbly, she went back to her room and lay on her bed. She marveled that this is what it felt like to be the most hated person at school. She was the only person who had no friends. Everyone knew she was a loser, and fat, and ugly. *They hate me because I look different from them.*

It really did make sense.

As horrible and mean as Jessica and her minions were, they did understand the true social order of teenagers. They could uncannily pick the value of each girl and boy, and rank him or her accordingly. Those who were found wanting, like Chloe, were treated as the worthless losers they were.

Chloe listened to her mom close the front door and drive away. She lay down on her bed and stared at the ceiling.

She was too empty, too numb to cry.

****

At the office, Dinah waited with great impatience for the time difference between Virginia and California to pass, so that she could call USC. In the meantime, Elise returned a call from Dr. Walker, who had done the autopsy on Lola/Rachel while they'd been in Norfolk talking to Flora Keenby.

"Hi, Detective. Hi, Dinah," the doctor said. "What a great morning!"

Dinah smiled. "Good morning to you, too! You did the autopsy on Lola Albright?"

"Indeed. Well, let's get straight down to business." He shuffled some papers. "Now. This woman was 37 years old, which matches the age given on her driver's license. She was in relatively good health, though she was a little on the underweight side of things. She was a reasonable consumer of alcohol; I wouldn't go so far as saying she was an alcoholic, but there was quite a bit of fatty tissue in her liver which is otherwise unusual on someone who wasn't obese."

That was interesting, Dinah thought as she wrote this down. Malia Shaw may have had a devastating and obvious addiction, but perhaps Lola had struggled to cope, too, and self-medicated with alcohol.

"She had never been pregnant, or birthed a child," continued Dr. Walker. "The remaining internal organs were quite unremarkable and consistent with a woman of her age. The manner of her death was very similar to that of Malia Shaw. Cause of death was asphyxiation caused by manual strangulation — again, I could find no evidence that a rope or cord was used in strangling her. I still tend to believe that the killer used his hands to kill her, and I say *his* hands because it's vastly unlikely that a woman would possess enough strength to both subdue *and* kill the victim. Though Malia Shaw was probably an easier victim, given her drugged state, Lola Albright was by no means a large woman. However, in this regard, I have some good news. Lola fought back."

"Really?" Dinah's ears pricked up and she looked at Elise, who leaned forward.

"I scraped some tissue from underneath her fingernails. Whoever killed her left behind some DNA."

"That *is* good news," agreed Elise.

"Now, although she was found on a rural property, I don't believe she was killed here. The time of death was about 12 hours prior to her being found there, and I believe the man who owns the property indicated he'd been in that particular part of the woods earlier that day to collect firewood."

Dinah remembered this. "Yes, that's true."

"So I would say that Lola was killed elsewhere, and dumped on that property under the cover of night — and snow," said Dr. Walker. "I didn't find any evidence of where the kill site could be, I'm afraid."

"So 12 hours prior would make it . . . Monday afternoon when she was killed?"

"Precisely."

Lola/Rachel's death had taken place exactly a week after Malia's. Whether that was a coincidence or not was beyond the scope of Dinah's understanding at the moment.

"Anything else of interest?" she asked.

"In summary, that was all you'd be interested in," said Dr. Walker. "I trust it was helpful."

After they'd hung up, Elise said, "I know you want to call USC, but I think we need to visit Angus Whitehall. What do you think?"

"Okay," agreed Dinah. She would be able to call USC later in the day. Elise took the keys and they drove to the First Baptist Church. This time, when his secretary Shana saw her coming, she didn't bother trying to stop her. Instead, Shana rolled her eyes melodramatically and picked up the phone, ostensibly to warn her boss.

Angus was leaning back in his chair with a wry smile when Dinah and Elise entered.

"I feel like we're spending so much time together, we've become friends," he said.

I'd rather swallow battery acid, thought Dinah, then she shook herself. *Don't be nasty.*

She smiled. "Hi, Mr. Whitehall," she said. "Just a quick visit today. I know you're a busy man."

He nodded. "Well, I did tell you that I didn't want to speak to you without my lawyer present."

"I understand," said Elise. "But I just wanted to go over your alibi for Lola's death, which you've already given. I won't ask any other questions."

Angus frowned. "I see. Wasn't it on Tuesday? I was home with my wife."

"That was when she was found. But she was actually killed on Monday afternoon."

She watched his face. He raised his eyebrows but showed no other concern. No dancing hands this time.

"So you're asking me where I was Monday afternoon?"

"Where were you on Monday afternoon?"

"I'm quite happy to answer that, because the answer is so easy," said Angus. "There was a communications meeting here at church. I was here for the whole thing, because I chaired it."

"What time?" Dinah asked, trying to mask her dismay.

"It started with lunch at noon and went until six in the evening." Dinah heard the note of triumph in his voice and had never wanted to punch someone so badly as right now.

She clenched her teeth together and counted to ten before asking, "You were at the meeting for the entire time?"

"Yes. Ask anyone. There were plenty of people here."

He met her gaze and for a moment she saw the depths of his relief. Yet he had still not been honest with them. In that moment, she just knew with every tendon, muscle, and sinew that lying was second nature to this man, that lying rolled off his lips as smoothly as oil, that deception came to him as naturally as breathing. She wanted to scream at him that she knew about him, that she knew what lurked in his dark heart. She knew lies festered there, lying coiled around each other like a nest of snakes.

"Thank you for your time," Elise said, standing up. "I'll be in touch."

"Please call my lawyer from now on," Angus suggested. "I really don't want to talk to you again without him present."

Elise and Dinah left. Dinah felt a flush creeping from her neck up to her face. Ordinarily, a solid alibi like that would rule somebody out as a suspect. But this time, Dinah wasn't ready to give up so easily.

For one thing, the medical examiner wasn't going to swear in court that Lola/Rachel had been killed between noon and six in the evening. The truth was that Angus could still have been responsible. Dinah just couldn't shake off the feeling that if anyone was capable of sneaking out of a meeting to kill a woman, it was Angus.

I know who you are, Angus. I know you are a pastor, but I see something else. I see cruelty and violence. I see a dark heart hiding something dreadful. I know you aren't who you pretend to be. I know you, Angus, because you remind me of me. I feel the weight of shame, just like you. I see the oppression of guilt in you because I know what it feels like.

The only way you will be free is to tell the truth. For the truth will set you free.

****

Dinah sat at her desk in the office and then prowled around for several minutes with such a cantankerous look on her face that even Elise left her alone. She tried to marshal her thoughts into some order, but stubbornly, her mind refused to consider anyone else could have murdered the women except Angus Whitehall. To that end, she wanted to drive back to his office and arrest him right then. Eventually, she sat back down at her desk and called the university in San Diego. A woman in the Student Affairs office answered.

"Hello, I'm Dinah Harris, a consultant with the Ten Mile Hollow Sheriff's Department in Virginia. I'd like to talk to someone about two former students, whose murders I am investigating."

"Oh, my!" said the woman. "How awful. I'll transfer you directly to the vice chancellor."

"Thank you."

Dinah listened to classical music interspersed with rousing descriptions of student life at USC.

Finally, a deep male voice said, "This is Vice Chancellor Jerry Shilberg. How can I help you?"

Dinah introduced herself again. "I am investigating the murders of two women here in Ten Mile Hollow. Several leads indicate that both women attended your campus, and I'd like to get as much information about each of them as possible."

There was a long pause. "Detective, you know we can't just give out private information."

"I understand," said Dinah, not bothering to correct him. "However, you must know that student rights are terminated upon death." She couldn't help adding, "Terminated much like these two women were."

"Very well, Detective," said Shilberg, with reluctance. "You've made your point. When were they students here?"

"It would have been in about 1994," said Dinah.

"What names?"

"The first one is Rachel Sutton."

There were a few moments of clicking.

"She was a student here in the mid '90s," said Shilberg.

"What about Theresa Scott?"

A few more moments of clicking led the man to confirm: "Yes."

"Thank you," said Dinah. "I'm not interested in her academic record. What I'm interested in is whether she got into any trouble while she was a student there. Police arrests? Disciplinary action? Anything like that?"

There were a few moments of silence as Shilberg looked through the students' records. Eventually, he said, "I'll start with Rachel Sutton. She was put on academic probation twice during her time here, and failed to enroll in the second semester of her third year. Her enrollment was cancelled shortly thereafter. Whether she had problems with the police, I don't know. You'd have to ask them."

"Campus police?"

"Right. Now, Theresa Scott. She didn't appear to have any record of academic probation, but her enrollment was also cancelled in the second semester of ninety-four. Rather abruptly, I might add."

"Okay. One last thing: would you mind emailing me any photos you might have had of either of them at the time?"

"Well, they'd be from their student cards," said Shilberg. "It's pretty grainy now, but you might be able to work with it. I'll have my secretary scan them and email you."

Dinah gave him her email address. "Thank you for your cooperation," she added. "I appreciate it."

Her next call went through to the USC Police Department. Dinah gave her credentials to the young man who answered the phone and asked for the chief.

"I can't help you there," the young man said. "The chief's been laid up with a serious heart problem for a while now. I can put you through to Captain Hamersley, who is holding the place together."

Captain Hamersley's voice was so creaky and old, he sounded like he'd been a permanent fixture at the department since before the Civil War.

Dinah told him the story of the women's murders and that the only key she'd found in the past were attendance at the same college, during which Rachel Sutton had completely changed and "done things she regretted." She ended by explaining how both student's enrollments were abruptly ended in the '90s.

"Well," said Captain Hamersley. "The name sure don't ring a bell, but I was here 20 years ago. We don't have computerized records going back that far. Can you give me the names again and I'll check our archives and call you back?"

Dinah did so and cooled her heels for a full hour. She was so edgy that she couldn't sit still, so she stalked around the office, her mind in high gear. When Hamersley called back, he sounded out of breath. "Where did you say you were from?" Captain Hamersley asked, the vigor fading from his voice.

Dinah's heart started beating faster. "I'm investigating their murders in Virginia," she said. "Did you find anything?"

"Now that I've had a look, I sure did," said the captain. "Scott and Sutton. Glory be; I didn't think I'd ever hear that unholy pair of names together again."

"Can you tell me what you know?" Dinah asked, so excited and impatient she could barely wait for the captain to spit it out. *Tell me, just tell me!*

"Those two were bad news, very bad news," said Hamersley. "Though neither of them were as bad as the fellow they associated with. His name was Robert Langer; a viler creature you wouldn't find here on God's green earth. There was an incident here on campus, but as I understand it, there were many more incidents off campus. The San Diego Police Department eventually took over the case as a result."

"There wasn't an incident report in her student file," said Dinah. She barely dared to take a breath, in case she missed something he said.

Hamersley sighed. "There wouldn't be. It was a long, complicated story and the university was trying to protect itself at the time. I'm not sure I even know the full extent of how it all went down. You'd best talk to the old San Diego Chief of Police. He'd remember it, I'm sure. It was a pretty famous case." He paused. "Although it sounds like you've never heard of it in Virginia."

"I will talk to the Chief of Police," said Dinah. "In the meantime, what do *you* know?"

Hamersley heaved another sigh, as if the burden of law enforcement was suddenly too great. "You ever heard of the Southern Cross Militia?"

The search warrant came through late that evening, and Dinah stayed at the office late with Elise and her team of deputies, explaining their individual roles during the execution of the warrant. Elise had to spend a lot of time explaining the case to Judge George Emmett, who was initially reluctant to agree to issue a warrant against the town's Baptist minister. But the probable cause was so strong, and Elise's stubborn refusal too strong to accept anything else, that in the end, he had agreed.

At seven-thirty the next morning, Elise knocked on Angus White-hall's front door. He opened it, and when he saw Elise standing on the porch with Dinah and the deputies behind her, his face faded to white save for two points of color high in his cheeks.

"Good morning," Elise said, her voice stiff and formal. "We have a signed search warrant, which gives us authority to search your home and office." She thrust a sheaf of papers at him. "The warrant is authorized in connection with the murders of Malia Shaw and Lola Albright."

Angus's wife appeared in the entry hall, drying her hands in a dishtowel. How awful the other woman looked struck Dinah. Though she was startled at the appearance of the police, Louise's face was gray with fatigue, her eyes encircled with shadows, her lips colorless and cracked. She wore an old bathrobe and fuzzy slippers, her fine, blonde hair pulled into a careless knot. She watched Elise, Dinah, and the police enter her house with resignation. *Interesting,* thought Dinah. *She doesn't seem incredulous or baffled or outraged that we're here. It's like she was expecting this.*

"Do you need me or the children?" she asked.

"No, ma'am," replied Elise.

"I'll take them to school," she announced, to no one in particular.

Angus was looking at the paperwork Elise had given him with one hand, his phone in the other as the deputies fanned out around the house, opening drawers, searching through cupboards and rifling through clothing.

"I'm calling my lawyer," he told Elise. Dinah heard the barely controlled fury in his voice.

"Certainly," she replied. "However, the warrant is legal, signed by a judge, and your lawyer will not be able to stop us."

She turned away from him and concentrated on the search.

Dinah couldn't technically execute the search warrant, and so she simply accompanied Elise. The detective was most interested in Angus's study, and that's where she headed first. It was a tiny room just off the landing, lined with bookcases and featuring one desk with a laptop computer. Elise unplugged the computer and packed it up to take with her, and turned her attention to the shelves. She and Dinah spent an hour in there, running gloved hands over book spines, hoping to feel for spaces behind them or crevices in which something might be hidden. Unfortunately, neither Elise nor Dinah found anything — the bookshelves were simply there to hold the books and had no ulterior purposes.

Elise walked into the master bedroom, where two deputies were in the wardrobes, looking through pockets and purses. It was unglamorous, boring work but it was vital.

Dinah looked through the night tables, each of which had a single drawer. There was nothing of interest there. She stood, massaging her aching back.

One of the deputies called out: "Detective? You there?"

Dinah and Elise entered the wardrobe, where one of the deputies had discovered a small stack of manila folders hidden on a shelf behind a wall of musty, bulky sweaters.

Elise opened the first folder and found a pile of bank statements in the name of Sons & Daughters, Ltd. Another folder held the bank account opening application, signed by Robert Langer and Theresa Scott. A third folder held bank statements for The Wellness Group Trust, and another folder held the authorities, signed by Robert Langer and Lola Albright. Finally, a fifth folder held bank statements for an investment account in the name of Robert Langer. It had slightly more than a quarter of a million dollars in it. The only withdrawals on the account were the amounts matching deposits into Malia Shaw's account, via the two corporations, as well as the half-yearly rent payments.

Dinah smiled to herself. *The money trail never lies.*

"Brilliant," she said. "Bag them up and bring them in."

She and Elise went downstairs to find Angus. He was in the kitchen, vigorously cleaning up after breakfast. He did not look up at either of them.

"So, Angus," Elise said. "You want to tell me about Robert Langer?"

He scrubbed the counter even harder.

"Well," she said. "I know that Robert Langer is you. I guess I'm confused. Who is the real *you*? Is it Angus or Robert?"

He remained silent, wiping out the waffle iron.

"We found all the bank statements, tracing the flow of money from you to Malia Shaw," continued Elise. "Did you have to try to make it so complicated? I mean, in the end, it was easy to trace. It was just a pain in the butt in the meantime."

Angus's face showed a flash of anger. "It wasn't designed to be complicated," he said. "Just to discourage over-enthusiastic bank employees from making connections they shouldn't."

"What connections?" pounced Elise.

Angus was silent for a while. "No big mystery," he said, at length. "Just that I didn't necessarily want the world to know that I was giving money to a drug addict."

"Why *were* you giving money to a drug addict?"

He shrugged. "I told you already: I felt sorry for her. I didn't want her to have to damage herself further to get heroin. So I enabled her."

"Why did you feel so beholden to her?" Dinah wanted to throw every question she could at him before his lawyer arrived.

"We were old friends," said Angus. "I felt responsible for her. That's all."

Dinah's patience with him was quickly beginning to expire. "Mr. Whitehall," she said. "I don't think you understand how serious this is. You are the only person who visited Malia Shaw and you gave her money. Then she is murdered. Next you lie about knowing the dead woman's friend, who is in turn murdered. Who do you think is the prime suspect? In a court of law, before a jury, the explanation that 'we were just old friends' isn't going to jibe. When we get to that point, it's not just the women's lives we'll be discussing, it'll be yours too. Virginia still has the death penalty!"

Angus dropped a plate he was washing. It slipped to the floor and smashed, the noise oddly appropriate, as if echoing the seriousness of Dinah's words.

Angus picked the pieces up carefully, then asked, "Has my lawyer arrived yet?"

Elise shook her head.

"Then I have nothing to say. Not yet."

Angus turned away.

****

A deputy found them, both still standing in the kitchen, staring at the minister with frustration as he picked up pieces of shattered crockery.

"Detective," the deputy said. "We found some things in the garage."

Angus kept his back turned to Dinah, so she couldn't see what his reaction was to this news, other than a possible slight stiffening of his spine.

Dinah and Elise followed the deputy to the garage, where one car was parked. A wall of open shelves at the back of the garage held gardening tools, car maintenance paraphernalia, a toolbox, and an array of gas cans filled with old fuel and oil.

The deputy showed them the toolbox. When it opened, it folded out concertina-like, so that the contents therein could be easily accessed. Elise looked at the selection of screwdrivers, hammers, and wrenches and frowned.

"What about it?"

The deputy smiled. "The toolbox struck me as being a little too shallow," he explained. "I've got one just like it at home, and the bottom compartment is supposed to be real deep, to store the bigger tools. This one just didn't seem right."

With gloved hands, he carefully moved the tools out of the way and smartly rapped the bottom of the toolbox. It rang hollowly and Dinah caught on.

"Oh!" she said.

The deputy used one of the flat-head screwdrivers to pry the bottom out of the toolbox, and it revealed a compartment underneath. A sealed plastic bag contained something that looked eerily familiar.

Elise picked the package up and opened it. Inside were identification documents — passports, a driver's license, and social security cards — and Dinah just knew that they would prove to be fake.

Elise opened one and showed Dinah the name — Robert Langer, the owner and signatory to the myriad of bank accounts.

There were two other names in the fake documentation — Leon O'Dempsey and Charlie White. It was anyone's guess with which moniker the man had been born.

Elise carefully bagged the documentation as evidence and visited the other officers, busy in different parts of the house. Nothing else of any peculiarity had been picked up, and the officers where finishing up.

Dinah found Angus still in the kitchen, nursing a cup of coffee with hands that were noticeably shaking. "Do you want to tell me about Robert Langer, or Leon O'Dempsey, or Charlie White?" she asked.

Angus was still, staring morosely down at the brown liquid in his cup. "I can't," he said, after a lengthy pause.

"Why do you have false identification documents in your possession?"

He just shook his head.

"Why did you buy fake identification from Richmond for you, Malia, and Lola?"

Still nothing.

"Was it the money?" she asked, bluntly.

He looked up at her. "What?"

"Was it the money? Did you get sick of paying her rent and living expenses, knowing full well she was shooting it into her veins?"

Angus shook his head. "You don't understand. I didn't kill her!"

"I think you got sick of paying money to a junkie," Dinah continued. "I mean, look at your comfortable life here. Your wife, your kids. A relationship with a junkie wasn't going to help with that, was it? Surely the money would be better spent putting your kids in a private school or their college fund."

Angus shook his head vehemently.

"Or did she try to blackmail you? Did she threaten to tell the truth? Was she endangering your job by having the audacity to keep living? Was she an addiction you just couldn't shake?"

"No, no, no," muttered Angus.

"It's so laughable," exclaimed Dinah. "A man in your position, using money you could have used for a renovation or put into your kids' college funds, and she was shooting it straight into her veins! What did she have over you?"

"Nothing!" shouted Angus, suddenly rearing up. His face was mottled red, and spittle flew from his lips. "She had nothing on me! You shouldn't feel so sorry for her, Detective. You don't know what she was capable of!"

Yes, I do, Angus. And I know what you are capable of, too.

Dinah watched him carefully, pleased she'd evoked a reaction. He stalked to the sink, flung in his coffee cup and stood there, breathing deeply.

"What did she do that got her killed?" she asked, quietly, wondering from where the man was operating: guilt? shame? fear?

But Angus appeared to realize he'd gone too far. "No," he said, his voice quiet once more. Dinah got the sense he was holding on to his emotions tightly, only barely succeeding in keeping them under control. "I won't speak to you without my lawyer present."

She waited for a few minutes, allowing some quiet time and space to calm the frenetic energy of their conversation. She couldn't force the issue any longer; if he truly didn't want to help himself, there was nothing she could do. Perhaps he didn't realize how much evidence they'd gathered against him; perhaps he didn't understand he was the prime suspect. But she'd given him plenty of chances to talk, to tell the truth. Instead, he obfuscated and evaded, under some shaky protestation of innocence.

Elise entered the kitchen and looked at Dinah, her eyebrows raised. Dinah just shook her head.

Elise said: "There is just one more thing, Mr. Whitehall. The search warrant included a request for your DNA."

He sighed. "Fine. What do you need?"

"I just need a cheek swab. It'll be painless and quick." Elise showed him the swab. "I just rub this across the inside of your cheek several times."

Angus submitted to the swab, and Elise quickly bagged it and labeled it.

"Thank you for your cooperation," she said. "We're finished."

He nodded and watched as she marshaled the deputies together and out of the house, gathering the evidence they'd collected and logging it in her notebook.

As he waited for the last of them to file out through the front door, he said, "You need to speak to my lawyer if you have any further questions about this case, do you understand? I will not say another word to you."

Elise looked at him squarely. "Yes," she said. "I understand."

****

Chloe stared at the phone and felt nauseous. The only time she'd ever felt worse was whenever she braved standing on the scales.

She was risking total rejection, and she knew there was a high possibility that it would happen. Yet she had reached a place of such desperation that she could see no other option.

Mrs. Whitehall answered the phone. Her voice was strained and tired. "Hello?"

"Hi, Mrs. Whitehall," said Chloe. "It's Chloe."

"Hi, Chloe. I haven't seen you around much lately. How are you?" Mrs. Whitehall tried to infuse some warmth into her voice, but Chloe could hear worry saturating every word.

"I'm okay. How are you all doing?"

Mrs. Whitehall sighed. "Well . . . we'll be okay. I suppose you'll want to speak with Gracie?"

"Yes, please."

"Hang on a moment."

Chloe's stomach danced violently. Her heart was beating so fast she actually felt faint.

It seemed to take a century for Grace to pick up the phone.

"Hello." There was flatness to her voice that made Chloe feel even worse.

"Uh . . . hi," said Chloe. "I just wanted to find out if you were, you know, okay."

"Yes, I'm fine."

Chloe heard voices in the background, slowly fading away, and realized Grace was being cordial because her mother was still in earshot.

As if on cue, Grace's voice dropped, fast and clipped with fury: "No thanks to your mother. Your *mother* is trying to put my *father* in jail. How do you think I'm doing? She was here today, you know. Ransacking our house, accusing my father of murder!"

Chloe fought back a sob. "I'm really sorry, really I am. I just, you know, have no control over that. It wasn't my decision."

"We have been friends for, I don't know, 15 years," continued Grace. "It didn't occur to your mom just once that there is no possible way my dad is a murderer?"

"I don't know," said Chloe, miserably.

"What it shows is exactly what your family thinks of my family. My parents would never have done anything like this to you."

Chloe was frightened by the coldness in Grace's voice. "I know. I'm sorry."

"Your mother turned up here and searched through our whole house. They even looked through my room — my drawers, my closet. How would you like it if a bunch of strangers went through your stuff?" Grace let out an abrasive chuckle. "I mean, you think you know someone. You've known my dad all your life. Do *you* think he's capable of murder?"

A hot fist of despair twisted in Chloe's stomach. "No, of course not."

"Well, your mom certainly doesn't seem to have any problems thinking it. She's the one in full public view, harassing my father. I can't even describe to you what this has done to my family, to my mom. You have betrayed us all in the worst possible way. I thought you were my friend."

Chloe watched her tears fall onto the handset. "Please don't be angry with me," she begged. "I need you. Please."

Grace didn't reply, and this gave Chloe the courage to plow on. "I don't have anyone at school anymore. Jessica is being really awful to me and I'm all alone. At school they threw a soda can at my head in the cafeteria. I don't have anyone else to turn to!"

Grace barked a peal of mirthless laughter. "You expect *me* to come running to your rescue? Just like you've come running to rescue my family and me? How hypocritical. No, now I see you for what you really are. And I understand why everyone at school hates you. You're pathetic, you're a loser, and you disgust me!"

Despite her best efforts, a sob escaped from Chloe's throat. "How . . . how can you say that?" she whispered.

"Your mom has forced me to choose sides," Grace hissed. "Do you really think I'd choose you over my own family? Like I'd be okay with listening to your mom call my dad a murderer?"

Chloe felt like her throat was stuffed with a tennis ball. She tried to speak, but Grace continued, relentlessly.

"I don't want to be friends with you. Not now. Not ever."

"But Jessica —" Chloe managed to rasp.

Grace gave a snort of disgust. "Well, could you at least try a bit harder to be *normal*? I mean, what's with the dumb hair, anyway? I've never told you this, but I've always hated your hair. You look stupid."

A choir of voices rose in the background. "I've got to go," Grace said, shortly. "Don't call me again."

Chloe dropped the phone back into the receiver, a shaky panic beginning to spread from her stomach. On cue, she heard the sound of Mom's car turning into the driveway and she ran upstairs as quickly as she could. There was no way she could explain to Mom why she was so upset.

She locked herself in the bathroom and stared at herself in the mirror. Her face was puffy, blotchy, and red from crying. A rash of acne pitted her forehead. The roll of fat underneath her chin was obvious. She tried to smile at herself. She'd always thought she had a nice smile.

Who cares if you have a nice smile when you are otherwise fat and ugly? I mean, face reality. Like any guy could possibly overlook the fat, the dumb hair, the glasses, the zits, and like me just because of my smile.

Chloe sank down on the cold tile floor, her mind awash with poisonous thoughts, voices that laughed at her and mocked her.

Fat, ugly, loathsome, unlikeable, unworthy, pathetic, a loser, a laughingstock.

Somewhere along the line, she'd started to believe them.

The Dark Heart

****

The following morning, Elise and Dinah executed the final part of the search warrant, at Angus Whitehall's office. When Shana Woolcroft saw her leading a pack of deputies down the polished hallway, she did a double take. "What are you doing here?" she demanded, her voice shrill. "You can't —"

Elise slapped the search warrant down on the girl's desk. "Please familiarize yourself with this. It's a search warrant, signed by a judge, and it's legal. The court will require your full cooperation."

"But — !"

"Call your boss. He'll tell you it's fine." Dinah didn't want to waste any more time arguing with her. She moved past the girl into the pastor's office.

Vaguely, she heard Shana dialing and speaking to someone with great outrage. Dinah thought about giving her the World's Best Secretary award for her efforts to protect her boss, but sensed her sarcasm would fall flat.

Angus Whitehall's office was large and well-appointed. Important tomes on the theology, philosophy, history, languages, law, and ethics filled two large bookshelves. His desk was large and covered with a map of the United States, but with no computer. A Rolodex sat to the right of the map. In the drawers of the desk, Dinah found some stationery.

The deputies carefully looked through each bookcase, opening each book and checking for anything hidden or suspicious. Dinah flipped through the Rolodex. It contained names, numbers, and addresses of associates and congregants. There were no surprises, except that neither Malia nor Lola appeared there, under their current or former names. Equally, there were no pictures of his wife or children, no sentimental items from home or even a potted plant. It was a sterile environment that reminded Dinah of the apartments of both Malia and Lola. Were the three of them running away from something so terrible that they dared not make memories of a new life?

The office yielded very little, and after several hours, Dinah and Elise returned to the office disgruntled. Waiting for her was the cell phone and computer taken from Angus Whitehall's home. While Elise started the computer, Dinah opened the cell phone and looked through the text messages.

There were several standard and generic messages between Angus and his wife — *What time will you be home? Can you pick up the kids? Are you free for a barbecue on Sunday?*

The messages between Malia and Angus were even shorter and to the point — *Are you okay? Yes. Do you need anything? No. Don't feel good today. I know.*

It was the text messages between Angus and Lola that were the most revealing.

> *Lola, I checked on Malia today. Haven't seen you around much?*
> *Is she okay?*
> *The usual. What's going on?*
> *I don't know. I'm not feeling safe?*
> *Did you see someone? Have you been contacted?*
> *No to both.*
> *So what's wrong?*
> *It's just a gut feeling. There's something bad in the air. I can feel it, but I can't explain it.*

Dinah wondered for a moment if at this moment, Lola had inadvertently alerted her killer to her suspicions.

Another exchange was started by Angus and read:

> *Should I be worried about my family and myself?*
> *I don't know. Noticed anything out of the ordinary lately?*
> *Not really. But you were always better at sniffing out danger than me.*

Finally, it appeared that Angus got frustrated with Lola's disappearance.

> *Lola, where are you????*
> *I felt I needed to get away. That town doesn't feel right to me anymore.*
> *Well, what about Malia and me?*
> *Can you watch out for her?*
> *Not really. I have my own family, you know.*
> *Yeah. Well, I probably should come back, I suppose.*

Had she just signed her own death warrant? Was Angus so worried about Lola freaking out on him, leaving him to potentially spill their secret, that he killed her?

In the days after Malia's death and before Lola's body was found, the text messages grew more frantic and were one-sided. At this point, Lola was no longer replying to Angus.

> *Lola, have you heard about Malia?*
> *Call me! Malia is dead!*
> *Do you know what happened to Malia? Are we in danger too?*
> *Are you okay? Call me or text me.*
> *Why aren't you answering? Where are you?*
> *Call me!*

Dinah frowned. Angus either truly didn't know what had happened to Lola, as evidenced by increasingly panicky messages, or they were a clever plant to mislead the police. She thought about what she knew of Angus: there seemed to be a cunning quality to him, a coldness, a self-absorption. These qualities made it possible for him to think he could outsmart her.

She scrolled through other text messages on the phone, but found nothing that seemed pertinent to the investigation. His call logs were very similar — most calls were to and from his home or office.

Dinah turned her attention to Elise, who had opened the laptop she'd found in his study. She could only do a cursory check here; any in-depth searches of the hard drive would need to be done by the forensic laboratory. But it was funny how many times criminals were arrogant enough to think the police would never find them, let alone look at their computers.

Angus's emails were uninteresting. He hadn't communicated with his family, Malia, or Lola by email, and it was all work-related. Most of the traffic came through Shana, the pastor's secretary. On the computer's desktop, she found icons for an Internet browser, the Microsoft suite of products and the church's internal software. The internal software was password-protected, and Elise couldn't go any further there. She opened up the Internet browser, where the homepage was CNN's website.

Elise immediately went to the browser's history to find out what websites the pastor had been accessing.

Surprisingly, there were few. He didn't have a Facebook or Twitter account, and used no other forms of social media. He checked out a dozen different news sites every day, and used the search engine Google. It was the search history for Google that proved interesting for Dinah.

Every single search Angus had undertaken involved the name Harry Purcell.

> Harry Purcell California.
> Where is Harry Purcell?
> Harry Purcell Virginia.
> Harry Purcell jail sentence.
> Harry Purcell parole?
> Whereabouts of Harry Purcell?
> What happened to Harry Purcell?

Dinah frowned. This was a new name, which hadn't come up in the investigation so far — what did it mean? Who was Harry Purcell and why was Angus so obsessed with him? Was Angus searching for this person in the role of predator or prey? Did Angus fear Harry or should Harry have feared Angus?

As Elise looked through the history of the computer, it appeared that Angus had done some kind of search on Harry Purcell every single day. Did it have anything to do with this investigation? Perhaps Harry Purcell was simply an old friend Angus was trying to locate.

However, Dinah's gut feeling was that this kind of obsession didn't exist for an old friend. Harry Purcell occupied a different role in the life of Angus Whitehall, and for that reason alone she meant to find out what that role was.

She glanced at her watch and saw that it was past nightfall.

"Yikes, it's late," agreed Elise. "Let's go home. Maybe one of us will have a dream that will reveal to us who on earth Harry Purcell is."

The former San Diego Chief of Police, Patrick O'Grady, had retired to the rolling green pastures of Lexington, Kentucky, to indulge in his beloved pastime of thoroughbred horse training.

Dinah and Elise took a 7:30 a.m. flight from Norfolk, Virginia, and knocked on the man's front door two and a half hours later.

O'Grady opened the door to reveal a tall, bald man with a bristling gray mustache, sharp brown eyes, and the slightly bow-legged gait of a lifelong horse lover.

"Hello, I'm Detective Jones with the Ten Mile Hollow Sheriff's Department," said Elise, showing him her identification badge. "This is Dinah Harris, former FBI agent and consultant on the case."

"Come in," he invited. "My wife has her sewing club meeting in town this morning, so we can speak freely. Can I get you a coffee?"

"Please," agreed Elise and Dinah, in unison. Plane flights always exhausted Dinah; not so much the actual flying but the hassle of airport lines, security, and delays. They made her cranky and impatient, although she was wise enough not to antagonize the security staff.

O'Grady had led them into a large living room with picture windows that overlooked his property. It wasn't a large house, done in a tribute to the log cabin aesthetic, but the views of the lush fields were priceless. A beautiful black horse flicked its head in a field nearby, its coat glossy in the sunshine.

O'Grady saw her admiring the horse. "That's my Dark Magic," he said, with pride. "Comes from impeccable stock. I think she'll make a fine racehorse."

"She is gorgeous," agreed Dinah. For a moment, she continued to watch the horse as she trotted away.

O'Grady sat opposite the two women, knees popping. As Dinah put cream and sugar in her coffee, he asked, "So this is about the Southern Cross Militia?"

Elise gave him a quick rundown of the case against Angus Whitehall, and their mission to find the killer of Malia Shaw and Lola Albright, previously known as Theresa Scott and Rachel Sutton, respectively. She finished by explaining her conversation with the campus and San Diego police departments.

He sighed heavily, stirring his coffee. "I remember the Southern Cross Militia," he said. "Took up a fair chunk of my time 20, 25 years ago or so. In those days, we weren't so worried about foreign terrorism and more concerned with local groups stirring up trouble. The Southern Cross Militia was a white supremacist group based in San Diego, led by a rather crafty fellow named Randall Shutter."

Dinah frowned. "White supremacy?"

"Yeah. They were just like the KKK in ideology, but left off the white hoods. Most of these groups were harmless, unless you count filling people's heads with hatred. They would get together weekly or so and have a rant about how much they hated equality and that would be that. The Southern Cross Militia, though, walked the walk. They were dangerous."

"What did they do?" Elise asked.

"Well, Randall Shutter was a former Marine with experience in explosives," explained O'Grady. "He was smart enough to realize that getting all his racist groupies together wasn't so smart, because it meant we, law enforcement, could keep an eye on things. So he formed what we now call cells — smaller groups of people who operate almost independently and communicate subversively. Cells are harder to track, harder to monitor. He put some of his most loyal lieutenants in charge of each cell, and they used a variety of communication methods without ever actually physically seeing each other or talking to each other by phone. Randall Shutter himself moved around constantly. The first thing they did was to mail a pipe bomb to the ACLU headquarters in L.A. The bomb killed two people and injured three others. Afterward, he sent a note to the press claiming responsibility with the words *agere sequitur credere* printed beneath their logo. That is Latin for *action follows belief.*"

O'Grady sighed. "There were two more pipe bombs, one at the State Legislature and one at the offices of a civil rights law firm. Both times, the Militia sent notes claiming responsibility, signed by Randall Shutter. A postal worker was killed at the Legislature, and the third bomb only injured two people. I think he grasped that eventually people would stop opening packages and he would no longer get the bang for which he was hoping. That's when he formed his cell groups. He'd arrange tasks for them to do and they would carry it out."

"What kind of tasks?"

"The murders of highly regarded African-Americans, for a start," said O'Grady. "High profile African-Americans, like Reverend William Shore and the civil rights lawyer Elijah Morris. Both were killed in drive-by shootings, and the next day the press received a note from the militia. But they hated almost everybody equally. They assassinated a well-known Asian heart surgeon. We think they defaced the Holocaust Museum in L.A. Aside from the high-profile people, they would also assault any African-American, Asian, and Jewish people they could find — harass and stalk them, graffiti their homes and workplaces. Anything to intimidate and frighten them. And it worked. They genuinely struck fear into minority communities all throughout southern California."

O'Grady poured himself another cup of coffee and refilled the cups of Dinah and Elise.

"It was particularly frustrating for the police," he continued. "We had no idea which cell group would strike next, or where. Shutter had trained them well in the art of evasion, and each attack was well planned and executed. As far as we could make out, each cell was trained for a specific purpose."

"And Angus Whitehall was part of the Militia?" Elise asked.

"Well, he wasn't called Angus Whitehall in those days," said O'Grady. "He was Robert Langer. He was one of Shutter's top-ranked lieutenants. He led a cell group that consisted of two males, including himself, and two females. Their modus operandi was to use the females to lure a victim into a deserted area, where the two males would attack. He and his cell were responsible for beatings all across the southern California area, usually targeting single men on their way home from work. It was a cowardly, vicious assault; the victim didn't stand a chance. The only favorable thing I can say is that at least his cell wasn't required to murder, although they came close at times."

"The two females in the cell — were they Theresa Scott and Rachel Sutton, by any chance?" Elise asked, sliding across recent photos of the women to O'Grady. "They've gone by the names Malia Shaw and Lola Albright recently."

He studied them intently for several minutes. "Yes, I believe so," he said. He indicated a thick folder on the coffee table. "I took copies from certain cases for my own files and I've refreshed my memory."

"So did you ever catch them?" Dinah asked, wondering if Angus, Malia, and Lola had set up life in Virginia, on the run from California law.

"No. We didn't catch that cell specifically, but we caught Randall Shutter. Bizarrely, because Langer's — that is, Angus Whitehall's — cell betrayed their leader."

Dinah was entranced by the story. "What do you mean?"

"Well, you have to understand what things were like back then. The city was going crazy; half the population lived in fear and the other half was furious. There was pressure for me to resign because we simply couldn't find the Militia. The FBI field office ran a joint investigation, which was as fruitless as our own. We managed to find and arrest a couple of cells, but we couldn't get to the leader. We knew that if we could shut down Shutter, the group would fall apart. That's the way these gangs are run — they rely almost totally on the charisma of the leader."

He shook his head. "The L.A. riots had happened only a couple of years prior, and the air of the place was like a tinderbox, just waiting to be set alight. I'm not sure what motivated Robert Langer, but perhaps he thought he could be a hero. In any case, it appeared that most of his cell wanted to get out of the gang."

"Most of the cell?"

O'Grady smiled briefly. "Right. Langer and the two women. The other member, Harry Purcell, did not want to leave the gang and had no idea what the other members were planning. Much like many of the gangs that still operate, the Southern Cross Militia had a blood-in, blood-out policy."

Dinah's ears pricked up. *Harry Purcell!* The person Angus had been obsessively searching for, every single day.

At this moment, she knew her case would be made for her.

****

"What does that mean exactly?" asked Elise.

"The Militia required evidence of one's commitment before being admitted as a full member," explained O'Grady. "Such evidence was the execution of an act of violence. Most members would be required to assault or kill a target. Equally, one was not permitted to simply leave the gang. Anyone who left was usually summarily executed."

If I'm wrong, and Angus is not the killer, could the three be under attack from their old gang? Is that why they have the fake IDs, the fake names, the new lives in Virginia?

"So what did they do to Randall Shutter?" Elise asked.

"The cells operated independently, as I've said. Shutter refused to allow most cell members, apart from his lieutenants, to ever see him. Very few people knew where he lived. It may surprise you to learn that he was supremely paranoid." O'Grady chuckled. "But Robert Langer had direct access to Shutter, and he used this access to sneak into Shutter's home, lie in wait for him, beat him senseless, and steal almost a quarter of a million dollars."

Elise sat back and stared at Dinah for a moment. "Huh! Really?"

"The full story is that the Militia had extorted a huge amount of money from various members of the minority community in return for 'protection' and the cash was sitting in Shutter's house. Only his top-ranked lieutenants would have known this. Langer and the two women broke into his home, waited for Shutter to arrive home, and attacked him with baseball bats. They took all the cash in the place and then disappeared from the face of the earth. Shutter was so badly injured that he was taken to the hospital after his cleaner found him. He was promptly arrested and eventually sentenced to life in jail. He has always professed vengeance against Langer, Scott, and Sutton."

"What about the other cell member, Harry Purcell?"

"He was loyal to Shutter. Tried to provide false alibis and that kind of thing. He went to jail too, but only for about five years on an assault charge. When he came out, he also vanished. As far as I know, he also swore revenge."

That changes things. How many people want to kill these three? Was Angus fearful of an attack from Purcell?

"And then Langer and the women pop up in Virginia," mused Dinah. "Still together, after all these years, using false names. Would it surprise you to learn that they stuck together, rather than splitting up?"

O'Grady smiled. "Heard of honor among thieves, Detective? There is none. No, it doesn't surprise me. The three of them disappeared with crimes more numerous than you have hairs on your head. They were wanted for attempted murder, assault, assault with a deadly weapon, extortion, harassment, and grand larceny. If there were two people in the world running around who know this about you, would you want to know where they were and what they were saying? I know I would. I think Robert Langer kept those two women close so that he could control them better."

"Both women have been recently murdered," said Elise. "What are your thoughts on that?"

"You're wondering who I think might have done it?" O'Grady scratched his head and smoothed his mustache. "Well, Robert Langer could have done it quite easily. Perhaps he was sick of the liability of having them around, and the chance they might talk. He had never shied away from violence. He could have done it in a heartbeat and walked away with a smile, make no mistake about that."

This observation about Angus Whitehall chilled Dinah.

"But it could have been a number of others, too. Purcell, for one. Like I said, he was loyal to Shutter and swore revenge. He might have finally found them and gotten rid of the easier targets first. Or it could have been someone else sent by Shutter. He's still well-regarded in prison by all the white-supremacist groups, and he could have ordered the hits through those networks."

Dinah remembered past conversations with Angus, who'd made vague references to people who might want to hurt him and his family. A few other things began to slide in place, gaining sharper focus, like when an optical illusion became apparent. The fake ID's had been necessary to hide from their old gang. The apparent inability of Malia and Lola to settle down and have normal lives, haunted by their past and the knowledge that it could catch up with them at any moment. The otherwise inexplicable relationship between the town's Baptist pastor, a drug addict, and a restlessly drifting woman, all bound together by invisible ties of mistrust, loyalty, and shared horror.

In the middle of these observations stood Angus. He had almost total control over the group's money, stolen from Shutter. He'd been able to marry, have children, and hold down a meaningful job. Perhaps this meant that the past bothered him less than it did the two women. It was this very past that made him *more* capable of murder, not less, in Dinah's view. O'Grady had said he could have murdered Malia and Lola with barely a rise in blood pressure, and Dinah could, from all that she knew about the man, imagine this. The question was, why? Had he wanted the nearly quarter of a million dollars for himself? Was he worried the women might one day expose him? Was he simply sick of looking out for them and wanted to be free of them and what they represented?

"How much did you ever find out about the members of the cell — Robert, Harry and the two women?" she asked.

"Well, we gathered as much information about them as we could," said O'Grady. "They were living double lives, you see. By day, they were harmless college students, and by night they were ruthless racists. So once we suspected who they were, we watched them and found out as much as we were able about them."

"What did you discover?"

"Randall Shutter and the Southern Cross Militia were on our radar for a long time. During the 1990s, they were the most organized domestic terrorist group in the country. Randall Shutter was already well known to us as a former Marine-turned-violent thug and we obviously felt that if we could incarcerate Shutter, the entire Southern Cross Militia would collapse." O'Grady stared out his picture windows, his mind far away in another time, another place that was as violent as his property was peaceful.

O'Grady continued, "We watched Robert Langer — or Angus Whitehall, as he's now known — for a long time. He was the most dangerous of the four members of the cell, not least because he was organized and intelligent. The attacks he executed were well planned and carried out smoothly. If I've mentioned that Shutter had charisma, Langer had as much of it, too. He was good-looking, smart, and disarming. He could tell you that the world was flat and the moon was made of cheese, and eventually you'd believe him. I believe that that's how he recruited the two women into the gang, and into his cell. The few times I managed to observe them together, he was always in control, and they were doing his bidding. They were certainly in his thrall. I don't know how he managed to maintain it, but he seemed to inspire their loyalty and entice them to commit violence on his behalf."

Dinah thought she knew. It wasn't uncommon for a vulnerable and broken woman to want to love and please a charismatic and powerful man, to be loved by him in return.

"We were never able to find out where the three of them had come from, or what their home lives had been like," continued O'Grady. "But violence ran in the blood of Langer. He was smart enough to be subtle about it while at college, but we found out about a few incidents from the campus police."

"What kind of incidents?"

"One young man in a class with Langer stood up to him in public, about what I don't know. Langer waited for him at his dorm room and beat him up pretty badly. He was given a warning and put on probation, but the damage had been done. From that moment, Langer was able to use the threat of violence to get what he wanted or to intimidate others. He had the history, and nobody wanted to take him on. Some of the students I spoke to said they could tell there was something very wrong with him, that he wasn't quite balanced. I have to agree. From what I knew about him, I'd say he was a sociopath who derived pleasure from violence."

"Were there any instances of violence against women?" asked Elise.

"There was an allegation that he tried to attack a young African-American woman on campus," said O'Grady. "But it was never proven and eventually it went away."

"What about Harry Purcell? What did you know about him?"

"I know he made a good soldier. He always did exactly as he was told. What he lacked in leader's magnetism he made up for with his enthusiasm. He was perhaps a less disturbing individual, but he seemed equally happy to carry out the violence."

"You mentioned he went to jail after the other three vanished?"

"Yes, but it was only a five-year sentence. He'd be well and truly out by now."

"Do you know what happened to him after he got out of prison?"

"No. I didn't hear anything from him. As far as I know, he stayed out of trouble, at least in my district."

"Do you think he could be capable of tracking down Angus, Malia, and Lola to exact revenge, even 20 years later?"

O'Grady thought about that for several minutes. "He wasn't as smart as Langer. He was a thug, a soldier. He was good at following orders. So if he'd been ordered by Shutter or someone else to find the rest of his cell, then yes, absolutely. He'd have no problem with killing any of them. He would have felt betrayed, just like Shutter did. They didn't split the money with him and they disappeared without him. So his sense of treachery would have been as high as Shutter's."

"What sort of thug was he? Did he favor a gun? His fists?"

"That cell had been armed with very few weapons, as I recall. Since their orders were not to kill, they often used their bare hands or weapons like baseball bats or tire irons." O'Grady shook his head at the memory. "Brutal stuff. In many ways, it's easier to simply shoot someone."

"If I told you that the two murdered women had been strangled to death manually, would you attribute that to Purcell or to Langer, do you think?" asked Elise.

O'Grady finished his coffee and stroked his mustache. "I tend to think that's the style of Purcell," he said, at length. "But Langer would be equally as capable. I wouldn't discount either of them."

Dinah digested that for a moment. It didn't allow Angus Whitehall clearance, but it added another suspect. The big question was whether he had been in Virginia at the time of the murders.

"Let me ask you something," said O'Grady. "Did you see the autopsies for either of the women?"

"I attended the first and read the report on the second. Why do you ask?"

"It's an irrelevant question," said O'Grady. "But I always wondered what they did with their tattoos."

"Tattoos? What do you mean?"

"Well, like most gang members of any color or creed, tattoos are a rite of passage. Members get the logo of the gang, or the number of kills they've made, or hate symbols like the swastika. All three of them had tattoos — Langer would have had more, but the women definitely had tattoos, too. It's also a way of marking a person for life as a member of the gang, to help ensure that they can never leave the gang. So I always wondered how they covered them up."

Dinah suddenly remembered the flat, bleached skin on the arms of both women. The medical examiner had thought they had been crude tattoo removal.

"I think they had laser removal," she said. "The autopsy reports found the scars from pretty crude treatment."

O'Grady nodded. "Well, it sounds like they thought of everything to begin their new lives, right?"

Almost, thought Dinah. *Except for the part where a killer re-emerges from the shadows to destroy the cell once and for all.*

****

Chloe hated gym class. In fact, to be truthful, she loathed it. In every other class she usually made an A, but she consistently scored D's in gym.

She stood listlessly on the volleyball court, watching the ball *thunk* from one side of the net to the other. When it was absolutely necessary, she made a half-hearted attempt to lunge at the ball.

Usually, she managed to work herself up into an outrage during every gym class, silently lambasting the faculty for making gym necessary, building arguments as to why it was a totally worthless class. But today, she was unable to muster even a solitary resentful thought, and she stood as usefully as a lump of wood as close to the line as she dared.

Ordinarily, the scathing looks sent her way by the athletic kids in class made her cringe and blush with embarrassment. But today, she returned their stares woodenly, barely registering their disgust.

It didn't help that the shorts highlighted the soft, pale pudginess of her legs, or that her face went an alarming shade of ketchup when she moved faster than a walk. All of these things added up to make gym class a thoroughly miserable affair. The only thing today's gym class had going for it was that it was the final class of the day, and at least afterward she could take a long shower and go home.

Finally, the teacher blew the whistle and Chloe sent her silent gratitude skyward. She trudged into the locker room behind the rest of class, and turned on the shower so that it was hot. Since she didn't have another class to get to, she luxuriated in the warm spray, scrubbing away the final remnants of gym class from her body.

When she turned the faucet off, the locker room was quiet. Everyone else must have showered quickly and cleared off. Chloe was glad to be alone.

She toweled off and dropped it on the ground, climbing into her underwear. A sudden noise made her look up.

Her stomach clenched in an icy fist.

Jessica Hunter stood in front of her, flanked by Sarah Mallister and Alice Greendale. Jessica held a cell phone up, the light on the camera steady and unblinking.

With a smirk, Jessica kept the phone trained on Chloe as she descended into panic, trying to pick up the wet towel to cover herself.

The towel had fallen into a patch of water and was thoroughly soaked. Jessica and her minions continued to laugh as she filmed Chloe try to pick up the towel and wrap it around herself, dripping with water.

"What are you doing?" Chloe shouted, angry and humiliated.

Jessica continued to film, laughing and showing Sarah and Alice.

"Give me that! Delete the photos!" Chloe cried. Grasping the towel in one hand, she lunged forward to try to wrestle the phone out of Jessica's hands. It was an instinctive urge, but in reality, Chloe had no chance. She felt the onslaught of tears, all at once; furious, frustrated tears.

Jessica deftly handed the phone to Sarah and laughed.

"Guess where this is going, Fat Cow?" she sneered.

Chloe realized that the echo of sobbing sounding off the walls was coming from her.

"Why are you doing this?" she cried. "Why do you hate me so much?"

She sank down to the ground, hunched over herself, trying to make herself less of a target.

"You are a disgusting, fat slob," snarled Jessica. "You make me sick. You don't even realize how gross you really are."

I don't look like you. That's the stupidity of this whole thing, right there, Chloe thought, wet hair strung across her cheek like a spider web. *She just looks at me and hates me, because I look different.*

Laughter rang out and slowly receded as Jessica, Sarah, and Alice left the locker room.

Chloe stayed hunched over herself, a slimy tendril of self-loathing worming its way through her body to her heart. *It's my fault. It's me.* Nobody else would be treated like a loser. Nobody else would end up being totally friendless, totally alone, like her.

Finally, she stood up and got dressed. The wet towel had left damp patches all over her underwear and her clothes stuck to her in places. She edged out of the gym, checking to see if any further attack might be awaiting her. But all was quiet and with thankfulness for small mercies, she walked home slowly, hoping that she wouldn't see Jessica again.

She arrived home, an empty, quiet house. She went, by default, into the kitchen and opened the refrigerator door. She blinked at the cool air, staring unseeing at the food therein.

Finally, she shut the door and wandered through the house until she found herself in front of her computer. Though a small, still voice was screaming at her not to look, she found herself logging into Facebook anyway.

The video Jessica had taken had been uploaded to YouTube, and shared on her Facebook page.

With sick dread, Chloe pressed play. She watched the video, vividly seeing her pale near-nudity, the white dimples of flesh nobody else had ever seen, seeing the pathetic look of humiliation crumpling her face. She heard, in supersonic quality, the sound of laughter, the words Jessica had thrown at her. She watched herself awkwardly try to cover up with the towel.

The comments underneath were scathing, from the usual suspects. But there were lots of comments from people she didn't know. People from other cities, other states.

And when she visited the video on YouTube, she saw a stream of comments from complete strangers.

Somehow they all knew the truth: that she was a loser, that she was fat, that she was ugly, that she was worthless, that her life meant nothing. They were saying as much in a steady trickle right underneath the video.

That's when the insidious thought popped into her mind: *Your life is not worth living.*

Suddenly, she felt calm and composed.

It was time to take care of a few things.

Chloe hadn't been to school in three days. She knew that her mother hadn't noticed, and her father would be none the wiser. But the school would notice and would start calling Mom soon.

She'd heard Mom leave early to catch her flight and knew that she had the whole day to herself. She'd slept in until about ten, and then had a long, hot shower. The weeks and months of roiling, retching anxiety had quieted down. She almost felt serene. She combed her hair but didn't bother with her teeth or face cream. Who cared about that stuff anymore? It was so superficial anyway.

She made herself pancakes for breakfast, covering them generously with maple syrup and butter. Instead of chastising herself for eating too many, she indulged in as many as she could eat. Afterward, the stomach uncomfortably full, she stretched out in contentment like a cat in the sun.

Chapter 15

Then Chloe returned upstairs to her room. She focused her energy first on her desk. She almost laughed. She opened her computer, and her Facebook account. She looked through the status updates and thought to herself how dumb they all were.

Look at all their pathetic little lives, trampling on each other to make it to the top, desperately hoping that each new update will bring popularity and validation. Look at their ridiculous profile photos, with their pouting lips and makeup. They are trying so hard to be pretty. And for what? Who is in the least bit concerned with what anyone else looks like? They are too self-absorbed to care about anyone else!

She felt almost high. She deactivated her Facebook account with a grin on her face. It was a giddy feeling — suddenly cast adrift from the artificial world of social media, no longer beholden to the unwritten rules of posting, no longer a slave to the sweaty palms and rising dread of checking to see what Jessica or her minions had written about her.

Next she deleted her emails, from her sent items to her inbox. Some emails required a reply, but she was sick of an inanimate object telling her what to do. Those people awaiting a reply probably wouldn't even realize she hadn't answered. People seemed to fire off an email every time a vague and stupid thought entered their minds.

Her computer suddenly clean and carefree, she looked down at her schoolbooks. Algebra, history, chemistry, and English. Two of those subjects required assignments to be handed in soon. She had started researching. The notes with her open, swirling handwriting were poking from the top of the books. She pulled out the notes and read them, laughing at the futility of it all. Did anyone actually use algebra while prepping for surgery or a court case or while fixing a car or scanning groceries? Did the history of the Second World War ever help anyone pay bills or save for college or buy a house? Did the ability to use semi-colons in a sentence correctly really help a person become a CEO or a senator or a mom?

None of it even matters. None of it.

She tore up her research notes into tiny pieces until it looked like her desk was covered with snow. She had no intention of completing the assignments. In fact, she wished she could simply write on the paper the teachers handed out: *This is stupid and I'm not doing it.* Just to prove her point.

Chloe swiped all the tiny bits of paper into her bin and stacked the textbooks up in a neat pile. They would probably be sent to the second-hand bookstore or sent to a poorer school somewhere who needed them. It no longer mattered to her. She wasn't going to read one more page of any of them. She could not care less about the value of *x* or *y*, or why the Japanese had used kamikaze pilots in their attack on Pearl Harbor, or the correct use of *effect* and *affect*. If colleges wanted to see good grades and healthy extracurricular activities logged and impeccable lineage descending from the *Mayflower*, it no longer troubled her.

Next she began to do a slow reconnaissance of her room, looking for things of value. It struck her that she didn't really own anything of real significance. It was a pretty pathetic showing for 15 years spent on the earth so far, she thought. Her parents were not wealthy by any means, and everything she owned was functional. She owned only the pairs of shoes than she needed. Only one purse, a closet of well-worn clothes. Her most treasured possessions were her classic novels in the bookshelves, where *Anne of Green Gables* nestled closely with *The Lion, the Witch and the Wardrobe*, *The Hardy Boys*, and *To Kill a Mockingbird*. They would mean very little to anyone else, she thought. Though she had sympathized with the scrawny, unloved Anne and been shocked by Edmund's betrayal, these scenes might not have moved others in the same way. Though she could find no other use for them, she couldn't bear to destroy them. And so she left the bookcase alone.

Finally, she came to the last possession of any significance. It was a C made of gold, hanging on a thin, gold necklace around her neck. Her friend Grace had bought it and given it to her on her 12th birthday. She had worn it every day since, a reminder of how close their friendship had once been. She hadn't been able to take it off since.

Except today.

Today, she unclasped the necklace and let it fall into her palm. It was warm and shiny.

She closed her fist around it, and looked at herself in the mirror briefly.

She didn't like what she saw, and averted her gaze.

Her tasks for the day completed, she left her room and went downstairs. For the first time in a long time, she was at peace.

****

Dinah and Elise flew home late that afternoon. Dinah's head was still buzzing with what she'd learned. She passed through the security checks and onto the plane without noticing anything around her. Her mind was too busy wondering if she had it right — was the killer Angus? Or someone else altogether? From her companion's silence, Dinah knew that Elise was wondering the same thing.

Elise drove them home from the airport in Norfolk down to Ten Mile Hollow. She could have been driving them to Mars for all Dinah knew, her eyes vacant, mind racing. It was a beautiful drive — the gray skies that brought sleet and rain had lifted, leaving behind a clear, crisp night. Dinah barely noticed until Elise turned into her driveway and found herself staring at the house as though she didn't recognize it.

"What if we've got it wrong?" she asked Elise as they walked from the car to the house. "What if it isn't Angus?"

"I don't know," admitted Elise. "I thought I knew, but it turns out I don't."

Elise called up to Chloe and looked marginally better when she heard her daughter's voice drift down. She opened the refrigerator door and Dinah saw that it was bare.

"I'll order pizza," she suggested.

"Great idea," agreed Elise. "Do you —"

She was interrupted by her cell phone buzzing on the counter. It was Dr. Walker.

"Hello?"

"Hi!" bubbled the medical examiner. "Thought you might find this tidbit of information useful: the DNA found underneath Malia Shaw's fingernails was a match with the swab you took from Angus Whitehall."

Elise sucked in her breath. "Really? Have you got any results back from Lola Albright's body yet?"

"Not yet. You'll be the first to know when we do."

"Thanks, doctor."

Elise hung up and Dinah felt as though she could no longer question Angus being the man who had killed both women. A sense of completion drifted over her. The last piece of the puzzle had fallen into place, and you couldn't argue with DNA.

Dinah and Elise met the following day with the Assistant District Attorney, Tony Steinhardt, for the first time. He wanted to know whether he should prepare for a grand jury. Steinhardt had been in the job for only a few years, but his reputation for being a fawning bootlicker was legendary. The District Attorney, Elliot Parker, was a very smart and very ambitious man, who unashamedly had his eye on the governor's mansion. As a result, he salivated over the high profile and controversial cases that came to their office. A whiff of a political scandal — he slavered. A celebrity misdemeanor — he drooled. A mass shooting or serial killer — he was a rabid dog.

Stature-wise, he was unimpressive. He made up for it with silvery hair and a chiseled face made for the camera. He cut a distinguished figure, sober and grave with the responsibility that rested upon his shoulders.

It was this salubrious example that Tony Steinhardt followed to the letter. Steinhardt was the DA's protégé, which was to say, he groveled at the man's feet the most. His groveling prowess seemed to overrule his less than stellar law school results. Still, as an ADA, he had performed solidly, and Elise grudgingly admitted to Dinah that the case would be in good hands with Steinhardt and his second chair, Elizabeth Masters. Elise knew Elizabeth in passing, and preferred her company to Steinhardt's. She smiled at Elizabeth briefly and turned her attention to Steinhardt.

Steinhardt was not one to engage in small talk, so over Elizabeth's embarrassed look, he said impatiently, "Well, what have you got?"

Dinah raised her eyebrows. She'd worked with prosecutors before and this one, in particular, seemed to lack certain social niceties. It was fortunate that he was such a skilled prosecutor. He'd entered the office empty-handed, but Elizabeth had a notebook and pen.

"Let me begin with Malia Shaw's murder. Several independent eyewitnesses saw the perp in the victim's apartment around the time she was killed. Both gave good descriptions of our suspect and his vehicle, because he'd been there many times before," began Elise. As she spoke, Elizabeth wrote notes at a furious pace.

"Are they reliable witnesses who could testify in court?" Steinhardt asked.

"Yes, I believe so," said Elise. "The perp's alibi is shaky at best and leaves a large hole of unaccounted time right around when the victim was killed. Secondly, we found in both the victim and perpetrator's homes a stash of professional fake passports, social security cards, and drivers' licenses, suggesting close links in the past with illegal activity."

"Really?" Steinhardt's eyebrows shot up. "What sort of illegal activity?"

"I discovered through the course of the investigation that Mr. Whitehall and both the female victims were members of a white supremacist gang years ago in California. They executed violent attacks upon racial minorities. Whitehall was the lieutenant of his group. Then they decided to betray the gang's leader, Randall Shutter, and steal almost a quarter of a million dollars from him. At this point, all three of them vanished. The fourth member of their cell, Harry Purcell, remained loyal to the leader. Both he and Shutter swore revenge against Whitehall and the two women."

"What happened to the money?" Steinhardt asked.

"We traced it to an account solely owned by Angus Whitehall, in his real name. I found that the victim, Malia Shaw, who was a heroin addict with no obvious means of supporting herself, received an amount of about $1,000 a month into her bank account. She also had the lease on her apartment paid for by cash six months in advance, which totaled $1,800. We ran traces on the money and found that via a system of dummy accounts, it came from this original account in Whitehall's alias."

"He was paying her?" Steinhardt asked. "Why?"

"He invoked his right to remain silent," explained Elise. "All he would say was that they were old friends and that he felt compelled to make sure she was okay."

"To the tune of what, $15,000 a year?" Steinhardt shook his head.

"I believe the money was in reality hush money," continued Elise. "Keeping Malia Shaw in plenty of heroin ensured that she wouldn't open her mouth."

"You think the money is the reason he killed her?"

"Yes, I do. We obtained DNA from Mr. Whitehall, and it matches the DNA taken from the victim's apartment and from beneath her fingernails," finished Elise.

"So what's your theory?" Steinhardt asked.

Elise paused thoughtfully. "I think that Whitehall and the victim have known each other for a long time, and share a shocking and violent past. They escaped the gang, knowing that their lives were forfeit once they'd done so. For whatever reason, they've stayed together ever since, relying on false identities to keep themselves safe. He's paying her money, maybe to protect himself, maybe in blackmail? He gets sick of shelling out so much cash and kills her. Though to be honest, she was doing a pretty good job of killing herself with drugs anyway.

The means of the murder is pretty simple. He was already a regular visitor; she knew him and she probably trusted him. She was tiny, only about the size of a teenager. The years of drug abuse left her frail, almost skeletal. Not to mention she was very high the morning she died, according to the medical examiner. He could easily have overpowered her, a small, drugged woman, and it wouldn't be difficult to manually strangle her.

"I believe his motive to be purely financial. He has kids who need to go to college and he wants to further his career, while he's watching the victim shoot *his* money into her veins. Getting rid of her makes perfect financial sense.

"As I've mentioned, his alibi is pretty wobbly. We have eyewitnesses who place him at the apartment the day she died, and he was inexplicably away from work for a good chunk of time, during which he could have easily driven to the victim's apartment, killed her, and gone back to work."

Steinhardt nodded enthusiastically. "And we have the DNA match."

"The case for killing Lola Albright isn't quite as straightforward. She shared the same violent past, but otherwise didn't have the same dependence upon Whitehall. I think that ultimately she was a threat to him in terms of wanting her share of the money and the possibility that she might talk, thereby endangering his life. He has a pretty decent alibi. His wife says he was at home the night Lola died, and she can't be compelled to testify otherwise. We still don't know where Lola was killed, so we don't have any witnesses, nor do we have any DNA linking them together yet."

Steinhardt looked pensive. "Okay," he said, after a few moments. "Here is what we'll do. The evidence for Shaw's murder will take us to a grand jury, and we'll sail through that. Once we've arrested and charged

Whitehall, we'll have some advantage to find out what happened to Lola. Can you keep working on that for us? The important thing, in the meantime, is to make an arrest."

Elise smiled. "Sure. Of course."

Steinhardt was now finished with the conversation and stood up. "Okay," he said briskly. "Let me know about the DNA. I'll organize a grand jury. Anything else?"

That was her dismissal. Elise and Dinah left the office, leaving behind a pumped-up prosecutor and his rather tired-looking second chair wilting beside him.

Now, their focus would be on Lola. There would have to be some way to tie in her murder to Angus Whitehall, and Dinah was determined to find it.

****

The sky was a meekly pale blue, as if too scared to wage a battle against the enormous forces of the cold. The sun watched on from afar, shedding light but no warmth on the frozen ground.

It was a Thursday morning, and Angus had decided to take the day off. He figured he wouldn't be in the role of Ten Mile Hollow First Baptist Church pastor for much longer, and he wanted to prepare. He knew that this would involve having to tell Louise the truth. The thought made him want to violently throw up, but he couldn't see any other way.

When he made his way into the kitchen. Louise was busy getting the kids ready for school, but she'd made him a coffee. "Sorry — you're on your own for breakfast," she said, with a forced smile that was a shadow of its former self. "Grace, we need to leave in ten minutes!"

"But I haven't done my hair!" Grace protested, jamming a piece of toast in her mouth.

"It won't make any difference," chimed in Marcus. "You'll still look like a freak!"

Grace tried to swipe her brother but missed and almost knocked over Angus's coffee.

"Enough!" he snapped. "Get ready for school and stop giving your mother a headache!"

Grace headed for the bathroom after shooting a murderous look at her brother, and Marcus, with a grin on his face, continued to eat his Cheerios. Louise rubbed her eyes, which were red with exhaustion.

Angus knew that it was his fault that his wife wasn't sleeping — he heard her get up several times a night. He hadn't been brave enough to get up to check on her, but his gut instinct told him she would be crying quietly in the family room. He'd rolled over in bed underneath a blanket of bleak shame.

The doorbell rang. Louise shook her head. "Great," she muttered. "I'll get it!"

Angus opened the newspaper and began to read, trying to tune out the chaos around him.

Moments later, the tone in his wife's voice made him start. "Angus. The police are here."

He looked up, and saw Louise's slight and bewildered frame, behind whom towered two uniformed police officers. They looked vaguely familiar. Behind them, stood Detective Elise Jones, her eyes narrowed as she surveyed the family. With her stood the former FBI agent and consultant, Dinah.

"Hi," said Angus. "What can I help you with?"

"You're Angus Whitehall?" asked one of the deputies, with a grizzled beard and weary eyes.

"You know I am," he said.

The other police officer seemed to move like lightning, and Angus felt himself being spun around and his hands wrenched behind his back.

"What —?" he cried, as Louise gasped.

"Mr. Whitehall, you're under arrest for murder in the first degree," explained the grizzled police officer. "You have the right to remain silent . . ."

He went on to recite the Miranda clause, while Angus felt the cold clasp of handcuffs close around his wrists.

"What on *earth* is going on?" Louise demanded, her voice shrill. She asked the question just as Grace appeared at the bottom of the stairs.

"Daddy?" she asked, sounding like a little girl.

Angus felt anger boiling up in his chest. It was precisely this devastating scene he had hoped to avoid. He wrested himself out of the deputy's grasp. "Please don't worry," he said, calmly. "It's just a misunderstanding, okay? I'll take care of it."

As the two police officers began to lead him toward the front door, he called out to Louise, "Call my lawyer, honey. Have him meet me at the police station."

She nodded, her eyes wide and frightened. There was something else in them, too: a resignation, a sad understanding that this had been inevitable.

He added: "I haven't done anything wrong!"

Louise's eyes betrayed her. She struggled to maintain composure on the surface, but he could see she was full of doubt. It had come as no surprise to her that he'd been arrested for first-degree murder.

With that, he was dragged unceremoniously to the police car. Once inside, Detective Elise Jones slid in beside him.

"Your timing was impeccable," he said, the shock making him feel like he couldn't draw a proper breath. "Thanks for doing it in front of my kids."

They sat in silence for several moments, then Elise said: "I'm sorry. It couldn't be helped."

Angus sighed. "Detective, I really didn't kill her."

Elise pursed her lips for a moment. "Then why won't you tell me the truth? I've told you repeatedly that I'm willing to help you if you'd only be honest. If you're not willing to do that, you tie my hands." She added, "I know who you really are, Robert Langer."

He nodded and sat back, closing his eyes. It was not the police he lived in fear of.

"Then you must know," he said, "that we have many enemies. They are the ones you should be looking for, not me."

"Like Harry Purcell?"

"Yes!"

"Well, Mr. Whitehall, the problem is that the evidence doesn't point to Harry Purcell. It points to you."

Several moments later, they arrived at the Sherriff's Office.

Angus was stashed in a gray, windowless room furnished with a rickety table and two hollow, metal chairs. His handcuffs were removed, but it seemed like he was in the room for an eon before Detective Jones appeared, accompanied by Dinah.

Dinah stood at the back of the small room with a thin file in hand. Detective Jones read him the Miranda clause again. "Do you understand?" she finished.

Angus nodded. "I'd like my lawyer," he said. "I don't wish to say anything else at this time."

Jones glanced at Dinah and shrugged. "He's on his way."

They both left the room.

Angus sat back in his chair. He looked down and noticed that his hands were shaking badly — from fear and dread. The truth would finally come out. Would it set him free?

Two hours later, Angus sat in that bare, cold police interview room with his lawyer, Julian Taylor, seated beside him, and Dinah Harris and Detective Elise Jones opposite him. ADA Tony Steinhardt stood with Sheriff Wilder behind the mirrored glass, listening.

"I want to reiterate," said Taylor, "that in return for my client's open and honest testimony, and for assistance in bringing the correct perpetrator to justice, you will give him full immunity from crimes committed while a member of the Southern Cross Militia."

"As the district attorney explained," said Detective Jones, impatiently. "There is no statute of limitations for attempted murder in the state of California. All we can do is recommend to prosecutors there that any charge be downgraded. Assuming your story checks out, of course."

Angus looked at his lawyer, who nodded. He took a deep breath, and mentally transported himself back to a time more than 20 years ago, when every base instinct was for violence and every moment of pleasure derived from hurting others.

"I was born in a small town in Southern California," he began. "My father was a metal worker and an alcoholic. My mother left us when I was about five. My father was a mean drunk, abusive to my mother and me. She eventually had enough and left. I haven't seen her since, although several years ago I heard that she'd been hospitalized for a mental illness and died there. Once she was gone, Dad drank more and I copped more of his abuse. I also got an earful of his hatred and prejudice.

"Dad always thought Mom had run off with a man she'd worked with — a Mexican man. I grew up hearing about how cunning and mean and dishonest minorities were, that they hated us and that we'd be better off without them. He hated African-Americans, Hispanics, Asians, Jews, Arabs, and anyone without white skin, equally. I heard my father call them every name under the sun.

"Growing up in southern California, I saw clearly that there were problems between different people groups. When the Rodney King riots erupted in Los Angeles, my father used them to hammer home the point that black people were dangerous and hated us, and that we should do everything in our power to eradicate them. He wanted America to be as it once had been — a nation of white people who held all the power. I agreed with him, because it was the only time that I felt close to him, that I felt he was proud of me. Instead of clipping me around the ear for being stupid, he'd clap me on the back and tell me that I understood life, the way things ought to be.

"By the time high school was finished, I was committed to the cause of hatred. I made life difficult for a few minorities in my grade. I was too smart to cause physical confrontation, but I'd deface their books and put KKK symbols in their lockers and call them terrible names. Then I'd go home and tell my father, and he'd laugh. He'd crack me open a beer and we'd sit down and drink together like we were good buddies."

He stopped and took a trembling breath. "You must believe me when I tell you that I don't believe any of that stuff anymore. I've changed completely. I became a Christian, and now I believe that every human being is created in God's image and is valuable. I no longer see people in terms of the shade of their skin or their facial features. I see them as brothers and sisters of mine, a blood relation. In fact, now I thoroughly believe that we are all one blood, as the Bible says. And that's exactly why I can't kill anyone, let alone Malia and Lola, Detective. I'm finished with violence and bloodshed. I want my life to be about the opposite now."

Detective Jones nodded. "Duly noted. Please continue."

"I met Randall Shutter after I started at college. We met at a bar and just started talking. We became friends and I guess we soon realized we shared a lot in common. He often talked about having a covert army undertaking attacks on minorities all across the region. Several meetings later, he told me about the Southern Cross Militia.

"He brought sophisticated planning, the cold, ruthless violence of an experienced killer. He taught me everything he knew, and I was a willing student. When I introduced Shutter to my father, Dad was enthralled. He saw in Shutter everything he'd wanted to be. I wanted Dad to be proud, so I listened to everything Shutter said. Dad admired him, and I wanted Dad to look at me the way he looked at Shutter."

Angus stopped for a moment to take a long drink of water.

"He was an experienced killer. He'd gotten a taste for it during the Vietnam War. Back on American soil, he had been murdering here and there, but what he really craved was attention and notoriety. He thought a militia could bring him some of that. Nobody had ever caught him, and this was why he was so charismatic. In our minds, we were freedom fighters. When he stood up to talk to us, we saw him as a fearsome and awesome leader.

"He planned everything to perfection. Each of us had a specific job to do, based on our strengths. I didn't know much about explosives or planning violence, but what I *could* do was recruit."

Angus stopped again as memory rose in him like a bitter wave. The room was silent and motionless, as if nobody dared moved or interrupt.

"I was young, cocky, and good-looking in those days," he continued. "Because my father had spent a lifetime teaching me about ways in which one could control and abuse others, I was able to pick out potential recruits who could be easily influenced.

"I'd pick the loners, those who were new in town, those with low self-confidence, those who wanted to fit in, those who desperately wanted friendship. I'd move in, strike up conversation, invite them to meet some of my friends, and eventually we'd reel them in. I didn't tell them that we belonged to the Southern Cross Militia specifically, or that we were white supremacists. They didn't need to know that initially. But over time, they would eventually come around to our way of thinking because they wanted to be part of our group.

"Meanwhile, while I was recruiting and swelling our numbers, some of the other guys were planning attacks. The way Randall Shutter wanted to do things was to make a big statement, something that would jolt the conscience of the mainstream. He wanted something big."

Angus looked up and he started to see recognition dawn on the faces of those around him. They were starting to remember Randall Shutter and the Southern Cross Militia atrocities of the 1980s and '90s.

"So he organized us all into groups of three or four and tasked us with various jobs. The jobs included things like harassment, stalking, intimidation, and violence. Those of us who were most loyal got the jobs that were the most difficult."

His stomach tightened, sick at the memory. A wave of nausea rolled over him.

"My group and I would go out during the night and prey upon minority people who were alone — walking home from work, going for a jog. We'd ambush them and . . . beat them up, kick them."

Angus remembered the feeling of splintering bone beneath his fist; the wet, gasping cry as his boot found purchase in the soft yield of an abdomen; the pouring, startlingly red blood.

There was more silence in the room, equally stunned and horrified.

The news reports of the attacks had warned minorities not to venture out at night alone. Yet, determined not to be cowed, many still did. Angus had not been the only cell targeting minorities; Randall Shutter had three other cells attacking at various points across the wider L.A. area.

"Who was in your group?" Steinhardt asked.

"Me, another guy named Harry Purcell, Malia Shaw, and Lola Albright," said Angus. "We had different names in those days. The girls would be the bait — they didn't look threatening. They'd pretend their car had broken down or that one of them had broken an ankle or something like that. When the victim stopped to help, Harry and I would jump out. The next day, Randall Shutter would call the press and claim responsibility, always giving them the message that minorities needed to leave the area, and that the attacks would continue until they did."

Angus remembered watching the nightly newscasts, proud that Southern California was gripped with such fear, proud that he was in part responsible for the terror lurking in the night. The Southern Cross Militia and their message of white supremacy became infamous.

He didn't tell the room how the savagery became satisfying; that the rush of adrenaline that accompanied each attack became addictive. He didn't tell them how he'd experimented with new ways to inflict pain, or that he read accounts of other attacks and copied some of their methods. He didn't tell them of his descent from violence into utter chaos, utter darkness, utter evil, nor of how easy it was to spiral into madness where the only bright spot was the anticipation of further harm. He shuddered, guilt and shame queasy bedfellows in his stomach.

"Shutter didn't participate in attacks himself. He planned them and provided us with weapons and other gear, but he never took part. I suppose this was to protect himself. I found out his activities involved extortion and blackmail, and that he'd been building up a nice chunk of cash for himself. I started getting a little angry. We were living like a true militia, never staying long in one place, always in shabby, backwater houses. Meanwhile, he was sitting on a mountain of cash. What's worse is that he lied about it. When I asked him, he pretended he had no idea what I was talking about. So I started to think about taking it."

"You wanted to leave the militia?" asked Elise.

"No," he said. "But I wanted the money. And the two were mutually exclusive. But I knew Malia and Lola wanted to leave; the violence had never sat well with them. They did it because I wanted them to, and I didn't know how long they'd be able to keep it up. So we hatched a plan, and I promised to share the money with them afterward and we'd look out for each other."

"That explains the false identity documents, the lack of personal history, the money, right?" said Elise.

"The Southern Cross Militia would never forgive me for betraying a brother. We needed to vanish and start new lives, with new identities. Initially, we moved around a fair bit, always worried they'd find us. Eventually, we picked a small town and settled down, thinking it'd be less obvious. I thought it would be difficult for Shutter to find us here."

Since then, they knew that Randall Shutter had been captured, charged, and now lived on death row in California. It had made sensational headlines at the time.

"So you came to Virginia, and Malia and Lola followed you here?"

"They didn't follow me, so to speak," said Angus. "We agreed to stay together. We felt there was safety in numbers; we could look out for each other. But Malia was starting to fall apart, so we agreed to use some of the money to help her." *And I wanted to keep an eye on them. I didn't want them to talk to the wrong people. I didn't want them to think they would ever be safe on their own, if truth be told.*

"What happened to Malia?" Elise asked.

She was forever damaged by the things I made her do. "She had participated in some pretty awful things," said Angus. "Terrible violence, and she just couldn't deal with it. She had already started to take drugs to distract herself from the guilt and shame. I understand what she was feeling; I felt it, too. So did Lola. But Malia had always been more fragile, more easily disturbed. I felt responsible for her, because I'd recruited her into the Militia in the first place. That's why I've taken care of her all these years."

"Were there any people in particular that you were afraid of coming to find you?" asked Dinah.

"I always thought about Harry Purcell, the only member of our cell who wasn't part of the deal," said Angus. "He could have been resentful or angry that we'd turned on Shutter, or that he'd been left out. Or someone come to do Shutter's bidding from prison."

"Let's talk now about Malia Shaw. You saw her on the day she died, is that correct?" asked Elise.

"Yes, I did. I checked in on her that morning. I'd taken an early lunch." Angus glanced at his lawyer, who was so far happy with the questioning.

"What did you find?"

"She was sprawled on the couch, a needle near her arm. It was obvious she'd shot up recently. I thought she should sleep it off in bed, rather than on the couch, so I picked her up." *She was a bag of bones*, he remembered. "As I was carrying her to the bedroom, she woke up with a gasp. She didn't recognize me straight away, and she lashed out at me, clawing my face. I put her on her bed, made sure she was safe, and left. That's the last time I saw her alive."

He leaned forward and looked Detective Jones in the eye. "I know I've done a lot of bad things in my life. But I did not kill Malia or Lola. I swear on my own life that I did not kill those women."

****

If Judge George Emmett was surprised to see friend and pastor, Angus Whitehall, in his courtroom for a bail hearing that afternoon, he didn't show it. He simply read the schedule, looked up at the lawyers and said, "This is a bail hearing for the accused, Mr. Angus Whitehall."

"Yes, Your Honor," the lawyers chorused.

"Let's make it quick," he suggested. He turned to the prosecutor. "What does the Commonwealth of Virginia have to say?"

"We'd like bail to be denied," Steinhardt said. "Mr. Whitehall is a man of means, with cash at his disposal. In addition, the police found several false identification documents in his possession, of which there could be more. He faces criminal charges in the state of California, where he once fled the law. It's clear he has a history of trying to escape the charges laid against him. These factors mean he poses a definite flight risk. He also has significant assets he could use to aid his flight."

"Counselor?" the judged asked of the defense table.

"Your Honor," began Taylor. "Mr. Whitehall is the pastor of this town and he vigorously defends his innocence. He is a citizen of good standing in this community, with a wife and children. He has lived here for 20 years, which would indicate that any past notions of fleeing are well and truly gone. He intends to fight all charges laid against him. He has an impeccable reputation with links to the community. We would ask that bail be set at a sensible amount of $250,000."

Angus knew that this was a ridiculous request; there was no way a judge would set bail so low for a capital crime. But the lawyers wanted to start low and negotiate up.

"Your Honor," protested Steinhardt. "The defendant is wanted in two states for violent crime and has a history of fleeing the law!"

"My client acknowledges crimes committed in his youth," said Taylor. "Despite many previous opportunities to flee, he has proven to be a man of his word and has stayed to defend all charges."

Judge Emmett was not one to listen to continuing flowery arguments by either side. He looked thoughtful for several minutes. "This is my ruling. The motion for bail is granted, set at one million dollars. If the defendant cannot afford to pay the bail, he must be taken back to jail." Emmett banged his gavel.

Steinhardt looked crestfallen.

Angus knew that his family home would now be put on the line as he fought to prove his innocence. The thought of telling Louise caused his heart to speed up with unease. He shook hands with Julian Taylor. "Thank you," he said. "It'll be good to go home."

"Of course," Taylor said. "There'll be some paperwork to fill out first, then you are free to go."

He turned to look at his family, who sat in the gallery behind him. Louise was dry-eyed and gaunt, her stare a long gaze at nothing.

He moved to the railing and reached over to his children. Grace and Marcus joined the hug; Grace was crying and Marcus repeated, "Are you coming home, Dad? Are you coming home?"

Angus put his hand on the boy's thin shoulder and said, hardly believing the words himself, "I'm coming home, son."

The bail paperwork was completed in the empty courtroom. Angus used his house to guarantee the bail, signed a small mountain of forms, and was now free to go.

Out on the front steps to the courtroom, a throng of media was waiting. As Angus and his family emerged into the sunlight, he stopped to enjoy the feeling of golden warmth upon his cheeks. The media converged on him, all asking questions at once, shoving microphones and recording devices in his face.

Angus blinked, and then Julian Taylor pushed forward to give a statement. Angus couldn't help but feel he'd fallen through the looking glass into a strange and confusing world. Finally, the family managed to get into the car, and Angus sat behind the wheel.

Louise quietly asked, "What happened?"

"I posted bail," he told her. "I used the house as surety."

She nodded and said nothing more. She was still so pale, her skin as white as bleached bone.

They arrived home ten minutes later, and Angus drank in the sight of his home, the place where he'd built his life with his family. He spent 20 minutes sitting in the living room, talking things through with Grace and Marcus, assuaging their fears and just enjoying their company. One of the reasons he would fight these charges vociferously was because he couldn't bear to be without his kids. Louise stayed in the kitchen, silently preparing lunch.

Finally, the kids had talked themselves out and went upstairs before lunch. Angus walked into the kitchen and found Louise, crying silently as she fixed sandwiches.

"I'm sorry," he said, miserable. The weight of all he'd done had never been so heavy.

"Uh . . . excuse me, sorry," said Grace from the entrance to the kitchen. "I found something Chloe must have left here accidentally. Can I quickly go to her place and give it back?"

Angus saw a thin, gold chain dangling from his daughter's hand.

"Sure," said Louise, her voice brittle. "She hasn't been around for a while, has she?"

"Uh . . . no," said Grace, a very strange expression crossing her face.

"Okay. Well, just be back soon for lunch, okay?"

Grace left, and Angus looked at his wife once again. "Please, talk to me," he begged.

Louise didn't answer, but took a plate of sandwiches up to Marcus's room. "You can eat up here," he heard Louise tell their son.

She returned, and the glassy, disassociated stare she wore on her face started to scare Angus a little.

"Louise?"

Louise put down the plate of sandwiches she'd been holding and turned to Angus.

She slapped him as hard as she could, right across the face.

****

Angus rocked backward, stunned by the fury in his wife's face. Her eyes burned hot and dangerous, like furious embers spat out by a brushfire. Angus held a hand to his face, where it stung, and backed away. He had never seen this side of his wife, who was normally gentle.

"Louise," he gasped. "What —?"

"Do you have any idea what you have done to me and this family?" she demanded, advancing upon him. Angus had never seen such raw, naked rage. It emanated from Louise like waves shimmering from the blacktop at the zenith of a summer's day. More surprising, it was coming from a woman who had never raised her voice to him in her life.

"I —" he began.

"You have *no* idea!" Louise informed him. "Your life — this life you've built with me — was founded on *lies!*"

"I —"

"You couldn't trust me with the truth of your life," she continued. "I fell in love with the man that I met, not the man that you once were. How many of us can lay claim to a perfect life? It might have surprised you to learn that I'd have been able to deal with the truth!"

Angus got the sense that he wasn't supposed to say anything.

"Not once during the last 20 years has it crossed your mind to tell me the truth, has it? Despite the fact that you've been secretly meeting with Malia and Lola every single week for those past 20 years, you never even tried to tell me the truth. It's nice to find out that I'm worth less to you than friends of yours. I am your *wife!*" She was shouting, tendons standing out on her neck with the sheer effort of channeling her anger.

"You —"

"I only find out when you are about to be arrested for *murder!* I mean, you were backed into a corner, and suddenly you needed my support. Suddenly, *you* needed *me*. Guess there's a first time for everything, right?" Louise gave a strangled laugh that contained no humor. "I don't even know your real name. I mean, can you believe that your wife of *20 years* doesn't even know your real name? You want me to tell you some truth now? I've been on the receiving end, and now I have some truth for you. I don't want you to come home!"

"Louise, I'm sorry," he pleaded. "How could I possibly tell you what I'd done? You were a beautiful woman from a Christian home —"

He was interrupted by the phone. With a jerking movement, Louise picked it up. "Hello?" she said, her voice shaky.

Even Angus, across the kitchen, heard the reply. "*Mommy!*" shrieked Grace, her voice hysterical. Angus felt fear shudder through him, bright and painful and quick. Louise gripped the phone with a clenched fist.

"What?" she asked, sharply. "*What?*"

"You have to come here! You have to come here *now!*" Grace was sobbing, almost unable to catch her breath. Then he heard her make an awful, keening noise that reminded him of a severely injured animal.

The fear grew teeth that bit into him.

"Where are you?" she shouted.

"Chloe's! Chloe's house!" There was a crash that indicated his daughter had dropped the phone, and he heard Grace crying out, almost screaming.

Louise looked at Angus, shaking all over, indecision on her face.

"Chloe's house," replied Angus, already moving toward the front door and their car. "Get Marcus, get Marcus!"

Louise dashed upstairs and came down again, dragging Marcus behind her. Once they'd all climbed into the car, Angus drove as fast as he dared, the two blocks to where Chloe Jones lived. They rocketed around corners, tires screeching, and it still felt entirely too slow.

Angus glimpsed Grace standing at the front of the Jones' house, and for a brief moment he was relieved to see she was standing, seemingly unhurt. But then he saw the wild fear on her face, and realized that she was indeed hurting.

He'd barely parked the car before he and Louise flew from the car. "What is it?" he asked. "What's wrong?"

Grace was trembling violently, pointing toward the house. "Chloe. It's Chloe." Then she collapsed in her mother's arms, sobs convulsing her body.

Angus raced through the front door, urgency eventually giving way to trepidation. "Chloe!" he called out. "Chloe, are you okay?"

The lower floor of the house seemed untroubled and quiet. He then walked up the stairs and instinctively knew to check Chloe's room first. The door was slightly ajar, and he pushed it open, unsure what would be facing him.

The horror was almost too much to understand at first. He saw her feet first, dangling six inches above the floor. His eyes traveled upward, hoping that his gut instinct was wrong. When he digested the entire situation, a choked sound burst from his throat. He rushed forward to undo the belt that Chloe had used to hang herself.

In the distance, he heard the wail of an ambulance.

He lay the still, pale girl down on the ground, took one of her cool hands, and placing his mouth over her blue lips began trying to breathe life back into her.

The case all but over, Dinah had spent lunch with Elise and Lewis, thinking about going home, about seeing Aaron again, and about returning to her church.

After lunch, Lewis drove them home. He was a steady and methodical driver, and Dinah felt much safer in the car with Lewis behind the wheel.

Lewis turned the car into their street. The strange flickering of light made Dinah look up. Because she'd seen them so many times in her work, she knew that they were the strafing lights of an ambulance, and it sent an electrical shiver of intuition up her spine.

As Lewis drew closer to his home, and she saw the ambulance parked in the driveway, Dinah realized with sudden, cold clarity that whatever was happening was happening to her friend. She saw a crowd of people, all looking at Elise's house, with the titillation disguised as sympathy she'd seen at so many crime scenes.

Then she saw the stretcher leaving the house via the front door. The still figure upon it was clearly Chloe. Wild instinct seemed to overtake Elise. She opened the car door and fell out, the car not quite at a standstill.

"Elise!" shouted Lewis. "Wait!"

Dinah jumped out, following Elise. Stumbling on her hands and knees, she looked up and saw Angus Whitehall alongside Chloe as the paramedics reached the ambulance. The only thought she could formulate was *what on earth is he doing here?*

Then she saw Elise. Fury that was perfect in its heat had consumed her. Elise pushed through the crowd of bystanders, shoving them aside with the strength of a mother desperate to get to her child. She ran as fast as she could toward Angus. Dinah followed her.

"What have you done?" Elise shrieked. "What have you done to my daughter!"

He turned, saw her and put his hands up in a protective gesture. It didn't help. Once she was upon him, Elise used her fists and feet, punching and kicking wildly. "What have you *done*?" she shouted. "If you've hurt my child I swear I'll kill you! I'll make you hurt! I'll —!"

"Chloe —!" Angus tried to speak.

"Elise!" Dinah tried to interject.

"You stay away from my family!" Elise shrieked. It was so raw and terrible that everyone fell silent.

Angus retreated, trying to protect himself. The paramedics loaded Chloe into the back of the ambulance as Lewis arrived, the only voice of reason amid the flooding wash of Elise's panic. He folded his arms around his wife. "It's okay," he said. "Let's find out what happened. Elise. Take a few deep breaths."

Elise's knees buckled, and she allowed Lewis's embrace to support her. Dinah took a step back, and only then she did see Louise, who stood with her arm around Marcus, her face white and shocked.

One of the paramedics put his hand on Elise's arm; an empathic gesture, but one to get her attention. "Are you Mrs. Jones?" he asked. His face was grave.

"Detective. I'm Detective Jones," Elise said, her voice weak. "What happened? What happened?"

"I believe your daughter has attempted to take her own life, Mrs. Jones," said the paramedic. "She was discovered by a young lady named Grace, who called her parents and 911."

His words tinkled around them like delicate glass. "Take her own life? What? Are you telling me she tried to commit *suicide?*"

"Detective Jones," he said. "Please get in the ambulance. We need to get her to the hospital urgently."

Elise didn't seem to comprehend his words. She turned toward Dinah. "This cannot be happening. This is not happening. Am I dreaming?"

Dinah didn't know what to do. Her feet felt stuck fast to the grass. "Elise, I'm so sorry, I —"

"Come on," said Lewis, gently. He guided Elise into the back of the ambulance, where the other paramedic was performing chest compressions on Chloe. Her whole body leaped with the force of the paramedic's ministrations. When Dinah saw this, her stomach twisted with a violent heave.

Elise moaned. "I can't, I can't," she cried. "Don't make me get in there. I can't watch that!"

Dinah knew how her friend was feeling. Despite being police, despite seeing death as part of their jobs, it was very different when it was your own child whose life was slipping away. She remembered the doctors working on her son, wondering how she could just sit there while the life of her son leaked out slowly, while the doctor cracked his ribs in an effort to keep his heart beating. She knew too much, she'd seen too much. She'd seen it happen to countless people she didn't know. When it was her own child, she couldn't bear it.

Lewis understood. "I'll go with you," he told the paramedic. "Someone, please drive Elise to the hospital." As quick as a flash, the ambulance doors closed, Lewis and Chloe inside, and it wailed off down the street. They all watched it go.

Elise looked like she was moving through a different world, thick and soupy as a dream. She walked jerkily five steps away and then back again.

"I'll take her to the hospital," said Louise.

Angus said, "Sorry . . . I . . ."

"What?" Dinah asked.

He took a deep breath. "I'm sorry, Detective," he said. "I . . . I cut her down. I tried to . . ."

Elise simply stared at him dumbly.

Louise touched her shoulder. "Detective, I'll —"

She was interrupted by a loud wail. Grace, who'd been standing near the flowerbed hugging herself, had turned an alarming shade of old bone-gray. She turned and threw up violently into the flowerbed, her entire body a convulsion. She took a few steps toward them, looking like a jittery newborn giraffe, unable to find its feet. Then her eyes rolled back in her head and she collapsed into a limp heap upon the lawn.

"What is going on? What is going on?" Elise demanded of no one in particular. "I need to get to the hospital! I need to —" She banged at her chest, as though something was clogging her airways.

Dinah stepped into the middle. Nearby, Louise and Angus picked up Grace, who had regained consciousness but was groggy and confused.

"Here's what we'll do," declared Dinah, taking charge. "Louise, take Detective Jones and Grace to the hospital. I'll drive Angus and Marcus home. Call me and I'll bring down anything you need, okay?"

Louise tried to pick up Grace, who had regained consciousness and was moaning. "Come on, honey," she said. "Let's get you to the hospital."

"You don't understand!" the girl sobbed. "It's my fault! It's all my fault."

Dinah sensed that Grace wasn't being melodramatic, but since she had completely lost the ability to understand what was happening around her, she said, "Please. You need to go to the hospital."

"It's my . . . my fault," hiccupped Grace, blonde hair covering her face. She struggled to stand up. "The others were so . . . horrible to her. I used to be her friend. I used to stand up . . . for her."

Louise supported her daughter toward the car and helped her in. Elise sat beside the girl while Louise climbed into the driver's seat and tried to start the car with shaking hands.

"What happened?" Dinah heard Elise ask.

Grace cried, shuddering for several moments. "Y-y-you," she said, finally. "You were trying to put *my dad* in jail! How could I be friends with her after that?"

Dinah saw the force of the girl's words slam into Elise as if they were a physical blow.

Elise gasped as if she suddenly couldn't breathe.

"I stopped being her friend," Grace was saying. "The others started . . . bullying her even worse. She begged me to make them stop, but I was so . . . angry with her I ignored her. I knew the girls were being really horrible to her. But I just didn't do anything!"

Elise tried to get some air into her lungs.

"After Dad made bail at the courthouse, I came home and found that she left her gold necklace here in an envelope."

"Yes," agreed Louise. Her voice was high-pitched and she spoke too fast. "She came by the house a few days ago, and asked me to give it to you."

"It was the necklace with a C on it," said Grace. "I . . . I gave it to her for her birthday and it was really special to her. I thought it was a mistake . . . but she was . . . she was . . . she gave it to me to say goodbye!"

Her last word was almost a shriek; so desolate it made Dinah's bones go cold.

Elise bent over double, hugging herself. Dinah could hear her struggling to breathe.

"If I'd just . . . if I'd been quicker . . . if I hadn't —"

Louise glanced in the rearview mirror, then put her foot down on the accelerator. She drove, erratic and jerky, down the street. Dinah stared after them, numbly unable to do anything except pray.

Please don't let today be the day Chloe dies. Not like this, Lord. Please.

****

Angus Whitehall found himself in a state of anxiety that was so bad he felt like throwing up. On one hand, he was still a suspect in two murders. On the other hand, he had just seen a beautiful 15-year-old girl, the best friend of his daughter, attempt suicide, and perhaps successfully so. Every part of his body trembled with fear and uncertainty. He sat in the passenger seat, his hands dancing all over his lap. He couldn't keep them still.

Dinah drove. She was quiet, concentrating on her task. He couldn't even imagine what she was thinking.

He looked around to the back seat and saw Marcus staring out of the window. He didn't look good either. His face was pale. "You okay, buddy?" he asked.

"Yeah," mumbled Marcus. "Can I go over to Jett's place?"

"Well, sure, if that's okay with Jett's mom. Do you want to talk about anything?"

Marcus hesitated. "Not yet, Dad. I just want to be with my friend."

He probably needed some normality, reflected Angus. A reminder of a place where he could just be a kid, without the burden of a father who had possibly murdered people and a mother and sister who were at the hospital with a suicide victim.

"Would you mind dropping Marcus off at his friend's house?" he asked. "I don't trust myself behind the wheel right now."

"No trouble at all," said Dinah.

They dropped Marcus off at Jett's house, where Jett's mother greeted him with a big hug. Marcus seemed relieved to be away from his father's company. It felt like a stab in the heart to Angus as he watched his son go gladly into someone else's house. *Is this just another of my failures? Failure as a father?*

At home, the house was quiet and empty. Dinah fixed them both a cup of coffee, and Angus sat down in the living room to try to make sense of what was happening.

Dinah entered the room and stood awkwardly. "I'm going to get some clothes and toiletries together for Louise and Grace," she said. "Is it all right with you to go into their rooms?"

"Sure," said Angus. He was numb, he was tired, he wanted to sleep through this entire nightmare.

She seemed to hesitate, then she said, "When things are tough for me, I usually go to the Psalms. It reminds me I'm not alone in my suffering and that God hears our cries."

Angus felt the onslaught of tears rush up his throat. "I'm . . . I'm not sure I deserve God at the moment," he whispered.

Dinah smiled. "I understand. Thankfully God doesn't feel the same way. When we are weak, he is our strength."

The bones in his body seemed to have turned to limp spaghetti. He could not hold himself up. "Thank you."

She nodded and left the room. Angus took a deep, shuddering breath. He tried to pray, to corral his thoughts the way a farmer tries to calm a jittery horse. But his sense of failure seemed too great. *I am so inadequate, Lord,* was all he could think to say. *So full of sin and so unworthy of You.* He could only repeat the same prayer over and over in his mind. Then he heard the front door close softly. *I didn't hear the car,* he thought, *but I'm glad they're home.* He wondered if Chloe was okay.

Strangely, he didn't hear the usual noise of Grace thumping toward the stairs or Louise dropping her belongings in the entry. He waited a few more moments, then got up with a frown. He had taken only a couple of steps when he saw the figure silhouetted in the living room doorway.

"Hello, Robert," the figure said, his face in shadow. "Or should I call you Angus?"

Angus gripped his coffee mug, his hands at once slippery with sweat. "Who are you and what are you doing in my house?"

The figure stepped forward, revealing a tall, thin man with a seamed face the shade of coffee, and grizzled white hair cropped close to his head. He had to be in his sixties, at least. He looked vaguely familiar.

"Don't know who I am, Robert?" He stood in a relaxed way, his weight on the balls of his feet.

"No," said Angus. His voice sounded weak. He cleared his throat and tried to speak with authority. "You have three seconds to get out before I call the police."

The man laughed. "The police are your friends now, huh? Guess things have changed."

Angus stared at him, trying to place his face. It took a few minutes for his fear-filtered brain to make the connection. "You're the guy from the pawnbrokers across the street!" he said. "I saw you there, near Malia's house!"

"Blake Watson," said the old man. "That's me. Guilty as charged."

"What are you doing here?" asked Angus.

Watson smiled. "I'm here to finish the job."

"What do you mean?"

All at once, Watson had a gun trained on Angus, pointed straight at his head. "I killed Malia. I killed Lola. Now it's your turn."

Angus dropped the mug in his hands. It fell to the hardwood floor and shattered. For one crazy moment, Angus remembered he had done exactly the same thing the night he had learned Malia had been murdered. "Wh — what are you talking about?"

"San Diego, 21 years ago." He looked at Angus sharply. "Do you know what happened in San Diego 21 years ago?"

"Oh . . . well. . . ." Angus searched his memory furiously, trying to remember what Watson knew about the Southern Cross Militia.

Watson crossed the room in two strides and put the gun to Angus's temple. Angus's knees went weak and rubbery, but he knew it would be over if he fell to the floor. So he forced himself to remain upright.

"Twenty-one years ago, my son, Jordan, walked home from work at about 11 o'clock at night. He was a respiratory therapist at a private hospital. My wife and I had come from long lines of poverty, and I had worked hard all my life so that my kids could get an education. Jordan was seriously considering applying for medical school. He was the smartest person I ever knew, that boy. So smart, just like his mama. In the meantime, he had a good job and he was a good boy. He was only three blocks from home when four monsters jumped him."

The old man's eyes were red and watery, but they did not waver. In that moment, he looked very old, the weight of grief heavy on his shoulders.

"There were two girls. They told him their car had broken down. He was such a nice kid he didn't think twice about helping them. The girls lured him to an alleyway, and two men attacked him. While he was down, they continued to beat him and kick him. Then they left him for dead, in a stinking alleyway, like he was worth nothing more than trash!"

Angus remembered now. The thrill had been hot lava in his veins. He had been consumed with desire to do nothing else but inflict pain and suffering on his victim. He remembered with the heavy coldness of shame.

"We always waited up for our kids. When he wasn't home by midnight, I knew something was wrong. I just knew. We started looking for Jordan at about two in the morning," continued Watson, not blinking. "We found him at about three. He was unconscious, but still alive."

He paused and jammed the gun roughly against Angus's head. "Jordan was in a coma and had suffered catastrophic brain injury. He's never woken up, to this day. He lives in a home and my wife visits him every single day. He's wasted away to almost nothing. He looks like a skeleton lying in a bed. He's fed with a tube. He can't think or speak or read or love. He might as well be dead."

Angus could no longer stand. He sank to his knees. "How did you find me?"

"Your friend Harry Purcell spilled his guts in prison, to me and to the state. He turned on you just as you turned on your leader. But by then you'd vanished, and so had my chance for justice. There was no justice for my Jordan or for my wife."

With his free hand, Watson took Angus by the chin so that he was forced to look into the sad eyes of the old man. "These hands, they earned a living for my family while my wife raised our kids. These hands loved my kids and trained them up right. When my Jordan was taken from us, I swore that these hands would avenge him because the law failed to do it. And so that's what I did. I used these hands to choke the life out of those two wretched women, and I'll use these hands to kill you, too."

Just like that, Angus realized his life was forfeit and that it was the right and just thing that ought to be done. He had run away; he had pretended to be someone else. But when all was stripped bare, he was who he had always been.

Violent, hateful, despicable, unworthy. That is who I am.

****

It was revenge; the whole thing boiled down to simple revenge. A man had lost his son and took justice for himself. Angus had to admire the man. Would he have done the same thing, if the roles were reversed? Didn't he understand his anger? There was something authentically basic about his desire for justice. It was human nature to try to right wrongs. He couldn't really blame the grieving father. For Blake Watson, Angus had escaped justice. It was therefore his job to seek it.

However, it was not easy to be pragmatic about this while a gun was pressed to his head.

"What did you do?" he asked Watson. "With Malia and Lola?"

Watson scratched a scrap of beard. "I broke into Lola's home pretty easily," he began. "The place was pretty dead. The door lock was pretty old and I used a screwdriver to break the lock. I went into the house and hid in her bedroom."

"How did you know she was coming home?"

"I watched her for a long time. I knew her routine. She went to work and she came home. Sometimes she stopped at Joaquin's for a drink. But even then, she'd always come home. I just waited for her. As soon as she walked into the bedroom, I attacked her. I strangled her, as you probably know."

Pretty straightforward, thought Angus, *when one is describing the method of murdering another human being.* He couldn't stop shaking. "But her body wasn't found there, was it?" Angus tried to recall what the detective had told him. "Wasn't the body found out in the woods or something?"

"Guess I learned my lesson," admitted Watson. "I hoped it would buy me time. I took her from the duplex and drove out of town."

"Did she fight back?"

"She tried, but it wasn't any good. I took her by surprise; I was taller and stronger than her. She flailed around some, knocked some stuff over. But I fixed it up before I took her away."

"How did you track us down?"

Watson smiled eerily. "That age-old mistake made by people who try to disappear; they contact loved ones from their old lives. Lola kept in contact with her grandmother. From there, it was easy. I didn't know that all three of you had stuck together and actually lived in this town. So I got lucky in that respect."

No, you didn't get lucky. We got what we deserved. "So what happened with Malia?" he asked, weakly.

Watson shrugged. "There's not much to tell. I walked across the street; I opened her apartment door. She was in the bedroom, half-asleep on the bed. I could see she'd recently taken a hit of dope. I walked right up to her, strangled her, and left her. Nobody came to check on her for two days. I know, because I watched from across the street."

"How did you get in the apartment?"

"I'd made myself a copy of her key," explained Watson. "She used to come into my shop from time to time. She told me once that she loved looking at pieces of other people's history. I lifted her keys once and made a copy."

Angus couldn't help but look at his hands, powerful enough to squeeze the life out of another. "When did you arrive in town?"

"About a year ago."

Angus nodded and then realized that he'd run out of things to ask the other man, and this meant Watson would probably pull the trigger soon. Panic seized him, despite the knowledge that had always existed deep within him that this day would come.

"Drop the gun," said a voice, low and calm, from behind him.

Dinah!

Angus had forgotten she was there. He closed his eyes and began to pray fervently.

Blake Watson started, taking his gaze away from Angus. His gun wavered. "Who are you?" he demanded.

"My name is Dinah Harris. I am a former FBI agent and I trained at the firing range twice as often as anyone else. You need to drop your weapon."

Watson shook his head. His gun hand jerked erratically. "Don't take my one chance for justice away from me!"

"I'm sorry for what you went through," Dinah said, still calm. "I can understand your pain. But this is no solution to that pain."

"Oh yeah? How would you know what it feels like?"

"My son died when he was only a little boy," said Dinah. "He was killed in a car wreck by a truck driver who veered onto the wrong side of the road. I understand what it's like to feel like nobody is held accountable for your child's death or injury."

Watson blinked. "I . . . well, I . . ."

"You need to drop your weapon. You know by now that taking a life in exchange for your son's life hasn't made you happier or made you feel better."

"It hasn't," admitted Watson. His gun seemed to have dropped to his side. Angus continued to pray.

"Your hatred and anger has only served to give you more pain," said Dinah. "You don't deserve to carry around so much pain. Don't make it worse now."

Angus heard a choked sound. He opened his eyes and looked up at Watson, who was weeping openly. "I didn't know what else to do," he whispered.

"I understand," said Dinah, still so calm she might well have been discussing the weather. "It is time to let go now. Drop your weapon and let go of the hatred that has consumed you."

Watson turned his gaze upon Angus, and Angus saw an utterly broken man. The gun wavering at his side in his grasp, great trembling rolled through Watson, his chest heaving, his face lined with pain, tears cascading from his eyes.

"I am so sorry," Angus said, meeting the man's gaze. "I'm sorry for the pain I've caused you and your wife, and for the life I took from your son. It was not my place to take. I am sorry for that with every part of me. I wish I could take back what I did. I regret it wholeheartedly."

The gun crashed to the ground. Blake Watson hugged himself as he continued to weep. Dinah picked up the gun in a flash.

Angus felt like he was in a surreal dream. The man who had tried to kill him was lying on the floor, consumed with grief. He himself was still sitting, not trusting in his ability to stand up. Dinah was on the phone, calling in the police, still cool and calm.

When she had finished, she knelt beside Watson. "Sir," she said. "You know that I am going to have to handcuff you." She helped him up to his knees, and then handcuffed him with plastic zip ties. She did so gently, as though she didn't want to hurt the man.

With the same gentleness, she helped Angus to the couch. Exhausted, he said, "Do you believe that I'm not the killer now?"

She gave a weak smile. "I do. Do you believe that God loves you despite everything you've done?"

Angus found that he could not answer.

Sirens wailed in the distance. Soon, the emergency lights would flood the street with their flickering, probing light.

Angus waited, thinking about the question Dinah had asked him.

****

Did they design these rooms specifically to suck the very last vestige of hope from anyone who dares enter? Dinah wondered. Her mind was randomly and strangely coming up with acute observations, while she, Elise, Lewis, and Louise waited in the hospital waiting room. Dinah found hospital waiting rooms extremely difficult. Memories of waiting to hear that her husband and son had been killed in a room like this one brought back a rush of pain. And so she could not sit still.

It was painted the same limpid greenish-gray of police interview rooms, she observed. Sickly lighting cast feeble shadows, struggling to light the entire room, as if itself in dire need of medical attention. From beyond the door, she could hear rapid footsteps and low, terse conversation; the controlled calm of professionals under enormous pressure.

Louise sat beside her, curled away; arms folded around herself, her face grim, staring blankly at the floor.

Lewis sat on the other side with Elise, stiff and still as a statue, as if not moving could somehow ensure Chloe's life would be saved. Elise seemed frozen with fear. Her face was as white as wax and only her lips moved, very slightly, as if she were mouthing a prayer.

Chloe had been rushed into the emergency room, while Elise and Lewis had been shown to this waiting room along with Grace and Louise. Only a few moments later, Grace had collapsed again, her face chillingly pale. She had been whisked away for treatment, leaving Louise shell-shocked.

Dinah had arrived, intending to tell Elise about the extraordinary events at Angus Whitehall's place. But now was not the time or place, she saw. She stood up, bouncing on the balls of her feet as she paced along the corridor to the vending machines. She considered their wares: coffee, chips, chocolate bars, and giant cookies, with more concentrated scrutiny than they deserved. She wrestled with the vending machine the way Isaac Newton had wrestled with calculus. Yet the thought of consuming any one of these items made her stomach curdle.

A sudden shout made her freeze, then she ran back to where she'd been sitting. A loud, insistent machine buzzed alarm throughout the ER beyond the flimsy door obscuring her view, and she heard the footsteps pounding as nurses and doctors poured into the triage.

The terrible memories threatened to send her into a full-fledged panic attack, making her movements jittery and urgent, like those of a trapped bird. When she arrived back to the quiet group, Elise was asking Louise, "What happened? At my house?"

Lewis stirred. "Elise. . . ."

"I need to know," she insisted.

Louise sighed. "We'd only just gotten home from the courthouse," she said. "Grace found something in her bedroom today. She thought it was from Chloe, and I caught a glimpse of it before Grace left. It looked like a gold necklace. Grace thought Chloe had left it at our house by mistake, so she went over there to give it back."

Elise stared at the ground intently, listening hard. Dinah sat next to her and took her hand.

"It was only a few minutes later than I got a frantic phone call from Grace. She was . . . upset, and we drove around there immediately. I stayed with Grace outside, and Angus went inside the house."

Dinah felt Elise take a deep breath, steeling herself.

"He . . . he found her, in her bedroom," Louise said, her voice thick. "She had used a belt."

"A belt to do what?" asked Elise.

The words seemed to stick in Louise's throat. "She . . . used the belt to hang —"

Dinah felt sick, the taste of bile bitter in her mouth. Elise whispered, "Chloe *hung* herself?"

Louise nodded. "Angus took her down, did CPR until the paramedics arrived."

Elise dropped her head, then started shaking it. "No, you must be wrong. You must have gotten her confused with someone else. I got up this morning, made breakfast. She was right there, dressed for school. She was right *there*. She was smiling, talking to me. It was just a normal day. She seemed so *normal*."

Louise said nothing. In her silence, Elise finally understood the truth. She put her head in her hands and let giant sobs wrack her frame, shuddering as though an electrical current was running through her. Lewis put both of his arms around her. Dinah felt useless, unable to stem the other woman's pain.

"How could this happen? I didn't know she was so sad! How could I not know my baby was in so much pain? How could I not see she was unhappy?" A high note of pain swelled in her throat, and Elise jammed her fist against her mouth as if to keep it in.

"Elise," said Lewis, his voice rough. "You cannot entertain thoughts like those. That way is madness. This is not your fault. Chloe very likely hid everything from us. She probably wanted to protect you; she probably didn't want you to worry about her."

Elise turned suddenly to Dinah, her burning, wet eyes staring at her. "We have to pray. God has to do something about this, right? I know God listens to you. You have to pray!"

Before Dinah could reply, the door separating the triage from the waiting room swung open. A young woman with a stethoscope around her neck looked around, a serious frown on her face. "Elise Jones?" she asked.

Elise moaned, standing up. "That's me," she said, voice little more than a croak. "That's me. Where is Chloe? Is she okay?"

The doctor pressed her lips together, perhaps trying to prevent the passage of bad news. "I'm so sorry, Mrs. Jones," the doctor said.

Dinah thought of Elise insisting to the paramedics: *I'm not Mrs. Jones! I'm Detective Jones!* The look on the doctor's face indicated that this was news she very much dreaded having to give. "Chloe was pronounced dead on arrival here at the hospital. We tried every method of resuscitation we could, but in the end, it was not enough. I'm so terribly sorry."

Elise stared at the doctor uncomprehendingly, her mouth agape, searching for a different answer. Dinah could feel the quaking in her friend's body. As the news sank in, Elise's face crumbled like ice sheets dissolving from a glacier, crashing into the sea.

"No!" she shrieked, voice raw and bleeding, suddenly falling.

Lewis caught her and helped her to a chair, while the doctor sat next to her and gently talked her through what had happened. Dinah sat next to her, knowing from experience that Elise would understand none of it. The doctor might have been speaking Swahili, for all she knew. Dinah knew that her friend's life had just been destroyed by a doctor's words, and where her heart had been broken, guilt would rush in rapidly to fill the void.

Eventually, the doctor left the room, leaving the stricken occupants alone. The feeling of incredible tragedy and loss enveloped the room thickly. The impersonal green of the hospital room, where a thousand other tragedies unfolded every day, would give no answers to Elise's questions.

Dinah felt as if she were sitting in a well thick with poisonous air, slowly suffocating to death. *This is how frail life is, how quickly it can be taken, how quickly the spark of life can be blown out. This is the futility of human life, barely more than a breath of wind across a cold earth. The Bible says life is nothing more than a vapor.*

Elise took a deep breath, seeming to calm herself. She turned to Dinah. "I know you will understand what I mean when I say this. I will never, ever recover from this."

Life at the Whitehall residence had not returned to normal. Angus no longer knew what normal even looked like.

Louise's anger toward him simmered and bubbled like a volcano: an eruption was imminent. She couldn't look at him, let alone speak to him. Grace had been so devastated by Chloe's suicide that she'd cried non-stop for two days now, refusing to eat or sleep. The hollow, deadened look in his daughter's eyes filled him with cold fear.

Fresh from a long, hot shower, he took a deep breath and went downstairs to where Louise was sitting in the kitchen with a cup of coffee. She was staring at a fixed spot, her eyes unblinking and unseeing.

"Good morning," he said, quietly.

She nodded, stood up, and turned away from him, wiping down a spotlessly clean counter.

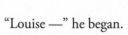

Chapter 18

"Louise —" he began.

"I know," she said. "I'm not being fair to you. Our children are going to need us more than ever, and they need us to be together."

What scared him most was the emptiness in her voice.

"Angus, I've been thinking. I've been thinking a lot, because I can't sleep and I can't eat. I'm worried that we could so easily lose our daughter. I've been thinking about our family, how important we have always been to each other. I built my life with you, but it was on a lie. I didn't even know your real name. I don't know who I am or who we are. And I am *so, so* incredibly furious with you that it takes all my strength not to hate you."

She fell silent, an excruciating stillness.

"But I am a Christian," she finally said. "And when Peter asked Jesus how many times he should forgive a man who wronged him, Jesus told him seventy times seven. Right? In other words, we are to endlessly forgive, just as God endlessly forgives us. We are to show love, just as God loved us while we still hated Him, to the point of sacrificing his own Son."

She finally turned to look her husband in the eye.

"God knows that I can't do it on my own strength. I'm so angry, so disappointed, so utterly destroyed by what you've done. Yet I will forgive you, with the strength of Jesus, I *will* forgive you. I can't promise that it'll be easy. But I have decided that I will obey."

She laughed softly, the whimpering sound of a wounded animal. "You know, on those talk shows when they talk about forgiveness, they tell you to just do it, as though it's easy. They don't tell you that forgiveness requires utter sacrifice, the loss of the anger and resentment and bitterness that fuels you. It leaves you empty, searching for some other way of trying to exist. They don't tell you that it's not just a one-time decision, but that it's a series of small decisions made every day — decisions not to hold a grudge, not to remember the past, not to allow anger to creep up. It's not a wash of warm and fuzzy feelings that conveniently wipes out all the wrong. It's the decision and determination to choose love despite the hurt."

Louise turned to face him. All that he had done to her was written on her face.

"I will stand by you. I will not leave. And although it'll take every ounce of strength I have, I promise you that I will forgive you and love you. Until death do us part."

The prison that had constricted his dark heart for so many years began to crumble; long-held secrets could no longer be kept, and truth had given wings to a bright, fresh future. Hope spread tiny wings in his heart as he went to his wife, and gently took her in his arms.

"Thank you," he whispered into her hair.

TWO YEARS LATER

She was a small and lonely figure, cutting through the section of the cemetery where the imposing marble headstones stood taller than she. In one hand, she gripped a fistful of flowers, in the other, a single white piece of paper. When she arrived at Chloe's grave, Grace Whitehall knelt beside it and laid the flowers down gently.

She closed her eyes briefly and then she laid the piece of paper underneath the flowers. It would not stay there long, she knew. The flowers would die, the paper would flutter away on the next strong breeze. She put her hand on the gravestone and whispered to herself. Nobody could hear her, but the words she spoke were a kind of therapy. They helped her work through the guilt and sorrow, which lay heavy on her heart for many months after Chloe's death. Now it was a habit, a way of honoring the memory of her friend.

Dear Chloe:

Nearly two years, and I'm still sitting here at your grave, talking to you like you can hear me. I still find it so hard to believe that you've gone. At first I was really angry with you, furious that you could be so selfish. Sometimes I felt like standing over this grave and just pummeling into the earth to try to hurt you.

Then, as time passed, I realized that I'd already hurt you in so many ways. Suddenly, I'm no longer angry with you but disgusted with myself. I am sorry that I let you down so badly. I'm sorry that I turned my back on you and didn't stand up for you when I should have. To think that I blamed you for your mom just doing her job burns me now. I don't know how many ways there can be to say it, but I am just so sorry.

The Dark Heart

Did you know that I flunked out of school last year? I made straight F's, for the first time in my life. But how could I go to that school and study and concentrate when I saw you everywhere? I saw you at your locker, your hair a crazy green stripe. I saw you in the cafeteria, saving a seat for me. I saw you passing me notes in English class.

Mom finally pulled me out of school, and gave me a few months off. Now Mom is homeschooling me, and will until I go to college. I can't do school anymore, Chloe. It's not the same without you, and believe me, I get that you're not there because of me.

Right after you died, Mom caught me trying to take her codeine pills. I told her I had a headache, but the truth was, I wanted to go to sleep and never wake up. I know that I wasn't thinking clearly. What I was feeling was . . . too immense, too big, to even think about. I wanted the pain to go away.

I hear that your Mom and Dad moved away. I didn't get a chance to talk to them before they left, but I hope and pray that they're doing okay.

My Mom and Dad didn't do so well after you died. Mom cried a lot for a little while. Dad had to spend a lot of time with the police, but you know what? Despite everything, he was different. Mom and Dad spent lots of time together; they talked until really late at night for a long time. I guess he was worried he'd have to go to jail, but I think he worked out a deal where he didn't get to keep the money he stole and got a suspended sentence, or something like that. I remember Dad always being a little distant, a little closed off from us until this whole thing blew up. Now it's like a weight has been lifted from his shoulders. The truth shall set you free — and so it seems.

He resigned his position as Senior Pastor at the church, even though they didn't ask for it. He has started up a ministry for perpetrators and victims of violence. He's making, like, zero money and I don't know how I'll be able to go to college, but I guess that's a problem we'll work out some other day.

It's very weird to think that my own father had once been so violent that he beat people unconscious. I mean, can you ever really wrap your mind around that? When he catches me staring at him, he tells me the story of the murderer Saul, who met Jesus on the road to Damascus, and became radically changed into the Apostle Paul. That is also his story, he tells me. He was once Saul, and now he is trying to be more like Paul.

Did I ever tell you that Jessica was expelled from school?

You want to know something funny? Not funny ha-ha, funny peculiar. Jessica is being homeschooled as well, and now I see her quite often. I've gotten to know her, and now I understand some things. Like, her dad would hit her if she made a bad grade. And that he used to call her all kinds of awful names. She was a bully because she was scared, Chloe. And I get that because that's exactly what Dad told me, too. He was a racist, violent bully because he was scared. He told me that he didn't like being scared, so he became angry instead. That's what happened with Jessica, too. Dad says that without an anchor, like Jesus, we try to manage our fear and pain ourselves. For some people, like Dad and Jessica, it's anger and lashing out at other people. For others, like you and that poor heroin addict who was killed, it becomes self-destruction or self-harm or addiction. We live in such a broken world, and we are all such broken people. Only Jesus provides us with a way out of our own mess.

Together, Dad and I worked through what it means to forgive, and why it was important for me to forgive Jessica. And it took some time, but I have.

Now I feel like I need to speak up. I need to tell your story and honor your memory, and include Jessica's story so that this tragedy stops happening. Next week I've been asked to talk to the high school in Suffolk. I'm going to tell everyone how awesome you were, and how your death has changed all of us. I'm going to tell Jessica's story, too. I'm going to tell them that anger and violence and cruelty destroys everyone. I'm going to tell the story of compassion and kindness, of love and forgiveness. It's the story of Jesus. I hope that even just one person will take notice.

You know, I really miss being able to pick up the phone and just talk to you. I miss you and your smile; wishing you

could be here. I got a gold chain, like the one you used to wear
— the one you left at my house right before you died. I put a
gold C on it, and I wear it every single day. It reminds me of
you, and you never feel far away.

Oh, Chloe, how I wish I could turn back time and change
everything. I wish I could change what I did. Every part of me
groans with your absence.

I miss you.

Goodbye, dear friend.

****

In coastal Maine in November, the sky was clear and cold, temperatures
plummeting. The cruise ships had left the terminal, and the summer
tourists had packed up and left. The locals began to bunker down. The
days grew shorter and darker, and all that was left to do was to watch
huge winter storms roll in from the Atlantic.

Elise Jones woke at 5 a.m., as was her new custom. In the cold
darkness, she sat in the small kitchen of the apartment overlooking the
sea. The water lay beyond her window, but it was impossible to see so
early in the morning. She wrapped her hands around a steaming hot
cup of coffee and reflected that living in an apartment in Bar Harbor,
Maine, was the not the life she'd imagined for herself.

She finished her coffee and pulled on a sweatshirt. Outside, the air
was bracing. She inhaled, enjoying the cold searing of her lungs, and
she began to jog, just as she did every morning.

Two years ago, she'd had a frenetic life, working in the sheriff's
department at all hours, taking care of her daughter and rushing
through life with her husband. Now, her days were ordered almost
to military precision. It had to be that way: it was the only way she
could keep from succumbing to the chaos that knocked on her door
relentlessly. She wrote lists every day, reminding her that she had to eat
breakfast, that she had to pay bills, that she had to go to work. If she
didn't write her lists, she forgot. Life was impossibly hard.

The town was deserted, but starkly beautiful, lit up with the soft
gray of an impending sunrise. Elise finished her jog, had a shower, and
ate a tub of yogurt for breakfast.

She remembered once being a little self-conscious about her
weight. Despite the cultural obsession with being thin, the nickname

Bonesy Jonesy had never been a term of endearment. If they could see her now, even the moniker Bonesy wouldn't do her justice. Now, she found it hard to eat. *The Profound Loss Diet,* she thought wryly, *could make me a fortune.*

Once she was dressed for work, she locked the front door and began to walk toward the small family law practice where she now worked as a part-time investigator, an office so small she had to type her own letters and fetch her own mail. It suited her just fine.

She made a short stop on the way to work every morning. Just as the sun began its ascent into the sky, casting pale, golden light to dance on the water, Elise ducked through the solid wooden doors of St John's Presbyterian Church.

She always went to the first row and knelt on thin carpet to pray. The first few weeks after she'd moved from Ten Mile Hollow, she'd walked past this church and glared at it. It reminded her of Pastor Angus Whitehall, of his lies and the hypocrisy of a double life, and of the person she'd blamed for Chloe's death: Grace Whitehall.

If they were the kind of people who were churchgoers, she swore she never would be. She remembered being inside her Ten Mile Hollow home after Chloe's funeral, her shock so enormous it blotted out the sun. She wandered around that house, bitterly recalling that when it was bought, she'd had both a husband and a daughter. Now the house was intolerably empty. Memories stretched like cobwebs across doorways and hallways and rooms; sometimes she walked right into them unawares and jumped with the visceral fear of having had a spider leap down upon her.

It hadn't taken long to realize that she couldn't stay there. She couldn't face the emptiness of Chloe's room, the echoing guilt that lay in wait for her around every corner, or the quiet desperation of the master bedroom.

Some days her phone had rung constantly, and she'd pick up the receiver and listen to whoever was on the other end. It seemed they had been speaking a different language. She'd listen in confusion for a few minutes and then gently hang up mid-speech.

Eventually, her phone stopped ringing. She had discovered that grief was too large, too raw, too personal for others to grasp, and when the pleasantries stopped and the awkward silences stretched on, people began to forget about her and go on with their lives.

The Dark Heart

Unable to restart their own lives, Elise and Lewis left for the eastern coast of Maine. She had not spoken to Angus or Louise since that awful day at the hospital, despite the messages they'd left on her machine.

For some reason, the small church on her way to work loomed large in her mind every time she walked past. Sometimes it seemed sinister and shadowy; at other times it seemed bright and welcoming. *All* the time, Elise knew it was crazy to be thinking so much about it all.

Finally, she relented and entered the church one bleak fall day. Inside, it was peaceful and silent, and Elise sat on a bench and rather enjoyed the meditative atmosphere. When she emerged, she felt calmer and more composed, and so she began to do it every day. *It's just a building,* she told herself. *It calms me down. It doesn't mean that I must associate with hypocritical Christians.*

Above the altar of the church hung a big wooden cross. Elise found herself staring at it each morning, taking in each detail intently. She realized that despite having been vaguely friendly with Angus and his family for ten years, she'd never really understood why Christians worshiped a man who had died upon a cross.

One summer's day, she caught herself talking to God as she sat inside the church.

Where exactly are You? Do You know who I am? Do You know about my life? Do You even care?

Well, she figured, she was inside a church. It was almost expected that people talk to God there. So she continued talking to God, telling Him about her life; the guilt, anger, and grief that consumed her heart in every moment, both waking and sleeping. She told Him about Chloe, about the waste of her life and how desperately she would give anything, including her own life, if only to give Chloe another chance. She told Him about the hatred she harbored for the Whitehall family, and how it felt like it was eating her from the inside out.

At the end of each talk, her eyes would inevitably drift back to the cross and she'd stare at it for several moments before leaving.

On the first anniversary of Chloe's death, Elise took the day off work and somehow found herself inside the church anyway. It was a difficult day, and she woke up after a patchy sleep, nightmares plaguing her. She was desperately sad and lonely, and on that particular day, she'd thrown her head back and silently yelled toward the sky: *"Do You even care, God? Do You care? If You care, show me. I'm sick of this one-sided conversation!"*

" 'You have sorrow now, but I will see you again; then you will rejoice, and no one can rob you of that joy.' "

The voice, ethereal and mesmerizing, floated to her as if she were dreaming. But the person who'd spoken them was real, and she was about Elise's age, reading from the Bible.

"I hope I didn't startle you," she said, gently. "But I often read aloud to myself while I'm in here. I didn't see you in here until I saw you move, and now I believe God wanted to tell you something."

Her name was Tara, and she often visited the church in the early morning, spending the quiet, still part of the day in prayer or reading the Bible. Today, she said, was no different except that she'd had an audience.

Elise had just experienced the full and relentless love of God, and it pierced the brittle shell surrounding her heart like an arrow into water.

Now, every morning, she came to the church to celebrate her salvation, her new identity in Jesus.

Father in heaven, how grateful I am that You loved me first, even while I was mired in hatred and sin. Thank You for showing me that, as great as You are, that You care for even the smallest, most lost person. Thank You that before I even knew what love was, You sacrificed Your perfect and blameless Son upon the Cross; that He bore the punishment for which I was due, so that I can call You Father. Thank You for Your love, so rich, so rewarding, so thoroughly undeserved. Thank You that in my utter weakness and helplessness, you are my strength and joy.

She stood, looking at the cross, before turning to walk back down the aisle. Then her face broke into a wide smile. Lewis had let himself into the church and in one hand, he carried his own copy of the Bible.

"Let me walk with you to work," he whispered, in that still sanctuary of God. "Shall we brave the weather and go out for dinner tonight?"

Lewis, my heart, my life, my love, my strength.

Elise took his hand and smiled. "Yes. I'd like that very much."

Julie Cave
AUTHOR

Julie has always been an avid reader, beginning with the adventure stories of Enid Blyton and the fantasy stories of C.S. Lewis's *Chronicles of Narnia* and Tolkien's *Lord of the Rings* series. In her teen years she gravitated toward mystery and thriller books, including the original Goosebumps series. During this time, she experimented with writing, penning her first novel-length story about kidnapping and teenage angst at the age of 12. She practiced her craft throughout high school, writing three novel-length stories, and then her writing took a back seat to university studies, marriage, and family. She returned to writing as an adult and a Christian, determined to combine her passion for writing with her faith. The result is the Dinah Harris Mystery Series, with *Deadly Disclosures* published in 2010, followed by *The Shadowed Mind* in 2011, and *Pieces of Light* in 2012. The fourth novel in the series is *The Dark Heart*. In between writing murder mysteries and reading the latest from John Grisham, Julie is a wife, mother to two daughters, the operator of a digital marketing and communications business, and resident on a Black Angus and Wagyu cattle property in Australia.

juliecave.com.au

A
Dinah Harris
MYSTERY

Don't miss out on the first
three books for this thrilling fiction series!

Deadly Disclosures | 978-0-89051-584-6

The Shadowed Mind | 978-0-89051-590-7

Pieces of Light | 978-0-89051-608-9

In these Christian fiction thrillers, author Julie Cave tackles the uncomfortable issues of the creation versus evolution debate, eugenics, domestic violence, and hypocrisy in the church with unflinching honesty. Cave's central character, Dinah Harris, is an ex FBI agent who deals with the real-world problems of alcoholism, depression, grief and more. With stories you might easily hear on tonight's news, Cave leads the reader to recall the authority of the Bible and our God of redemption.

THE REMNANT TRILOGY
BOOK 1

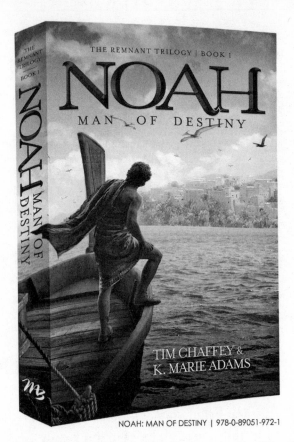

NOAH: MAN OF DESTINY | 978-0-89051-972-1

Most people think of Noah as the man who built a large ship and spent months caring for thousands of animals. But who was he and what events shaped who he would become? *Noah: Man of Destiny* takes readers on a captivating, coming-of-age journey through the pre-Flood world. Noah learns more about the Most High while standing against a sinister belief system emerging throughout the land. Whether escaping legendary beasts, tracking kidnappers, or pursuing his future wife, Noah acquires the skills he will need when God calls him to his greatest adventure: surviving the global Flood. Explore what it may have been like for a righteous man to relate to God before the Bible was written.